SIMEON'S TOUCH

BOOKS AUTHORED OR COAUTHORED BY BRENTON G. YORGASON

The Garrity Test (coauthored with Richard Myers)
Ty: The Ty Detmer Story
NAMINA—Biography of Georganna Bushman Spurlock (private printing)
Six Secrets of Self-Renewal and Relationship Enhancement
The First Christmas Gift
Prayers on the Wind
Spiritual Survival in the Last Days
Here Stands a Man
Roger and Sybil Ferguson History (private printing)
Little-Known Evidences of the Book of Mormon
Sacred Intimacy
Receiving Answers to Prayer
Obtaining the Blessings of Heaven
Pardners: Three Stories on Friendship
In Search of Steenie Bergman (Soderberg Series #5)
KING—The Life of Jerome Palmer King (private printing)
The Greatest Quest
Seven Days for Ruby (Soderberg Series #4)
Dirty Socks and Shining Armor—A Tale from King Arthur's Camelot
The Eleven-Dollar Surgery
Becoming
Tales from the Book of Mormon
Brother Brigham's Gold (Soderberg Series #3)
Ride the Laughing Wind
The Miracle
The Thanksgiving Promise (made into Disney classic TV movie)
Chester, I Love You (Soderberg Series #2)
Double Exposure
Seeker of the Gentle Heart
The Krystal Promise
A Town Called Charity, and Other Stories about Decisions
The Bishop's Horse Race (Soderberg Series #1)
Windwalker (movie version—out of print)
Others
From First Date to Chosen Mate
From Two to One (out of print)
From This Day Forth (out of print)
Creating a Celestial Marriage (textbook)
Marriage and Family Stewardships (textbook)

SIMEON'S TOUCH

BRENTON YORGASON
AND RICHARD MYERS

Bookcraft
Salt Lake City, Utah

Library of Congress Catalog Card Number: 93-73464
ISBN 0-88494-899-4

First Printing, 1993

Printed in the United States of America

To Margaret and Susie,
whose continued encouragement has seen us
through to the end once more

Authors' Note

Doctrinally speaking, we have been taught that periodically the Lord has arranged for some of his children to undergo a temporary change in their physical makeup, which change continues from the time they lived here upon the earth until the moment of their personal resurrection. After this change has taken place, they have been known as *translated beings*. Included in this number would be the inhabitants of the city of Enoch, Moses, Elijah, and Alma the Younger. Four others—John the Beloved, as well as the three Nephite disciples—were given a special blessing by the Savior, that of being able to tarry upon the earth, in their "translated state," ministering to the inhabitants of the earth until the Savior comes the second time, this time to usher in the Millennium. (See *Mormon Doctrine*, 2d ed. [Salt Lake City: Bookcraft, 1966], pp. 804–8.)

The Apostle John's translation is referred to in John 21:20–23; Revelation 10; and Doctrine and Covenants 7 and 77:14. The account of the translation of the Three Nephites (see 3 Nephi 28) is discussed by Elder Bruce R. McConkie as follows: "It is from the account of the translation of the Three Nephites that we gain most of our knowledge of the present ministry among men of translated beings. It is very evident that such persons 'never taste of death . . . never endure the pains of death'; that they have undergone a change in their bodies, 'that they might not suffer pain nor sorrow save it were for the sins of the world'; that they were holy men, 'sanctified in the flesh'; 'that the powers of the earth could not hold them'; that 'they are as the angels of God,' ministering to whomsoever they will; that they 'shall be changed in the twinkling of an eye from mortality to immortality' at the Second Coming; and that they shall then inherit exaltation in the kingdom of God."

It is from the doctrinal premise of these four translated beings that we have taken literary license to create a fictitious "what if?" scenario of our own.

In three of the New Testament Gospels a brief reference is made to a man named Simon. It is mentioned that he is from Cyrene, a town in Libya, North Africa. (See Matthew 27:32.) It is this Simon who is given the unlikely task of having to carry the heavy cross up to the hills to Golgotha. This cross, of course, is the same one on which Jesus Christ is ultimately nailed and crucified—and upon which he eventually dies.

The premise of this fictional story centers on two theoretical questions: What if there was a fifth man alive in the world today who was once, along with John the Beloved and the Three Nephites, a personal friend of the Savior? And what if, just prior to His death, this same Jesus Christ bestowed the gift of translation upon his head, thus transforming his body chemistry so that he would never taste of death—but would continue to live here upon the earth?

Moreover, consider the implications of such a man, alive and well in the twentieth century—a man more than two thousand years old with a specific calling from Christ Himself to assist His latter-day prophets in preparing the way for His second coming.

While all of the events in this novel are fictitious and reflect our imagination, they have been woven together to provide the reader with reason to pause, to ponder, and to give credence to the fact that many calamities and extraordinary events will precede the Savior's second coming. The value of considering this inevitability is to simply allow each of us to make even greater resolve to prepare ourselves and our families for this event, as well as our friends and other loved ones around us. This is done, of course, by more fully keeping the Lord's commandments and by following the counsel of those Brethren who have been called to assist us in this effort.

PART ONE

The Coming Winds

For kingdoms, and for men,
　　there comes a time
That change is wrought
　　by Hands unseen.

The stirrings flow
　　from deep within,
Giving life anew,
　　time and again!

CHAPTER 1

The early-morning offshore winds rolled gently across the vast, open expanse of the Pacific Ocean, bathing the southern California coastline in a warm tropical breeze. The air, thick and dense, pressed steadily against the ominous land mass and rose skyward with the towering cliffs that lined the quiet beaches.

A few miles north of the city of Los Angeles, high above the ridge tops, a lone seagull banked slightly eastward, hooked its wings into a smooth updraft, and began a slow, spiralling ascent heavenward, above a beautiful finger of land known simply as Point Dume. As it did so, its senses became suddenly aware of an elderly man, a human, standing alone at the summit of the point.

Slowly the sleek white bird circled twice, effortlessly rising aloft with the winds. At last, sensing the moment to be correct, the seagull began its slow descent and glided silently through the grey, predawn light toward its final destination point, just inches away from where the curious stranger was standing.

The bird landed with a barely audible sound, shook its tiny head with a quick snap from left to right, then looked up at the figure before it. Still, the man did not move. Instead, his eyes, green as emeralds, stared out across the vast Pacific as if in search of some faraway place which could not be seen but which was apparently vivid and real inside the pages of his memory. He did not seem to notice the feathery figure which had suddenly dropped out of the morning sky, and which was now nestled between his feet.

Like a house cat starved for attention, the seagull moved gently in and around the old man's ankles, brushing its warm feathers against the grey sweats and tennis shoes covering the man's legs and feet. Quietly then, it began to murmur a soft cooing sound. Finally, as if the audible tones were meant to call out to the kindly gentleman seemingly mesmerized by the sea, the old fellow turned his gaze downward and looked pensively at the small creature.

"Why, hello there, my friend," he whispered calmly, stooping down, then sitting Indian fashion on a smooth, windworn rock. "Were you hunting for food, my little one, or were you simply enjoying an early-morning flight in these warm winds?"

The seagull swayed back and forth in a rocking motion, then cooed once more.

"Oh, I see," said the stranger. "Looking for food, then, is that it? Well, let me see what I have here."

The pleasant-tempered old gentleman retrieved a backpack from his shoulders, untied the two leather straps that secured the contents inside, and lifted the vinyl flap. In a small sandwich bag, three freshly-baked slices of whole-wheat bread produced a tantalizing aroma that quickly scented the immediate area between them.

The bird was clearly excited.

"My wife, Sarah, makes these," the man whispered calmly, while extracting one of the delicious-looking bread slices and replacing the others back into the small pack.

"Oh, yes," he continued, "she's a marvelous cook, and a true sweetheart. Here," he motioned, a small morsel of bread on his fingertips. "Come, my little friend; eat with me, and enjoy the miracle of another new day."

The seagull climbed up onto the old man's lap and began eating the bread directly from his fingers. There was harmony here—no danger whatsoever. The two new friends ate in silence and eventually finished the last remaining crumbs of the bread.

The old man looked out across the sea and watched the first rays of the rising sun in the easterly skies as they painted soft morning colors over the surface of the ocean. It was the work of God himself! Beautiful and magic! And when the grey shadows of the predawn darkness faded at last, another day was born.

"It is time, my little friend," the old man stated, softly stroking the back of the bird's coat of white, fluffy feathers. "We must be on our way."

The seagull hopped down from the old fellow's lap, waddled a few steps off toward the edge of the towering cliff, then quietly spread its wings and lifted off into the gentle, rising winds coming up from the waters far below.

Meanwhile, cinching his green backpack securely over his shoulders, the man rose slowly to his feet and watched as his feathered friend circled upwards. Carefully then he proceeded over to the edge of the precipice and at once entered a small narrow path that wound down the side of the cliff's face to the water's edge.

CHAPTER 2

"It's not really worth an argument, Larry," Eddie said calmly, lifting the heavy scuba tank into the bed of his Chevy S-10 pickup truck. "Besides, for the hundredth time, I *like* what I do. Can't you understand that?"

"You're totally misunderstanding my point, Eddie. No one faults you for your love of diving. As far as that goes, little brother, Warren, Kenny, and myself enjoy the sport as much as you do! It's just that *we* think you're throwing your life away! Really, Ed, what kind of money can you make as a gung-ho lifeguard?"

"I'm not a lifeguard, Larry! You know perfectly well what I do!"

"Oh, yeah," Larry mocked. "You're an important *dive master* with the L.A.P.D. Aquatic Rangers! I seem to forget just how *important* that really is! Frankly, Eddie, we've all forgotten how important you've become—ever since you joined the Mormons!"

Eddie spun around and faced his older brother with a fierce, angry look in his eyes. "You know," he replied, disgusted with his brother's callous attitude, "sometimes you can be the most adolescent adult human being I've ever known! Why don't you grow up, Larry, and quit being such a first-class jerk!"

"Hey, man," Larry answered, retreating just a little, "I was just kidding. Chill out a little, will ya?"

"You're the one who needs to chill out, Larry! Stop riding me! I happen to find a great deal of satisfaction in both my Christian beliefs and my professional endeavors. I enjoy what I do, and I couldn't care less what you, or Warren, or Kenny think about my lifestyle! I'm not interested in your money. I get an honorable day's wage for an honorable day's labor, and I'm perfectly content with the system of budgeting that my son and I have created to care for our needs. Can you ever get that through your head?"

"Sure, Ed, I can get that through my head, all right," Larry answered defiantly. "But I'm not buying into your little 'I don't care about the money' routine. If you didn't care so much about the money, or about a position with the firm, then why did you ask Dad to make the down payment on your house out in Malibu?"

Eddie stared at his brother in disbelief, desperately fighting the emotional responses surging inside him. And in moments his face began to redden with anger and his hands began to tremble. Still, he suppressed the almost overwhelming urge to land a bone-shattering right hook into Larry's left jaw. Instead, he silently gritted his teeth and walked to the driver's side of the pickup. As he stepped one foot inside the vehicle, Eddie turned casually forward, looked his insensitive brother squarely in the eye, and said simply, "Have a nice day, Larry."

Outside, on Rockingham Avenue, Eddie paused for a brief moment and stared back at the long, red-brick driveway from which he had just emerged. The tall, cast-iron gates vibrated slightly as they continued their motorized journey that would theoretically shut out the world and its twentieth-century madness from the massive estate within.

"Thirty million dollars," he mumbled to himself, thinking back to a conversation he'd had with his father several months before. "Thirty million. And Dad seemed completely undaunted! Can he really be worth so much?" Eddie shook his head, thought about the phenomenal wealth to which he was an heir, then threw the Chevy into gear and drove off down the road. As he drove, he thought of his work, and his mind flashed back to his learning of the newest tragedy.

Two weeks earlier, a couple of teenage brothers—both quite young—had been in a small fishing boat, apparently drinking heavily. They were unexpectedly caught in a powerful riptide and held captive as the motorless craft was swept mercilessly out to sea. It was suspected that the small vessel had capsized, because from that day forward no one had heard from, or seen, the two boys again.

Eddie had made more than a dozen dives in the area but simply could not come up with so much as a single clue as to the whereabouts of the wreck or the victims. "What a horrible way to die!" he said out loud, as if speaking to some unseen passenger sitting there beside him.

Sadly, he thought, few people give heed to the dangers of drinking. He couldn't count the number of times he had boarded a sea vessel, only to find a stash of liquor. It wasn't against the law for a passenger of a given boat to drink while out at sea, or for an ocean-worthy craft to set sail with alcohol on board. But it *was* illegal for the captain of the vessel to drink, and unfortunately, if the crew and the passengers were in that festive, partying mood, then it was almost certain that the ship's captain would partake as well.

Needless to say, Eddie Allen Russell, son of the world renowned multi-billionaire, Allen Scott Russell III, did not drink. He simply valued his health and was determined to live a long, healthy, sober life.

After approximately ten minutes of driving in and out of the traffic on Sunset Boulevard, Eddie pulled out onto the Pacific Coast Highway. From there, he turned north and drove faster until he finally arrived at the beachfront office of the Los Angeles Police's Search and Rescue Division, the fledgling team of professionals known as the Aquatic Rangers.

He pulled the Chevy pickup slowly into the parking lot and rolled comfortably into his personally marked parking stall. There was a white-painted concrete tire-stop at the head, which simply read, "Sergeant Russell."

Eddie turned off the ignition, extracted the keys, and climbed out of the pickup. He stood for a brief moment, drew in a deep breath of fresh ocean air, then went inside.

"Oh, hello, Sarge," Janie Hamblin said cheerfully from her station at the dispatch console. "I've been trying to reach you all morning. Called your house, but no answer. Tried to get you on the radio, and still no answer. Did you turn the radio on in your pickup this morning?"

"Whoops!" Eddie responded guiltily. "I forgot. Sorry about that, Janie. I wasn't home last night, either. But never mind that. What's up around here?"

"Nothing much, really. Tommy Cosland called. Said he'd

like you to meet him up at Point Dume, ASAP. He figures that's the best place to get started on the final sweep of the search for those two Hansen boys. But also, you need to call Captain Mitchell. He says it's nothing earth-shattering, but kind of important. You want me to get him on the phone?"

"Not just yet. I've got a couple of things I have to do first."

Eddie walked into his office, pulled a small plastic bottle of orange juice out of the little refrigerator situated neatly in one corner of the room, then poked his head back out the door, and said, "Hey, Janie, where is everybody?"

"You already know where Tommy is, and, uh . . . Art and Gene said something about having to stop at Lock Port. Said you'd know about it."

"Oh, yeah, that's right," Eddie answered, remembering the conversation with Art Sackler the night before.

Half an hour later, with tasks completed, Eddie was once again inside his pickup truck, driving north toward Point Dume, his rendezvous point with his diving partner, Tommy Cosland, whom Eddie affectionately referred to as "TC."

Eddie was in a pensive but pleasant mood and looked forward to the dive. Frankly, although his underwater experiences often revolved around tragic or even dangerous events, he was generally enthusiastic with anticipation whenever his work called him to the sea.

TC was already suited up and rechecking his diving gear when Eddie arrived and rolled out onto the overlook. There was no direct route for a motor vehicle down to the oceanfront itself, so it required that the two men don their wetsuits and carry the remaining equipment down a narrow path to the scenic cove far below.

"Well, it's about time!" TC scolded, looking up from the pressure valve he was working on. "Where've you been, Eddie?"

"Sorry about that, partner. Got tied up at the office. Captain Mitchell called."

"Oh?"

"Yeah, it seems that the news media is interested in doing a little story on the Rangers." Eddie reached into the back of the Chevy, extracting his diving gear and laying each piece separately and neatly out onto the ground in front of him.

Tommy Cosland continued the questioning. "What kind of story are they looking for?"

"Well," Eddie said, "I'm pretty sure it's a public relations kind of thing, actually. Mitchell said they're interested in our recent work with the Coast Guard. The whole concept of the Aquatic Rangers, an L.A.P.D. extension, is still very much a novelty, TC. You've heard the criticisms. Some people call us a 'needless waste of taxpayers' money.' But with the highly publicized cooperative efforts with the Coast Guard, especially with the two recent drug busts, we're starting to get some serious support! Mitchell's *way* happy about that!"

"So," TC said, "it's a good thing, then, this media stuff, right?"

"Well, Mitchell thinks it is, anyway. Especially in the wake of all that happened with the L.A. riots, and the rest of the police force there."

"How about you?" TC asked. "Are you in favor of this media hype for our department?"

"I'm not sure, really. I just don't want the Rangers to be looked upon as *vice* cops. You know what I mean?"

"Sort of," TC replied, paying more attention to the final adjustments he was making on the pressure valve than to the conversation with his sergeant.

"Well," Eddie continued, "if you think about it, the Rangers program was initially conceived with one purpose in mind: a search and rescue operation that would assist people in trouble. You understand what I'm saying, TC? We're policing, instead of helping people. The point is, if I had wanted to be a cop I would have enlisted as a cop."

Closing the valve and attaching the regulator to the air tank, TC looked up at his diving partner and said calmly, "Now that you mention it, Sarge, we *have* been working a lot more like police, haven't we? So, what're ya gonna do, Eddie? You gonna give the interview?"

"I don't really have a choice, TC. But I'll tell you this much for certain: I'm going to put in every plug possible for the Rangers' principal scope and mission!"

The two men became silent as they readied themselves and put on their wetsuits. Then, in continued silence, they hoisted the remaining scuba gear over their shoulders and carefully made their way over the ridge and down the narrow path that led to the beach below.

Fifteen minutes later, the two divers slipped on their fins, masks, and snorkels, popped their regulators into their mouths, and began the cautious backward walk down into the ocean. Once away from shore, they found the underwater visibility better than average for the Point Dume area, and Eddie was immediately grateful for that added luxury. Together they dived, down to the first search level of forty feet.

The vast, gently swaying forest of green and gold kelp was teeming with life. This, Eddie knew, was a regular playground for hundreds of seals who used the kelp beds for hunting. Two of the creatures suddenly entered Eddie's field of vision. They were playful animals, to be sure, but Eddie knew that they could also get a bit frisky. He was cautious and alert, always keeping his hands close to his side.

Twenty minutes into the dive, Eddie retrieved the depth gauge from his side. It registered sixty-four feet. Next to it, inside the same console, was a pressure gauge. By reading it, Eddie knew that he had used up about one-third of his available air. Another forty minutes, and he would have to surface. Moving steadily, just inches above a tremendous outcropping of oceanrock, Eddie glanced at the compass on his wrist. He got a visual fix on his position, then began swimming to the west, a direction that took him further out into the ocean.

By now, the tall vines of the thick kelp beds towered above him like hundreds of magnificent bean stalks from Jack's fabled garden. It wasn't unusual for divers to become easily separated in such a forest, and Eddie—though clearly aware of the textbook regulations suggesting that one should never dive alone or become separated from his partner—was not unduly alarmed when he noted that TC was nowhere to be seen.

"He'll turn up," Eddie reasoned mentally. Both men were experienced divers, and each adhered to the customary precautionary measures.

Eddie swam on. As he continued to weave in and out of the giant kelp vines, following the steadily descending terrain of the ocean floor, something with a slight reflective surface suddenly caught his eye. He paused for a moment, then slowly initiated a 360-degree visual. Still there was no sign of TC.

Drawing the maze of tangled vines out of his way with his hands, Eddie moved silently forward until suddenly he came upon a sunken vessel, long forgotten. It was a fishing boat, an old trawler, but not the one he had been hunting. Undoubtedly, this was a boat which had sunk years ago. He noted an old Mercury inboard still intact at the stern, rusting slowly with time, then moved in for a closer look.

Barely visible, painted on the outside of the old hull, was a name. It was hard to read at first because of all the slime that had grown over the surface of the craft through the years. With his left hand, Eddie reached over and wiped away the mossy buildup. It was difficult to read what had been painted years earlier, but with a little effort he could read a name.

The *Bonnie Marie*.

"Bonnie Marie?" he mumbled into the mouthpiece. "I wonder who that was."

There were other markings. A set of numbers. Registration numbers. The trawler would undoubtedly have been registered with the licensing bureau of L.A. County. If that were the case, he might be able to identify it if that became necessary. Carefully, then, he washed away the greenish vegetation until the numbers could be read: PW-2833.

Just then something moved.

"What in . . . ," he said, jerking his head to the left just in time to see several large marine animals swim into his immediate area. There were dozens of them.

"Sharks?"

His heart raced, and absurd amounts of adrenaline surged into his bloodstream. His breathing increased, and valuable oxygen was expended rapidly. But it wasn't a school of sharks. Something else—dolphins. Twelve, maybe fifteen or more altogether. And *something*, he wasn't sure what, was swimming in their midst. In between the two larger mammals, holding firmly onto the dorsal fins, was . . . was . . . a man! An old man with piercing eyes and thick white hair.

The dolphins ceased their forward momentum, then hovered just a few feet above the ocean floor, as if following some unspoken directive from the pilot animal directly in front of them. But then, ever so slowly, the man in the midst of the sleek creatures uprighted himself, turned in Eddie's direction, looked him squarely in the eyes, and smiled. Eddie's heart raced wildly. His breathing increased for a second time, expending the oxygen remaining in his air tank at nearly three times the normal rate.

"What's going on here?" he screamed into the mouthpiece. "Who *are* you?"

The old fellow's thick hair danced and swayed gently with the soothing underwater currents. He did nothing unusual—except that the event itself was remarkably unusual. Here was a human being nearly seventy feet under the surface of the ocean, *without* breathing gear, *without* a mask, *without* fins, *or* a snorkel! Just floating there under the water with a school of dolphins! How was it possible?

And there was something else. His *eyes!* When Eddie shined his light directly into the man's eyes, he saw that they were uniquely emerald in color. Not frightening eyes, but strangely luring, in fact even comforting. And they were soul-piercing eyes as well, penetrating deep into Eddie's mind and heart, as if searching for something good! Something good? What kind of thoughts were these?

Eddie wondered for a moment if he was dreaming the entire experience, and he considered the need to wake up. He blinked his eyes and looked again at the floating form just ahead of him. But the man was still there, and still looking curiously in his direction.

Then, quite suddenly, the old fellow waved his right hand through the water in a wide, sweeping arch, and Eddie felt a feeling he'd not experienced for more than four years, as energy surged through his entire being. It took his breath away and filled him with a sense of euphoria that was impossible to describe—a soothing rush of gooseflesh and warmth that permeated his entire self. His eyes widened with wonder.

Without warning, the old man smiled again, grabbed hold of the two dorsal fins of the creatures that flanked him, and vanished upward, deep into the dark expanse of the kelp forest that seemed to extend forever toward the surface.

Forgetting everything he had ever been taught about safe surfacing maneuvers during emergency encounters, Eddie panicked and swam frantically upward. Finally, breaking the glassy surface of the water, he yanked his mouthpiece free and screamed for help.

But neither the old man nor Eddie's partner, TC, was to be seen. Eddie knew instinctively that something eerie—ungovernable—was happening. And, as he struggled to stay afloat, he sensed the uneasiness of the approach of a mild state of shock as it began to take a firm hold.

CHAPTER 3

By midafternoon the San Fernando Valley was a boiling pot of lung pollution and suffocating heat. The news reports confirmed several pollution-related deaths, all of them senior citizens.

Far to the eastern end of the San Fernando Basin, in an old, run-down apartment complex, Salvador "Chava" Ayala finally arrived at the top floor of the building. Cautiously the young Mexican immigrant, illegally residing in the United States, withdrew a small key. He looked around for any signs of unusual activity, unlocked the dead bolt in the wooden door in front of him, and quietly slipped inside.

The apartment was a small, barely functional residence that was in desperate need of repair. Chava, however, didn't care about that. He walked over to the small living room window, drew back the musty brown curtains, and slid one of the panes of glass to the side.

The instant movement of air was refreshing. He stood there for a moment, focusing his attention on the streets below. They were busy mazes of confusion, teeming with under-privileged youngsters anxiously engaged in play. These were the street urchins of West Coast America. Poor, to be sure, but enviably wealthy compared to the kids in *his* neighborhood back home.

Chava watched for several minutes, then noted scenes of merriment. He was glad that such was the case, for his eyes had seen the opposite. His neighborhood had its playful children, just like all neighborhoods, but the significant difference from what lay out below him and the dismal streets of his home was that many of the children could *not* spend their days romping freely with friends and playmates. Instead, they were forced to search relentlessly for the basic necessity of life itself—food! His thoughts were painfully disturbing.

Turning from the window, Chava walked wearily into his small bedroom, just down the narrow hallway from the living area, and over to the wooden table standing at the right side of the bed. Carefully, he lifted the tiny reading lamp from the table and placed it on the faded carpet at his feet. Then, gently tipping the nightstand backwards, he stooped and retrieved a small, grey-colored metal box hidden underneath. It was a typical cash-box that required a tiny key. Chava would take that as well. It was dangling on a thin gold chain next to a miniature crucifix hanging around his neck. He took the items and went into the kitchen.

Sitting contentedly at the small dining table, with the metal cash-box opened in front of him, Chava began piecing through the contents. There was a small, black-and-white photograph, wrinkled from years of use, that showed his parents standing affectionately with arms around one another. Plus a second snapshot of his brothers and sisters—all five of them. Chava looked at the photographs tenderly. Then he held the photo of his brothers and sisters up close to his face, peering deeply into each of the faces, and whispered their names out loud.

"Juan Carlos"—just ten years old.

"Elias"—the eight-year-old mischief-maker.

"Norma Angelica"—seven. And what a sweet sister!

"Pedro Antonio"—his little five-year-old brother, the curious one.

"And precious Sylvia Maria"—the four-year-old baby of the family, the sick one.

"Oh, Sylvia, my little sister," he pleaded. "Hold on please, baby, hold on!"

Wiping tears from his eyes and replacing the photographs, Chava considered the emotional despair to which he had succumbed. He desperately disliked the ease with which he lost control. Whatever happened, he had to be a man—and deal with it as a man—even if Sylvia *died*.

"No!" he cried out, the emotions welling up inside him again. "Hold on, my Sylvia!"

This time Chava placed the photos face down inside the box

so that he wouldn't be tempted to look at Sylvia's saintly, sickly face. Then, reaching a little deeper, he withdrew a yellowish-white envelope and poured its contents out onto the table before him.

The envelope had been filled with newspaper clippings, each one different and yet each essentially the same. But Chava was particularly interested in the newest of the clippings—one he had cut out of the *Sud Californio* last week, before he started the nearly thousand-mile journey up the Baja, toward his current residence here in the United States.

The news clipping was a front-page article from the Latino paper. It described in detail a multi-billion dollar contract Mexico's president had made with a U.S. industrial giant. The article said that the American-based "Hospital Planning and Engineering Company" had been given the go-ahead to build fourteen modern medical facilities in and around Mexico City.

But what interested Chava more than the article itself was the newspaper's photograph depicting two men standing side by side, smiling into the photographer's camera. The man on the right was Mexico's elected president, and the stately gentleman on the left was the fourth wealthiest man on the earth—the sixty-nine-year-old billionaire, Allen Scott Russell III.

Chava's stomach churned; his adrenaline pumped uncontrollably. His errand, filled with risk to his life *and* his freedom, had now, irrevocably, changed its course.

CHAPTER 4

Six and a half miles north of Malibu, nestled away at the end of a remote stretch of road aptly called Pacific View Circle, Eddie Russell sat quietly out on the oak veranda of his ranch-style, all-stucco beach home.

Pacific View Circle, as its name implied, was a dead-end street, finished properly with a small cul-de-sac. Eddie's was the only house at the far end of the private road, and he liked that very much. It provided the seclusion he had dreamed of all his life, and the desperately-needed proximity to the sea—his lifeblood.

Inside the living room, a compact-disc player sounded a soothing melody. It played a selection of classical pieces from Eddie's library. At the moment, it was Bach's Brandenburg Concerto No. 3, and Eddie's favorite, Pachelbel's Canon in D. The latter provided the mental panorama of a soothing, dream-like vision. It was a reminder of a moment, long ago, that was both painful and sweet, bringing with it tears to Eddie's eyes. The emotion was a natural response, for it came from the memories of his beloved Andrea lying at the very brink of death in a sterile hospital bed.

Presently, he could shake free from neither the memorable scene nor the feelings that came with it. And of course, Pachelbel's inspiring canon served its purpose well, providing the means for retrospective stimulation.

Sometimes Eddie yearned for that unique emotion, a curious mixture of pain and unutterable love, that had accompanied Andrea's passing. It had been a profoundly painful experience, to be sure, and clearly he had not expected the peaceful euphoria that had swept through him at the moment of her death. Yet it was *that* single element of the ordeal that had provided the desperately needed comfort that was to aid him during the soul-shattering aftermath.

In fact, many nights thereafter, when he believed that he could not make it without his wife, the gentle whispering of her precious spirit would echo once more through Eddie's heart. It served as a reminder that she had moved on to that eternal world of peace and had left behind the relentless agony of her three-year battle with cancer.

The peace itself had come precisely at that very instant when Andrea had expelled her last breath. Eddie had been there at her side, holding gently onto her thin but ever-so-beautiful hands. She had somehow sensed that the time was rapidly approaching, and had asked him to play *their* song, Pachelbel's Canon in D, on the cassette player.

Then suddenly it was all over. One moment they had been staring longingly into each other's eyes. Then, as if the clock had finally wound down, Andrea had smiled softly at her beloved husband, then whispered a barely audible, "I'll love you always, Eddie. . . ."

Moments later, she died.

"No!" he had cried desperately, cursing the fact that no amount of money or medical technology had been able to save her. But as he did so, something totally unexpected happened. He had been holding on to her, trying desperately to support her fragile frame and render what comfort was possible. And as she breathed her last words into his ear he experienced an event that was unlike anything he'd ever imagined. He had not been able to describe his emotions in words, and so had called it the *touch* every time thereafter, when mentally referencing the experience. He did, that is, until Jennifer had entered his life, six months later, and had introduced him to what she called "the gospel of Jesus Christ."

Then there had been the missionaries, the discussions, and finally the day when both he and his then fourteen-year-old son, Jeff, had entered the waters of baptism and then received the gift of the Holy Ghost. It had almost seemed like a dream, it was so compelling. And then, a week later, he received the Aaronic Priesthood under the hands of his new bishop, Randy

Grimshaw. That moment had been surpassed only by the one, immediately thereafter, when he conferred the same priesthood on Jeff's head.

It all seemed so unbelievable, so unreal! But it *was* real, and Eddie knew in the succeeding months, as he prepared for and then received the Melchizedek Priesthood, that he had been taught more about spiritual impressions and truths than he could ever have thought possible.

The sensation he had experienced at his beloved Andrea's passing was a once-in-a-lifetime experience. It was her spirit passing beyond mortality. And with her passing was a gentle momentary commingling—a remarkably soothing yet breath-takingly powerful touch of her spirit with his own. He'd felt it—like a warm spring breeze passing directly through his body.

And what added dramatically to the experience was An-drea's voice—a still, small voice deep inside him, that was piercing and pleasant, whispering gently to his soul, "Be at peace, my beloved husband . . . be at peace . . ."

That had been over four years ago. And except for the ordi-nances performed by him, or in his behalf, inside the Church, he'd not felt that remarkable sensation of pure love, until this very day.

A voice broke through Eddie's pensive silence. "Dad?"

Sixteen-year-old Jeffrey Phillip Russell emerged cautiously from the living room and walked out onto the veranda. "Dad?" he said again. "Are you all right, Dad?"

Eddie looked up at his son. He could see him standing now, just inches away, but was still mesmerized by the subconscious page-turning of memories.

"Dad? Are you okay, Dad? You're scarin' me! You've been sitting out here ever since you got home, listening to those same classical CDs over and over again! You haven't said a word to me! What's the matter, Dad?"

"Oh. Sorry, Son. I guess I've been doing a little reminiscing about . . . your mother. . . ."

"Oh," the boy answered, feeling the impact of his father's words. "I understand, Dad, believe me. But there's something else. I can feel it. What happened today that got you all weirded out?"

"Weirded out?"

"Yeah, you know, all shook up and quiet, and all. . . ."

"Well," Eddie began, then thought about the awkwardness of trying to explain the feeling inside him, or the experience under the sea. "It wasn't so much something that happened, actually. It was, well . . . just some difficult memories that brought your mother to my mind."

Eddie turned then and looked deeply into the boy's eyes, thinking about the uncommonly solid relationship they'd developed over the years—especially since Andrea's death and their conversion to the Church. They had made a promise never to hold back. It was the glue of their relationship, born of mutual respect.

They did not lie to each other, or mislead each other. When there was a problem, the two of them worked it out like responsible partners. After all, that is exactly what they were. Partners. They shared everything. And in Eddie's eyes, Jeff had matured rapidly. He was far from the typical adolescent so common among his peers, and Eddie could only attribute that to their relationship, coupled with the growth that had followed their introduction to the gospel.

"Oh, Dad," Jeff sighed, reaching down to offer a needed embrace. "I'm sorry. I miss her too, you know. But like you said, we gotta be tough!"

Tears formed again in Eddie's eyes. He held onto his son with gentle gratitude, silently thanking God for so great a blessing.

At that moment the doorbell rang. "That must be Jennifer," Jeff said with sudden vibrance, pulling away from his father.

"Jen? And just how would you know that, young man?"

"'Cuz I'm the one who asked her to come over, that's why."

"You did *what?*" Eddie asked, attempting to understand what was going on.

"Yeah. I told her to come over when she called earlier. I tried to tell you," Jeff continued, as he made his way over to the front door, "but you were daydreamin', remember? I'd better let her in."

Jennifer Lee Lapman was, without a doubt, the best thing to come along in Eddie's life since Andrea's death. And with her, of course, came the gospel. She was outgoing, charming, extremely intelligent, and nearly flawless in personal integrity. She was strikingly beautiful, with thick brown hair, hazel-colored eyes, a small, slightly upturned nose, and a womanly figure that clearly revealed her passion for a health-conscious lifestyle.

Eddie and Jennifer had met a little more than three years ago, at a martial arts seminar in Burbank. Both were students of a highly energetic, rigorously disciplined school of self-mastery called the Elysium. The mutual attraction between them was initially rooted in their shared admiration for the pursuit of physical health, but this quietly evolved into a healthy, normal bonding that was so essential for the kind of relationship they both sought.

Stated simply, over the course of the next two years, they had fallen in love.

"Eddie?" she probed, with obvious concern, upon entering the living room. "I came over as fast as I could. Are you all right?"

He smiled at her. "I'm fine, really."

"But Jeff said. . . ."

"I'm okay, really. Had a rather peculiar experience this morning during one of my dives, that's all. It kinda set me thinking a little. But you're certainly a breath of fresh air! Look at you, honey, how beautiful you are!"

"Wow!" Jennifer responded, "What brought all that on?" She moved slowly into Eddie's arms, never once taking her eyes away from his. They embraced, exchanged a warm, reassuring kiss, then pulled back and smiled at each other. Meanwhile, Jeff, who was standing over by the doorway, quietly slipped outside. And as he did so, carefully closing the door behind him, a smile of satisfaction drew across his face. He knew he had done the right thing by inviting her over.

Turning now to Eddie, Jennifer said, "Now, what's all this business of your supposedly 'weirdin' out' that Jeff was talking about?"

"He shouldn't have asked you to come over like that, Jen," Eddie said apologetically. "I hope this didn't inconvenience you."

"Nonsense, sweetie. I was looking for an excuse to come over, anyway."

"Sure you were," he joked playfully.

"Are you telling me that you don't think I enjoy being around my two favorite men?" she countered.

"Well, no . . . I would hope. . . ."

"Then I won't hear another word about it! Let's talk about you. Want to tell me what happened?"

"It's nothing, really," Eddie answered, feeling suddenly very warm inside. He then began to describe the curious events of that morning, pointing out that the whole thing began with his continued efforts to locate the missing Hansen boys who had vanished weeks before.

"Did you find them?" she asked, thinking that it may have been their discovery that haunted him so.

"No," he said. "Something else, though. There was this old trawler, the *Bonnie Marie*. . . ."

"A what?"

"An old fishing boat, Jen. It caught my eye about seventy feet down. Must have sunk years ago, though, because it was nearly overgrown with crustaceans, barnacles, and sea vegetation."

"Well, so what'd you find, Eddie . . . some kind of sea monster?"

"No, no monsters. Something totally unique, actually. But I'm not sure you'll believe me, even if I tell you."

"Try me," she said, offering reassuring support.

"The problem, Jen," he said cautiously, "is that I'm not sure I believe it myself!"

"What? Believe *what*, Eddie?"

"Well . . ." He fumbled awkwardly with his choice of words. "There were these dolphins . . ."

"You saw dolphins?"

"Not just dolphins, sweetheart . . . something *with* the dolphins . . ."

"*What?*"

"A man. Some old guy with thick white hair. He was . . . well . . . swimming with the dolphins!"

"An old man was training some dolphins?" she quizzed, trying to picture some retired worker from Sea World so infatuated with aquatic mammals that he had continued his efforts in the open sea.

"No, Jen. Not training—*swimming* with them! Hanging onto

their dorsal fins while they propelled him through the deep ocean waters!"

"Is that really so unusual?" she questioned, remembering the times she had seen similar interactions between humans and dolphins—and even killer whales—on television programs, at Sea World, and other places.

"At seventy feet under the water in the open sea?"

Suddenly the images he was trying to paint began to focus in her mind. "You mean this guy didn't have any diving gear? Is that what you're trying to say?"

"Exactly. He just came out of nowhere! One moment I'm there surveying this old wreck, then suddenly out of the kelp come these dolphins with the old guy hitching a ride. No diving gear of any kind. I'm telling you, it was the wildest thing I've ever seen!"

Jennifer just looked at him for a moment, trying to picture the scene in her own mind. Slowly, then, she spoke. "Well, how was he breathing then, Eddie?"

"That's just it, sweetheart. I don't *know* how he was breathing. In fact, I'm still curious just how it was possible for him to be down at that depth in the first place. It's nearly impossible for a human being to dive that deep without an air supply. It takes too long to swim down to that depth and return to the surface, especially with the stops you need to make along the way to equalize the sinus pressure that inevitably builds up in your head. It's impossible, I'm telling you, impossible!" Eddie looked long and hard into Jennifer's eyes, hoping for a response that would give him the go-ahead to continue the fabulous tale. He found one.

"Besides," he continued, "the weird thing was the guy's expression. . . ."

"Expression?"

"Yeah. The old guy just floated there at the bottom of the kelp beds and looked at me with a weird smile on his face."

Jennifer sat motionless on the sofa next to Eddie, trying again to visualize the scene of the remarkable tale. She stared into Eddie's eyes, searching, probing for perhaps a sign that would tell her that he was just teasing her, playing some kind of ridiculous game, or something of the sort. But in an instant she knew that he was serious—dead serious. He continued.

"Do you remember my telling you about the experience I had when Andrea died?" he questioned, attempting to address the sensations that had accompanied the experience under the sea. "It was a *feeling* I had at the precise moment of her death. A feeling even stronger than the one I had when I knew the Church to be true. Do you remember me telling you about it?"

"Well," she responded uneasily, "sort of . . . something about her spirit connecting to yours. Is that what you're talking about?"

"Yeah, that's it. The *touch*."

"Yes, I do. So?"

"Well," he continued, "this may sound a bit farfetched, hon, but what happened to me on that dismal day when Andrea died was that her own spirit somehow connected to mine. It was the most remarkable sensation I've ever experienced."

Eddie looked longingly into the hazel eyes of his girlfriend, hoping beyond hope that she was beginning to understand. He wanted the reassurance that she was there for him, supporting him, despite the unusual nature of his tale. She must have sensed the longing need, for without a word she reached over and cupped one of his hands in her own, then said softly, "What happened, Eddie?"

"I felt the *touch* again, Jennifer. It took my breath away, just like the first time! And I've not been able to get it out of my mind since." He paused for a moment with tear-filled eyes, never removing his gaze from the beautiful woman to whom he had become so devoted. Then, in a quiet, almost inaudible whisper, he said, "I've got to go back, Jen. I've got to go back to the *Bonnie Marie*."

CHAPTER 5

High above the eastern province of France, quietly passing over the picturesque city of Dijon, Captain Steven Stewart checked with Robert Kevin, his navigational officer and a skilled jet pilot, and reset the vector heading before initiating a gradual descent.

He reached over and flipped a small switch that in turn illuminated a miniature red light on a private telephone receiver back inside the plush solid oak office in the rear of the luxury Boeing 727 jet.

A buzzer sounded.

"Yes?"

"Excuse me, Mr. Russell. We've started our descent, sir."

"Oh, good. How long before we touch down, Steve?"

"We should be in Zurich in about twenty minutes, Mr. Russell."

"That's fine. Thank you, Steve. Let me know when we're on final approach, will you please?"

"Certainly, sir."

Allen Scott Russell III placed the ivory-colored telephone receiver back onto its resting place at the corner of the desk, then turned back to the two gentlemen sitting in front of him. "We're approaching Switzerland," he said casually. He then arose slowly from the thick, soft-leather seat, moved over to a portside window, and peered out at the earth passing beneath him, some thirty thousand feet below.

"Excuse me, gentlemen," he said, "there's something I need to attend to. It was nice doing business with you. There'll be a limo waiting for you on the tarmac when we touch down. The chauffeur is at your complete disposal. He'll take you to your hotel suites near the lake. I will give considerable thought to your proposal, then call you in a couple of days.

"In the meantime," he continued, smiling graciously as he spoke, "go out and see the sights. Zurich is truly beautiful this time of the year. I trust that will be all right with the both of you?"

"Oh, certainly, sir. Thank you, Mr. Russell. You've been too kind," they chorused, obviously pleased.

Smiling genuinely, Allen Russell turned, exited the small aerial office, and closed the door behind him.

His mind deep in thought, he went to a small circular booth and picked up another extension of the Boeing's onboard telephone system.

A buzzer sounded in the cockpit.

"Yes, sir?" came the captain's voice.

"Steve, connect me with an overseas operator, will you, please?"

"Certainly, sir."

Captain Stewart flipped a switch that instantly put Mr. Russell on a standby mode, then turned to his navigator. "Bobby, patch us into an overseas operator through Zurich International. The boss man wants to make a call."

"Done, and—done!" the young, energetic pilot-navigator responded cheerfully, while making the radio-linked contact.

Moments later, with the connection made, Captain Stewart once again flipped a small switch, released his employer from the standby mode on the intercom, and alerted his employer.

"Your call is ready, sir."

"Thank you, Steve," Mr. Russell responded. "You do good work."

Inside the small stucco house at the end of the cul-de-sac on Pacific View Circle, thousands of miles to the west, the light brown telephone hanging on the wall in the kitchen began to ring, as did the other phones throughout the quiet residence. However, since the occupants were temporarily absent, the call was picked up by a small answering machine.

"You've reached the Russell residence, and we're not at home at the moment. And, since this is just a machine . . . well . . . you know the routine."

There was a short, silent pause—then, "Beeeeeeep."

"Hello, Eddie. Sorry I missed you, Son. I'm on my way to the family chalet in Zurich. Would you please call me collect if you get a minute? And oh, yes—tell that good-lookin' grandson of mine "Happy Birthday," will you? Sorry I missed the festivities."

CHAPTER 6

By ten-thirty Friday evening Eddie was finally beginning to feel at ease and appeared to be returning to his normal self. He and Jennifer had decided to go out for a bite to eat at a small restaurant in Santa Monica called Pickle Bill's. They ate roast beef sandwiches piled high with the famous pickles on which the mom-and-pop restaurant laid its claim to fame. Although Eddie attempted to enjoy himself, Jennifer could clearly detect the mental distance that was evident in his repeated stares out the window.

She wondered at times if she would ever be able to fulfill the needs of her companion, because she realized that even though Eddie's former wife had long since gone physically, Andrea continued to live on in his heart. Nevertheless, she loved this man dearly, and inwardly she pleaded for the day when he would ask for her hand in marriage—if in fact he ever would.

Eddie, she thought pensively, was wonderfully different from most other men. His moral integrity was above reproach, as he openly expressed that he wanted to share his feeling of love and intimacy only within the bonds of marriage—even before his conversion to the Church. And for an extremely handsome, middle-aged guy of the nineties, that *was* unusual.

And it wasn't just that that drew her to him. There was much, much more. He seemed to thrive on quiet and reclusive acts of charity, never allowing those he would help to know who he was. And, more than anything, Jennifer loved that particular trait. In an almost reverent kind of way, Eddie had become a thoughtful, caring man who seemed to go out of his way to ensure that those around him felt important and cared for.

Jennifer remembered the incident . . .

It had been the single kindest act of human caring she had ever been part of, or witnessed. It literally took her breath away, because it had come at a time when Eddie was so close to realizing a personal dream of his own. And not just *any* dream. As the memory of it came back to her, tears suddenly surfaced in her eyes. It had been this particular event which had captured her heart, and which had planted the fertile seeds of love.

When the Aquatic Rangers celebrated their second anniversary, just two months after she and Eddie had met, she learned that he had finally saved enough money to purchase the home he and his son, Jeff, had longed and planned for. However, just two days before they were to close escrow—after they had made a substantial non-refundable earnest money deposit—Eddie had met a young, homeless mother with three children. He had found them sleeping among old blankets and torn-up sleeping bags under the Malibu pier. Without hesitation or fanfare, Eddie had taken them in, fed them, clothed them, and eventually used the money he had been saving to purchase a small condo for them out in Thousand Oaks. He had even gone so far as to insure the family's future by finding the woman a full-time job as a secretary and assisting in enrolling her children in a local school. Somehow it didn't surprise Jennifer, just three months later, that Eddie had deeded the condo to the little family of four.

That was when Eddie finally broke down and asked his father for assistance in purchasing his and Jeff's home out on Pacific View. And she knew how much that had distressed him.

The Russell family, no matter how hard they tried, were never able to learn what Eddie had done with his and Jeff's savings. And even though it had never really seemed to matter to Mr. Russell, himself, others in the family used the event as a reminder that, as far as they were concerned, Eddie would do well to abandon his "childish" lifestyle with the Aquatic Rangers. He could then don a suit and tie and assume his rightful role as another of the privileged heirs to the financial holdings created and maintained worldwide by his billionaire father.

Their urgent prodding, of course, consistently yielded the same fruits. Eddie had borrowed the money out of need, and need only, and intended to pay back every dime of the "loan." And push and persuade as they did, his mother and brothers simply could not alter Eddie's professional mind! He was a Ranger! He enjoyed the work, and he planned on working with the L.A.P.D.'s unique aquatic division until, at the right moment, he would retire with honor. In the meantime, he would live completely within his means.

For Jennifer, the single greatest hope inside her heart and soul was that one day she would become *Mrs.* Eddie Russell. "Oh, yes," she whispered inwardly. "I do love you, Eddie Allen Russell! Ask me to marry you, my darling, and I will!"

During the extended drive homeward, out along the Pacific Coast Highway, Jennifer decided to probe a little further into the events to which Eddie had alluded earlier. In her mind, it seemed to be the best method of helping to bring her dearest friend out of his unusual mental state.

Jennifer wasn't convinced that he had actually *seen* the "old man of the sea," with his supposed escort of dolphins. But she was certain that something had happened—if nothing more than some unusual hallucination caused by heaven only knew what.

In her dealings with the many patients who regularly received psychological counseling at her clinic in Santa Monica, Jennifer had learned that people generally opened up when they were given the chance to just speak their minds to a friend who cared about them—or more importantly, who loved them. She was trained to listen, to learn, to observe, and then to seek out and find the mental difficulties that so often whirled around inside minds filled with anguish, despair, or loneliness. But, most significantly, she was trained to help.

Jennifer loved the way Eddie accepted her chosen profession as a licensed clinical psychologist, and his occasional reference to her being a "physician of the mind." That seemed a fitting title to her quest in mortality.

Indeed, her observations of Eddie through the course of the evening had given her reason to suspect that he *needed* to talk— to open up. Perhaps more time was needed to heal the heart which had broken as a result of Andrea's death. And oh, how she prayed that the pain would ultimately pass, and that he could simply go on living.

Nevertheless, Jennifer understood the unmistakable need for patience and unconditional love, and she resolved to extend them to Eddie, no matter what! As she thought about that need, a warm feeling of renewed hope entered into her heart, and ever so softly she whispered the words, "Unconditional love . . ."

"Huh?" Eddie said, looking momentarily her way, then returning his gaze to the highway in front of them.

"Oh, nothing," she responded, a gentle smile sweeping softly across her lips. "I was just thinking about you."

"About me?"

"Yes," she answered, trying to direct the conversation properly without his sensing that she wasn't entirely convinced about his dolphin story. "I was just thinking about some of the things you said earlier, when we were at your place."

"You mean the guy in the ocean at Point Dume?"

"Yes. A fascinating story, Eddie."

"You don't believe me, do you?"

"I didn't say that, sweetie!" she said defensively, angry that she had tripped herself up. "The idea just sort of takes your breath away, that's all."

"You're telling me! I haven't been able to get it out of my mind all evening!"

"Yes, I noticed."

"That bad, huh? I'm sorry, Jen. I didn't mean to spoil your evening."

"Nonsense, Eddie. You haven't spoiled anything. On the contrary, I was curious about the part of the story you left out."

"Left out?" he queried, looking again in her direction.

"Yes, hon. Remember when Jeff came into the living room and announced his wanting to spend the weekend with some friends?"

"Yes . . . so?"

"Well, if you remember correctly, you had been telling me about how, after the old guy with the dolphins swam away through the kelp, you suddenly disregarded everything you had ever been taught about safe surfacing maneuvers during a crisis situation and swam as fast as you could to the top. Remember?"

"Wow!" he exclaimed, clearly surprised. "You were really paying attention back there, Jen! But, what'd I leave out?"

"Well, you said something that kind of puzzles me about your buddy, Tommy Cosland. You said you felt frightened when you broke through the surface of the water and discovered he was nowhere to be found. You remember that?"

"Yes, I do remember. I was describing the panic." Eddie looked over at Jennifer, searching for her support. Then he said, "That's unusual, you know."

"What?" she questioned. "Your panicking like that?"

"That's right. I don't think I've ever panicked, Jen. At least not during a dive. I've tried to pride myself on the fact that I earned a 'dive master' status, never having panicked a single time. But I'm telling you, hon, when I saw that old guy swimming with those . . . well . . . with what seemed to be remarkably well-trained dolphins, there was this almost haunting feeling, or déjà vu that seemed to sweep over me—reminding me of Andrea—and well, I panicked!"

"Good heavens, Eddie, you don't need to apologize. Just because you panicked one time is certainly no cause for alarm. But you still haven't answered my question, sweetie . . . What happened to TC?"

"Oddly enough, Jen," Eddie responded pensively, "that's one of the reasons why I want to go back to the old sunken fishing trawler, the *Bonnie Marie*. One of the reasons why I panicked was that I wasn't able to find TC or his bubbles. According to my compass, while I was still under the water I hadn't wavered so much as two degrees from the search grid pattern. But when I looked around for TC, thinking that he was just a few feet to my right or left, I was startled to discover that I couldn't locate him."

"You mean you lost him under the water *before* the incident with the old man?"

"Right. It happened sometime after we entered the kelp beds."

"Why didn't you surface then, and look for his bubbles right away? Weren't you afraid that he was in trouble or something?"

"Actually no, I wasn't," he answered. "You see Jen, we've been separated before, and we have this kind of emergency plan we follow. If one or the other doesn't swim into view within, say, three to five minutes after we discover we've been separated, *then* we initiate surfacing maneuvers. But in the past, we've always found each other long before the required ascent, which, by the way, expends a great deal of valuable air from the scuba tanks."

"Yeah, I'll bet it does," she agreed. "But what about your compass? You started to mention something about your compass—"

"I was just getting to that. Like I said, I was searching along the charted grid when I first spotted the trawler. Something on its hull caught my attention. And anyway, I looked at my compass, checked my coordinates, and then did what we call a 360-degree circular rotation under the water, in an attempt to locate TC."

"Did you spot him, then?"

"No. I couldn't see him anywhere. That's part of what worried me—because in order to get a closer look at the sunken fishing boat, I had to veer off in a northerly direction, leaving the search grid where TC would be looking for me."

"So, what happened, Eddie?" she quizzed, growing more intrigued with each passing minute.

"Well, from my vantage point under the water, the old trawler didn't appear to be much more than ten, maybe fifteen degrees off to the side of the search area. So I figured I could swim over to her, take a quick peek, and return if it was of no further interest to me. But when I got over to her and saw the old guy with his dolphins, I surfaced in a panic and eventually rechecked my compass above water.

"I was astounded to discover that instead of having swum fifteen or twenty feet away from the search site, I had actually distanced myself by more than a hundred yards! I couldn't believe it, Jen! No wonder I couldn't see TC anywhere. It wasn't Tommy who got lost, it was me!"

"A hundred yards? How was that possible, sweetheart?"

"I don't know, Jen, any more than I understand any other part of this unexplainable encounter. The point is, when I finally got a hold on my emotions, inflating my buoyancy compensator so that I could just float there, out past the breakers, I looked around and took a visual reference on the cliffs at Point Dume.

"And sure enough, I was a good hundred yards past the

spot I'd calculated earlier on my compass. It was then, after I had finally realized where I was, that I scanned the surface of the water in the direction I should have been. And there was TC's head—just a small dot of a thing—bobbing out of the water where I should have been."

"Did he see you?" Jennifer asked anxiously.

"No, not at first. I had to do some considerable swimming. He wasn't looking for me out in the open sea, where I had mysteriously surfaced. He was searching in what he figured was the right location—where I should have been! And he was obviously terrified, because when I finally swam to where he could see me I could tell that he was not just frightened, but had begun to panic as I had done."

"Poor guy!"

"Yeah, he was really worried about me. Anyway," Eddie continued, "I never did tell him about the old fishing boat, the *Bonnie Marie*, or the experience I had just had. Instead, I just sort of made up this story about a slight undertow. Besides, I didn't think he'd believe me, anyway."

"Wise choice," Jennifer said reassuringly.

Eddie wrapped his arm around her shoulders and drew her close. Their eyes met, and she reached up and gave him a quick reassuring kiss on the lips. "So," he said affectionately, "what do you think, Doctor Lapman, my beautiful physician of the mind? Am I losing mine?"

"Oh, I don't think so, Sergeant Russell. But I would suggest that you try to relax a little more, and maybe spend more time with the lady of your choice!"

"And is that your professional opinion, Doctor?" he asked playfully, as they pulled into the driveway at the end of the cul-de-sac.

"That, and *this*," she responded, turning toward him and putting both arms around his neck just as he was shutting off the engine. They held each other close and kissed tenderly.

"I love you, Jennifer," he said contentedly.

"That's a reassuring thought, Sergeant, because you know what?" she said, whispering softly into his ear.

"What?" he responded, feeling a ticklish chill run up and down his neck.

"I love you, too."

By midnight, Jennifer was backing out of the driveway with a lingering smile on her face.

"Be careful, my lady!" Eddie called.

"Don't worry about me, good lookin'," she answered playfully. "You just go in and get some rest. I'll come out tomorrow afternoon and cook you some barbecue chicken. Sound good?"

"Does it ever!" he said cheerfully.

"Good! See you at noon, Sergeant!"

Eddie stood silent out by the curb and watched Jennifer's Audi 100 sedan scoot out along Pacific View, disappearing finally up over the small hill at the end of the street. The sound of the car faded, and everything was silent except for the soothing whisper of the gently rising and falling waves that caressed the sandy beach far below. Off in the distance, in a northerly direction, Eddie could clearly see the dark but distinct features of the rocky cliffs that outlined Point Dume.

Then, like a silent, furtive voice in the night, calling out to him, Eddie sensed a curious compelling need—a beckoning call to go back—a desire to feel again, the *touch!*

He stood, straining his eyes to see through the darkness. Point Dume. He *had* to go there! It was only three miles to the north. He could drive there now—look around—maybe even make a quick dive.

"What?" he whispered, with a clear strain in his voice. "What am I saying? It's nearly one o'clock in the morning! Am I losing my mind?"

Then, as if drawn by some magical magnet of pure curiosity, Eddie was suddenly racing in an activity of sheer madness. He hurried back through the living room and out into the garage without even shutting off the stereo player. Quickly, but carefully, he lifted his diving gear back into the bed of the pickup, changed into a full-body wetsuit, and jumped into the truck.

There was no more time for retrospection. The course was clear. He drove off down the quiet oceanfront road of his little neighborhood, up and over the small hill at the opposite end, and out onto the Pacific Coast Highway beyond.

For a moment, he drove in complete silence. Then, in a barely audible whisper, he heard himself saying, "I've got to go back . . . I've got to go back to the *Bonnie Marie.*"

CHAPTER 7

The winds that blew steadily in from the Pacific seemed unnervingly cold and eerie to Eddie Russell as he stood at the narrow overlook at Point Dume. He hadn't remembered, in fact, when nighttime winds during the summer months of southern California's coastal regions had been this cold. It wasn't normal.

Dressed from head to toe in his heaviest wetsuit, Eddie checked his diving gear, then stepped back. There was a sudden queasiness inside his stomach.

He tried to rationalize the seemingly irrational decision he had made back at the house: this maddening compulsion to return to the sunken fishing trawler—alone, at night! But he could not make sense of it. And although he was just about to violate every diving regulation to which he had sworn his allegiance, he could not—literally could not—turn around, get back into his pickup, and drive back home where he belonged.

He was going to make the dive, no matter what frightening consequences lay ahead. After all, nighttime only existed above the ocean. Beneath, his searchlight would give him all the visual assistance he would need. As these thoughts raced through his mind, neurological impulses inside his brain suddenly dispatched a series of signals to his arms and legs, and without knowing why, he simply threw the heavy scuba tank over one shoulder and simultaneously entered the narrow trail that descended gradually toward the sandy beach.

Once he was in the frigid water, it took just a minute for Eddie's body temperature to normalize itself. Before long the initial shock and trauma ended, and he began swimming slowly out into the darkness. Of course it wasn't totally dark.

His six-volt rechargeable underwater lamp helped him get a visual "fix" on his surroundings, and he received further guidance from one of the two compasses strapped on his wrists.

He had brought two compasses this time. After checking to see that they were both operational, pointing due north, Eddie took in a deep breath of oxygen, pointed his lamp toward the west, and slowly propelled himself out into the deeper waters of the open sea.

At thirty-five feet, floating just inches above the sandy bottom next to a field of crusty-looking coral reefs, Eddie paused briefly and pinched his nose in an effort to neutralize the sinus pressure. As he did so, he noted with a sense of anxious uncertainty that feelings of increasing uneasiness began to sweep over him. The thoughts troubled him, and he felt suddenly compelled to initiate not one but two complete 360-degree visuals, shining his light into the voids and reassuring himself that he was, in fact, alone.

Checking his depth gauge, Eddie figured that he was approaching the spot where he had originally seen the old fishing trawler. He halted for a moment, pulled his pressure gauge up into view, and marked his remaining air time. Plenty of air.

With the underwater lamp in his left hand, he began a slow sweeping search of the immediate area. The *Bonnie Marie* was close by—he was sure of it!

But . . . nothing.

He checked his compasses again. According to both units, he still needed to swim another ten to fifteen yards west. From there, he was fairly certain that the sunken trawler would come into view. Another five minutes passed. Still nothing. Eddie was beginning to feel disoriented. So where was the *Bonnie Marie?* He checked his pressure gauge again. Ten, maybe twelve minutes of air left!

Where *was* it?

He had never had this much difficulty relocating an underwater destination when he had been there before. Especially if he had charted the position. But mysteriously, nothing in the immediate vicinity looked to be even remotely familiar.

Suddenly, something—he wasn't sure what—shimmered slightly as he passed the underwater beam of light across its surface. Yes! There *was* a reflection! Slowly, he swam off in that direction and at last emerged from the tangled vines of the kelp beds to find the upturned skeletal remains of a small fishing boat.

But it was not the *Bonnie Marie*.

He moved in for a closer look. The markings on the hull were familiar—yes, it matched perfectly the description of the small fishing craft that had vanished just a couple of weeks before.

The Hansen boat!

A shudder of anxiety seared through Eddie's body as he began surveying the wreckage. He envisioned a familiar scene from an old Hollywood picture show, where a lone diver had come upon a similar vessel, peered into its sunken hull, and been met by a pair of haunting eyes attached to a decaying corpse.

He of course didn't particularly care to find one or both of the Hansen kids in that same fashion, but he reconciled himself to the responsibility that was his. He'd have to bring up the body—or bodies—if, in fact, they were here. His heart began to race while his breathing increased.

Then slowly, and ever so cautiously, Eddie grabbed onto the underside of the small boat, shined his lamp underneath, and forced himself to look. No bodies.

He marked his position and depth, then immediately began to surface. By now, he assumed that he was probably several hundred yards out into the cove and would have to swim his way over the surface toward the shore. No big deal. An inconvenient swim above water, that's all. The only real hassle would be the tedium of making his way through the giant lily-pad-like entanglements of seaweed that floated on the surface. He had done it before.

It was time to go home and get some sleep.

Eddie Russell broke through the surface of the water at approximately 1:40 A.M., and the first thing that caught his eye was the full moon overhead, flanked by an impressive ocean of stars. With the little air remaining in his tank, he filled the buoyancy compensator to near capacity, then began his swim back toward the shoreline.

With barely two hundred yards remaining before he would

be able to touch the rising shoreline, Eddie felt a sudden chill of anxiety surge throughout his body. His every sense became aware of something that seemed to have triggered an internal alarm!

He halted his forward progress for a moment, bobbed gently in the surf, then turned around and gazed back out across the open expanse of the sea behind him. The constantly churning waters sparkled mysteriously, as if under a spell of magic, reflecting the shimmering glow of the moon and stars.

But there was something wrong—something *very* wrong! He didn't quite understand, but he knew somehow that there was something out in the water, just beyond his field of vision. He floated in silence, never moving a muscle, and strained with great difficulty to see what, for the moment, he could only feel.

Eddie was about to turn back toward the coastline and resume his swimming when a dark, shadowy silhouette of something incredibly large broke through the surface of the water about seventy-five yards behind him. He whirled around in the water, causing a considerable splash in the process.

Then panic took over, and instinctively Eddie turned toward the shoreline, swimming for all he was worth. He felt suddenly grateful for the large, effective flippers attached to his feet, and he hoped beyond hope that what he believed he saw was simply an illusion of the night instead of a sea creature that was about to devour him.

Off in the distance he could hear the waves crashing onto the beach. "Faster!" he willed himself. His swimming became frantic, and with every physical effort possible he pushed ahead. He heard another sound. But this time it wasn't the surf against the shore. Nor was it the near thrashing madness of his hands and feet desperately slicing through the waters. Instead, it was a terrifying sloshing sound just five, maybe six, yards directly behind him. The sound of *something* chasing him!

For a brief second, he strained his neck to look back. It was grey, and it was at that very moment submerging again into the darkness of the deep. There *was* something behind him! The fear was suddenly overwhelming. And thinking that at any moment he was about to feel a vice-like bite from some ferocious beast, he screamed!

That was when his hands slammed suddenly onto the sand.

Out of sheer panic, not even watching where he was going, he had propelled himself right through the small waves and up onto the beach! Frantically, he crawled out of the water and onto the shore, gasping for air. He threw his tank and regulator onto the beach, sat up, and stared out into the murky waters.

His shivering became intense—completely out of control. But strain as he did, he could see nothing. There was only silence and the relentless motion of the small, gentle waves lapping at the wet sands just feet away from his flippers.

He dropped onto his back from sheer exhaustion, stared up at the moon and stars, and tried to get control of the panic that had overcome him. All was quiet for a moment, except for his heavy breathing.

"What next?" he wondered. "What in the world was—"

There was a noise behind him. Something just a few feet higher up on the sand!

He leaped up onto his feet, staggered wearily, then spun around. There directly in front of him, standing almost motionless, was the figure of an elderly gentleman.

"Hello, Eddie," he said calmly.

CHAPTER 8

The debate that raged inside Chava Ayala's mind was the single greatest mental contest he had ever faced. It was a loathsome task, having to deal with this new form of mental reasoning referred to as rationalization.

He hated it. For it was extremely foreign to his otherwise honorable, even noble character. There had never been a reason for Chava to rationalize. Especially when it came to compromising his strict Christian principles. Yet here he was—already neck-deep inside the initial phase of the most degrading debauchery he could possibly have imagined.

"What else can I do?" he sighed audibly. It was either follow the outlined plan or do nothing at all. If the latter course were taken, he would wearily witness the slow death of his little sister, Sylvia Maria. And in the end, he rationalized his actions with his sense of duty and love.

As he drove the well-used Ford Escort south along the San Diego Freeway, up and over the Santa Monica mountains, and finally onto Sunset Boulevard, Chava rationalized again that when it was all over, Jesus would forgive him, since He knew that Chava's only motive was to save the life of his so-very-fragile and innocent baby sister.

He simply could not stand by and let her die.

When Papa had passed away, the family had been catapulted headlong into a world of poverty that was beyond the reaches of human endurance. Eventually it had become a monumental effort just to find a simple morsel of bread with which to fill the starving bellies of his brothers and sisters, his grief-stricken mother, and himself.

Chava pulled the light tan-colored rental car over to a gas station and up alongside a corner phone booth. Turning off the engine and positioning his hands on top of the steering wheel, he hung his head between his arms and offered a silent prayer. He prayed that his dear mother would be able to care for Sylvia until he could return with the desperately needed financial aid that would allow them to pay for the expensive medical treatment Sylvia needed if she had any hope for a chance to live. Time was running out. And if the "plan" did not work, Sylvia would be dead in a matter of weeks—months, at best.

Determined, therefore, to go through with his plan, Chava climbed out of the car, retrieved a crumpled-up piece of paper from inside his shirt pocket, then walked slowly over to the telephone booth. "Russell," he said quietly, looking down at the name written in his even penmanship. "Warren A. Russell; Brentwood, California; the oldest of the four sons. Hmmm."

He paged through the directory that lay before him. There was no listing for Mr. Allen Scott Russell III. He had already tried that. But maybe the older son . . .

As he continued his search, he came at last to a list of "Warrens." He withdrew a wooden pencil and copied each of their telephone numbers and addresses. That accomplished, Chava carefully scanned through the telephone numbers, selected three that impressed him, and dropped a quarter into the money slot. There was a slight pause following his dialing of the first set of numbers, then a ring.

"Hello, Russell residence," a female voice answered.

"Hello? Yes, pardon me, ma'am. I am looking for Señor Warren Russell."

"Yes, this is Warren's residence. How may I help you?"

"Is this the same Warren Russell whose father is president of the hospital company?" Chava inquired politely.

"No, I'm afraid you've got the wrong Warren, Mr. . . . . uh . . .'"

"Señor Carlos Antonio. I'm a reporter, ma'am, with *La Opinión*."

"La what?"

"I'm sorry, ma'am. It is a Latino-based newspaper here in Los Angeles, for the Spanish-speaking citizens."

"Oh, yes," the woman replied, "I've seen that on the newsstands. And you're a reporter, huh?"

"That is correct, ma'am."

"You're doing a story on the billionaire family, the Russells, you say?"

"Again, you are correct, ma'am. Do you happen to know them personally?"

"Oh, I wish!" the woman said eagerly. "But actually, no. The only thing I do know is what I read in the newspapers, or hear on the TV. They're very wealthy, you know!"

"Yes, ma'am, I do know. However, I must be going now. I need to locate the correct Warren Russell."

"Well, you might try the Russells in Santa Monica. If I'm not mistaken, I believe the Warren you're looking for lives on a street called La Mesa Drive, just off San Vincente Boulevard. My husband, Warren, is often mistaken for the billionaire's son, and we get phone calls all the time from people trying to contact him for some reason or another. Well, anyway," she continued, "my sister and I were curious ourselves about the family, and we went up to look at their beautiful home in Brentwood."

"Whose home?" Chava queried excitedly.

"Why, Mr. Allen Russell's home."

"And you know where he lives?"

"Certainly. Everyone knows where the Russell mansion is. Don't you?"

"I'm afraid that I do not, ma'am. You see, I just recently acquired this assignment, and had not really paid too much attention to the Russell family."

"Oh. Well, that's easy, Mr. . . . ."

"Carlos, ma'am."

"Well, it's easy, Carlos. As I said, the family estate is up in Brentwood, on Rockingham. You know where that is?"

"Not exactly, ma'am. But I do have a map."

"Well . . ." she said a bit fidgety, "I'm not supposed to give it out, you understand, but if you can keep it a secret, I've got both their addresses, as well as the telephone number of the Brentwood mansion. Shirley Wilcox down at the beauty parlor gave them to me. Would you like to have them?"

Chava's eyes widened with delight. "Well, yes, ma'am. That would be most helpful."

CHAPTER 9

Jennifer was weaving in and out of the traffic on the Pacific Coast Highway. She was thinking about the evening before and considered herself marvelously lucky to have such a wonderful boyfriend as Eddie.

Today was going to be a special day, after a grueling week of work. She had stayed up the night before, preparing everything just right. Barbecue chicken and the works. And what a splendid day to be on the beach—Eddie's beach—with no one around but the two of them to enjoy the afternoon and evening together.

The phone message from Jeff had informed her that he was away for the weekend, enjoying "Carmel by the Sea." "Good for Jeff," Jennifer thought. He had gone with a group of priests from his ward. She appreciated his call, letting her know that she was just preparing for two—Eddie and her.

By eleven-fifty Jennifer was less than a mile from the Malibu city limits, and she noted with casual interest that nearly all of the public beaches were already teeming with sunbathers and ocean-goers.

Summer was here!

Just past the old Texaco station, she spotted Eddie's office. "I wonder if he came into work," she whispered quietly. She noted, however, that Eddie's S-10 was not in his usual parking stall, and she was about to continue her drive toward his house when a pleasant little thought entered her mind. She would stop for a minute and leave a little note on his desk.

Janie Hamblin, Eddie's dispatch operator, was there—her little Mazda RX-7 was parked just to the right of Eddie's spot.

Jennifer liked Janie. The two had become almost best friends, and had often gone out to lunch together.

She pulled off the coast highway and into the small parking lot, parked her Audi 100 alongside Janie's Mazda, then went inside.

"Oh, good!" Janie said upon seeing Jennifer enter the office. "I'm so glad you're here! Is Eddie with you?"

"Well, no, he's at home, isn't he? I was just on my way there, as a matter of fact. We're having a picnic this afternoon. Why? What's wrong, Janie? You sound worried."

"I am worried!" Janie exclaimed, clearly flustered. "I've been trying to get Eddie on the phone all morning. But all I get is that blasted recording. In fact, I can't even get him on the radio. Do you know where he is, Jen?"

"Why? What's the matter?"

"He's got an important television interview today, Jennifer! It surprises me that he didn't tell you about it. When did you talk to him last?"

"Well . . . we were together last evening, actually. But he never mentioned anything about a television interview."

"Oh, *rats!*" Janie exclaimed. "What am I gonna do, Jen? He knew the interview was scheduled for this afternoon! I must have reminded him a dozen times before he left the office yesterday."

"Why don't I run out to his house?" Jennifer answered anxiously. "I've got my own key to the place, and I can call you from there if I find out anything. Does that sound good?"

"That sounds great, Jen. If you find him, though, tell him that Captain Mitchell is going to be arriving around three this afternoon. And the reporter with his news team is supposed to be here promptly at four. In any case, please call me the minute you arrive."

"I will. But don't worry, Janie, we'll find him," she said reassuringly.

Jennifer turned and headed directly back out the door of the office, beginning to wonder for a moment if, in fact, there *was* cause for alarm. The thought worried her briefly, and as she left the building she distinctly heard her friend's voice at the radio transmitter, frantically calling out once more—

"One-W-Sixteen . . . come in Sixteen. . . ."

*   *   *

Jennifer pulled into the driveway at the end of the cul-de-sac on Pacific View Circle and immediately noticed something *very* wrong!

In the first place, it was completely out of character for Eddie to have gone off without remembering to close the garage door behind him. In fact, with the remote control device inside the cab of the S-10 it was an effortless process, anyway. And she just knew that Eddie would never leave the place unattended like that. Something *was* wrong!

Cautiously, she parked the Audi to one side of the driveway, climbed out of the vehicle, then walked slowly into the open garage. Immediately she noticed that something else was wrong. The kitchen doorway that led into the garage, was also open—wide open. Obviously, when Eddie had left the house—and she was reasonably sure that he had, since the Chevy was gone—he had done so in a hurry.

She poked her head into the kitchen. "Eddie? Jeff? Anybody home?"

No answer.

"Hey, you guys! It's me, Jen. Is anyone here?" Still silence. Clearly, the house was deserted.

Jennifer stepped over the threshold and moved cautiously through the kitchen area and into the living room. There was music playing on the CD player—classical music, in fact—one of Eddie's favorite pieces. It was a disc she had heard many times in the past. Apparently, Eddie had left recently. Or . . . maybe not. She remembered that the stereo player was equipped with a computerized continuous-play device that allowed the scanners to play, then replay over and over again. It could have been playing for hours.

Carefully she walked over to the machine and shut it off. Then, for a moment, she stood in the living room in complete silence. That was when she noticed the sliding glass doors. They, too, were open.

"What's going on here?" she said, quite puzzled by the unusual series of unexpected discoveries. "Eddie? Are you here, honey?" But just as she expected, there was no response.

"Maybe he's asleep," she thought irrationally, looking down at her watch and noting, with obvious concern, that it was almost one in the afternoon. "Of course he's not asleep," she answered herself sarcastically, rebuking the question. Nevertheless, she walked carefully down the narrow hallway from the living room and entered Eddie's bedroom. The room was, as she had expected, deserted. In fact, the bed was made, and the room was clean. It had not been used all night. She felt sure of it.

Moving timidly back up the hallway toward the living room, growing more and more worried as she went, Jennifer decided to call Janie back at the station and get an update, if there was one. She hoped, of course, that by now Eddie might have called in on the radio.

In the living room, she walked over to a small end table next to the sofa and reached for the telephone. Before she could pick it up, however, it began to ring.

She grabbed at it anxiously, hoping to hear Eddie's voice on the other end.

"Hello?"

"Hello. Who is this?" came a male voice at the other end of the line.

"Jennifer," she said timidly. "Eddie's friend . . ."

"Oh, hello, Jen. Warren here."

Jennifer recognized the voice of Eddie's eldest brother. She really liked Warren.

"Is Eddie there? We've been trying to reach him all morning," he said politely, though with urgency.

"No, Warren, he's not. As a matter of fact, I just came from the station where I talked with Janie Hamblin. She's looking for him, too. I was hoping you might be able to give *me* some information. It seems that no one knows where he is."

"What about Jeff? Does he know where his dad is?"

"I'm afraid Jeff's gone as well, Warren. He left last night while Eddie and I were preparing to go out for a bite to eat. Said he was going up to Carmel for the weekend."

"Did he say who he was going with?"

"Just some boys from his Church . . ."

"Do you think Eddie might have gone to help Jeff out, or something . . . maybe a problem on the road?"

"I really don't know, Warren. He didn't leave a note, and things just aren't right around here . . ."

"What do you mean, Jen?"

"Well," she said nervously, looking around the room and feeling a bit panicky, "the garage door was open when I got here, and so was the kitchen door leading into the garage. It's not like Eddie to leave things wide open like that."

"And his truck's gone, as well?" Warren questioned further.

"Yes."

"Does it look like anything's missing from the house? A burglary, maybe?"

She looked for a second time around the living room and the adjacent kitchen area, searching for clues. But she couldn't see anything that would lead her to believe anyone had broken in or stolen anything.

"No, not that I can see, Warren. In fact, his CD recorder was playing when I got here . . ." Clearly, she was becoming more unnerved by the minute.

"Listen, Jen. Kenny, Larry, and I have to leave sometime tomorrow afternoon for Zurich. Dad's out there for an important meeting with several of our top Swiss and German companies, and he fully expects us to be present for Monday's business. I really need to talk with Eddie before I go. If you see him, will you tell him to call?"

"Sure, Warren, no problem. Should I have him call you at home, or at your parents' place in Brentwood?"

"Try our house first. But if you can't reach me there, call Mom's place, okay?"

"All right, fine," she said calmly, writing down the message.

"Hey . . . and Jennifer?"

"Yes?"

"Call me yourself when you find out anything about Eddie, will you?"

"Of course. I'll do that. Bye, Warren."

"See ya later, kiddo."

With anxiety swelling in her stomach, Jennifer hung up the phone and walked slowly through Eddie's home, peeking timidly into each of the bedrooms, closets, and storage areas. She knew that the search was silly and chastised herself for the effort. But for some unknown reason, she found comfort in this little exercise.

She ended up out on the veranda, Eddie's favorite place of solitude. Slowly, she walked over to the oak railing, placed her hands gently on its surface for support, and stared out at the sea.

She heard noises in the distance: the ocean, the birds, the winds, and subtle sounds of children playing on the beach. But suddenly her thoughts were interrupted by another sound altogether, coming from nearby.

Quickly she turned on her heels and ran back through the living room, toward the garage. She hadn't remembered closing the garage, since she still had to bring the food in. But she *had* remembered closing the door that led out through the kitchen into the garage.

As she approached the door, someone on the outside grabbed the door handle and began turning the knob slowly, clockwise.

Someone was coming *in!* Yet she hadn't heard Eddie's truck pull into the garage! She froze, feeling a sudden shiver of nervous anxiety. Her heart raced wildly.

"Who is it?" she called out fearfully. The door opened, and there standing at the threshold was Eddie! But *not* Eddie!

She put her hand over her mouth and stared in shock at the figure before her. It was Eddie, all right, but his *hair!* His hair—which had always been a deep, handsome brown—was completely white!

CHAPTER 10

Several miles away from Eddie's Malibu home, and less than a block away from the Russell mansion on Rockingham Avenue, Chava had set up his surveillance. There hadn't been much activity for the past hour, and he was progressively more nervous about being exposed to the passersby. No one, however, seemed even to notice him sitting there, so he remained poised and ready with his camera.

As the morning gave way to afternoon, Chava was able to take about a half-dozen photographs. Each of these, he had reasoned, would eventually lead him to the individuals he sought—if he would just be patient.

But that was the problem. Time was running out. He knew it, and it worried him more than ever. He realized that he had two or maybe three weeks, at most—and by then, without help, Sylvia would be dead!

"Oh, dear God," he cried miserably, "please preserve my dear sister . . ."

Sylvia was dying! The symptoms, he remembered, were deceptive at first. Who would ever have thought? They were symptoms any child could have had. But there was nothing simple about her illness. Sylvia Maria Ayala, his angelically beautiful sister—then two years of age—had been diagnosed with acute lymphoblastic leukemia (ALL).

How appropriate! In English, "ALL" meant everything. And now this dreadful disease was consuming *all* of Chava's time, efforts, earnings, and attention. Moreover, it was consuming all of the remaining life of his stricken sister. Chava thought back to the moment when he and his mother had received the terrible news.

"The stem cells," the aged physician had said, "those that divide to produce both red and white blood cells, become somewhat defective."

"Somewhat *defective?*" Chava had questioned. "What does that mean?"

"These stem cells," the doctor had continued, "produce defective cells that suppress the formation of normal cells and infiltrate some of the body organs. For example, the liver, spleen, lymph nodes, and sometimes even the kidneys will accumulate the defective cells, and swelling will begin to take place inside the body."

Chava and his mother stared nervously at the old doctor, patiently waiting for him to continue.

"The greatest concentration of these stem cells," he said, "is found in the bone marrow itself. You see, little Sylvia will need a bone marrow aspiration to confirm what I am afraid we already know."

"A bone marrow *what?*"

"Aspiration, Mr. Ayala. Your sister is very sick, and although we are relatively certain that she suffers from the acute form of ALL, as I have said, we cannot be sure until we perform a bone marrow aspiration."

As the doctor continued to explain the procedure, Chava could clearly see the long needle in his mind—the needle that would have to be pushed into his sister's tender flesh until it penetrated the bone. Even Sylvia, who had been very brave to this point, had a worried expression on her precious little face.

"My poor Sylvia," Chava moaned.

"ALL," the doctor had said, "is the most common form of leukemia among young children. And the likelihood of remission is greater than ninety percent! This, however, depends to a great extent on the treatment. You see, Sylvia will need to be taken to a specialized treatment center for chemotherapy. The process may last up to three years."

"*Three years?*" Chava echoed desperately. "How can we afford such treatment?" He looked over toward his mother, who was herself clearly struggling with the helplessness of their situation. They were poor people. There was absolutely no way for the Ayala family to come up with the kind of money that would be required to pay for such treatment. Moreover, the funds that had been saved in their tiny bank account were depleted.

Still, Sylvia had received months of intense treatment, on credit and promises to pay, and in time it had begun to pay off. The waxy pallor of the young child's face had eventually given way to her original healthy bloom of color.

Slowly her appetite and energy had increased, and it seemed that God Himself had intervened. Even so, all of this, in terms of cost—both in human suffering and in monetary expenditures—had been staggering for the Ayala family. And yet, for the moment, it had appeared to work.

"Remission," he whispered aloud.

That's what the doctors had called it. For within two short years, Sylvia's fragile little body had grown stronger, and the doctors had proclaimed the disease to be in complete remission.

"Remission!" he said again, feeling suddenly very bitter inside. The deadly symptoms had returned. And Chava had felt as though his life and that of his dear, poverty-stricken family were falling apart.

The doctors, this second time, had made things very clear. Only a full-scale bone marrow transplant could stop the cancer from snuffing out Sylvia's life. There would be more tests. More costs!

But for the moment, due to the complete lack of funding, Sylvia Maria would not, or could not, undergo further testing or treatment of any kind. Instead, she had been left with Mama back in La Paz, with nothing more than a rapidly diminishing hope in the Lord Jesus to see her through.

Sylvia was *dying!* And if her brother, Chava, did not come up with the required 160,000.00 U.S. dollars needed for the tests and subsequent transplant, she would soon be gone.

First Papa, then Sylvia. Who would be next?

Something desperate had to be done, and although it went against everything Chava believed in, the corrupt scheme was all that was left. It was simply do, or die!

Again getting a grip on his emotions, Chava turned his attention toward the immense Brentwood Heights estate across the street. Several hours had passed, and still there was no sign

of the individuals he sought. But somehow—sooner or later—
he just knew they would show. And he would be ready. He
would see them, photograph them, develop the prints, and
drive the four hundred miles to California's Folsom prison
before Tuesday.

He would wait.

CHAPTER 11

For a moment, Jennifer could not speak. She remained transfixed and immovable at the sight of her boyfriend's sudden change in appearance, and she wondered if her eyes were deceiving her. Eddie looked into her startled eyes and spoke softly.

"Hello, Jen . . . Sorry I'm late."

"Wh . . . *what?*" she responded, still very nearly overwhelmed with confusion and a sense of fear that she could not understand.

"Our barbecue . . . remember?" he said, maintaining the air of calmness that, to Jennifer, seemed totally out of place and completely deceptive. "You did say that we were going to have one of your famous barbecues today, didn't you?"

"Eddie?" was all she could get out. "What . . . what are you talking about? Barbecue? Everyone on the entire planet has been looking for you, Eddie. Your brother, your office, your father in Switzerland, the television reporters, your captain downtown at the precinct . . . *everybody!* You've got a television interview in about two hours from now, and I've been worried half to death wondering where you've been all morning. Then you suddenly show up here at one o'clock in the afternoon, looking like you've seen a ghost. Look at you! Look at your hair! It's all *frosted*, Eddie! I mean . . . I can't say it! Obviously something terrible has happened, and all you can say is 'barbecue'? What's going on, Eddie? Where've you been?"

"My hair?" he questioned, singling out the one thought only. "My hair is what?"

Eddie walked quickly past his girlfriend and over to a full-length mirror that was mounted just to the right of the front living room door. He stood for a moment, staring at the reflection in the glass, but he did not seem the least bit surprised or even concerned about what he saw. His hair *was* white. Hardly a trace of the original color was anywhere to be seen.

"Well, what d'ya know about that?" he said with remarkable composure. "It *is* white. Doesn't look too bad, though, does it? You still love me, I hope."

"*Love* you?" she exclaimed, still as confused as ever. "Oh, Eddie, of course I love you." She then reached up and put her arms around his neck, squeezing him with all her strength. "I'll always love you, Eddie, but I just don't understand . . . Tell me—what's going *on* here?"

He drew her back and looked longingly into her eyes. He then kissed her gently on the forehead and thought for a moment. What could he say? Even with her knowledge of the gospel, there was so much to tell that he really didn't know where to begin.

His mind raced, and he considered the events of the previous night—and the subsequent hours of the morning. So much had happened. And although he had been thoroughly active all night long, and had never so much as slept a wink through the morning hours, his body and mind felt completely invigorated.

In his mind, Eddie knew that some things could not be revealed. Some of the events to which he had been a part would ultimately remain—forever—his experience alone. He simply couldn't share everything.

Even as it was, Eddie was sure that Jennifer would consider him crazy if he were to open up wholeheartedly and tell all. It fascinated him that the physical appearance of his hair color had changed, but he understood why and was therefore completely accepting of it.

Again, in a very tender way, he gave his girl a warm embrace, drawing her close and holding her for a moment longer. He would tell her what happened, but not just yet. There were other matters that needed his immediate attention, and they were matters of importance. The television interview was one of them. He had forgotten about it, just as his dispatch operator, Janie, had suggested that he might.

"Listen, Jen," he said in a quiet tone of voice. "Something *has* happened. Something wonderful and frightening, all at the same time. When I can, I'll tell you everything. But for now, love, we've gotta get down to the station. I'm sure Janie's worried sick about me. She tried over and over to remind me about the TV interview, and probably told you I'd forget it, right?"

"Well, as a matter of fact—"

"I knew she would. But no matter. She was right as usual, bless her heart. I had so much on my mind yesterday, things I didn't understand."

"So that's it!" Jennifer said excitedly. "That old man and his dolphins! You went back, didn't you, Eddie! Is that what happened? Did you go back there looking for the old fishing boat? Did you find it? Did you see the old man?"

"Whoa! Hold on there, Jen! One thing at a time."

"You did, didn't you! You went diving alone!"

Jennifer stepped back, held firmly on to Eddie's shoulders, and looked apprehensively at the obvious changes that had come upon this man she so deeply cared about.

He was dressed from head to toe in his dark grey-and-red wetsuit. His hair was uncombed, and obviously unattended since his dive in the ocean. She hadn't noticed at first, because of the dramatic change in his hair color, but she now saw that Eddie had, in fact, been out on a dive—alone.

"How could you, Eddie? You promised me that you'd never do that," she said with painful disappointment in her voice. "Why?"

"Please, Jen," he countered. "There's nothing you need to worry about."

"Well, no," she said angrily, "not *now*. The damage is already done! You could have been killed out there, Eddie!"

"You don't understand, sweetheart," he answered calmly, doing his best to soothe her anxiety, "but you will. I promise you that."

He pulled back, and seeing the emotion and concern that was in her eyes, he began to apologize. "Oh, Jen, I'm *so* sorry. It's hard for me to explain what should never be rationalized, and you're right, I did promise you that I would never dive alone, or risk my life unnecessarily. I don't blame you for being angry, or even skeptical, about the tale of my friend and his dolphins."

"Your *friend?*"

"Yes, sweetheart, my friend."

"You saw him again, then? You met him? Talked with him?"

"All in good time, Jen, I promise. But you've got to trust me on this one, okay? I did what I *had* to do."

Eddie carefully detailed every thought so that when the moment was right he could describe the events he longed to relate to his girlfriend. He made a commitment to meet with her later on that evening and tell her what he could. Meanwhile, they set about the tasks of the afternoon.

"Eddie," Jennifer said as they were carrying into the house the food that she had prepared for the picnic, "you can't show up for the interview with pearl-white hair. Not without being fully prepared to give an explanation to everyone down at the station, including the captain and the TV crew. And, since you won't even tell *me* why your hair has turned white, I think maybe we'd better think about getting you some mild hair-coloring shampoo."

Eddie nodded at her, thinking that the suggestion was an excellent forethought on her part.

"You want me to drive into Malibu and pick something up?" she suggested.

"If you think it will work," he said, feeling a bit timid about the idea of putting some sort of unnatural dye in his hair.

She reached up, kissed him on the right cheek, grabbed her keys on the countertop, and headed out the door. "Please call Janie down at the station and tell her you're all right. Let her know that you'll be there for the interview at three. I'll be back shortly. You don't have much time, you know . . ."

And with that, Jennifer turned and walked out the kitchen door. Eddie followed her. Getting into the driver's seat, she buckled her seat belt, poked her head out the window, and called, "Hey, you'd better call your brother Warren, also. He's been trying to reach you all morning."

"Did he say where he was calling from?" Eddie called back.

"Try him at his house first. If he's not there, he said for you to call your parents' place. See you in a few minutes, sweetie."

"Thanks, Jen. Thanks a lot."

The television interview went well—far better, in fact, than Eddie had expected. And in the end, except for the news team's reference to Sergeant Eddie Russell being the son of the famous billionaire, Allen Scott Russell III—which Eddie felt was completely irrelevant to the interview itself—the Aquatic Rangers received a noteworthy appraisal from the interviewer, as well as from the program directors.

Eddie knew, as did Captain Mitchell and all who were present at the broadcast, that when the story aired on the ten o'clock evening news, the Malibu Aquatic Rangers would receive a tremendous boost.

By seven-thirty, Eddie had tied up all of the loose ends at the office and had thanked Janie for her devoted persistence in seeing that the interview ran smoothly. In addition, he had diagrammed a map for divers TC, Art Sackler, and Gene Boylan, all of whom had agreed to make the dive Sunday morning off Point Dume and recover the remnants of the Hansens' fishing boat. And so, he sat in his S-10, thoroughly exhausted, and took in a deep restorative breath of fresh ocean air.

Before he turned on the ignition, however, Eddie was intrigued to hear Janie talking with TC in the parking lot. Of course, neither suspected that their sergeant could hear them, for their voices were hardly more audible than a whisper.

"Did you see his hair?"

"Yeah," TC answered, "I think he had it colored!"

"I think he did, too," she responded with a giggle.

CHAPTER 12

Chava sifted slowly through the small stack of photographs and carefully pasted them, one by one, inside the large scrapbook he had assembled. Altogether now, he had accumulated eleven full pages of worthwhile photos, and he had meticulously labeled each one.

It was late, and he was anxious to crawl into bed for the night. He had spent more than seven hours taking photographs and felt reasonably sure that he could now find and photograph the younger generation of the Russells' homes, as well as their respective occupants, before Tuesday.

By then, in any event, he supposed that he would be ready. He could make his selection before driving to Folsom. If not, he could always get his friend Romero to help him. Together they would choose the right one—he was sure of it. After all, the right choice was important. That alone could very well determine the success or failure of the plan.

Setting the scrapbook on the kitchen countertop, Chava walked slowly over to the old vinyl couch in the living room. He then kicked off his shoes and sat down. He thought for a moment about his friend Romero Valdez and wondered how he had made out over the past three years inside the penitentiary.

Folsom.

That was supposed to be a hard place to do time. Romero said it was, anyway. Chava silently prayed that he would never have to find out for himself. And yet, here he was, risking that very possibility! Was it worth it? For Sylvia, it was.

In fact, it really didn't matter anymore. He had to go through with it, despite the risks and conceivable consequences. The life of his baby sister was far more important than a few crummy years behind bars.

"Besides," he considered out loud, "they'll have to catch me first."

Chava decided to watch the local news, then get some sleep. He reached over and flipped on the switch of the old black and white TV. It finally showed a picture, even though the reception was poor.

There wasn't much that caught his attention at first, and he was just about to call it a night when he heard the newscaster say something like, ". . . the son of wealthy billionaire Allen Scott Russell III. . . ."

Quickly Chava leaned over toward the set and turned up the volume.

". . . And how long has the program been operational, Sergeant?" the reporter asked.

"A little more than five years now," the man responded. "But I want to add that the effectiveness of the Aquatic Rangers program lies primarily in the skill and professionalism of all our divers. Our principal scope and purpose, after all, is search and rescue operations. We tend to shy away from the idea of police work, although our work with the Coast Guard *has* given us a chance to join the fight against drugs. . . ."

Chava carefully studied the face of the man being interviewed—Eddie Allen Russell. The youngest son of the Russell family. He would memorize the face, for he was fascinated that this particular heir to the Russell fortune was not an active participant in the family business.

"Very interesting," he whispered quietly. "Very, very interesting."

CHAPTER 13

Sitting back on the couch in Eddie's living room, with her inexplicably changed man next to her, Jennifer considered all of the things she had been told. She didn't know whether to get up right then and there and run Eddie down to the psychiatric ward at St. Johns in Santa Monica, or to slap him in the face for being untruthful with her.

In any event, the entire story was impossible. And since the man she loved seemed so completely adamant about the story's authenticity, she began to worry.

Something, it was clear, had happened to Eddie. But *what* exactly, she just couldn't be sure. His hair had turned completely white in less than twenty-four hours, which certainly accounted for something. And what bothered her the most was that there was no evidence of any injury, which might have given credence to a more logical—and certainly more rational—explanation.

Eddie obviously hadn't been in an accident, so what had happened?

"You don't believe me, do you, Jen?" he said, sliding away from her on the sofa to look more directly into her eyes.

"Well . . ." she answered nervously, not wanting to sound offensive, "it's just not possible, Eddie. But I'm not saying that it's wrong for *you* to believe it. One thing is clear, and that is that *something* happened—or else the sudden change in your hair color could not have occurred—biologically speaking, that is.

"Sometimes, sweetie," she continued, caressing his arm as she spoke, "things happen to people that cannot be explained. The mind, as you well know, is vastly complex. It is still so thoroughly misunderstood that even the most brilliant psychologists, psychiatrists, and neurologists are discovering new things every day. The point is . . . well, it doesn't matter what really happened last night and this morning. Because any kind of trauma—mental *or* physical—could have accidentally triggered a series of powerful hallucinations that may very well have been profoundly realistic. Do you understand that, sweetheart?"

Jennifer shifted her position just enough so that she could look directly into Eddie's eyes and monitor his reaction to her words. In trying to reason with him, she paused for a moment and recalled that, as an experienced "physician of the mind," she had known others with similar tales. They, through therapy, had ultimately regained a hold on reality. She was sure that Eddie could do the same.

"Can you see what I'm getting at, darling?" she asked lovingly, then paused again for a response.

Eddie smiled calmly, then spoke, almost in a whisper. "There's something you don't quite understand, Jen. Perhaps it is time to show you."

He smiled a second time and looked deep into her eyes. For some strange reason, Jennifer suddenly felt a warm and abiding love for Eddie that left her speechless, but wonderfully content inside. She couldn't take her own eyes away from his.

For what seemed like an eternity, Eddie just looked at her, never blinking at all, but staring and studying her as if it were the last time they would ever see each other. And yet, she wasn't angry or the least bit offended by Eddie's having suddenly cut her short as he had done. She was mesmerized by the near-mystical spell he seemed to have cast upon her.

"Come with me, Jen."

Very tenderly Eddie reached down and took Jennifer's hand in his, assisted her in getting up from the sofa, and walked her out onto the veranda.

Moving out into the moonlit night, Jennifer felt yet another surge of soothing warmth pass through her body. It was a feeling like nothing she had ever before experienced, leaving her quite literally overwhelmed with a sense of infinite peace and happiness. She did not understand but was so completely overcome with the sensation that tears welled up in her eyes and fell, unchecked, down her cheeks.

"Oh, Eddie . . ." she tried to respond, searching for the right words, "what's happening to me?"

"Look!" he exclaimed, pointing at the sea and the distant horizon. "What do you see out there, Jen?"

"Well . . ." she whispered, trembling just a little as she spoke, "I see a very beautiful ocean . . . I see the moon, and the stars . . ."

"And beyond those?" he pressed.

"More stars . . . the galaxies, the . . . heavens. *What?*" she asked.

"You said it, Jennifer! The stars. The heavens. *Life!* All of it created by Him! Don't you see? Everything you can see, and far, far beyond. Other worlds, other suns—stars without end! All of it created by the hands of the Master. Everything with its purpose. Right down to you and me, just as you taught me when I was investigating the Church.

"And yes, my lady, you are absolutely right. We do not understand the marvelous workings of the human mind. We may never understand it! For it is *His* to understand! He created it, and all of the ideas that originate from it." He paused.

"Look at me, Jen," he said softly, turning his gaze once more at her. "What I saw, and what I felt, was *not* a hallucination. . . ."

He placed his hands softly on top of her shoulders and stepped back slightly so as to see her features entirely. She was trembling.

"The old man's name," Eddie continued, "is Simeon. He is a messenger, really, working, in his own way, for the Master. He is not a figment of my imagination any more than you are, my love. His purpose for being here is clear to me at last, even though there are many marvelous things I've yet to learn from him.

"But what is most important, Jen, is that I can finally say I do understand! My eyes have been opened, as well as my heart and my mind. I see what I must do—while there is still time.

"Simeon knows Him personally, Jen. He, quite literally, is His *friend!*"

"Eddie, I . . . I just—"

"And he reminded me," Eddie said, interrupting her with kindness, "that He is coming back again. A second time. And if we are ill prepared, if we are not ready, if we have not been diligent in our own tasks, doing all we can to assist others and lift and build them, then we will have failed. We will simply not be worthy to meet or be with Him when He comes!

"Now," Eddie continued, "look at me, Jennifer. My heart whispers that you too can be trusted—which allows me to open your eyes as well."

Eddie bent over slightly and kissed her on the lips, then pulled back and said, "Watch."

For a moment all was quiet, except for the whisper of light winds and distant surf. But then, as if by magic, a magnificent pearl-white seagull seemed to fly out of nowhere. It landed on the wood railing before them. Then slowly a second gull, then another, and still another—until momentarily the railing and the veranda itself were covered by an extraordinary array of white-feathered, curiously tame and clearly affectionate gulls, all milling and cooing contentedly.

Jennifer stood silently, transfixed by the scene before her.

"There is a great danger awaiting us, Jen. But a marvelous experience and tremendous responsibility, as well. I'm not sure what it is just yet. But I do know that it awaits us both."

"Oh, Eddie . . ." she responded tenderly, her voice filled with emotion and her eyes moist with tears, "I didn't know . . . I didn't know . . . "

The danger, the nightmare of overwhelming proportions, was at that moment beginning to unfold.

PART TWO

Force Five

There are moments, suspended,
    in the lives of men,
When forces, unseen and uninvited,
    alter destiny forever.

But always, when confronted,
    a higher force is sought and named.
Building and lifting, not destroying,
    this force prevails forever.

CHAPTER 14

The light rains and gentle winds blowing out of the north made hardly a sound. They were a mere forerunner of the violent squall line that was moving inland. And for that reason, Eddie Russell allowed his fantasies to carry him to new heights—quite literally—as he parachuted from "Captain" Steve and Donna Stewart's private plane and floated effortlessly toward the small island far below.

From this lofty height, Eddie could see the lighthouse on Santa Rosa's northern point. A thick fog was moving in from the open waters and just now sending tendrils of dense mist into many of the lower regions of the island's rocky cliffs and lagoons.

Although usually afraid of heights, Eddie did not seem to mind his present altitude. Something more significant had given him cause for concern.

For a moment, Eddie's attention was focused on the island itself, where the terrain was kept out of the fog by its very height above the waters. Most of the lower beaches were quickly becoming obscured.

But what was it? What was his concern?

Slowly, hoping to zero in on the area that seemed to trouble him most, Eddie pulled on the right stall-line of his chute and initiated a wide, sweeping twelve-degree bank toward the San Miguel Passage and the lighthouse overlooking the passage.

That was when he spotted the fishing trawler. It was headed through the strait between the two islands of Santa Rosa and San Miguel but was obviously lost in the fog. And if the lightkeeper didn't turn on the giant lamp, the fishing boat would inevitably crash into the rocks.

Simeon! he thought. Someone had to awaken the old man—
the light-keeper. What about Simeon's wife, Sarah? Where was
she? Weren't they aware of the fog? Eddie knew that he had to
do something on his own, so, using all of the strength he could
muster, he maneuvered his chute toward the lofty cliffs below.

Setting up a careful approach against the growing winds,
Eddie stalled to a feather-soft landing just at the edge of the
rocky cliffs, discarded his gear, then edged slowly to the point
and looked out over the rim. The ocean could no longer be
seen; for in its place was an extremely dense ocean of fog. And
Eddie was poised at the highest pinnacle of the island that jut-
ted out of that fog.

Quickly he turned and ran over to the little picket fence that
surrounded the front yard of Simeon's lighthouse. The small
gate was already open.

"That's strange," he whispered under his breath, thinking
back to when he had seen the gate close on its own, when he
and Simeon had come here the night before. "It must have broken."

He took a second to look. The spring was gone.

"Now, who could have taken that?" he found himself asking. "It was just here last night." But he didn't have time for
missing gate-springs. The passengers on the fishing boat were
in grave danger.

Back to the task, the errand, the rescue.

He walked briskly up the narrow cobblestone path leading
to the entrance and knocked on the oversized wooden door. No
answer. It was clear that the lighthouse was vacant, and that
meant that he would have to handle this one on his own. So he
ran quickly back out of the well-manicured front yard, and hurried once more over to the edge of the cliff.

Having searched for mere seconds, he stumbled on a small
trail, Simeon's trail. Without hesitation, he began his descent.
About halfway down the steep slope he began hearing the
sounds of the surf splashing against the rocks. But still he could
see nothing. Seconds later, he entered the thick greyish mist and
vanished into its obscurity.

Surely by now the crew aboard the old trawler would have
sent out a call for help—an S.O.S. But neither the blast of a

foghorn nor the high-pitched gonging of a bell could be heard, and Eddie feared the worst.

"Maybe she's already gone down," he considered out loud, his chest heaving. "Maybe it's already too late." Cautiously, he worked his way to the water's edge and stared numbly out into the wall of fog. There was, of course, nothing to see—and nothing to hear.

For several moments things remained as they were. And then, something out past the breakers made a distinct noise. It was a familiar sound. Not an engine, not a blast from a foghorn or a distress call from the boat's bell, but something different— quiet and steady in rhythm. An in-again, out-again dipping of a set of oars in the water.

A rowboat! Yes. That was it. Someone was approaching the shoreline in a small rowboat. But *who?* Eddie stepped into the water and craned his neck to see. But again the visibility was so bad that he saw nothing. Yet, by the ever-increasing sound of the oars steadily splashing in and out of the waters, he knew that the rowboat was getting closer. Someone was *definitely* approaching!

"Ahoy there!" he yelled into the fog. "Who goes there?"

No response.

"You need to watch out for the rocks. There are some large jagged rocks just ahead of you. Can you hear me?" Another moment of silence. But then, quite unexpectedly, someone *did* answer.

"Eddie?" the voice called, "is that you? Is that you out there, Eddie?"

"Yes!" he screamed back, "it's me. Over here. A little more to your left."

"Eddie!" the voice called out again. "Help me, Eddie . . . they're chasing me!"

Eddie froze. For a moment he was caught in a grip of paralyzing anxiety, fear restricting his breathing and racing through him like lightning. The voice was horrifyingly familiar—it was Jennifer's voice!

"Jen!" he screamed, "is that you?"

"Save me, Eddie! They're getting closer!"

Just then he heard a splashing noise, altogether different

from the steady rowing that had been cadenced seconds before, and then a muffled scream. "Jennifer!" he screamed in response, diving into the icy waters and swimming frantically out toward the spot from which he had last heard her calls for help.

Someone, it seemed—judging from the sound of the thrashing about in the waters—had yanked Jennifer into the ocean and was trying to carry her away.

"Jen!" he called out between breaths, "Hold on, Jen! I'm coming!"

But by the time he arrived at the small rowboat, it was too late. Jennifer was nowhere to be seen, and all that remained was a battered wooden skiff with its two oars fastened to both sides, drifting aimlessly with the outgoing tides.

Eddie sat upright in his bed with a start. He was perspiring profusely and breathing rapidly, and had awakened at the sound of his own voice calling out into the otherwise-silent Sunday morning calm.

He opened his eyes, saw the familiar sights of his bedroom, blinked a couple of times, and then slowly got control of himself. This he did despite the paralyzing images of the dream still vividly displayed in his mind.

A full minute passed before he was able to free himself completely from the chilling effects of the dream. But strangely, unlike most images born of sleep that fade almost immediately after waking, the eerie drama lingered on, leaving a disturbing sensation in his heart and mind.

"Now, what was that all about?" he mumbled sleepily.

He decided to call Jennifer, to assure himself that she was all right. But then, looking over at the alarm clock situated on the nightstand and realizing that it was barely six o'clock in the morning—Sunday morning—he reconsidered the idea. It was, after all, just a dream . . . Wasn't it? That particular thought was unsettling.

"Get a grip on yourself, Sergeant Russell. That's an order. Besides, she deserves to sleep in."

He did so, and a moment later he slid over to the side of his bed and stared blankly out through the narrow gap in the curtains which were drawn over the sliding glass door. It was raining. Raining?

Slowly he lifted himself up off the bed, walked over to the sliding double-panes, pulled back the curtains, and looked outside. Every inch of the morning sky was under siege. The storm that had blown in through the night was dark and ominous. In considering the storm, however, he realized that the magnificent front was long overdue. California had been in the grip of a horrible drought for almost a decade and desperately needed the moisture. The dark clouds reminded Eddie of the dream he'd had. The massive fog bank in the dream was still a vivid image in his mind.

He and Jennifer had often discussed their dreams, and he remembered her saying that most often we dream about events that occur in our conscious experiences. One thing in particular that he had remembered was her reference to characters that played roles inside the dreams themselves. Something to the effect that, for the most part, the players in a dream were usually individuals familiar to ourselves—and that the central figure, or the "star" of the dream, was usually the one having the dream. That seemed fairly accurate in his experience. He was always a main character in his own dreams.

But why was this one dream lingering so, and in such vivid detail? Could it have been, like Lehi's dream in the Book of Mormon, a type and shadow of things to come?

In quiet solitude, Eddie stood transfixed at the window and looked out at the heaving sea. He thought about the intriguing experience he'd had with Jennifer the night before and the warm and refreshing feelings they'd both enjoyed. He was grateful beyond words that she had been able to witness for herself the power of the Holy Spirit. Those feelings took him immediately back to the meeting—the first wonderful encounter with the old man Simeon.

Even now, the kind gentleman's voice reverberated through his mind . . .

"Hello, Eddie," the old fellow had said, somehow already acquainted with him even though Eddie was certain they had never been introduced.

"Who are you?" Eddie had inquired, clearly startled to see the elderly figure on the beach that night—so late at night. He couldn't remember ever having swum so rapidly over the surface of the water, or having crawled out of the ocean with such

speed. Indeed, the physical display of human strength and out-
right stamina, had it been recorded, would surely have been a
world record.

His fear vanished, however, when he met the old man. Another emotion took its place in his mind. It wasn't fear, actually,
but for a while there he felt a great deal of curious apprehension.

"I am Simeon," the aged stranger said, "the light-keeper."

Instinctively, Eddie stepped back. "Light-keeper?"

"You've no reason to be afraid, Eddie. There is nothing here
that will bring harm to you."

Eddie, however, wasn't taking any chances. After all, there
had been something in the water—something frightfully vicious. Perhaps the old gentleman wasn't a threat, but the creature in the sea had one thing on its mind, and that was dinner. *It*
would have torn him to pieces; Eddie was sure of it!

"Even the beast in the water could not have harmed you,
Eddie," Simeon continued, as if somehow able to read Eddie's
very thoughts. And for some peculiar reason, Eddie suddenly
knew that the old fellow was right.

Although he could not understand it, Eddie felt curiously
drawn to the old man. There was a compelling radiance of
goodness about the fellow, and Eddie realized immediately that
he could be trusted.

"And . . . how would you know that?" Eddie asked, still
thinking of the razor-sharp teeth that he had imagined during
his frantic swim toward the shore. "I mean, how do you know
that the beast, as you call it, wouldn't have harmed me,
Simeon?"

"It could not have, my young friend, for it was not real."

"Not real?" Eddie queried. "I saw it with my own two eyes.
What do you mean, not real? What was it, then?"

"It was a beast of your own creation, Eddie, a ploy from the
source of darkness to frighten you away from the ultimate
quest and destiny that is yours."

"Quest? Destiny? What are you talking about, Simeon? And
how is it that you seem to know so much about me, yet I know
absolutely nothing about you?"

For a moment Eddie became defensive again. He was not
frightened, but he remained cautious. Then, having given a

little more thought to the man's remarkable words, Eddie continued. "Who *are* you? What brings you out here in the middle of the night?"

"I am the light-keeper, young Edward. But that is not important at the moment. We are here for a reason, you and I. You seek answers to the multitude of questions racing about in your mind, and each of these—I can assure you—has an answer. But this is not the place for teaching. It would be well with us to leave this place and sit together before a warm fire . . . perhaps share a meal. Come, my friend, let us depart. . . ."

Right then, Simeon leaned forward and touched Eddie on the shoulder. Instantly, a feeling of tremendous belonging permeated his entire being. His whole body literally tingled with warmth, a sensation similar to being unbearably cold one moment and then stepping into the soothing comfort of a hot sauna the next.

Thinking back to the experience, Eddie concluded that describing the event would truly be a difficult task. For what occurred next was so extraordinary, so completely distant from the norm of reality, that words were inadequate. Something happened at that precise moment that was both exhilarating and frightening. It had literally taken Eddie's breath away.

They had stood there on the beach at Point Dume, looking into each other's eyes. And then, quite suddenly, in the time it takes to blink an eye, a spontaneous and curiously natural feeling of transformation occurred. Without having the slightest clue as to how the event transpired, physically speaking, Eddie blinked once, then twice, and was astonished to find himself standing *not* on a sandy beach overlooking the lagoon at Point Dume, but instead on a rocky ridge in front of a marvelously well-constructed and well-preserved lighthouse. Simeon's home.

"Welcome to our home, Eddie," Simeon stated matter-of-factly.

"But . . . How did we . . . ?"

"Be at peace, young friend. There is nothing to fear. You are welcome in our home. Come. My companion, Sarah, awaits our arrival. She will have a warm broth prepared. Please," the old fellow said, raising his hand and pointing toward the front entrance of the beautiful structure. "After you, my son."

Cautiously, Eddie proceeded in front of his elderly host. After passing through a small, well-kept picket fence that encircled the neatly manicured front yard of the lighthouse, he walked up to the front door.

Politely, Eddie waited for Simeon to open the door. But before the old fellow reached the red-brick landing, the handle on the old wooden portal turned slightly to the right and the door swung quietly open.

"Do come in," came a voice from within—a kind, maternal voice that seemed to fill Eddie's entire soul with sudden joy and an overwhelming sense of well-being.

The woman was beautiful!

Eddie stood there with his mouth agape, paralyzed by her majestic beauty and mesmerized by her soul-soothing voice.

"You must be Edward," she said pleasantly, offering a hand. "So you've come at last, have you?"

"Eddie," Simeon interjected, "This is the beautiful bride of my youth, Sarah."

"Uh . . . how do you do, ma'am?" Eddie said awkwardly, extending his hand to meet hers.

"I am well, Edward, thank you. But do come in, won't you? You must be freezing."

A few moments later, while seated in front of a crackling fire in the old couple's living room, Eddie tried to make sense of the events that were taking place. He was still dressed in his wetsuit, although Simeon had provided an old faded flannel shirt for him to slip on over the rubbery fabric.

Simeon's wife, Sarah, was angelic in appearance. Her sparkling, dancing eyes, the soft and perfect contour of her nose, and the beauty of her smile were captivating beyond words. It was clear to Eddie that she and her husband were in the twilight years of their lives. Her hair was snow-white and thick like Simeon's, and was beautifully done up on top of her head. Her skin was curiously soft, like a child's, and seemed to radiate a rich, healthy luster.

Without knowing why, Eddie felt strangely drawn to lightly kiss Sarah on the cheek, but he restrained himself. The woman's face, which seemed to be perfectly symmetrical, was stunningly sleek and elegant—not at all like the face one might have expected from an elderly citizen.

"That's odd," Eddie whispered under his breath, considering the unusual appearance of the two. "They *seem* old, yet there is something different, unexplainable about them."

Still dazed by the miraculous transfer to the lighthouse off Santa Barbara, Eddie wondered if the whole thing was nothing more than some weird dream or hallucination. He wanted to awaken, if possible, and step back into the real world.

But it *was* real, all of it!

"You are not dreaming, Eddie," Simeon stated matter-of-factly, as if once again having access to his thoughts. "It will all be clear in a matter of time. But first, be at ease, lad, and allow us to properly introduce ourselves and explain our purpose for summoning you here at this hour.

"I am Simeon, the 'Old One.' In truth, I use my father's name, rather than my own, for reasons that are sacred to me. My real name is Simon. Simon of Cyrene. I come to you from a country in the northernmost part of Africa, quite distant from here, and now nothing more than a faded memory.

"My companion is Sarah Ozias, daughter of the noble Jechonias of Bethany, near Jerusalem. She has adopted another name as well, out of respect for an old friend who has long since passed beyond the veil of mortality.

"Like ourselves," Simeon continued, "you are here because you were chosen, because of your inner character and the integrity with which you now honor your priesthood."

"What do you mean, sir?" Eddie questioned, his mind reeling from the eerie and unexplainable nature of the conversation.

"Yours is a pure heart, Eddie, a heart that can be molded for the good of all the children of men. You see, my son, long ago . . . long before you were even born into mortality, the Master knew who you were. He selected you, as he has many others, because of your noble spirit and birthright. He knew that you would possess all of the qualities needed to bring hope into the lives of others. Indeed, young Edward, noble son of Allen, you were chosen and foreordained before you were born!"

"Chosen for what?" Eddie asked timidly, trying to remain as polite as possible.

"Greatness beyond your fondest dreams!" Simeon answered excitedly, his bushy-white eyebrows lifting upward and his eyes widening as he spoke.

"But I don't care for greatness, Simeon! I've tried to convince my parents that money and fame are not important to me."

"It is not the glory of the world that will be your gift, young lad. That could have already been yours. Oh, no, Edward of the pure heart, it will not be gold or silver, or the precious riches of this planet. Not at all. You would not be here if that was the treasure of your heart.

"I refer to the lasting glory, Eddie, the ultimate pinnacle of greatness, wherein you, because of your triumphant conquest over self, will sit with the Brethren to the right of the Master!"

"What are you talking about, Simeon? I'm afraid you're losing me."

Simeon stood and walked slowly over to the fireplace. He looked for a moment into the flames, then turned and faced his guest, meeting Eddie's eyes with his own.

"Great things will happen to you and to members of your family, Eddie. There will be events both wonderful and frightening. Nevertheless, the way will be open for you to overcome the darkness and eventually stir the souls of many with the gospel knowledge that is now yours.

"It is often by small things that the Master makes his will known. He was, after all, a carpenter's son."

The telephone rang, and Eddie was suddenly jarred loose from the retrospective images of the man Simeon, the lighthouse off Santa Barbara, and the kind woman who had prepared the warm meal. There were tears in his eyes, causing the scenes outside his bedroom window to become blurry and distorted. He wiped them away and redirected his thoughts to the here and now—focusing once again on the massive cloud cover and the increased intensity of the winds and rain.

The phone sounded a second time. "It's gonna be a real thunder-bumper!" he said aloud, mentally assessing the magnificent squall. "I wonder if we need to batten down the hatches?"

Eddie turned away from the window and walked over to the nightstand next to his bed. He glanced at the clock while retrieving the telephone receiver, and noted that it was 6:20 A.M.

"Who could be calling at this hour?" he moaned.

"Hello?"

"Dad?"

"Jeff?"

"Are you awake, Dad?"

"Should I be, at six-twenty Sunday morning?" Eddie said playfully.

"Well," Jeff apologized, "I hope I didn't ruin a good dream or something, but you did remember that we gotta be at grandma's by eight o'clock, didn't you?"

"Oh, yeah!" Eddie responded with sudden recollection. "That's right! They're all leaving for Zurich this morning. I nearly forgot!"

"What's new?" Jeff teased. "You comin' to pick me up, then? I'm back at Scott's place. We had the greatest time up the coast!"

"Yes, of course. Glad that your weekend has been good. I'll be there in a few minutes, Son."

"Okay, Dad, see ya in a few. . . ."

"Hey, Jeff?"

"Yeah?"

"I love you, Son. Thanks for calling and reminding me."

"Love you, too, Dad. Besides, someone's gotta look out for you!"

CHAPTER 15

By the time Eddie and Jeff were turning off Sunset Boulevard onto Rockingham Avenue, the downpour had begun. The rain fell in sheets. Water was already collecting in the streets and gullies and rushing downhill like thousands of swollen streams and rivers. This was not a normal California downpour, here for a moment and gone the next. To the contrary, this was a tropical monster destined to flood hundreds out of their homes, fill the aqueducts and culverts to capacity levels, and transform all of the low areas of the greater Los Angeles basin into veritable lakes, swimming pools, and unwanted ponds.

Many would suffer because of this storm. However, the dangerously low reservoirs would fill again. And so, in the end, though burdens and trials of desperation would have to be endured by a few, the greater part of the state's population would recognize this summer storm for what it really was—a profound blessing.

But Eddie had other concerns.

Every time a major storm front moved into the area, the Aquatic Rangers, local lifeguard units, and Coast Guard had their hands full. For without a doubt, some daredevil would sail out to sea a half mile or more, brave the explosive gale forces of the prevailing winds, and ultimately end up another victim to Mother Nature. Sunday or not, this was not a day to drift too far from the Malibu station.

Eddie looked over at the two-way radio just below the dash and made sure the little red power-light was illuminated. It was. Eddie was relieved to know that most of the Rangers had already showed up at the station and were monitoring the storm's progress. For the moment, in any case, he felt reasonably sure that he could enjoy a few hours at the Russell estate, visiting with his mother and seeing his three brothers and their wives off to the airport.

As the two of them pulled into the long, narrow driveway of the magnificent estate, Eddie noticed that Jeff had been staring at him from the passenger seat of the Chevy.

"What did you do to your hair, Pop?" Jeff suddenly asked, breaking the silence. "Did you put some coloring in your hair?"

"Yeah," Eddie answered playfully, not wanting the conversation to develop much beyond the hair issue. "You like it?"

"Well, I don't know. Who'd ya color it for, Jennifer?"

"No, not really. For me, I guess, to cover the grey."

"What grey? I don't remember grey in it, Dad. I think you're losin' it!"

"Think so, huh?"

"You don't need hair colors and tonics, Pop! That's just for old people. This is the nineties. Stay with the natural look, Dad. So what if you got a little grey showin' through. I think it'll make you more distinguished looking. It'll embarrass me to see you put any more of that greasy gunk in your hair. The natural look. Remember that, will ya?"

"Well, thanks for the perspective, Jeffrey. I'll try to keep that in mind."

And then, as an afterthought, Jeff said, "There's something different about you, Dad. And it's not just your hair. I'm not sure exactly, but I think something happened to you over the weekend. I'm not complaining, mind you, 'cuz I think it's a good something . . . Anyway, you're all right with me, Dad, even if you do put greasy stuff on your dome."

Eddie drove the pickup to the front walkway, shut off the engine, and looked thoughtfully over at his son.

"I did have a few interesting experiences over the past couple of days, Jeff. You're right about that. One, in particular, has had a rather profound effect on me. You could say that it has kind of changed the way I look at things," Eddie said with a serious expression on his face. "Sometime soon," he continued, smiling softly, "I'd like to tell you about it. It has something to do with the Melchizedek Priesthood."

"Well, I'd like for you to, Dad, 'cuz whatever it was seems

to have brought out the best in you . . . Ever since I climbed into the truck this morning at Scott's place, well . . . there's been this really neat feeling inside me . . . something that I think has to do with *you*."

Jeff turned away briefly and stared out the windshield. Then he turned back to face his father. There were tears in his eyes. "You're all I've got, Dad! And though I don't quite understand why I'm suddenly feeling all mushy inside, I just got to thinking how much I really love you, and how much I don't ever want to lose you!"

"You're never going to lose me, Son." Eddie responded tenderly, reaching over to embrace the boy. The two held each other for several seconds, then pulled back.

"You just remember," Eddie continued, "we're going to have our whole lives together, you and me. We're a team! The Russell team. A bona fide partnership that can't be broken! You got that?"

"Yeah," Jeff answered, smiling and feeling curiously reassured.

"Good! Now come on, let's get out of this storm and see what your grandmother has cooking!"

"Rockingham Palace," as it was affectionately called by the Russell grandchildren, was a truly splendid mansion. With more than sixteen thousand square feet of enclosed living and recreational areas, it was a veritable castle of wonderment. It contained every conceivable luxury and means of entertainment.

Grandpa Russell delighted in spoiling the grandkids. Nevertheless, he was equally fervent in his consistent concern for the education of each one, and he instilled values of good, hard work, insisting that Jeff, his only grandson, assist the groundskeepers. He cooperated, and whenever he was at the estate he spent his Saturday mornings in hard, physical labor. The granddaughters, on the other hand, washed windows, vacuumed, and helped the maids wherever they were needed.

Because of Grandpa Russell's education ethic, the wise man had made sure that his home contained facilities for learning as well as recreation. For instance, having himself always been intrigued with the stars and the surrounding heavens, Mr. Russell had gone to great lengths to create an extraordinary alcove which he called the "Window To Heaven" room. It was an oval-shaped edifice, built into the second floor east wing, which in many ways resembled a small observatory.

He had had his dear friend, Jerry Foote, who had installed one of the most sophisticated observatories in the country, design and build it. Jerry was a scientific genius, and Mr. Russell valued such intellect. In fact, this philosophy was borne out again and again in the mansion, with his oft-quoted guideline: "You pay for the best, and only cry once!"

There was also a rich and completely stocked library. Its collection of books, journals, manuscripts, microfiche, and research information on seemingly endless topics made it a wonderful place for the grandchildren's studies.

And for that matter, the aging patriarch and his companion were forever encouraging their descendants, children and grandchildren alike, to utilize the vast warehouse of knowledge for whatever purposes they saw fit. "The doors to the library," they had said time and again, "are always open."

The mansion was kept in immaculate order and in perfect repair by a staff of ten servants. Among these were cleaning maids, two full-time cooks, a groundskeeper with two assistants, and an extremely likeable butler, Charlie, and his wife, Virginia. The latter were a middle-aged black couple. All of the Russell's servants were governed by Charlie and Virginia, who, in turn, reported directly to Mrs. Russell.

Delores Russell delighted in her matriarchal stewardship, not just because Rockingham Palace was indeed her very own creation but also because of the relationship she'd developed over the years with Charlie and Virginia.

Charlie and Virginia were family. They were trusted, loyal friends who had been in the service of the Russell family since Eddie was but a teenager. And moreover, they lived on the estate, inside the spacious servant's quarters at the west end of the mansion, just over the six-car garage.

The Russells also employed two skilled pilots and a full-time helicopter and Lear jet mechanic. These three men had each served two tours of duty in the Vietnam conflict, the second time by volunteering, and had been attached to the 101st Airborne unit outside of Phu Bai, in an aptly named compound, Camp Eagle.

And so, as lifelong friends and comrades, these men worked with and flew the family's two executive-class Bell Jet Ranger helicopters, both of which were stored in the specially designed and camouflaged hangar on the estate. The pilots also flew Mr. Russell's personal Lear jet, which was maintained and stored in the private section of the Burbank airport.

Eddie's son, Jeff, was particularly fond of the pilots, Tom Geddess and John Ferguson. These men shared equally in the maintenance and flying of the entire aviation operation, although the fleet operation itself was under the direction of senior pilot and captain, Tom Geddess.

When Eddie and Jeff entered the house, moving at last out of the rain, activity inside was already in full swing. Charlie, the butler, met them at the door.

"Well, now," he said with a smile, "Mister Edward and Sir Jeffrey, how nice to see you both this morning."

"Hi, Charlie," Jeff said cheerfully. "What's goin' on?"

"It's all a bit confusing, Jeffrey, but it would seem that your uncles and aunts are preparing for a business trip to Switzerland."

"Oh?" Eddie questioned. "All of 'em?"

"It would appear so, sir."

"That sounds nice," Jeff said, as he and his father stepped past the butler and walked into the ornate foyer. Just then a voice sounded from the adjacent living room. It was Larry's voice.

Uncle Larry, to Jeff. *Brother* Larry, to Eddie. Insecure and condescending Larry to both of them. "Well, well, and triple well," Larry uttered. "If it isn't the star of the 1960's TV drama, Mr. Lloyd Bridges, in the flesh! The finest lifeguard ever to hit the beaches of Los Angeles!"

Larry climbed the two steps from the sunken living room and stood in the foyer in front of his younger brother and Jeff, then smiled and added, "And you've decided to leave the set of 'Sea Hunt' for a while so you can spend some time with us? How kind of you, Ed. And who's this young man with you? Beau . . . er . . . no, it must be *Jeff* Bridges!"

Neither Eddie nor his son was the least bit offended, or amused, by the flippant Larry Russell. Instead, they just looked at each other briefly and smiled. Besides, they had talked about

Larry on several occasions and had agreed that his eccentricity and self-importance were character flaws that would undoubtedly catch up with him one day. Perhaps then this unfortunate man would get a good, long look in the mirror.

"Hi, Uncle Larry," Jeff answered politely, extending a hand. "Uncle Warren said we were havin' some kind of family meeting this morning. Something important before you guys go off to Switzerland, huh?"

"Yep, that's right, kiddo," Larry said, a little more courteously than usual, while slapping Eddie on the shoulders. "We've been waiting for you guys. Everyone's down in the theater room." Then, speaking to Eddie, he continued, "Glad you could make it!" Eddie just smiled and followed his brother into the estate's theater room.

None of the three saw the look in the butler's eyes. It was a look of concern and disgust, very atypical of the aging black man. But it was not directed at Eddie or his son. It was instead an indication of the inward loathing that Charlie nurtured toward the pompous Lawrence David Russell.

In fact, there were secrets in Larry's life that were truly dark. Skeletons lurking in his closet. But then, that was no one's business except Larry's. Charlie only wished he had not known about them.

"Okay, everybody . . ." Eddie's brother Warren said from his position up on the family stage, "sit down, please, and listen up." He was waving his arms up and down, desperately trying to get his family's attention. But all of the young cousins, seven girls plus Jeff, were busily trying to catch up on all the latest gossip and family events.

Jeff felt unique and proud in the presence of his all-girl cousins. In fact, it was for that reason that he sensed his special place amongst them. He was the only male grandchild of the famous Mr. Allen Scott Russell III, and he liked that. He liked being with all of them but had developed a special friendship with Megan Lynn. For some reason, she had captured his heart.

"Oh yes," he whispered to himself, looking over at the small-framed ten-year-old sitting quietly by herself on the front row. "What a precious little girl—Megan Lynn."

And she *was* precious. Megan Lynn Russell was the youngest daughter of Larry and Elizabeth, and for some inexplicable reason, was quiet and reserved. She rarely spoke but seemed to wear an eternal smile on her face that had a magnetic impact upon all who knew her. *Everyone* loved Megan!

"Hey, everybody!" Uncle Warren called out again. Only this time he had turned on the theater's public address system and was holding a microphone in his left hand. "Please! Will you all sit down, please, and let us begin." The theater grew quiet.

"Okay, thanks," Warren continued. "Now, if I can have your attention for just a few minutes, there are some things we need to discuss before our trip this afternoon." He looked over at his brother Kenny, who was standing by the projection room at the rear center of the theater, and asked, "Are we ready with the satellite hookup?"

"Ready," Kenneth called back.

"Okay, Ken, stand by," Warren instructed, then turned once more to the small audience of family members in front of him. "As most of you know," he continued, "Jeff just had a birthday . . . ."

Jeff suddenly turned a little red in the face. He looked over at his dad, who was sitting next to Grandma Russell near the front of the theater, and caught a quick wink. Everyone in the seats around him was looking his way, as well.

". . . And although many of us celebrated his birthday last Thursday, here at Mom's and Dad's house, there were a few of us who weren't able to make it."

"That's okay!" Jeff blurted out. "I'll accept checks, credit cards, or cash." There was a wave of laughter in the group, then Warren continued.

"Well, Jeff," Warren countered, "we'd like to give you some cash, but Grandpa insisted on something a little different. And as you know, he wasn't able to make it to the festivities last Thursday. But . . . well . . . he's the one who asked us all to gather here this morning. Ken?"

There was a short pause, and then slowly the lights began to dim and the curtains behind Warren separated electronically. Warren moved over to one side. A large projection screen appeared from its resting place high above the stage and slowly came to life.

Jeff felt like he was suddenly aboard the fictional starship the U.S.S. *Enterprise* depicted in the television series "Star Trek:

The Next Generation." Any moment now, he expected to hear the voice of the ship's captain, Jean-Luc Picard, give the command to place the incoming message "on screen." And sure enough, as if the scenario were indeed being carried out just as Jeff had envisioned it, the scrambled static on the giant TV monitor faded slowly, giving way to a bright and vividly detailed image.

It was Grandpa, beaming in through a satellite link, all the way from Zurich.

Warren walked over to the microphone still resting on the boom-stand on the stage. He then retrieved it and brought it to his lips. "Testing . . . ," he said timidly, "testing, one, two . . . You there, Dad?"

"Well, hello, Warren," came a sudden voice over the theater's P.A. system. "Have you got the signal?"

"Yes, we sure do. You're coming in crystal clear. How's everything in Alpine country?"

"Beautiful, Warren, just beautiful. The sun dropped down over the lake a few moments ago, and I'm telling you, it was a sight to behold!"

"Good weather, then?" Warren inquired.

"Outstanding weather, Son. Can hardly wait for you and the others to get here. But hey, is everyone there in the viewing room? Eddie and Jeff there?"

"Yes, Dad, they're here. We're *all* here, just as you requested."

"Excellent!" the old man said excitedly. Hello everybody! Can you all hear me?"

A sudden chorus of young, energetic voices sounded in the small audience. "We hear you, Grandpa!"

"Hi, kids!" Mr. Russell said enthusiastically, hearing the faraway voices being picked up by the sensitive microphone in Warren's hand. He was loving every minute of this activity, for the single greatest thrill for the aging billionaire was the unity of his family. They were his joy and happiness, and he thoroughly delighted in doing extraordinary things for them— things that bordered on the spectacular, like an expensive satellite transmission from one side of the earth to the other—all in the name of fun.

Grandfather Russell's philosophy, right or wrong, was that

one of the privileges of the rich was to be able to do whatever their hearts desired. Especially, in his case, if this meant bringing a smile to a young grandchild's face—or a look of satisfaction to one of his sons, or to his beloved wife, Delores.

And this was one of those moments—a pre-planned, costly moment of sheer joy—one that he was certain that his only grandson, Jeffrey Scott Russell, would long remember and cherish.

"Jeffrey, you out there?" Mr. Russell continued.

"Yes, Grandpa, I'm right here!" Jeff shouted, hoping his voice out in the audience would be picked up by the cordless microphone in his uncle's hand.

"I'm here, too, dear," Mrs. Delores Russell added. "Don't forget me, honey!"

"Of course, Grandma," he countered. "Why do you get all the fun with everyone, while I have to sit in this lonely Swiss chalet, talking into an absurdly wonderful device that looks nothing like you?"

"You're charming, Grandpa, but you'll be home next week, and perhaps you'll find something 'fun,' as you say, to help you forget about the hard life there in Switzerland!" Everyone laughed at this familiar banter and sensed the enduring love between the aging couple.

"Perhaps . . . ," he answered, his face smiling on the large screen before the group. "But when I arrive, I'm going to need a hug and kiss first. I miss you something awful!"

"I miss you too, dear."

"Warren," the proud grandfather continued, "hand the microphone to Jeffrey, will you, please?"

"All right," Warren responded obediently, motioning for Jeff to come forward. "Handing it to him . . . right . . . now. . . ."

"Good!" came the aging patriarch's voice. "You there, Master Jeffrey?"

"Yessir!" Jeff said enthusiastically. "I'm sitting on the fifth row, Grandpa, over to the right. I have the mike, and I can see you just fine."

"Well, good! Now, young fellow, this is directed to you. First let me apologize for not having been able to attend the birthday festivities last Thursday. I had an important commitment in Amsterdam that I couldn't get out of." On the screen,

Mr. Russell stood up and began pacing the floor of his office on the other side of the planet. Someone working the camera and satellite equipment followed the billionaire's every step.

"Anyway, Jeffrey, I do hope that your birthday celebration was eventful."

"Oh, it was Grandpa! We had a great time, thank you very much."

"You can thank your grandmother for that one, Son. She's the one who made all the arrangements. But let's see. You turned sixteen, am I right?"

"Yessir."

"Now, that's a fun age to be, Jeffrey. Sixteen is also a responsible age. It's a time when certain rights and privileges are granted to those who can be trusted. And from what your father tells me, you seem to have become a trustworthy young man. Am I right?"

"I . . . I like to think so, Grandpa," Jeff answered shyly, quite embarrassed by the focused attention he was getting. But he continued, being quite serious. "Dad and I have a pretty open and honest relationship. But he's also quite biased, as you know."

"Yes, that he is. But Jeffrey," Mr. Russell continued over the satellite communicator, "I have a special gift I'd like you to have for your birthday celebration."

"Oh?" Jeff said anxiously, his heart beating faster and faster with anticipation.

"It's right here in my coat pocket. . . ."

The old billionaire stopped his pacing, walked a few steps toward the camera—growing larger in size as he did so—and looked directly into the lens. Slowly, he reached inside his suit-coat pocket and pulled out a large, white envelope.

"Warren?" he said, still looking directly into the lens, "I'm going to hand this to you. . . . You ready?"

"I'm right here in front of you, Dad!" Warren said, enjoying the extravagant game.

Mr. Russell inched the envelope closer and closer to the camera lens, as if suggesting that he would actually be able to pass the article directly through the video camera, out through the satellite link hundreds of miles above the earth, and into Warren's outstretched hands. And as he did so, Warren, who was playing right along with his clever father, inconspicuously placed his own hand inside his coat and withdrew an identical white envelope.

The screen turned dark for a brief instant as Mr. Russell covered the lens completely and Warren pretended to reach up and retrieve the incoming birthday present.

For the younger children, the process actually appeared to have worked! Everyone cheered.

"Jeff," Warren said proudly, "come on up here and join me on the stage, will you?"

Jeff jumped up from his position out on the fifth row, microphone in one hand, and walked up onto the stage to face his uncle Warren.

"Well, Master Jeffrey," Mr. Russell began calmly, after having returned to his comfortable sofa in the Swiss office, "I know that you're up there on the stage with your uncle Warren, and probably wondering what's inside the envelope, right?"

"I'm right here, Grandpa. Should I open it?"

"I think you'd better, young man, before we all die of curiosity."

Warren handed the envelope to Jeff. Jeff, in turn, handed his uncle the mike and opened the envelope. Inside were two documents.

The first was a letter of acceptance into the prestigious undergraduate school and School of Law at Princeton University, based upon a continuation of the grade point average that Jeff was presently enjoying in his high-school advanced placement courses. It was signed by the president of the university, a Doctor Anthony Barrett; and signed as well by the dean of the law school, Doctor Arthur C. Wiscombe.

The second document was a trust fund, which had been established in the name of Jeffrey Allen Russell. It was made for the amount of $150,000.00, with Eddie as trustor of the account. The fund, of course, was for Jeff's future college expenses. It promised to increase substantially in value over the next few years.

"I know that you're not yet finished with your high school years, Jeffrey," Grandfather Russell said over the satellite link, "but I wanted to make sure that your goals were lofty, so I telephoned my associates at the university, who sit with me on the board of directors. I persuaded them to open the doors for your future at Princeton! That *is* where you said you would like to go, isn't it, Jeffrey?"

"Oh . . . ah . . . yessir!" Jeff said with embarrassment, looking down at his father in the audience.

Eddie was already in on the little birthday present, as he and Jeff's grandfather had enjoyed a special father-to-son visit regarding the trust. And although Eddie did not particularly care for the flaunting of wealth, he was inwardly thrilled that his son's university expenses would be met. In addition, he appreciated the value his parents had placed on education, as that value filtered down to their posterity. Eddie had found it difficult to maintain his independence and at the same time respond appropriately to his parents' generosity. He recalled that Theodore Roosevelt, Senior, was named "Greatheart" because of his philanthropic nature. His parents were of the same mold. More than anything else, they enjoyed sharing their wealth and allowing others to enjoy a better life as a result.

Eddie winked at Jeff, and the young man took it as a sign that it was all right to accept the generous endowment.

"Thank you *very* much, Grandpa!" Jeff responded cordially, " . . . Very much, indeed! And yessir, Princeton is where I want to go to college. This is a wonderful gift, and I thank you and Grandma so very much." Jeff smiled at his grandmother in the audience, and she, in turn, smiled and winked approvingly at his comment.

"You're all too welcome, Jeffrey," Mr. Russell continued. "We're all counting on you to earn your doctorate so that you can represent the firm one day. Sound good?"

"Uh . . . sure!" Jeff agreed, then looked again at his father. Eddie just shrugged his shoulders.

"And now, of course," Mr. Russell stated, standing again in front of the faraway camera, "it's your grandmother's and my opinion that any responsible sixteen-year-old should be given certain opportunities to prove his maturity and good common sense. And, since you're a legal, licensed automobile driver now, we think it's time you had your own set of wheels—"

"Huh?" Jeff blurted out suddenly.

Mr. Russell walked over to the left corner of the room, where he stood by a large easel that was draped with a red silk cloth. "And so, my finest and only grandson, after consulting with a few of my friends last week in Germany," he said, reaching over and lifting the silken canopy away from the wooden easel, "we decided that an ideal first car for a young, respectable lad like yourself should be this 1994 Strosek Porsche 911 Turbo Carrera 2!"

"What?" Jeff blurted out excitedly, feeling his knees grow weak. There on the easel, just now coming into focus on the screen, was a brilliant photograph of an all-black Turbo 911, with specially designed wide front and rear fenders, brown leather interior, tinted windows, rear scoop for the air intakes, and state-of-the-art spoilers. It was a dream car!

"But," Jeff squeaked, looking down a second time at his father, who was clearly not at all happy. In fact, although Eddie had been a part of the decision to create a trust fund for his son's future scholastic needs, he had not known about the absurdly lavish and foolishly expensive Porsche. He was angry, and Jeff could tell.

However, Eddie reasoned, this was not the time or the place to make a scene. They would discuss it later. But one thing was certain—Jeff was *not* going to keep the expensive toy! In fact, he wasn't even going to accept it. It would ruin him!

"I had the Porsche shipped over last week, Jeffrey," Mr. Russell continued, smiling and clearly delighted with himself. "But it didn't arrive until the day after your birthday."

"But Grandpa . . . I can't—"

"Nonsense, my boy. Never deprive an old man of the pleasure of gift-giving. Besides, if you felt deserving of such a machine, I would think it unwise to give it to you. But your head is on straight, Son, and after all, my money has to do good somewhere."

"Well—"

"Well, nothing, Jeffrey. You've earned it! Warren has the key. Warren?"

Warren turned to Jeff, still standing beside him on the family stage, and handed him a gold ring with three keys attached, as well as a small leather piece that had the expensive car company's logo printed on its surface.

"Happy birthday, Jeffrey!" Grandpa said, and Warren as well as everyone else in the room chorused in celebration.

Everyone, that is, except Eddie. Instead, he just turned to his mother, who had been sitting at his side in silence, and gave her that "What the heck's going on?" look.

"Mother!" Eddie stated impatiently. She just shrugged her shoulders as he had done earlier. And that gesture made Eddie even *more* frustrated.

"I can't let him have that car, Mother . . . you know that!"

"You'll have to take that up with your father, Ed. There's certainly nothing I can do about it."

"But how could you let him—"

"I don't *let* your father do anything, Son!" she countered. "I made a decision long ago never to be critical of a decision he makes, and this non-response has worked marvelously for both of us, because he treats me the same way. But if it's any consolation to you, I didn't think it was such a good idea, either.

"But your father insisted," she continued, whispering even more softly. "And Edward, you *know* that when your father insists on something . . . well . . ."

"I guess I do, at that, Mom. Sorry. I'll take it up with him, as you've suggested, when he gets home. But in the meantime, you know I can't allow Jeff to take the car. . . ." He looked up at the boy, who was still standing in front of the projection screen, celebrating uncomfortably with his cousins. Turning back to his mother, Eddie continued. "Where is the Porsche, anyway?"

"Out in the garage," she answered quietly, smiling with empathic understanding of her son's concerns.

"What should I do, Mother?" Eddie pleaded, truly too stunned to think through the situation.

"Well, Son," Mrs. Russell sighed, "now that you ask . . . if I were you, I would let Jeffrey enjoy this moment with his cousins. He can't take the car with him now, anyway, since it still needs to be serviced before driving. Time will sort this out, as I'm sure you know. Just allow Jeffrey his birthday moment with his grandfather. It will always be a special memory that way—don't you agree?"

"I guess you're right. But I still have great concerns over what this will do to Jeff's opinion of himself."

"You're the finest, Edward." His mother smiled again, taking her son's hand in her own.

A few minutes later, after the satellite connection had been shut down and after everyone had had a chance to see the sports car in the garage, Warren, Kenneth and Larry—and their wives—made all of the final preparations for their flight to Zurich. It had been decided that the granddaughters would spend the next two weeks at the elegant Rockingham Palace with their grandmother. The others would make their journey to Europe by way of the Boeing 767 which Mr. Russell had sent back to the States to retrieve them.

Because of the continued downpour, it was decided that the three couples travel to the airport by way of one of the family limos. The largest of these was an elegant Cadillac that was chauffeured by Charlie—and as it drove off down the driveway, Eddie and Jeff, as well as the granddaughters and Mrs. Russell, stood at the door and waved good-bye.

No one saw the small rental car—the obscure Ford Escort— as it pulled away from the curb and followed after the limo. But Eddie stood, nevertheless, at the front door and watched with concern as the heavy rains pounded the pavement.

The fierce nature of the storm was unsettling. It left an eerie feeling inside Eddie's stomach, and for a moment he thought he heard a noise—Something over to the left, out there on the circular drive where he had parked the Chevy earlier, seemed to be hissing—

"Someone there?" he called out.

No response. But then the noise came back a second time . . . a crackling sound . . .

And it wasn't the rain, Eddie was sure of it! For suddenly a curious sense of concern swept over him, and with it, a slight but notable fear.

CHAPTER 16

Kenneth Sean Russell was worried. He sat silent by one of the windows in the back seat of the elegant limousine and stared out at the intense downpour. The wind had increased overnight and through the morning, and he was worried about the storm itself. Still, he was unable to vocalize his concerns to those sitting in the limo with him—his wife, his two brothers, and their wives.

In truth, he didn't want them to think that he was frightened—scared, quite literally, out of his wits!

Early that morning, Ken had kept a vigilant ear tuned to the television weather reports. Consequently, he knew that this was a very unusual storm. Its origin was an out-of-season hurricane just a few hundred miles off the coast of Baja, California.

Hurricane Bard. That was a weird name—Bard. That's what they had called it, though, and it was a *strong* one!

Wave after dark wave of storm clouds had windmilled off of the whirling mass of unsettled moisture out in the Pacific and had rolled in to cover Baja as well as the entire southern half of the state. He and his family would have to hurry in order to fly out of L.A. before the really bad weather hit.

Yes, Ken was scared! This whole idea was nuts!

Still he felt incapable of voicing the fear. He was, after all, the quiet one, the soft-spoken brother of the family—a good *follower*, his brother Warren would say.

And so Ken kept his fears tucked safely inside and just watched in silence as Charlie, the driver, turned out onto Interstate 405 from Sunset Boulevard North and headed south toward the Los Angeles International Airport. "Why couldn't the

Boeing have been in Burbank?" he asked himself, knowing even as he asked the question that Steve and Bobby had flown into LAX *from* Burbank because of a much-needed equipment check.

As the group sped southward on the San Diego Freeway, Larry suddenly announced the need to stop at a convenience store.

"What in the world for?" Warren asked, feeling a bit put out. "We haven't got time for that, Larry! We've gotta get up over this storm front before it's too late! What do you need at the store?"

"I need some gum and a few other things I can't get at the airport," Larry said defiantly.

"*Gum?*" Warren countered, "Are you serious?"

"Well, of course I'm serious, Warren. My ears can't take the ascent without some gum. But, don't worry about it. I'll only take a second." And then, turning to Charlie, Larry ordered him to turn off at the next exit.

"That'll be National Boulevard, sir, just past the Santa Monica and San Diego Freeway interchange. Is that all right with you?"

"Sure, Charlie. Get off on National."

"No, *don't*, Charlie!" Warren objected. "You just stay right on the freeway and get us to the airport!"

Charlie looked briefly back at the two brothers, then faced forward again.

"No, Charlie!" Larry said, "You get off where I told you to, find the first convenience store, and let me out! You hear me?"

"Yes," Charlie answered, feeling desperately locked in a no-win power struggle.

"I need some gum, Warren. I always chew gum when I fly so I won't get sick!" Larry's wife, Elizabeth, tried to intervene but was quickly shut down by her husband.

"For pete's sake, Elizabeth! Why do you have to jump in all of a sudden? It's just a couple of packs of gum. You and Warren are acting like this is some gigantic inconvenience. I mean, what gives? It's just a quick stop—is that all right with you?"

"Hey, hey, Larry—" Warren interjected, retreating at last. "*Fine!* You want some gum, that's fine! But let's stop this senseless bickering."

Then, turning to the aged butler/chauffeur, Warren said, "Pull off at National, Charlie. Let's find Larry some gum."

"Yes, sir. National it is, sir." As they drew nearer to the designated off-ramp, Charlie secretly knew why Larry insisted on turning off toward a convenience store. And it *wasn't* for the simple purchase of a pack of gum.

When the limo pulled into Dan's Cash 'n Carry, just off Barrington and National, the otherwise jovial mood of the three Russell brothers and their wives had fallen to a level that was sullen. For the most part, the others were internally angry with Larry. Even his sweet and supportive wife, Elizabeth, was feeling a bit uncomfortable. Nevertheless, the idea of the upcoming fourteen-day trip to the lavish Russell family chalet in Zurich was paramount in everyone's minds, and as if by unspoken agreement, they began to refocus on the excursion, rather than on the childish selfishness of Larry Russell.

"You want me to come in with you?" Elizabeth asked her husband as he started to climb out of the car.

"No, you stay right here, babe! No sense in both of us getting wet. I'll only be a minute."

At that moment, two parking stalls to the right, Chava was shutting off the motor of his rental car. He too was concerned about the rain. Not because he had an important flight to catch, like those he had been tailing ever since Rockingham Avenue, but because he had also been listening to the continued weather reports over the small Ford's AM radio and was distressed to learn that the center of the mammoth hurricane was a few hundred miles out in the Pacific, just off the coast of Cabo San Lucas. He knew that if the dreadful "force five" storm continued along its present course, the destruction to his small hometown of La Paz would be tremendous. His family could be killed, and he would not even be there to assist them in their most desperate hour.

They'd be all right, he convinced himself. If things got too bad, the neighbors Chava had called upon to look out for his family would assist in every way they could. And so, putting the troubling thoughts of home behind him, Chava refocused his attention on the luxury limousine. Someone was getting out of the back seat. He wasn't sure, but he thought it was Larry. And sure enough, as he watched the neatly dressed executive step awkwardly through the puddles toward the entrance of Dan's Cash 'n Carry, the identity became certain.

Chava wondered if he should follow Larry inside the store. He decided that if, in fact, anyone from the stately limo had seen him along the way, or even saw him now for that matter, they would consider it suspicious that he had remained behind the wheel. He decided to go inside.

Just then he noticed a man in a wheelchair—a veteran, judging by the Air Force field jacket he was wearing. He had apparently gotten stuck just inside the doorway and was desperately struggling to free himself. And that's also when Chava got a better, closer look at the face of Lawrence Russell.

The billionaire's son was standing directly in front of the disabled man, just out of the rain, and seemed angry that the fellow was blocking his entrance. Staring directly into the eyes of the handicapped man, Larry mumbled harshly, "You guys are all the same. You never can think of people who might be in a hurry!"

Chava was surprised by Larry's cruel words and stood back out of the way, next to the telephones mounted on the outside of the building. He couldn't believe what he had heard from Lawrence Russell's mouth. What kind of a man was this, anyway?

"I'm sorry," the man in the wheelchair replied sincerely. "I didn't know I was—"

"Look, pal," Larry continued callously, "I haven't got the time to parley words with you. So if you'll get out of my way, perhaps I'll still have time to make my appointment!"

"Hey!" came a sudden voice from inside the market. "What's going on? Is there a problem out here, Stan?"

A man dressed in a freshly pressed United States Air Force uniform, with the bird-rank of a colonel on each shoulder, handed his son the small sack of groceries he had just purchased. In doing so, he said, "Little Jack, hold this. We may have a problem here." The lad obediently backed away, and the officer stepped up behind his friend in the wheelchair and carefully inched him through the doorway. The man then walked over to Larry and stood less than two inches, in front of his face.

Larry was just under six feet tall, with a well-deserved pot-belly on an otherwise slender frame. But the man who squared off with him was at least six feet two inches tall, well-built, and obviously a seasoned veteran—judging by all of the medals pinned to his coat. Larry also noticed a Purple Heart award. It was clear that this man and his disabled friend had seen combat, probably the Desert Storm conflict.

Larry swallowed nervously and glanced back at the limo.

"You got some kind of problem, sir?" the uniformed Air Force officer probed.

"Who are you?" Larry countered timidly. He then backed away and looked down at the polished name tag that read "Col. Jack Garrity." "Are you this guy's friend?" he asked, desperately looking for a way out of the conversation.

Just then the door of the limo opened at the driver's side and Charlie climbed out of the car. "Problem, Mister Russell?" he asked, eyeing the proud-looking Air Force officer.

"No, Charlie. Get back in the car. Just a little misunderstanding, that's all."

"Yeah, Charlie!" Colonel Garrity reaffirmed, turning to the driver of the limo, "that's right. Just a misunderstanding, and your boss is doing all he can to learn a few manners. Isn't that right, sir?"

"Uh . . . yeah, sure. Uh, sorry," he mumbled to the man in the wheelchair, and then disappeared quickly into the market, past the lad with the groceries, and out of view of those in the car.

Colonel Jack Garrity then spoke to the youth, who was still inside the store. "Come on, Son. Can you believe some people think they're so important that they treat others that way?" The officer winked at his friend and motioned for his son to follow, and within seconds the three had disappeared into a new Ford Bronco that was parked next to the limo.

Chava, meanwhile, had picked up one of the telephones and pretended to be talking with someone on the other end of the line. And as he spoke absently into the receiver, his eyes watched with curious fascination as Lawrence Russell entered the men's room at the far corner and shut the door behind him.

From his vantage point outside, Chava reasoned that the Air Force colonel, had he been a violent man, could easily have hurt Larry. Obviously, the man was a well-disciplined veteran, and Chava inwardly respected the cool restraint exhibited by the combat pilot. He also respected the teaching moment the man had with his son.

Meanwhile, Larry Russell stood inside the small bathroom and glared hatefully into the mirror. But his hatred was not for the man he had just confronted. Rather, it was for himself. He was out of control, and his entire life seemed in shambles. Steeling himself against his thoughts, Larry then retrieved a miniature one-gram vial from a small pocket sewn into his coat.

There was a little gold-plated spoon attached to a tiny chain. This, in turn was attached to the lid of the vial. He used the spoon to dip into a crystalline substance, then brought it up to each of his nostrils—once, then twice—as he snorted the white powder into his lungs.

A few moments later, as the limousine pulled out of the parking lot and resumed its journey on toward LAX, Chava left his place at the pay phone and walked slowly back to his tan-colored Ford Escort.

He did not pursue the limo. There was no further need to do so. Instead, he dried himself off with a small towel that was on the back seat, then pulled out his scrapbook with the pictures inside and found the one he was looking for.

The photograph depicted four individuals—each was at one stage or another of exiting a truly elegant BMW 735 I. The four individuals who had been photographed by Chava's camera were Lawrence Russell, his wife, Elizabeth, a pre-teenage girl with her hair all done up, who Chava had heard referred to as Heidi Marie, and a much younger child, whose name was Megan Lynn. Chava stared at the picture, trying to memorize the faces. He then returned the photograph to its designated spot inside the scrapbook. He was, at last, ready to proceed.

Several blocks away, not far from the southbound ramp onto the 405, a very pensive Charlie gripped the wheel of the limousine with both hands and initiated a lane change. He had seen the Ford Escort. He had seen it all the way back at Rockingham Avenue, as it had pulled away from the curb and followed their limo. He had watched it through the side and rearview mirrors as they exited the 405 and headed west on National. And he had grown concerned when, bringing the limo to a stop at Dan's Cash 'n Carry, he had seen the little vehicle enter the same parking lot.

Back at the market, when Larry had almost gotten popped in the mouth by that Air Force officer—something Charlie was certain Larry had deserved—Charlie had stepped out of the car and had taken a good, hard look.

He hadn't done so for the purpose of assisting Larry. No, not at all! He wanted to get a look at the driver of the Escort, license plate number CA 14799. He had written that number on a small tablet of paper inside his pocket.

The driver had obviously been of Mexican descent—young, dark hair, dark skin, and a bit chubby. Maybe eighteen, nineteen years old. He had made another note of those observations, as well. But now the Escort was gone. Maybe it had all been a coincidence. Then again, perhaps not. In any case, Charlie turned onto the 405, kept his thoughts to himself, and merged quickly into the late morning traffic. It was raining outside—really raining! Charlie leaned forward a bit to get a better look at the sky. "This has got to be the mother of all storms!" he whispered, then looked into the rearview mirror. He could see Larry.

And he watched with growing concern the gestures Larry was making—for indeed, he was sniffing and wiping at his nose with such relentless regularity that Charlie was amazed and bewildered that others in the family couldn't see through the obvious facade.

CHAPTER 17

The sound of the torrential downpour made it nearly impossible for Eddie Russell to identify the noise coming from somewhere over by the parked cars in the circular driveway. But whatever it was, he was certain that it was *not* the rain. Slowly, he moved away from the protection of the mansion's front entry and walked out into the downpour.

"Who's there?" he called out again. But still there was no response, and as before, there was an interval of silence, then the crackling, hissing sounds continued. But he could see no one, and no one answered.

"Wait a minute," he whispered. "The *radio*. Janie's trying to get me on the radio."

Quickly he ran over to the pickup, soaked to the skin from the ongoing downpour, and opened the driver's side of the cab.

"One W-Sixteen! This is Malibu dispatch! Come in, Sixteen!"

He picked up the mike. "Malibu dispatch, this is Sixteen. Go ahead, dispatch. Over."

"Oh, thank goodness!" he heard Janie shout. "Is that you, Sarge? Over."

"Affirmative. What's up, Janie? Over."

"We got problems, Sarge! Four separate Code Blue's! Five or six persons on one skiff alone. Calls have been coming in all morning. We need your help desperately!"

"Ten-four, Janie. I'm on my way. Keep the radio channel open, and I'll be back with you in a couple of minutes. Over."

"Roger, Sarge. Radio channel two-seven to remain clear. Dispatch out."

Frantically, Eddie dropped the radio-set microphone onto

the front seat of the pickup and ran back inside the mansion. "Jeff!" he called out upon running in through the front doorway. "Jeff, where are you, Son?"

Hearing Eddie's shouting, his mother, Delores, came into the foyer. "What's wrong?" she asked excitedly.

"There are some reported MP's out in my district, Mom. I've gotta get to the station and lend a hand. This storm's a real kicker."

"What are MP's?" she questioned anxiously.

"Missing Persons. They're reported as a Code Blue, which refers to a possible drowning. They've been coming in all morning, and I've gotta go! You seen Jeff?"

"I'm right here, Dad," came a sudden voice from the living room. "What's up?"

"Grab your things, Son. We've gotta get back to the station." Then, turning to his mother, he said, "Gotta go, Mother dearest. Thanks for the marvelous Sunday morning . . . *and* for Jeff's gifts."

"Yeah, thanks a bunch, Grandma!" Jeff said, "We'll come by tomorrow and pick up the car, if that's okay."

"We'll talk about that later, Jeff," Eddie said with a somewhat stern expression on his face. "You ready to go?"

"Yeah," the boy answered, sounding a bit downhearted.

"See you later, Mom," Eddie continued.

"Well, all right, then," she said, still feeling a bit anxious. "You be careful now, you hear me?"

Without speaking, each of the men kissed the aging matriarch, then turned and ran back out through the rain to the pickup. They waved good-bye as they pulled out and then drove off down the long driveway exiting the Rockingham estate.

Each passing minute meant that a human life was more in peril than the minute before. And only now, through his continued radio-link with the Malibu station, was Eddie able to visualize the nature of the distress calls.

After getting a thorough debriefing, Eddie concluded, "Okay, Janie, I'm close to the turnoff onto the Coast Highway. We should be there in just a minute. What's available for the operation? Over."

"The Bayliner's still moored at the Malibu pier. TC and Jo Ellen took the Sea Ray. Over."

"Have you got 'em on the Marine Band? Over."

"Affirmative, sir. Over."

"Any sight of the dinghy?" he queried with growing concern. "Over."

"Negative, sir. No word yet, but they're keeping the lines open. Over."

"Okay, listen up, dispatch," Eddie directed. "Who's with you at the station? Over."

"It's just me at the moment, Sarge. But Bev's on her way in. She'll help me monitor the storm, as well as the operations. Over."

"All right, Janie. Have her get my diving gear ready. You copy? Over."

"Roger, sir. But you can't dive alone, Sarge! Over."

"Where's Howie? I thought you said he was coming in. Over."

"Negative, sir. Howie's still up in Ventura with Sheriff Haas. They've been at it all weekend. I haven't even heard from him since yesterday. We're on our own, Sarge. Over."

"What about the Coast Guard? Can we get an assist on the—what'd you call it? The Netherman's vessel? Over."

"That's Neberman, Sarge. James Neberman. And that's a negative on the Coast Guard. They've got their hands full. Lifeguard units are swamped, as well. From what I've been able to monitor on the Weather Band, we're in for the ride of our lives! Over."

Eddie held the handset away from his mouth, then looked anxiously over at his son, who was sitting quietly, but even more anxiously, next to him. There was real concern in Eddie's heart. He knew that the kids in the Neberman sailboat were in serious trouble, for undoubtedly the swells out at sea were already white-capped and dangerously turbulent! Any one of a dozen surges could capsize an eighteen-footer. With the storm growing in intensity, as it was, and if indeed the craft did flip in the water, it would be virtually hopeless for those aboard.

"Janie?" he radioed again, "can you give me an update on the storm forecast? Over."

"Roger, Sixteen. National Weather Bureau reports a force five hurricane, just off the coast of Todos Santos, north of Cabo San Lucas at the tip of the Baja. Barometric pressure is at twenty-four and dropping! It's moving right up the coast, Sarge! Over."

"Then this is only the front? Over."

"Affirmative, sir. Like I said, this one's gonna be a real donnybrook. Over."

"All right then. Get that gear ready for me! Jeff and I will take the Bayliner." Eddie paused and looked again over at his son. Jeff didn't say anything but simply nodded his head to confirm his willingness to assist his father in the rescue operation. "You copy? Over."

"Ten-four, Sarge," Janie responded obediently, but with frustration and concern mounting in her own mind. "But I still hope you're not planning to solo dive! You still need another diver! Over."

"I'll dive with you, Dad," Jeff interrupted suddenly. "If you can get someone to pilot the Bayliner, I'll dive with you—if we need to dive at all—"

"Not on your life!" Eddie stated conclusively. "You don't have near enough experience to dive in a turbulent sea!" Jeff said nothing. He just turned and stared out the front window while Eddie got back on the radio.

"Actually, Janie, there probably won't even be a need to dive. I'm sure that if the sailboat has capsized, the survivors will all be floating on the surface. We'll just be providing a taxi service. But get my gear ready, and an extra set, just in case. Over."

"Ten-four, Sixteen. Ready equipment. We'll have it waiting for you when you get here. Dispatch clear."

When at last they turned onto the Pacific Coast Highway and shot northward along the slippery surface of the winding stretch of road, Eddie and his son had lapsed into an uneasy silence. Each was caught up in his own thoughts, and each was concerned about the upcoming rescue operation. But that was not the only focus of their thoughts.

Like most kids Jeff's age, Eddie's son had become preoccupied with glorious visions of driving around town in his own car. His very own Porsche! The sleek, black, lushly-upholstered leather interior Turbo Carrera 2 that was sitting in the garage at the Rockingham mansion.

And although Jeff was grateful for the magnificent scholastic endowment, it just wasn't quite as exciting as rocketing around the neighborhood in a precision machine that would undoubtedly be the envy of every guy on campus.

Stated simply, Jeff was extremely frustrated about his father's attitude toward the car. Sure, they'd talked—many times, in fact, about Eddie's wish that he not accept handouts and lavish gifts bestowed by his grandfather. They had even agreed that earning their own way in life was, by far, the best way to go. But what harm was there in accepting a gift or two along the way? Whose car was it, anyway? It had been given to Jeff, not Jeff's father! And as far as the youth was concerned, it should have been his decision alone when and how—and if—he should take possession of the expensive automobile.

Then, on top of everything else, he'd made a truly noble gesture in offering to assist his father in a very dangerous rescue operation. And instead of his father treating him as an adult, as he could have done, he had treated Jeff like a runny-nosed kid with zero diving capability!

Jeff's thoughts brought a bitter taste to his mouth, and he found himself suddenly feeling strangely defiant. Subtly, he peered out from the corner of his eyes and looked at his father's concerted gaze at the highway stretched out before them. Strangely, he then thought that even though he was upset, this was not the time to abandon his father. In fact, his father would need him. Jeff would use his maturity and show his father that he was capable of accepting and driving the new car.

"And so . . ." he whispered under his breath, "if you're gonna dive, Dad, I'm gonna dive with you. You want me to grow up? You want me to make responsible adult-like decisions? Well, okay then. I hereby forbid you to risk your life unnecessarily by attempting an insane solo dive in a stormy sea. I love you too much to allow you to make such an irrational choice. I'm diving with you, Dad, whether you want me to or not."

The barely audible whisper of Jeff's voice did not register in Eddie's ears. He was too far away. He had been keeping a vigilant watch on the massive swells pounding at the beaches along the coastal route to the Malibu Ranger Station. Images of an old man and his wife sitting in an island lighthouse were the central focus of his thoughts.

Simeon had told him that great things were in store for him and his family. Yet these, he had said, would be the rewards of long-suffering and a painful endurance of trials that were yet to come.

With bold sincerity, and with an air of humble reverence, Simeon and his wife, Sarah, had spoken of a *Second Coming*, an event that was to transpire shortly, although no one would know exactly when. And although Eddie had not fully understood, he knew somehow in his heart that the remarkable couple had spoken the truth.

And, oh, how sobering the feeling when they had declared that Eddie had been chosen to assist in the preparation for this event!

"Eventually," Simeon had said, "your actions and intervention in the lives of many will change hearts and open doors for thousands of non-believers. They will see hope once more! They will *believe* because of you! And for this reason, young Edward, many who would have been lost will arise and come forth to greet the Savior of the world—the Son of the God of Heaven and Earth.

"And He *will* come, my son, as surely as the night follows the day! And the world will know that He is come, for there will be signs from the earth herself!"

"What do you mean?" Eddie had probed, trying desperately to understand.

"There will be earthquakes, the likes of which no man can comprehend, that will shake the mountains and the valleys, the cities and the open plains! There will be great wonders in the heavens, events seldom seen by man, which will cause many to wonder and to speculate. Even the sun will refuse to shine!

"In the end," the old man had continued, "all who failed in this life to live honorably—to give freely of themselves, to assist the needy and the homeless, to speak truths, or to bestow good rather than evil—will perish!"

"Perish?" Eddie had queried, feeling frightened and unworthy of the task ahead. "Well . . . who is to determine which of us will . . . perish, Simeon?"

"All men, Eddie, wherever they are, in whatever capacity they serve, and in almost all circumstances, are clearly capable of discerning right and wrong. How simple it is, really. One does not need a tutor at every turning. Our human souls are endowed at birth with a noble conscience that whispers, every day, approval or disapproval of our choices.

"But, my good friend, if we become sensitive to the needs of others, if we set aside the lures of self-gratification and instead give completely of ourselves, then we will be prepared when the Master comes. And thus we will *not* perish. Regardless of whether or not we are members of the Church, we will fall to our knees and acknowledge that He is the Master, and that He can now lead us into further light and truth!"

Eddie remembered, as he continued north along the highway, the sensation of warmth and peace that had accompanied Simeon's insightful tutorial.

"Then what you are saying, Simeon," Eddie had continued, "is that the choices we make are either right or wrong. Correct? There is no in between?"

"Men know, noble Edward, even if their hearts are past feeling. Still, they know! They are not so naive as they would have others believe. It is right, or it is wrong. And in answer to your question, there is no in between.

"We search our hearts for hope, for happiness, and for peace. We know that each of these are measurements of light. Why, Sarah and I even heard a man named Randy Travis singing a song of such light on the radio. "A Thousand Points of Light," I think it was called. To my understanding, there is a right way and a wrong way to fulfill the desires of our hearts. How we fulfill them is the important thing.

"If it is right, there is light in our hearts, and strangely, in our countenances. But if it is wrong, darkness! We have but to look upon the heart and countenance of Saddam Hussein, as he justified the brutal murder of over one million of his Christian citizens, the Kurds, to see evidence of this. And as the great prophet, Mormon, once explained, it is people of this nature who experience the sorrow of the damned! It is they who curse God and wish to die, and yet who fight for their very lives.

"We know, Eddie. We know because it is given to us to know. And so, in the end, before the great earthquakes and calamities are upon us, preparing the way for His coming, we will know!"

"We will know," Eddie whispered to himself, still eyeing the beaches and thinking back to the sobering conversation with the old man and his wife.

"Unusual storms?" he thought pensively, weaving in and out of the traffic along the coastal route and watching the hypnotic swiping of the windshield wipers. "This is an unusual storm, if there ever was one!"

Hurricane Bard, an out-of-season hurricane of incredible "force five" magnitude, was bearing down on the coastline of southern California and the Baja Peninsula.

CHAPTER 18

Warren Russell sat without comfort on the plush sofa at the farthest end of the Boeing 727 luxury jet and held firmly onto his wife, Jodi. His discomfort stemmed from his concern for his brother Kenneth. Trying not to draw attention to himself, Warren had been watching Ken out of the corner of his eye and had seen the terror that was bottled up inside his quiet, unassuming brother. Warren knew that Ken desperately disliked airplanes. He was uncomfortable in any form of aircraft, in good weather or bad.

The difficult part was that coupled with the fear itself was the frightening scenario outside—Hurricane Bard.

Warren knew that there really wasn't much to worry about. The company Boeing jet was a state-of-the-art executive luxury cruiser, flown by two of the best pilots money could buy. Both had made so many transoceanic flights that for them it was as routine as climbing into a car and driving down a familiar neighborhood street.

Only yesterday, Captain Steven Stewart and his skilled navigator, Robert Kevin, had taken off from Switzerland again, at the request of their billionaire employer, and had rocketed through the skies over the Northern Hemisphere. Landing first in Burbank, then LAX, they had slept through the night and then returned to the cockpit to head back to Switzerland.

All of that didn't seem to matter to Kenneth Russell. He remained fearful, cradled by his protective Monica, and spoke no more than a sentence or two during the entire flight.

"Poor Ken," Warren whispered in Jodi's ear. "I just wish that there was something I could do for him."

Warren and his wife stared out the window and held fast to each other as the sturdy jet blazed a turbulent path through the fierce winds and freezing rain. Even at forty-five thousand feet, they had not risen above the voluminous clouds. And although Warren knew very little about aviation and aircraft, he did have to admit to himself that flying in this kind of weather made him uncomfortable.

For that reason, Warren was truly curious when he noted suddenly that his other brother, Larry, was up and about, consuming drink after drink without the least bit of concern for safety. For some reason, the bumpy ride didn't seem to affect him in the least.

Up front, in the cockpit, there were other concerns. Captain Stewart thoroughly disliked the violent conditions through which he and Robert were flying and was anxiously awaiting a weather update.

"Okay, I think I have it, Steve," the young navigator said finally, after a prolonged search through a set of radio frequencies. Both pilots wore headsets that fed continual oxygen into their systems, allowed them to communicate through small electronic mouthpieces, and monitored all audio transmissions, either incoming or between themselves.

"I'm monitoring a conversation right now, and I'll feed it to you as I get it." Robert paused for a moment and listened intently. He then continued. "Bingo!" he said. "It's definitely a 141 . . . a Starlifter out of McClellan . . . And . . . here comes the update from the meteorologist on board!"

Quickly the young pilot-navigator whipped out a mechanical pencil from a shirt pocket and began scratching down the incoming data.

"They're right inside the eye!" he said, fascinated with the gutsy Air Force crew whose job it had been to fly into the storm and collect data for the National Weather Bureau and defense depots monitoring the massive hurricane.

"Windwall speed has increased," he continued.

"What is it now, Bobby?"

"Two hundred . . . eighty-seven and increasing! Gusts as high as . . . Wow! Three hundred and ten miles per hour! I've never heard of anything like it! But . . . wait. There's something else."

His mouth slightly agape, he looked over at his flying partner, and his eyes filled with an expression of horror that was altogether foreign to Captain Stewart.

"What is it, Bobby?" Stewart pressed.

"It's headed north, Steve . . . north by northeast. . . . And according to the radar on the 141 Starlifter, Bard is on a wide, sweeping collision course with . . . with the city of . . . Los Angeles!"

CHAPTER 19

Chava fiddled with the little knob on the radio, trying to tune into the emergency weather report that was just now coming over nearly all the stations, AM and FM. He was fascinated with what was being said, but he was also scared.

According to the reports, Hurricane Bard was increasing in intensity and weaving a destructive path northward along the coast of his beloved Baja. Its intense fury remained unchecked about two hundred miles out at sea. The windmilling spin-off clouds, winds, and rains were already doing their damage to his hometown of La Paz. Nevertheless, he was immensely grateful for the near-miraculous directional change that the furious monster had made in recent hours.

But this new information was also unsettling. The radio reporter's update had frightened him sufficiently that he decided to drive immediately northward toward Sacramento and ready himself for Romero's release from Folsom prison early Tuesday. According to the news report, Hurricane Bard would hit the Los Angeles basin sometime Wednesday afternoon. And so, as far as Chava was concerned, there simply wasn't any time to waste. He would have to pick up Romero at the front gate and make a mad dash back to L.A., and to their business. It was a risky plan. But then the whole thing had been risky right from the beginning. The storm might serve as a protective cover if they played their cards right.

As Chava continued his drive northward into the San Fernando Valley, the small Ford Escort felt like a flimsy cardboard box on wheels. It swerved this way and that with the buffeting winds. Chava felt a giant knot form in his stomach. The next forty-eight hours would be the most perilous of his entire life.

CHAPTER 20

As Eddie and Jeff pulled into the parking lot at the Malibu Aquatic Ranger station, they heard a horn honking directly behind them. Whirling around, they both caught a glimpse of the Audi 100 just as it pulled up next to them. It was Jennifer. Eddie had no idea why she was there, but he was pleasantly surprised and grateful that she was.

"What are you doing here, sweetheart?" he asked, helping her out of the compact car and heading for the sturdy sanctuary of the Ranger station.

"I thought you could use a hand," she said, shielding her face from the fierce winds and rains that pelted them. "Have you been listening to the radio?"

"Of course," he said, grabbing hold of the front door and gesturing for her and Jeff to go on in ahead of him. "I know all about the hurricane."

"Did you know it's moving up the coast of Baja and is scheduled to hit L.A.?"

"What?" he exclaimed, astonished at the report. "Where'd you hear that, Jennifer?"

"Over the Emergency Broadcast System on the radio, just a minute ago. They say it's going to smash into the L.A. basin sometime on Wednesday, and it's going to pulverize us!"

Eddie considered that sobering thought and felt a slight chill. He had considered the storm carefully but had not kept a vigilant ear to the police radio for further updates. For indeed his thoughts had been elsewhere. Quickly the three of them rushed into the station and right past the dispatch console.

"Is the gear ready?" Eddie asked Janie Hamblin, who was walking on his heels.

"All set," she answered anxiously.

"Jeff?" Eddie said, turning to his son, "Will you bring the truck around to the back? I'll pop the garage door. Back it up right to the table here, will you, please?"

"No!" Jeff said quite suddenly, with a tone of absolute defiance in his voice. Everyone turned and stared—

"Not until you hear me out!" he demanded. "Ladies, maybe you can help me talk some sense into my dad—"

"What are you talking about, Jeff?" Eddie asked with anxious concern.

"I'm talking about your decision to dive alone in this rescue operation."

"Hey, now," Eddie countered, "we may not even *need* to dive, Son. And we've already talked about—"

"No, Dad! *You* talked . . . *you* demanded! And I was forced to listen!"

"Jeff," Eddie interjected patiently, "we don't have time—"

"Let me finish, Dad!" the young man interrupted a second time. "You said I wasn't adult enough to dive with you out there in that choppy surf—"

"No," Eddie corrected, "I said you weren't *experienced* enough—"

"Adult enough, experienced enough, it's all the same thing. And that's not what matters, anyway," Jeff countered, taking command of the conversation for the third time. "It implies that I'm not a responsible diver—that I'm not good enough to dive at your side and assist you when you need me the most!"

Eddie felt suddenly a bit awkward, even ashamed. But he stood silently, listening to his son without comment.

"Your message to me, Dad, back in the truck was like this: Even though I've made hundreds of dives all on my own, and was taught by the best—by you, Dad—my age somehow discredits my abilities and my competence. You are the one who taught me that a professional diver *never* dives alone!" Jeff paused for a moment, then walked over to his father and stared into his eyes.

"Well," he continued, "here it is, Dad. I'm not going to

allow you to risk your life needlessly! If you're going to make a dangerous dive out there this afternoon, then I'm diving with you. We'll perform the rescue operation together, but you're *not* going alone. I lost Mom to cancer, and I'm *not* going to lose you to the sea!"

Both women felt an emotional tug and were unable to hold back their tears.

Eddie finally accepted the profound thinking and very adult reasoning of his son. He felt more ashamed than ever, yet he was equally proud. Affectionately he reached over and drew his courageous son into his arms.

"You're right, of course," he said tenderly. "I guess I have been a bit unreasonable."

He pulled away and looked into Jeff's eyes.

"I'd be honored to have you assist me in the operation, Jeff. But we'll have to find a pilot and navigator for the Bayliner."

"I'll go with you, Sarge!" Janie Hamblin volunteered readily. "I know that boat like the back of my hand! I'll pilot it for you!"

"Me, too!" Jennifer chorused, though she wasn't even sure yet what the operation was all about.

Eddie looked at the two women, took in a deep cleansing breath of air, then said in a proud, confident voice, "Well, then, what are we waiting for?"

By the time the four of them arrived at their destination at the extreme west end of the Malibu pier, Eddie had become concerned that the rising tides and growing intensity of the surf would render a launch impossible. And so, as fast as they could, the small team loaded the Bayliner with all of the diving and rescue equipment stowed in the back of the pickup. They then lowered the sleek craft down into the angry sea and sped off northward toward Topanga.

Twenty-five minutes later, a mile or more due west of Topanga, Eddie powered the Bayliner down to quarter speed. Jeff, like everyone else, was dressed head to toe in a yellow raincoat, hip waders, and a protective head cover. He stood high atop the cruiser's crow's nest with a pair of binoculars in his hands.

"Can you see anything, Jeff?" Eddie shouted above the wind and pelting rains.

"Not yet, Dad!" the young man called back, carefully scanning the surface of the turbulent waters.

Just then Janie picked up something on the Marine Band. "Sarge," she yelled, "Listen to this on channel sixteen—sounds like a fading S.O.S.!"

Rushing to the forward cabin, Eddie called, "Wherever it's from, it's a long way out! Pray to heaven it's not the vessel we're looking for, because if it is . . . well . . . I don't think there's much hope. Keep an ear to the channel, Janie. The best we can hope for is that the Coast Guard will pick up the distress signal further out at sea. Call me, though, if you hear anything else."

"Roger, Sarge," she answered sadly, thinking to herself how dreadful it would be to be lost at sea in such a miserable storm.

Back up topside, Jennifer, who had relieved Eddie at the helm, felt fatigued. She had only been at it for a few moments, but the relentless rocking motion of the craft played havoc with the hydraulic steering system. Although she had repeatedly readjusted the trim tabs, the violent motions yanked at her wrists, leaving them painfully weak.

Momentarily, Eddie was back on the flybridge and once more in command of the sturdy vessel. "Thanks, Jen!" he shouted. "See anything yet?"

"Nothing," she responded wearily, shaking her hands and wrists. Jennifer turned away for a moment, and looked out at the raging waters. Inwardly, she was more frightened than she could ever remember. Just then, her eyes caught sight of a momentary flash of something due west that had surged upward with a giant wave out in the deep.

"What's that?" she screamed.

Eddie quickly responded, looking at her briefly to see in which direction she was pointing. He then turned his gaze west across the water. "What do you see?" he called back.

"Something orange! Or red, just a half mile or so that way!" she screamed, her right arm extended and her index finger pointing westward. "There! There it is again!"

Eddie saw it as well.

Jeff lowered his binoculars and looked down at his father. Eddie was pointing directly out to sea. No words were necessary. Jeff instinctively knew to raise the glasses a second time and scan the direction indicated by his father's gesture.

That's when he spotted it. "Yeah!" he screamed at full pitch. "Three hundred yards off the starboard bow!"

"What is it, Jeff?" Eddie screamed back.

"A raft! An orange raft! There are people on board."

The small survival raft was nearly three miles out in the open ocean. It was west-by-northwest of Topanga and turned out to be the missing teenagers from the Neberman sailboat. But not everyone.

"Where are the others?" Eddie yelled to the two boys as he was pulling them onto the rescue boat.

"Don't know," the one lad said, shivering uncontrollably. "We couldn't find 'em."

"Who?" Eddie pressed. "How many others are there?"

"Sharon and Mike," the lad said.

"Mike?" Eddie pressed again, "Mike Neberman?"

"Yeah. It was his dad's boat! I told him we should have gotten permission . . . honest!"

"It'll be okay," Eddie responded, trying to calm the lad down.

There were three survivors—two young men and a young woman—each so traumatized by the ordeal and so cold from the icy winds, surf, and rains that they were almost incoherent.

"Tell me," Eddie continued, realizing that the lad was shaking violently and that his mind was nearly paralyzed "how long ago did the sailboat capsize? It did flip over, didn't it?"

"I don't know how long . . . "

"Think!" Eddie shouted with pressing urgency. "The lives of your friends may depend on it!"

The boy shivered and closed his eyes.

"Five, maybe ten minutes ago . . ." he said finally, though clearly without confidence in what he was revealing.

"Jeff!" Eddie shouted abruptly, "take this boy downstairs with the others. Get all the information you can about what happened! Have Janie call in on the Emergency Band, and have an ambulance waiting for us back at the Malibu pier! You got that?"

"Yessir!" Jeff replied confidently.

"Then come back up topside. I'm gonna need your help. Have Jennifer look after the kids."

"Okay, Dad."

Eddie stood on the flybridge and scanned the turbulent

surface of the water in a southwesterly direction. Judging by the direction of the winds, he was certain that the raft and its occupants had drifted a mile, perhaps more, from the original location of the accident. And if he was correct, they would eventually come upon a widespread area of floating debris.

Eddie followed his hunch and powered at three-quarter throttle through the churning waves in that direction. But after twenty minutes of brutal swells pounding at the hull, he began to sense the hopelessness of the quest. "How could anyone survive out here?" he thought morbidly. "They've drowned . . . they just couldn't have made it!"

He pulled back on the throttle and looked back toward the coastline. It had vanished. With the steadily increasing downpour and cloud cover, the view in every direction had become dismally obscure. All that could be seen was the magnificent white-capping of a furious Pacific Ocean—an *immense* Pacific Ocean!

He brought the stalwart Bayliner to a full stop and let the powerful engines idle for a moment. That was the instant that something unique and totally unexpected occurred.

It was a slight sound at first, not unfamiliar. Beginning deep inside his mind, and slowly, ever so slowly moving outward until finally, the raging winds were blocked out altogether. He could hear nothing but the sound—penetrating and reassuring—humming from some faraway place. Yet Eddie could hear the tender sweetness with perfect clarity. And the voice and melody were familiar—very familiar! He recognized both simultaneously.

The voice was that of his beloved departed Andrea! She was *alive* and was acutely aware of him! And the melody was *their* song—the soul-soothing classical piece by Pachelbel—the Cannon in D.

"Andrea!" he shouted, whipping his head this way and that as if to spot her suddenly poised on deck. But she was nowhere to be seen. "What's going on?" he called out, surprised to hear his own voice alongside her gentle humming. "Andrea?"

"Eddie, my noble companion, be at peace," she directed, her voice coming to his inner, spiritual ears.

With his wife's words, Eddie was suddenly calmed and comforted. "I have come to assist you, at Simeon's request."

"Simeon? He knows where I am?" Eddie inquired with increasing calmness.

"Yes, my love, and you must have courage. There is a great need for haste! For the two whom you seek are near unto death. Ahead, my love, with the greatest of speed! Follow your impressions and use the Holy Spirit to assist you. Otherwise, you and they will perish."

And with those words ringing softly and surely in Eddie's mind, Andrea's voice began to fade and the sounds of the thunderous storm returned.

"But which way? How will I—" he called out desperately, not wanting her to leave. But before he could finish his pleading calls, he *did* know!

"Hold on, Jeff!" he called. "I know where they are!"

Then frantically he slammed the throttle forward as far as it would go, made a hard right rudder, and sped due west, directly out into the obscurity of the tumultuous winds and rapidly rising waves.

Five minutes later, after everyone on board was certain they'd just experienced the wildest and most chaotic ride of their entire lives, Jeff spotted a few scattered objects floating directly ahead.

"Dad!" he screamed.

But Eddie had seen the objects as well, and he suddenly throttled back, killed the engines, and leaped off the flybridge. "Come on, Jeff!" he called, peeling off his raincoat and weather-protective clothing. "This is the spot! Hurry! There isn't much time." Together, they rapidly changed into their wetsuits, donned their tanks and equipment, and waddled over to the swim platform.

"It's deep here, Son," Eddie cautioned with loving concern, "and I'm going to need you every step of the way!" He reached over to where Janie was standing and grabbed hold of the life tether-line she held.

"Hook this onto your weight belt, Son," he said, "and don't even think of losing sight of me! This may be our only means of getting back safely to the Bayliner! Are you with me?"

"All the way, Dad!" Jeff answered, feeling more nervous than he'd ever known. "Let's do it!"

"Okay, girls," Eddie shouted reassuringly, "we're going to need your prayers on this one."

"You got 'em!" Jennifer said, leaning over and kissing Eddie firmly on the lips. "Please be careful!"

"You, too, Jeff," Janie Hamblin chorused, also leaning forward to give her boss and his teenage son a reassuring embrace. "Go get 'em, you guys! You're their only hope! Pray to God they're still alive."

Under questioning, the two women had learned from the Richardson boy that when the sailboat had capsized, Mike Neberman and his girlfriend, Sharon Atwater, were locked inside the cabin. According to Richardson, there were two rooms inside the small vessel, a forward galley and a smaller sleeping cabin—airtight—just beyond.

The thought was chilling, but what appeared to have happened was that the rapid inward rushing of ocean water had somehow imprisoned the two unsuspecting teenagers inside the smaller cabin, and the boat had sunk!

The Richardson boy had also indicated that the boat had carried a partially-filled oxygen tank, and that even though the vessel's capsizing had occurred with no warning, his last sight of his friend Michael revealed the sinking lad waving the tank frantically in the cabin window, giving hope, at least, that they might still be alive.

Eddie and Jeff plugged their regulators into their mouths, looked cautiously over their shoulders, then fell backwards off the small platform into the water. Both had extra weights tied around their waists to facilitate the most rapid underwater dive possible, and they began sinking like two doomed sacks of concrete.

Down, down, down they plunged, each holding onto the other with one hand while tightly clinging to an underwater lamp with the other hand.

A few minutes later Eddie gave the signal, and they began to slowly inflate their buoyancy compensators, which allowed them to slow their descent just long enough to equalize the pressure that had been building in their sinuses.

"Are you okay?" Eddie said to his son using coded hand signals. The boy nodded.

"We'll wait here at this depth for a couple of minutes, then continue," Eddie scripted with his hands, using the depth gauge to get his message across with better clarity.

While they waited at forty feet, allowing their bodies to compensate for the pressure, Eddie moved slowly all the way around his son and double-checked the boy's diving equipment. More particularly, he checked the life tether-line connected to Jeff's belt. Everything looked fine. Then slowly they released some of the air in their B.C. units and started to sink deeper into the ever-increasing darkness below.

And dark it was. Jeff was not the kind to panic, but this prolonged descent was as eerie as anything he had ever imagined. He scanned the area with his lamp but could see nothing other than an occasional school of small fish and the comforting view of his father nearby.

By now, twelve minutes into the dive, Jeff was deeper than he had ever been before. He looked at his own depth gauge, saw the numbers, and felt a sweeping sense of fear and panic.

Sixty feet! And still no view of the ocean floor.

For a second time, he made eye contact with his father.

"Okay?" Eddie signalled.

"Yes," Jeff responded, although in truth he could hardly wait for this nightmare to end. He was frightened almost beyond panic! It was like falling off a darkened cliff—falling, falling, forever falling without reaching the bottom—having no idea what was awaiting him in this bottomless abyss!

The paralyzing fear began to take its toll. Jeff was hyperventilating.

"Relax," Eddie signalled calmly, "You'll be okay. Just breathe normally and relax."

Jeff nodded again and really tried to follow his father's advice. But his *heart!* The pounding in his chest was incredible, and there was nothing he could do about it. Nothing, that is, except pray.

Moments later, and with a great sense of relief, Jeff and his father spotted the sandy surface of the dark ocean bottom. Together they touched down with a gentle thud, kept their balance, and remained standing. Slowly, Eddie swam around his son, reaffirming to himself that all was well and that the diving gear was functioning properly. Also, of course, he fingered the life tether-line and rechecked the coupling at his son's waist.

At last Eddie felt ready to proceed. He looked at his compass, decided on his direction, then swam off to the northwest at three to four feet above the surface of the ocean. Jeff followed at his side.

Twenty minutes into the dive, they spotted the upturned sailboat. At the stern, a devastating gash in the hull was now filled with sand and debris. The midsection was flooded, although it remained in pretty good shape. It was clear that it had stayed in one piece. Eddie wasn't sure how rapidly the vessel had sunk to the bottom, but he figured it had happened fast. And when it had finally come to rest, the bow was pointed upward at an eighteen to twenty-degree angle. Unbeknownst to Eddie and Jeff, the two teenage victims were trapped inside, near death's gate, with hopeless anxiety and fear in their hearts.

There were three tiny windows in the little cabin: one forward, and the others on each side. Quickly Eddie swam over to the left side window and directed a beam of light within. A terror-stricken, alive Michael Neberman leaped forward with a startled jerk, put his hands on the glass, and began screaming. Eddie knew that Michael couldn't see him outside in the murky water, so he shined the lamp back into his own face to calm the fears of the near-hysterical Neberman boy.

Already, Jeff was at the outer galley door, inching his way upward and into the flooded compartment. At length, he reached the smaller portal that accessed the sleeping cabin where the two youths were trapped. Jeff tapped on the door, signalling that he was about to pry it open. Michael knocked back.

Jeff knew that if the sailboat had come to rest in any position other than with the bow angled upward, his opening the hatch would have been risky if not impossible. It would have flooded the tiny compartment immediately, and there would have been profound panic on the part of the two victims. Fortunately, the bow was positioned correctly, and with a little effort Jeff swung the small door open and popped his head inside.

"You made it! Thank God you made it!" the boy screamed, looking pale and starved for oxygen.

Quickly, Jeff yanked the regulator mouthpiece free and stuffed it into the girl's mouth. Already her eyes were rolled back toward the top of her head, and judging by the stench of the air that remained in the stuffy compartment, Jeff knew that what had been left of the oxygen tank had been exhausted and that the girl was near death.

Her lungs expanded gratefully, and the restorative air from Jeff's tank rapidly brought life to her depleted body. Jeff transferred the mouthpiece to the boy, then back to himself, repeating the cycle several times over a period of two or three minutes. Jeff noted that no blood was coming from their ears, and aside from the effects of oxygen deprivation, the two seemed in remarkably good condition. It had truly been a miracle.

"You all right?" Jeff asked between breaths.

"Yeah, I'm all right," Michael said.

"We've gotta get you guys outta here, and I'm gonna need your help!"

He turned his attention to the girl. She was clearly in a state of extreme shock, and her wide-eyed stare filled young Jeffrey Russell with grave concern. "We've gotta help her first," he declared, looking back once more at the very shaken Neberman.

"Wha . . . what do you want me to do?" he inquired.

"Talk to her! Tell her to breathe slowly into this regulator. We'll swim out together. Then I'll give her to Dad, and they can buddy-breathe all the way to the surface. We have a rescue boat on top, and they're waiting for us. I'm gonna swim outside with Sharon. You just hang tough, and I'll be back for you as quickly as I can. My dad will start the ascent with Sharon, and you and I will follow. Got it?"

"Y-yeah," the boy answered, his teeth chattering mechanically.

Somehow, and without too much difficulty, Jeff managed to squeeze in and out of the small portal two separate times and initiate a successful buddy system of breathing.

Slowly, then, the four of them began the long, intensely dangerous ascent, following the life tether-line up through the ever-pervading darkness. At about fifty feet, Eddie signalled for his son to stop and release a portion of the compressed air from the B.C.'s so they could decompress properly and neutralize the life-threatening nitrogen bubbles that had been accumulating in their bloodstreams.

They would have to stay put at this depth for about five minutes, at least.

But not more than a minute later, the first curious and famished blue shark suddenly bumped into Sharon's thigh. The shark, having approached Eddie and his near-lifeless passenger from behind, caused Eddie to wonder if they could risk it. Within seconds, there were seemingly hundreds of them—an enormous school of aggressive predators, each one more curious than the last.

Quickly Eddie signalled to Jeff to draw in close. They had to watch each other's backs. Since Michael Neberman and the Atwater girl had their eyes closed, it fell to Eddie and Jeff to somehow thwart off the inevitable attack.

"What shall we do?" Jeff gestured with his one free hand.

For a brief moment Eddie began to panic. These sharks were an aggressive breed, unlike so many of their placid cousins, and Eddie knew that it was only a matter of time before one or more would muster the courage to attack. If even the smallest amount of human blood was spilled, the four would perish! It would be a frenzy!

While these thoughts raced about wildly inside Eddie's head, sending chills up and down his spine, a sudden prompting awoke inside his heart. The priesthood! "Use it as you must," Andrea's voice had whispered, "but call upon the Lord with reverence, and use it righteously."

That had been the dictum of Simeon himself. And here was a moment of great need. A moment when he could call upon the powers of the Almighty for a righteous purpose. Life's forces were at stake, and he knew that Simeon's God, his God—*their* God, the omnipotent creator of the world and its oceans—was genuinely concerned about life. And so, he reasoned as the others hovered nearby, the moment was right. He knew it!

Slowly then, with Jeff looking on in curious fascination, Eddie stretched forth his own free hand and made a simple command. "In the name of Jesus Christ, and by the power of His holy priesthood, *be gone!*"

Suddenly, a brilliant white light shined around the small

cluster of swimmers, and every predator in the immediate vicinity turned tail and swam frantically off into the dark void below them!

"What?" Jeff breathed, nearly losing hold of the struggling passenger who was clinging desperately to his side and using up vast quantities of his precious oxygen.

"It's all right," Eddie motioned. "Let's go! We haven't a moment to spare!"

Jeff jerked his head back and forth, scanning the area for what he was sure would be additional sharks poised and ready to strike. But there were none. They had simply vanished.

When Jeff, Eddie, and their passengers broke through the surface of the water, there was a wild chorus of jubilant cheers. Everyone on board the Neberman sailboat had been rescued!

Forty minutes later, the frantic parents of five teenage sons and daughters wept tears of unutterable and unsurpassed joy. Their childrens' lives had been spared. And, as Mr. Russell explained, they were spared by Him—by Him, and by the matchless power of His touch!

CHAPTER 21

By dawn Monday morning, all of Los Angeles was under siege. Hurricane Bard was gaining strength by the hour, and its force five strength was knocking at the door. Throughout the night, literally hundreds of thousands of people had fled the city, while millions more had set about the task of reenforcing their homes and businesses against the magnificent oncoming force of nature.

Most of the coastal inhabitants had long since driven inland, where there seemed to be a greater chance for survival. Forecasters, particularly a special team called "Bard Watch," monitored the hurricane's path and promised the die-hards remaining along the beaches the latest information about the most massive surge of water ever to hit the California coastline.

Eddie, Jennifer and Jeff were three of those who chose to remain. As the monstrous storm approached, the three fearless survivalists remained busy—taping windows, nailing up sheets of heavy plywood, and securing everything outside that could take flight and cause damage. In the end, they were determined to defend themselves, their home, and their little piece of earth. It was an insignificant dot on someone's map, but they would do all within their power to protect it from Bard's cataclysmic force.

Somehow they would be ready, and *somehow* they would survive!

CHAPTER 22

Romero Valdez looked around the small confines of his cell. Cell number 228. The ugly, dreary compartment, which he referred to as the "Romero Meat Locker," had been his home, his *casa*, for the past three years. It was his only place of solitude, which came late at night during periods of "lockdown." It didn't really belong to Romero, of course. It was, instead, just another cage among thousands which made up this demon city-within-a-city. Just one single cage inside the massive prison known as Folsom.

There wasn't much to the one-man cell, really. Just a single bunk, a metal desk built right into the wall, and a lousy toilet-sink combination made of ice-cold polished steel! How glad he would be to be free, at last, of that abomination.

During the time that he had been locked up for two armed robberies in San Diego County, he had done his best to turn the Romero Meat Locker into a livable, tolerable retreat. But that was all behind him now. Tonight was Romero's last night in the "big house." Tonight he tied up all of the loose ends, said goodbye to the handful of individuals he called his friends, and made ready to walk out of the place bright and early tomorrow morning.

Romero was on his way home.

At nine o'clock the following morning, when Chava pulled up in front of the fortress-like main gate of Folsom, there was fear in his heart. He didn't quite understand, at first, but thought maybe it had something to do with seeing a part of his own future.

He hoped not. He didn't think he could withstand a long, lonely stretch inside the gloomy fortress before him. In truth, the more he thought about it, the more he was convinced that he would not be able to endure being treated like garbage, abused, and tossed around like a piece of meat. That's how Romero had described it.

No, Chava did not want to end up with a number written across his shirt, or to be forced to live inside the numbing, chilling confines of a meat locker. So, he prayed silently that the feelings he was experiencing were not insights into a future of darkness and misery. Perhaps he was just feeling homesickness for his mama, his sweet little Sylvia Maria, and his other brothers and sisters.

"Dear Lord," he pleaded in a whisper, "please don't let me end up in that awful place! I'm doing what I must do to save the life of my little sister! I have no other choice, Lord. . . ."

And with that, Chava thought about his plan, his brief reunion with Romero, and the long drive the two would have to make back toward Los Angeles—back into the powerful unrest of Hurricane Bard!

CHAPTER 23

Megan Lynn Russell stood at the picture window inside the gameroom of Rockingham Palace and stared out into the fury. The massive storm that everyone had been so worried about— so preoccupied with—was on its way here! From what she had remembered her grandmother saying, it was somewhere out in the Pacific Ocean. But this morning, Wednesday morning, it seemed to her that the giant storm was already here.

"Uncle Charlie," the nice black man who worked for her grandparents, was usually her favorite friend in the whole world. He did things with her. He taught her how to play checkers, and how to use many of the video games in the gameroom. He even took her to the stables and taught her about the great Arabian horses. Oh, yes, Uncle Charlie was her best friend!

Patiently, the little ten-year-old daughter of Larry Russell stood alert at the window and waited. She was genuinely concerned about Charlie and hoped that he was okay. After all, the giant storm was blowing everything around so much that, in her mind, she was sure that it could very easily pick a man right up off the ground and carry him away like Dorothy in *The Wizard of Oz*. And right now she couldn't bear such a horrible thing, because everyone needed Charlie! He was the busiest of them all, doing everything Grandma asked of him, and much, much more.

Inside her ten-year-old mind, Megan needed Charlie. She had been very concerned about the horses and wondered if she and Charlie should do something. Maybe they should go out and check to make sure that all of the doors and windows were tightly secured, so that the nasty winds and rains wouldn't set inside and frighten the poor creatures.

"Hurry, Uncle Charlie!" she thought with growing concern. "The horses *need* us!"

Everyone around the Rockingham Palace seemed frantic. They were doing their best to prepare for the powerful on-slaught still to come. Grandmother Russell worried about her family, although Eddie had called to indicate that he and Jeff were okay.

The Rockingham estate, thanks to the foresight of Allen Russell, was fortified against the storm's wrath. But no one could foresee everything, and as the winds had increased in strength, some of the windows were shattered. The devoted butler remained ever alert and was quick to respond to these crises.

By ten-thirty A.M., the city was in a state of sheer pandemonium! The winds of Bard's outer reaches were gusting up to one hundred and ninety miles per hour. An untold number had been killed or injured, and hundreds of thousands more were huddled together inside basements, garages, family rooms, and all sorts of makeshift sanctuaries—praying, weeping, and hoping that by tomorrow at this time they would still be alive.

By 10:44 A.M., Megan decided to do what she knew in her heart she must. She had not seen the old butler finish his errand out in the generator shed, and so she figured he must still be inside the little concrete structure. With growing determination and courage, she zipped up her coat, put the hood over her head, pushed through the small gameroom door that accessed the backyard area, and went out into the storm.

At first the powerful winds were too much, and Megan was swept off her feet and thrown forcibly to the muddy pavement. "Help!" she yelled. But no one heard her.

Fear gripped her heart, and she was just about to turn and crawl back to the sanctuary of the gameroom, when thoughts of the equally frightened Arabian horses raced through her mind. She had to help them! Even if it meant crawling all the way to the stables on her hands and knees—which, in the end, she did.

Back out along the Pacific Coast Highway, Eddie, Jennifer, and Jeff huddled in one corner of the living room. They sat now with their backs against a sturdy wall, staring silently at a small candle flickering on the floor.

"It's almost here," Eddie said morbidly. "I hope we don't discover that our decision to remain here was a foolish one."

"We'll make it," Jennifer said reassuringly. "We just have to have faith."

A few miles north of the great coastal metropolis, one man, at least, was *not* concerned. He was sitting in his favorite rocker, gazing at the pelting rains outside. "Sarah," he called out. "Would you care to join me?"

"I'll be right in, dear," the elderly woman called back. She was just now tending to a fresh pot of beef stew. Quietly she stirred the deliciously aromatic contents one more time, took a taste from the spoon, replaced the lid, and then walked into the small, neatly decorated living room.

Together, the two walked over to a window and looked out at the sea, which at that moment was tearing away at their island retreat. The storm had become a magnificent spectacle, and Simeon wondered if it would ever let up.

"This storm worries me," Sarah sighed quietly. "So many will die. Do you think the time is come, Simeon?"

"I am not altogether certain that the people are ready, my love. Perhaps this has opened a few of their eyes."

"Then why don't you intervene, Simeon? I believe that what they have seen is enough, don't you?"

"Perhaps," the old man whispered.

Simeon thought about the merciful request from his beloved companion, and he knew that it echoed the words of literally hundreds of thousands on the mainland. He felt good inside. Perhaps it would be better to stay the onslaught and hope for a change in the hearts of so many who would otherwise perish.

Quietly, then, Simeon took his companion's hand in his. The two went silently to their knees, and after petitioning his God for direction and for strength, Simeon arose and assisted his wife to her feet. "Come, my love," he whispered.

A moment later the two were climbing the circular stairway upward, until at last they reached the magnificent perch high above their cottage residence. "This is a fearsome storm, Sarah,"

Simeon said. "And you are right. If we do not intervene, tens of thousands will die in a matter of hours. But it is not the time. It is but a warning, a very strong and visible warning."

Slowly, the pensive, white-haired seer raised his hands above his head and looked heavenward. He then called on his Creator, in the name of his Master, while his wife, Sarah, bowed her head respectfully.

After a brief pause, he commanded with a voice of noble authority that the elements—the wind, rain, lightning, and thunder, indeed the very oceans—hear his bidding.

"Be still!" he cried.

And someone far away gave heed to the words spoken. For true to the natural laws of the priesthood, there came a response. The heavens complied.

At the mansion on Rockingham, however, something was wrong—terribly wrong! Grandmother Russell picked up the phone for the third time and frantically dialed the number to Eddie's house. This time, however, she got through.

"Hello?" Eddie answered, still stunned by the storm's miraculous abatement.

"Eddie!" Mrs. Russell screamed hysterically, "Is that you?"

"Yes, Mama, it's me. And we're fine, Mama. Jennifer's here with us, so please don't worry about us."

There was a slight pause and an audible sobbing over the phone line.

"Mama, what's wrong? Is something—"

"It's Megan, Eddie. . . . She's *vanished!*"

PART THREE

A Hostile Flurry

Destiny beckons to each,
     in its way,
As willed by a caring Creator.

But Agency also exists,
     which allows us to choose
The light we will have in our future.

CHAPTER 24

Allen Russell couldn't take it anymore. He had been sitting for hours in front of the television set with his eldest son, Warren, trying to assess the damage that the terrifying hurricane was doing to the county of Los Angeles. In all his life, Mr. Russell had never known such total and consuming concern. And in this particular instance, there was nothing he or anyone with him could do to assist his wife and granddaughters back at Rockingham Palace. He felt utterly helpless, yet he *had* to do something!

Communications linking Europe to the United States were jammed. And although he had tried repeatedly to get through on his private satellite hookup with the California mansion, the entire Los Angeles basin was in such an extreme state of turmoil and confusion that, in the end, he had simply given up trying.

For the moment, all he could do was wait it out, and hope and pray that between Charlie, Eddie, and his dear wife, Delores, they'd somehow be able to weather the storm.

"Are you all right, Dad?" Warren asked, watching with concern his father's emotional response to the events unfolding before them. "Honestly, if we'd only known that Bard was headed directly to L.A. before we took off from LAX, I would have insisted on postponing the trip so that Kenny, Larry and I could have stayed behind and helped Mama and the kids!"

Mr. Russell didn't respond. He simply stared blankly out at the lake.

"By the time we heard the report from Bobby up front in the cockpit," Warren continued, "we were already up and over the storm."

Mr. Russell stood stoically as if he were a soldier at attention. For a moment, Warren wasn't altogether sure whether or
not his father was listening to him. "Dad," he asked timidly,
"are you all right?"

"They'll be fine," Mr. Russell blurted suddenly, not hearing
the question. "I just know they'll be okay. Charlie's there, and
so is Eddie. They'll know what to do, I'm sure of it!"

For a moment, except for the muted noise coming from the
television set, the exquisitely decorated den in the Swiss chalet
was silent. And although Warren felt guilty for not having remained behind to assist his mother and the children in this disturbing crisis, he was even more concerned about the emotional
stress being endured by his father.

It was an extremely painful sight for Warren to watch him
stare out the window, knowing full well that despite his massive fortune, he was helpless to assist. Warren hated seeing his
good father so completely distraught. And judging by the look
on his dad's face, Warren knew that he was suffering—really
suffering.

Warren thought for a moment about what he could possibly
do to ease his father's pain, but nothing came to mind. It was
then that he realized that, to a large extent, they were all suffering. He and his father, his wife, Jodi, his brother Ken and his
wife, Monica, and even Larry and Elizabeth.

Mr. Russell turned his attention to the lake. "Funny, isn't
it?" he said calmly, "All my life I've lived in Los Angeles.
Moved there when I was just a kid. Met your mother out there.
And in time, all you boys were born there, as well. And for as
long as I can remember, I've seen California storms come and
go. Even so, there's something peculiar about this one. It almost
seems to be a follow-up to the record-breaking March storm on
the east coast, earlier this year."

"Why? Because it's so intense?" Warren probed.

"It's more than that, Warren. Ever since we first heard about
it—the fact that it represents the first ever recorded hurricane to
hit the basin directly—I've had this unusual feeling in my heart
that . . . well . . . perhaps there's more to it than we understand
. . . ."

"What are you driving at, Dad? What feeling?"

"It's not natural, that's what feeling! There's something behind this horrible storm! Something that seems to be directing its path . . . as if . . . some awesome power is actually willing Bard's ultimate destination!"

"What?"

"I mean it, Warren. That's what I'm feeling inside. I believe a *Creator* from the galaxies in space, if you will, has something to do with all of this! In fact, like I've tried to tell you boys for years, I believe that there is an omnipotent power . . . a being of marvelous intellect, who somehow watches over the earth. He *is* the Creator, I feel it. And I believe that the stars and planets in the firmament were created by Him, as well."

"You mean God?" Warren questioned timidly.

"Yes," Mr. Russell affirmed, "God! I believe that He truly exists, and that Christ is His son. Since Eddie joined the Mormon church, he and I have talked about it several times, and I know that he believes it too. I'm convinced that this strange set of natural occurrences along the California coastline has something directly to do with His will."

"You mean God intends to kill us?"

"No, Son, I don't mean that, at all. I think this storm is a *warning* of some kind."

"A warning?"

"Yes, that's what I'm feeling inside. And I don't know exactly how to describe the sensation, other than to say exactly that. All I do know is that there is an out-of-the-ordinary hurricane spinning disastrously out in the Pacific, windmilling its way toward Mom and the grandkids! And, judging by the reported strength of its center, I'm scared to death that it's going to *level* Los Angeles!"

"How's that supposed to be a warning, if, as you say, it's going to kill everyone in its path? I mean, what kind of a God would destroy His children and call it a warning?"

"I don't have the answers, Son. I'm just telling you what I feel."

"Well," Warren continued, "what do you think the warning is about, Dad? Do you have any feelings about that?"

Mr. Russell turned and gazed deeply into his son's eyes. Warren could see the intense seriousness in his aging father's face and wondered exactly what he was thinking.

"This may sound silly," the billionaire said, "but after

speaking with Eddie two weeks ago, my mind focuses on the upcoming turn of the century. The year 2000, or sometime shortly thereafter."

"The turn of the century? What on earth are you talking about, Dad?"

"According to Eddie, something incredibly wonderful—and yet for some, incredibly disastrous will someday happen. He doesn't know when, but I keep thinking about the upcoming turn of the century. More than that . . . the upcoming ushering in of a new millennium."

"Millennium?"

"That's correct. A new thousand-year period is about to begin. And from what Eddie related to me, apostolic writers of the New Testament, as recorded in the Holy Bible, made claims that . . . well, that Jesus Christ was to come back to earth a second time—presumably sometime after the second thousand years."

"You actually *believe* that, Dad?"

"I'm not altogether sure what I believe, Warren. I know that Eddie surely does. And I've just had this feeling since I first learned of the unusual nature of this massive hurricane. I can't explain anything beyond that, except for the fact that I'm worried for Mom and the kids, and I wish there was something we could do for them."

Warren sensed his father's continued concern and was grateful to be with him, even though in truth he wished desperately that they could help their family at the Rockingham Palace.

"I'm going out for a walk, Warren," Mr. Russell announced unexpectedly. "I need to be alone for a few minutes, down by the lake." The aging patriarch then stepped out into the night. There was a warm rush of mountain-fresh air that whirled into the den behind him, caressing Warren's face and providing for the eldest son a momentary exhilarating sense of well-being that could not be explained.

A few moments later, after his father had disappeared down across the meadows, Warren turned from the window and went back over to the television set. Quickly, he grabbed the remote control and began running through the channels of their satellite-dish TV link. Eventually he found what he believed to be the best twenty-four hour news source, a British cable station linked directly with the BBC. For several minutes, he watched various videotaped scenes of the damage that Bard was doing to his home city, and he noted that the camera crews themselves were struggling against the awesome winds and fury. It was just as he had imagined it! Maybe even worse! He was witnessing the greatest natural disaster that he had ever seen!

Suddenly, Warren thought more about the discussion he and his father had just concluded and the inner feelings his father had shared about Hurricane Bard somehow being the will of God in heaven. "Dear God," he whispered, tears welling up in his eyes, "Unlike Eddie, I've never really been a religious man. But Dad has always instructed me correctly, and I know *he* believes in you. And right now, God, we're all of us in a real jam! We need your help!

"As you probably know—"

At that instant, the television news was interrupted by an update that caught the humbled Warren Russell by complete surprise, jarring his attention back to the newscaster.

"We interrupt this broadcast with a special bulletin just in. An astounding phenomenon is occurring at this very moment over the skies of Los Angeles, California! For some unexplainable reason, Hurricane Bard's tremendously destructive winds have suddenly ceased blowing! The rains have stopped falling, and as our camera crews in west Los Angeles are this very minute recording, the massive cloud cover over the region is dissipating completely!"

Warren's eyes widened in disbelief as the scenes unfolded before him. Above the city, for all the world to see on television, was a scene that was nothing short of miraculous! The clouds were rolling back and disappearing with such unusual speed that it appeared to be a replay of an incoming storm front, rolling backwards at high speed.

The storms and fury of Bard had simply stopped! And if this was not enough, Warren watched, as if in a stupor, another spectacle even more magnificent than the receding cloud cover. There on the screen, still being taped by the camera crew in west Los Angeles, was a pair of exquisite rainbows that seemed suddenly to grow out of the Pacific Ocean, bend slowly up and over the tattered coastline, and settle into the very heart of the Los Angeles basin!

"What?" Warren cried out in disbelief. "How could—"

Suddenly, with a comforting dose of renewed hope surging inside him, Warren turned away from the TV, ran over to the French doors, and sprinted out into the starlit meadow beyond. He had to find his father! "Dad!" he called. "Where are you, Dad?"

Mr. Russell heard the distant voice and arose from his knees. He was standing on top of a grassy knoll that rose about twenty feet above the lake, providing a splendid view of the surrounding meadows, mountains, and forests. There was a tall spruce on top of the knoll, under which Mr. Russell had been kneeling in fervent prayer. Now, almost absently, he looked back toward the chalet and saw a dark, barely visible figure running toward him along the lakeshore. "Warren, over here," he called out. "Up here, Warren . . . up on the knoll!"

A moment later, as the pensive billionaire walked down the grassy embankment to greet his son, who arrived and blurted out the message he'd seen on the television set, an enormous wave of emotionally charged gratitude swept over his heart, and the two of them wept in each other's arms. "Quickly," Mr. Russell instructed. "Let's get back to the chalet."

Once inside, the two men sat on comfortable easy chairs, keeping their eyes glued to the broadcast, and watched in fascination while history was recorded live before their very eyes.

"A warning," Mr. Russell whispered almost inaudibly. "It really is a warning!"

Warren heard the quiet remark but said nothing.

Meanwhile, thousands of miles away in a small, weather-beaten dwelling next to their old lighthouse, the ageless couple, Simeon and Sarah, stood in front of their kitchen window and gazed seaward.

Their time-worn hands were intertwined, and their breathing came and went in perfect harmony. They had also witnessed and understood the miraculous and all-encompassing power that had been made manifest, moments earlier, by the great Creator. Though neither spoke, each said volumes as they searched the other's tearful eyes—sensing, together, a deep and abiding gratitude to be on the earth at such a moment in the Saturday evening of time.

CHAPTER 25

"I *still* can't believe it!" young Jeffrey Russell was saying to Jennifer. "It's like we've just witnessed the single greatest magic act ever conceived! What do you make of all this?"

Slowly, the woman turned to face Eddie's teenaged son. She looked him directly in the eyes for a moment, then refocused on the ocean beyond. "Are you a believer, Jeff?" she breathed quietly.

"Believer?"

"Yes, a believer. From what I've experienced, some members of the Church are, and some aren't. Do you believe in things you cannot always see . . . that there may be greater powers somewhere in the universe which influence our choice-making and our destinies?"

"Well, of course," he whispered back. "But I'm not sure I'm following you."

"Well, I *wasn't* a believer," she answered shamefully. "But that has all changed now. I'm ashamed, actually, that even as an active Latter-day Saint, I chose to live much of my life relying on the secular knowledge I believed was so important!"

"What are you talking about, Jennifer?"

"Humility, Jeff!" she exclaimed. "I'm talking about a second chance!"

Jennifer knew that her thoughts were skipping around and would undoubtedly confuse the boy. But she didn't care. Right now, she felt overwhelmed with gratitude for the way her eyes and heart had, at last, been allowed to *see*. And in her own way, she felt like her sole expression, for the moment, should be sincere, heart-felt gratitude.

"Clearly, Jeffrey," she continued, "you've seen, as the whole world has seen, an extraordinary elemental event that will never be explained by our scientists and meteorologists. It was a miracle that, until now, we've only seen in Hollywood movies."

"Yeah?" Jeff began, "I think—"

Just then Eddie walked out onto the veranda and interrupted the conversation. "I just spoke with Mother," he said worriedly, facing his girlfriend and son, who had simultaneously turned to greet him. "Megan's missing!"

"Megan?" Jennifer responded, trying desperately to remember which niece she was and who she belonged to.

"Larry's youngest daughter," Eddie clarified, sensing her confusion. "Mom said they've searched everywhere around the estate, and she is simply nowhere to be found!"

"Oh, no!" Jennifer gasped, putting a hand up to her mouth. "Do you think—"

"She's gotta be there somewhere, Dad!" Jeff interjected, visualizing the precious little ten-year-old in his mind and remembering how much he truly loved her. "Maybe—"

"Mother's worried sick," Eddie interrupted, "and I'm going over to lend her a hand."

"What about the roads?" Jennifer protested. "I would imagine that the mud slides in Malibu will be blocking traffic in that direction. You probably need to—"

"Mom's sending one of the choppers," he answered. "I'll fly over there with John, find out what's going on, and see if I can help them find my niece."

"You want me to come with you, Dad?" Jeff inquired earnestly.

"No, Jeff, I'd prefer that you stay right here and start the cleanup. We'll need to take down all of that plywood, as well as the other reinforcements we nailed up to block the storm. And looking around the yard and down the beach, it looks like we're gonna have our hands full helping the neighbors—"

"You go on, Eddie," Jennifer interrupted. "Help your family. We've got a lot to do around here. Jeff's going to need help, and besides, I've got to get in touch with my bishop and my counselors to make sure our ward members are okay." Eddie agreed reluctantly, recognizing more than ever before Jennifer's unusual capacity to serve and to sacrifice.

Within the hour, John Ferguson, one of the family's pilots, banked slightly to the north and began a smooth, gradual descent toward the beach. He could see Jeff and Jennifer standing out on the porch with their hands held up over their foreheads, blocking the sun from their eyes. Eddie was making his way down the small path that accessed the beachfront and was signalling the chopper pilot to set her down close to the water's edge.

John did just that, and within seconds Eddie climbed into the forward right seat, donned a flight helmet, and keyed his cabin-mike a couple of times.

"Hold on," John instructed. "We're outta here!"

"Let's do it," Eddie answered, giving a thumbs-up sign.

The luxury Bell Ranger lifted off nearly as quickly as it had set down, and together pilot Ferguson and his passenger, Eddie Russell, flew out over the sea, banked inland at four hundred feet, then initiated a gradual climb over the Santa Monica mountains.

Once airborne, Eddie was able to get his first serious look at the extreme devastation wrought by the forces of the hurricane. Everywhere there were signs of destruction, chaos and disorder. Many of the less-sturdy beach homes had been uprooted from their foundations and had been thrown about mercilessly, leaving huge piles of twisted steel, concrete, splintered wood, and other materials heaped up onto the highways and cliffs in every direction.

It was a somber and sobering ride for both of them. Twenty minutes later, as they circled Rockingham Palace, Eddie thought about his niece—his helplessly dependent niece, Megan.

Was it possible that she could somehow have been killed by the storm? Was she hiding somewhere inside the immense mansion, curled up in a fetal position, just waiting for her would-be rescuer? Was this to be part of the pain and sorrow that Simeon had predicted would come into his and his family's lives? Was Megan's name soon to be added to that lengthy list of persons killed or missing as a result of the ominous fury that was Hurricane Bard's?

Silently, Eddie prayed that it would not be so.

Delores Russell was nearly hysterical when Eddie arrived. It was clear that she had been crying, and for the first little while

Eddie concentrated on providing what comfort he could for her.

"We'll find Megan," he repeated, doing all in his power to reassure his mother of the girl's eventual and ultimate safety. "She's around here somewhere, no doubt curled up in an out-of-the-way hiding place, frightened to death by the storm."

"But she's not here, Eddie!" Delores sobbed. "We've been throughout the house . . . every nook and cranny! She's gone, I tell you! Vanished!"

Once more, as if consumed by personal guilt, feeling that Megan's absence was entirely her fault, Delores Russell laid her head on the consoling shoulder of her son and wept.

Throughout the early evening, and on into the night, everyone at the estate continued the search. While Eddie and his mother talked, they considered, then reconsidered, as many options as possible. They contacted the police and every other public agency they could think of, but all of them had been flooded by calls from storm victims. It became clear that there would be no outside help. If Megan was to be found, they would have to find her themselves!

Precisely at 9:20 P.M., Mrs. Russell collapsed in despair. At first Eddie thought she'd had a heart attack from the stress. An hour later, however, she resumed consciousness and was resting in her bed.

By ten forty-five P.M., the others of the Russell household were also exhausted. They had searched throughout the day and evening, but all to no avail. Even the neighbors had become involved in the search. But in time, all came to the same bitter conclusion—Megan had simply vanished. In any event, they would resume the search tomorrow morning.

The collective anxiety was overwhelming for everyone. All of the young granddaughters shared in the blame and lamented the loss of the little girl they'd so often rejected from their adventures. Hurricane Bard had visited the Russell mansion with a vengeance and had left an indelible mark on the family therein.

Late in the evening, long after Eddie had returned to his home in Malibu, and long after everyone else had fallen asleep from exhaustion, a very pensive Charlie stared into the darkness of his bedroom at the west end of the mansion. From the sound of her breathing, and the steady rise and fall of her chest,

Charlie knew that Virginia was asleep, obviously overcome like everyone else. His thoughts centered on the fragile and ever-so-innocent child, Megan Lynn. He had seen her that morning, although he hadn't mentioned it to anyone. And what troubled him the most was the sketchy memory he had of the event.

"What was it she had said?" he probed his mind, searching, seeking, groping for answers. "Somethin' she'd wanted me to do with her. Let's see . . . where was she when we talked?"

Slowly, Charlie put a dark hand to his brow, rubbed his temples, and stared at a small crack, barely visible, in the dimly-lit ceiling. "Concentrate!" he commanded himself. And carefully he flipped through the pages of his memory. At some time during the day—early, as he recalled—the little girl had come to him about something.

For several more agonizing moments, Charlie lay quietly, staring at the ceiling and focusing on the small crack in the corner. And when he was ready to give up altogether, roll over onto his side, and try to get some sleep, he finally remembered the seemingly insignificant conversation that had eluded him all day long!

"Horses!" he cried out abruptly, momentarily startling his companion, who let out a slight groan, then drifted back into the dreamy abyss from which she'd come. "That's what she said! Something about seeing the horses!"

Quietly, the old butler slipped out of bed and pulled on a pair of well-worn overalls. Then, careful not to disturb his wife a second time, he crept quietly into the enormous garage beneath their apartment and walked out into the night.

A short while later, having equipped himself with a powerful flashlight and a warm coat, Charlie headed for the Arabians' stables. It was a bit of a walk even in the light of day, but it seemed even further in the dark. And in the aftermath of the storm, with fallen tree branches and scattered debris still tangled in large heaps around the yard, the midnight investigation was actually somewhat perilous.

Nevertheless, with determination to follow his hunch and search the stables—even though they had been thoroughly searched earlier in the day—he plodded on through the darkness.

"Wait a minute!" he exclaimed suddenly, surprised by something he believed he had seen down by the gate. "What's that?" Quickly, the old man spun around on his toes and pointed the flashlight at the four-by-four concrete post sticking out of the ground.

"Somethin' there!" he whispered again, eyeballing a barely visible piece of colored something. A familiar colorful something, lying in the mud at the base of the post. Several months before, Megan had visited the Rockingham estate and had approached "Uncle Charlie" with a gift.

"I made this for you!" the little girl announced proudly.

Charlie knelt down beside the little girl, looked at the slender bands of colored, carefully-woven threads in her hand, and commented on their beauty.

"Why, child!" he said, "you made these all by yourself?"

"I sure did," Megan responded proudly.

"Well, what are they, honey?"

"Bracelets! Friendship bracelets," she said, handing a red, blue, and green one to the old butler. "And this one's for you!"

"Well, now," Charlie responded, "Isn't that the most beautiful thing you ever did see! Thank you, child. I surely do appreciate that special gift."

"You're welcome, Uncle Charlie," the little girl had said. "Now, let me help you tie it on. Hold out your hand."

Even now, as Charlie was approaching the west gate, he held out his wrist, shined the flashlight on it, and noted with a tear in his eye that the "friendship bracelet" was still there, right where she had tied it.

And when he knelt down beside the concrete post and retrieved the muddy remains of a similar woven band, he remembered with perfect clarity that the bracelet Megan had worn was red, yellow, and blue. Here in his hand was that same carefully crafted bracelet—Megan's bracelet!

Carefully the anxious black man scanned the immediate area, then unlatched the gate and walked cautiously outside the property and onto a narrow dirt access road. This was used primarily for bringing feed to the Russells' Arabians and other supplies to the massive stables. But as he studied the muddy tire tracks and deep footprints left behind by two individuals— a *big* somebody, and a *little* somebody—Charlie's heart skipped a beat!

Someone had kidnapped Megan!

CHAPTER 26

During the past twenty minutes, Chava's heart rate had doubled. And even though the outside temperatures were cool, he couldn't remember when he had perspired so profusely.

The idea of crossing the border just south of Tecate, California, had been perfect. Of course, it was always easier to cross the border into Mexico than to come the other way into the United States. He had guessed that U.S. customs officials wouldn't concern themselves with one lone Mexican leaving their country, and he was right. Why, not only did they not care, they didn't even peek into the backseat of his car!

Everything had gone well—too well, in fact. And all Chava could conclude from the experience was that God must have been with him. God must have truly wanted to assist him in this "unlawful" adventure, for the sake of little Sylvia Maria!

On the other side of the border, Chava veered south almost immediately, driving directly toward Ensenada. For the first time in days, he felt like he had an opportunity to clear his mind completely and to thoroughly consider everything that had transpired, and everything that would take place in the future.

Earlier, a good forty-five minutes before they had crossed the border, Chava had provided the frightened Russell child with a warm cup of cocoa to which he had secretly added two teaspoons of liquid Benadryl. The drug had produced the desired effect, and sure enough, Megan had fallen into a deep sleep.

Chava never intended to harm the little girl. Still he knew that she would unavoidably suffer some fear and anguish. Such trauma, of course, could not be avoided. And for that reason, his plan included a very well-thought-out anti-trauma campaign, which had apparently worked. Megan and Chava were already becoming friends.

Deep in his heart, Chava knew that there was no justification for the lawless act of kidnapping and extortion. Nevertheless, what was done was done, and if he and his convict friend were caught . . . well, he supposed they'd have to suffer the consequences. They may very well end up in Folsom prison together, but at least Sylvia Maria would have the lifesaving bone marrow transplant she needed.

"You will be okay, my little one," he whispered, looking tenderly at Megan. "No one will hurt you, I promise." He then turned around and drove off into the night. But before he did so, he set "The Russell Chart" onto the passenger seat and glanced at it one last time. The name at the bottom of the paper, Eddie Russell, strangely teased his mind. It was an unusual feeling, to be sure, and definitely an uneasy feeling.

Uncomfortably then, Chava drove on, and in the ensuing moments he focused his attention on the glimpses of desert terrain illuminated by his headlights. Somehow, he would forget the silly name written on the notebook paper. Yes, indeed . . . somehow he'd forget the name of Eddie Russell.

Besides, there were far more important matters to which he must attend. Among these, was his friend Romero. The fact that Romero had spent the past several years at Folsom made Chava more than a little uncomfortable. In addition, Romero had already gone too far, in the initial phase of the operation.

Why, he'd nearly frightened young Megan Russell to death! And yes, in his interpretation of the proposed stratagem, Romero had acted properly; but it had angered Chava when, during his intervention, he had found the little girl not just afraid of Romero, but downright terrified of him!

It had been Romero who had actually pulled off the kidnapping. And, like he had said, it had been a stroke of luck to have spotted the little girl, off by herself, behind the Rockingham stables.

During the storm, Romero and Chava had separated. The idea was that one or the other would pretend to be the bad guy, abduct the tiny child, instill an appropriate fear into her heart, and then ultimately whisk her away from the Russell compound. But shortly thereafter, following Chava's anti-trauma approach to the ongoing plan, Romero was scheduled to meet—and in fact *did* meet—Chava, in the corner of a large, abandoned parking lot, in Inglewood. It was there that Chava had assumed the unlikely role of "Prince Charming." When pretending to spot the tied-up and unnecessarily gagged Megan Lynn Russell in the backseat of the rental car, he had rushed over to the vehicle and had engaged in a make-believe fistfight with the abductor, Romero.

All of which had been nothing more than an act to spare the defenseless child from unnecessary emotional despair.

"What's happening?" he had demanded to know, acting out his role with all of the finesse of a well-seasoned actor. "What are you doing to this little child?"

Romero, of course, had played his particular role with equal skill, leaving Megan with the impression that, in fact, the two men were strangers to each other, and that this man, Chava, whoever he was, would rescue her and eventually return her to her family!

And, of course, in the end, Chava did rescue Megan—or so she was led to believe—and did actually "beat up" the bad man, Romero.

Chava thought back to the event and smiled to himself. He had never been much of a fighter, but it felt good to have knocked Romero out with a left uppercut and a hard right hook, even if it was an act. And all the while, a very wide-eyed Megan Russell looked on, inwardly applauding the apparent skills of her rescuer.

They had become good friends after that, making it easier—much easier, in fact—for Chava to persuade the young, impressionable child that he needed her assistance.

"What is your name, young lady?" he had asked her in perfect English as he was freeing her mouth and hands of the duct tape Romero had bound her with during the abduction.

"Megan Lynn Russell," she had answered timidly, still very frightened and struggling to hold back a fresh batch of tears. Her tiny hands touched her mouth, where the cruelly strong and sticky tape had rendered the skin sensitive.

"I know some Russells," Chava answered, acting out the preplanned charade.

"You do?"

"Oh, sure," he lied, smiling reassuringly. "They live somewhere up in the Brentwood Heights area. They're a very wealthy family, a big family."

"That's my grandfather's house!" Megan exclaimed enthusiastically and with growing confidence. "I was out helping the horses when the bad man came and took me away."

"You mean he kidnapped you?"

"Yessir," she answered politely, her little chin quivering from the fresh memory of the trauma. "Doc needed my help," she went on, "and that's when—"

"Doc?" Chava queried, "Who's Doc?"

"He's one of our horses."

"Just one of your horses, huh? Well, how many horses does your grandpa have?"

"Oh, he's got a whole bunch!" she responded with mounting enthusiasm. "They're a family! There's a mommy and a daddy, and lots of cousins and brothers and sisters."

"Really?"

"Yes, really. And when we get home, Uncle Charlie could help you ride one. He's Grandpa's helper, and he's very nice. Have you ridden horses before?"

"No, not really," he admitted. "But I'd love to learn how. And, well . . . so would my baby sister."

And that, of course, had been the lead-in Chava wanted. He began to tell the young girl the tragic story of his four-year-old sister, Sylvia Maria. He told Megan about the extreme poverty in which his family was forced to live, and all about the deadly disease, leukemia, that was depleting the life from Sylvia's tiny body.

He did not describe his criminal scheme. But he rapidly won the confidence of the tenderhearted Megan, and he used this rapport to persuade her to go along with him.

"Sylvia likes horses so much!" he said, steering the conversation where he knew it needed to go. "And you know something, Miss Megan? I think you could really help her prepare for the dangerous operation in the hospital if you would be willing to come to our house for a few days and tell her stories about your grandpa's horses."

"Well, I would," Megan said, "but my grandma doesn't even know where I am. I think I should go home first, and tell her."

Looking around at the destruction the storm had caused, Chava told Megan that it was virtually impossible for them to get back to the Rockingham estate for at least a day or two. He, however, would contact Mrs. Russell over the telephone and inform her that Megan was well and in caring, capable hands. He would also inform her that the girl would be returned in a couple of days when it was safe.

In the meantime, they would travel together to a place called La Paz, which Chava represented as being quite close to Megan's home. Here, she was informed, was where her new friend, Sylvia Maria, lay desperately awaiting word from her big brother. And in the end, although extremely hesitant and clearly unsure of herself, little Megan Lynn Russell trusted her Hispanic benefactor. She agreed to go with him—as long as he promised to tell her grandmother where she was going. "I promise," Chava lied, hating himself for saying the words. And so, without further words, the two travelers began their lengthy journey down the Baja.

Driving now at a steady speed, Chava experienced a sudden surge of guilt for all of the lies and mischievous acts of which he was now, unalterably, an integral part. He hated telling lies—let alone to an innocent child. Surely, God could not have condoned this terrible act. He was wrong to have assumed otherwise. Nevertheless, it was too late to turn back the hands of time. His hands were soiled, and scrub them as he might, or rationalize as he felt he must, he could never again come clean.

When at last Chava reached Ensenada, he was tired and overwhelmed with guilt. He pulled off the interstate at the Costero Boulevard exit, looking for an all-night gas station.

A few moments later, after reaching the downtown area, Chava turned south again onto a small avenue called Calle Tercera. An all-night service station appeared in the distance. There wasn't a great deal of activity anywhere at three-forty in the morning, but it was somewhat refreshing to be back in his own country, speaking his native Spanish.

"Excuse me, my friend," Chava said politely to the young attendant on duty. "Do you know where I might find a hot cup of coffee, and perhaps a small bite to eat?"

"Si, Señor," the boy answered, gesturing to the south. "There is a place on Calle Novena called Bahia de Todos Santos. They are always open."

"Thank you," Chava responded gratefully, looking off in that direction. "Please," he continued, "fill it up for me, and check the oil. I still have a long drive ahead of me."

"Si, Señor," the boy said agreeably.

After using the service station's rest room, Chava sat still in the front seat of his vehicle and recounted the remaining U.S. dollars from his pocket. Altogether, he counted 9,846 dollars— money he had received from his friend Romero. He'd better be careful not to spend much more. It was money that he needed to get Sylvia Maria's operation underway, and money that would need to be repaid to the Mexican mafia in San Fernando, California.

This frightening, unexpected arrangement had been conceived by Romero himself, who through powerful "contacts" inside the prison had made a connection in the San Fernando Valley. This "connection" had given the funds to Chava so that the doctors in Mexico could proceed with Sylvia's pre-surgical procedures, and Chava had promised to repay the entire ten thousand, with an additional ten thousand in interest, within two weeks.

In fact, so convinced was Romero that the Russell family would pay for having their granddaughter returned to them, he had not hesitated to agree to the loan's outrageous terms. And, of course, his promise became Chava's promise. He had taken the money, abandoned his rented Ford Escort, and borrowed an old Chevy from another of Romero's Chicano friends in the L.A. basin. He was grateful for the immediate hope that the funds would bring to Sylvia, but he remained worried that something—he didn't know what—might go wrong.

Slowly then, with mounting anxiety in his heart, Chava reached for the keys in the ignition, started the engine, and threw the old Chevy into gear. With so far to go, he sighed audibly, then sped south toward La Paz.

CHAPTER 27

In the days immediately following the climactic and abrupt ending of Hurricane Bard, the city of Los Angeles and its occupants fell into a paralyzing state of aftershock. The impact to the area was very similar to the hurricanes which had paralyzed southern Florida, Louisiana, and Kauai during the summer of 1992. The powerful shock, however, was not confined solely to the city's inhabitants. The entire world was stunned by the sight of Bard's awesome power.

When the billionaire patriarch of the Russell family arrived back in Los Angeles on Thursday afternoon, with his sons, Warren, Kenny, and Larry, chopper pilots John Ferguson and Tom Geddes welcomed them at LAX with the executive Bell Ranger. The Russells were helicoptered immediately back to the Rockingham estate. Along the way, they were increasingly silent as they flew over the terribly shaken city and its residents.

Larry, however, could not sit still. Nor was he able to voice an emotional concern for the thousands of terrified men, women and children left homeless and destitute from their suffering. In fact, he didn't care! Those people, however they might be hurting, were of no concern to him. His concerns were far more important, for Megan, his beautiful little Megan, was missing.

And although Larry did not outwardly voice his feelings, he had become obsessed with anger. If his mother, to whom he had entrusted the life of his youngest daughter, had been more responsible, Megan would not be missing. If his "no-account" brother, Eddie, had been more concerned for the family, instead of being off in the world of that silly lifeguard business, he would have been with Mother and the girls, and would have been able to protect little Megan. But no, Eddie had never shown signs of maturity. And because of it, Megan was gone.

Inwardly, Larry's anger mounted and a fierce rage crept into his heart. He had long since lost his ability to cope rationally with the matter. Instead, he turned more and more to the maddening solace of his seemingly endless supply of cocaine. And in the days that followed, his mourning for his lost daughter gave way to a cancerous spirit of revenge.

Eddie was responsible for Megan's absence—not Mother, but Eddie. And although he did not know *how* his pathetic younger brother would pay, Larry was determined to unleash a just and painful vengeance!

By Sunday morning, four days after the hurricane had passed, Allen Russell III was painfully convinced that his youngest granddaughter was, in fact, gone. And as oddly morbid as it may seem, he believed that Megan had very likely been killed by the winds and unearthly deluge. It was a terrifying thought, really—a helpless child being killed so easily.

For several hours, Mr. Russell had sat alone in his beloved "Window to Heaven" room. He had been wide awake since before dawn and had come to the observational retreat to watch the final stars of a predawn darkness give way to the first rays of light that eventually ushered in another Sabbath day. He was still feeling the pain of Megan's death, which he now fully accepted, but he had an additional concern.

Ever since they had arrived home from Switzerland, he had noted that his own wife, Delores, had grown progressively burdened by the guilt she felt over Megan's disappearance. The result, of course, had been devastating.

By Saturday night, Mr. Russell had become frightened and had consulted with their doctor for over an hour. Mrs. Russell was suffering from acute depression, and until she could mentally free herself from the caustic burden of guilt over the loss of her grandchild, she would remain bedridden.

A small electronic clock sitting next to one of the computer consoles told the heavyhearted Mr. Russell that it was fast approaching six o'clock in the morning. The mansion itself was breathlessly quiet. There were no granddaughters running about, no more confused sons with their wives, hopelessly searching in remote corners for a child they could not find. No more police officers asking questions. And no more insensate accusations from an irrational Larry, who had willfully blamed Delores and Eddie for the awful tragedy.

Thinking back on it, in fact, Mr. Russell concluded that here was another concern. What was wrong with his son, Larry? How could he have carried on so?

"This hurricane . . ." Mr. Russell whispered sadly, "has done its job well. Not only has it destroyed buildings and businesses, but it has also destroyed lives." People were dead, he considered silently, and families—many families like his own—had been pulled apart and were blaming each other for their grief. How would it all end? To whom could the people turn for relief and peace?

In his heart, Mr. Russell knew the answer. And today—in fact, at this very moment—he would fall onto his knees and voice his grievances heavenward. And so, slowly closing the door to his beloved observatory, he walked over to one of the chairs and knelt reverently in front of it. He then removed his glasses, rubbed his newly moistened eyes, and began a very simple but earnest prayer.

CHAPTER 28

While the very troubled old man knelt in the early morning solitude of his observatory, his youngest son, Edward Allen Russell, several miles away, had also initiated a heavenly plea. He, too, had risen early and at this moment was standing in the silence of his secluded beach home, looking seaward as the first heavenly lights broke through the morning darkness.

He was glad that it was Sunday. He desperately needed to attend church, partake of the sacrament, and gather strength from those he had come to appreciate as his brothers and sisters. But their three-hour block of meetings did not begin until noon. He would take advantage of that fact, climb back into bed, and do what he could to reclaim a few hours of desperately needed sleep.

Eddie somehow sensed that tired as he was, drifting off to sleep would not be as easy as simply closing his eyes. For like his father, he too had been troubled and downhearted, and had knelt earlier at the side of his bed, prayerfully petitioning the heavens for courage in the face of so many trials.

Megan was still unaccounted for, and almost everyone, except for Charlie, had already concluded that she was dead. Eddie's mother, Delores, had taken a serious turn for the worse, and that only added to his despair.

Drearily, then, Eddie climbed into his bed and ruffled his pillow to make himself comfortable. He desperately needed sleep. That's all—just sleep. And so, without further delay, an emotionally and physically exhausted Eddie Allen Russell pulled the covers up around him and answered to the demands of his body.

Before he slept, however, an image of sheer beauty appeared inside his mind. It was Megan. A content and happy Megan, with a lovely smile drawn across her lips.

"Where is she?" he whispered quietly, trying to memorize the features in her tiny face. "Where is she?"

CHAPTER 29

When at last Eddie awakened, he noted immediately that it was nearly 11:00 A.M. Slowly, resisting the urge to lay back down and sleep, he stood, walked over to the sliding glass door, mechanically threw back the curtains, and then began dressing himself.

It occurred to him that he had not heard from Jeff this morning, and he wondered if his son was still sleeping. Momentarily, he'd go quietly downstairs to Jeff's room and check things out. Just then there was an abrupt and aggressive pounding on the front door.

"Who is it?" Eddie shouted as he headed to the living room entrance.

"Open this door," came an angry, yet oddly familiar, response. "Open it before I break it down!"

"Huh?" Eddie mumbled, trying to match the voice to the individual he was sure that he knew. As he unlatched the dead bolt and reached for the doorknob, the heavy, solid-oak panel swung suddenly inward. Behind it stood a fiery-eyed Larry Russell, who, without words, stormed into the room.

"What in the world—" Eddie managed to say, but he was instantly cut off when, to his surprise, his brother drew back and delivered a powerful left hook to his right jaw. The force of the blow knocked Eddie off of his feet and sent him to the ground with an awkward flailing motion.

"You killed my daughter!" Larry blurted out mindlessly. "You killed her, just as sure as if you'd put a gun to her head and pulled the trigger!"

Having spoken these words, Larry lunged at his brother a

second time and revealed the shocking secret behind the unexpectedly powerful punch that had sent Eddie to the floor. His brother had hit him with a force that was surprising, considering the fact that he had always been something of a weakling. But when Eddie collected his wits and zeroed in on his fierce assailant, he noted, with sudden horror, that Larry meant business. For there on his right hand was a set of brass knuckles.

In Larry's eyes, Eddie could see a hatred that was unnatural. There was no way for him to reason with this madness. His only choice was to defend himself. Quickly, Eddie started his body into action. Because of his training at the Elysium, he instinctively knew what to do. He braced himself on the floor, assuming a push-up position for balance, then used his left leg for a skillfully executed 180-degree low-level windmill sweep that caught his unsuspecting brother just behind the right knee and dropped him instantly to the floor.

"Ahhhh!" Larry yelled, reeling in pain and falling awkwardly onto his back. "You no good—"

"You're totally out of line, Larry!" Eddie shouted, springing instantly to his feet and seizing the opportunity for a final and very persuasive offensive. "And brother or no brother, you don't come into my home with your idiotic antics, however angry you may be! Not in my home, Larry! And especially not with brass knuckles!"

And with that, Eddie lunged forward and threw a supremely well-executed rolling scissor-sweep with a forward snap kick that connected with perfect accuracy. The blow caught Larry just below the left temple and sent him backwards a second time. The move was meant to immobilize an assailant, rather than to seriously injure him, and it achieved its intended effect. Larry was knocked out cold and rendered completely harmless.

Moments later, when Larry regained consciousness, he bolted into a seated position and swung his arms wildly. "Where am I?" he demanded to know.

Eddie, still very angry at his brother's assault, was standing nearby with an ice pack. "Here, put this over your eye, Larry," he said, "or the swelling won't stop."

"Put it over my eye?" Larry countered angrily, grabbing the ice pack and throwing it against a nearby wall. "You put it over *your* eye, you jerk!" And with that, he stood up, steadied himself for a moment, and headed straight for the door. "This isn't over, Mr. Mormon Lifeguard!" he blurted defiantly. "You killed my little Megan, and no matter how long it takes, I'm going to see that you pay for it!"

"Pay for it?" Eddie interjected, trailing close behind. "How can you be so stupid, Larry? It's nobody's fault. I'm just as shook-up as you are about Megan's death. Still I—"

But Larry slammed the door on his brother's protests before Eddie was able to vocalize them. He crossed over the front yard to the driveway, climbed into his Mercedes, and started the engine. Then, before Eddie could respond, Larry screeched out of the driveway and disappeared down Pacific View.

The entire episode had been profoundly unsettling for Eddie, and for some time afterward, he didn't move from the front porch. He was grateful beyond words that Jeff hadn't witnessed the horrible scene.

In the hours that followed, Eddie and Jeff dressed for church, attended the services, and then returned home. The spiritual uplift had been a soothing balm, and each, in his own way, felt a greatly needed sense of renewal. Unfortunately, however, Larry's senseless assault still weighed heavy on Eddie's heart, and he thought that if he and Jeff could share a good meal, perhaps he'd be able to forget about the incident for a while.

"Jeff?" he called, poking his head over the railing. But there was no answer.

"Hey, Jeffrey," he shouted again, this time a little bit louder. "Hey, buddy, you down there? What d'ya say we cook up something to eat?" Quietly, Eddie waited for his son to respond. But when, after a short pause, that didn't happen, Eddie called out one last time.

"Jeff! Are you down there, Son?" Silence.

Feeling very uneasy, Eddie raced down the stairwell, through the family room, and into Jeff's room. The boy's bedroom was a mess. That in itself was extremely unusual. Here was the apparent aftermath of a private hurricane, and Jeff was nowhere to be seen. First Megan, and now Jeff! Feeling somewhat overwhelmed, Eddie collapsed onto his son's bed and tried to think.

As he let himself go, a quiet, unexpected thought came into

his mind. What had become of Simeon? Wouldn't he have the answers everyone sought? Perhaps he knew the whereabouts of little Megan. And maybe, just maybe he could assist the Russell family in this, their greatest hour of need. Why hadn't he thought of this sooner?

Eddie leaped to his feet, ran upstairs to the sliding glass doors overlooking the ocean, and scanned the beach. He had hoped to spot Jeff somewhere in the distance, perhaps wading pensively in the shallow surf. But he saw nothing more than a few of the neighbor children.

"Hmm," he thought out loud, "what to do?" If indeed something had happened to Jeff, Simeon would know. Besides, there was probably nothing wrong. Eddie felt strongly that his son was all right and that he should go see the old man. He grabbed a piece of scratch paper and scribbled a note to his son:

Jeff—

It troubles me that you would leave
without at least telling me. But I know that
you probably have a good reason, and I
forgive you.
Something important has come up that
requires my immediate attention. I'm not
sure when I'll be back, so make yourself
something to eat, and try to relax, okay?
I love you, Jeff. And don't you ever
forget that. We've been through a lot
together, and continue to grow because
of it. And that's what it's all about, bud!
So be tough, and enjoy the rest of the evening.
Meanwhile, I'll see you when I get home.

Love, Dad

Eddie folded the note into a neat little packet and placed it in an envelope. Then, with a bright red magic marker, he wrote Jeff's name on the outside. After sticking it on the front of the refrigerator so that Jeff would be sure to see it, Eddie went back into his room, slipped on a pair of tennis shoes, grabbed a light jacket and his wallet, and headed into the garage.

It was time to visit again with Simeon.

Just north of Point Dume beach, where the Coast Highway changed from a divided two-road interstate into a two-way road, Eddie was struck by the sight of the forces that Bard had unleashed.

Entire homes in the area had fallen into the sea. In addition, massive amounts of real estate had given way in the furious deluge. Crews were working around the clock to clear away the mudslides that continued to block the road.

The journey, to this point, was slow. A drive that would normally have taken no more than five minutes now took more than forty-five minutes. Nevertheless, Eddie felt an urgent need to see Simeon again. He didn't know whether the drive would take all night or just an hour, but Eddie resolved to press forward. He would go to Ventura and use Sheriff Haas's offshore patrol boat for the trip to the island.

It suddenly occurred to Eddie that he really didn't know how to find the island, or where he would moor his vessel when and if he did find it. In fact, all he did know was that Simeon's lighthouse was located on the northwest point of the island, where the San Miguel Passage divided the smaller island of San Miguel from the larger land mass, Santa Rosa.

A few miles past Zuma beach, still crawling at a snail's pace behind the cleanup crews, Eddie decided to contact the Malibu dispatch and have Beverly call on ahead to the Ventura sheriff's office. He had hoped, of course, to commandeer the sheriff's rescue vessel and save time by having it readied in advance.

The radio link went through quickly, and Beverly was both responsive and eager to assist her supervisor.

"Affirmative, sir," she said over the radio connection. "I have it all written down, just as you requested. Over."

"Read it back to me, will you, Bev? Over."

"Roger."

There was a moment's pause; then, as instructed, the skilled and dutiful Beverly Stratton keyed her station-mike and read back the proposed message to Eddie.

Repeating his location, she added, "Anything else, Sarge? Over."

"Negative. That ought to do it. Just hold down the fort for me, and keep those Indians at bay! Over."

"Hey, Sarge. Over."

"Go ahead, Bev. Over."

"What's the rescue boat for, just in case Haas wants to know? You following a lead on a Code Blue? Over."

"Negative, dispatch. Just tell Haas it's something I needed to check out. And call me back on this channel just as soon as you get through, okay? Over."

"Roger, sir." Beverly answered agreeably, but she was somewhat curious about her boss's intentions. "I'll get him on the horn right away. Over."

"Ten-four, dispatch."

By the time Eddie reached San Buenaventura beach, just south of Ventura, Beverly had gotten through to the sheriff's office and a young deputy named Lance LeCannon was down at the docks, ready with a forty-foot cabin cruiser called *Sheriff's Rescue One*.

"Hello, Sergeant Russell," LeCannon said to Eddie just after he had pulled up and stepped out of his Chevy. "What brings you all the way up to our neck of the woods?"

"Oh, nothing, really," Eddie lied, somewhat embarrassed that he could not be fully truthful. "Just wanna check a couple of things out, that's all.

"Say," he continued, "how far out are those islands?" As he spoke, he pointed seaward toward the Channel Islands, which could just barely be seen through a blanket of haze.

"Not that far, sir. Twenty-five to thirty miles to the first island—the eastern tip, anyway. Why, sir?"

"How about the Santa Rosa Island?" Eddie pressed.

"That's the second island, sir. It's closer to forty-five miles from here. Why do you ask? You planning on heading in that direction?"

"I was thinking about it, yeah. You think this cruiser will make it that far?"

"Oh, sure, Sergeant. It's not that far, at all."

With that, the young Lance LeCannon gave Eddie some brief instruction in operating the cruiser and assisted him in launching the vessel. "Good luck, sir!" he called out as Eddie piloted the craft at a wakeless speed through the small marina. "Keep your Marine Band open, if you need anything."

"Thanks, Lance!" Eddie called back. "I'll do that, and I'll see you in a few hours."

The late-afternoon ocean waters were unusually calm. And remembering well the turbulent adventure of the week before, when he, his son, and two very courageous female companions braved several hours of the most violent surges he had ever seen, Eddie was truly grateful. Within a short while, Santa Cruz, the first and largest island, began to loom up before him. It was a tremendously beautiful island, teeming with wildlife.

About twenty minutes later, after rounding the northwestern tip of the large island and crossing the Santa Cruz Channel, Eddie arrived at the northernmost peninsula of Santa Rosa. Slowing the rescue cruiser to one-quarter speed, he rounded this finger of land and stared in awe at the towering majesty of Santa Rosa's sheer cliffs and rocky beaches. The island was spectacular, just as he had remembered it. It was a setting of exquisite beauty, sculpted by the hands of the Creator. However, it troubled him that he still could not find any sign of human activity. He knew, though, that Simeon did in fact live on this particular island, and that if he would just be patient, he would eventually spot the lighthouse on the west end.

As Eddie navigated cautiously just outside the island breakers, moving westward, he began rehearsing all of the things he hoped to say to his light-keeper friend. There had been an unusual magic about the abrupt ending of Hurricane Bard, that Eddie felt certain was—in some way—linked to Simeon. And although he had instinctively known this to be so, he still wanted to discuss the matter with the old man. He remembered, too, that Simeon had spoken of great signs and natural wonders that were, according to the prophets of old, supposed to occur prior to the Master's Second Coming. He suspected that Bard was one of these wonders. The storm had held dark terrors, but what had effectively humbled the hearts of so many was the miracle of its passing. Simeon, Eddie was certain, would know about that. And Eddie felt sure that Simeon would be able to ease his mind about the other matters, Megan, in particular.

Slowly, then, Eddie trolled into the next inlet and noted with relief that at the far end of the small bay there was a weather-worn landing. And although it was an old dock, to be sure, and in need of repair, it would clearly suffice for his purposes. Skillfully, then, Eddie throttled down even more and slid the craft alongside the rickety wooden structure.

He killed the engine, secured the expensive cruiser to the dock, and went ashore. All was silent except for the sound of a gentle surf lapping at the rocks and an ever-present squawking of birds overhead.

Immediately to Eddie's right, winding upward and over the top of a towering ridge, was a narrow path that looked like it hadn't been used in years. It seemed eerily reminiscent of the one Eddie remembered seeing in a dream, and he felt an uneasy sense of déjà vu.

"I know this place," he thought, remembering the dreams in which the area about him was enshrouded by a heavy fog. He could almost swear that he'd seen it before.

Without hesitation, Eddie began climbing the trail before him. For, if indeed this was the spot, Simeon's lighthouse would be somewhere near the summit. Eddie soon spotted the lighthouse and cottage, and before long he arrived at the main gate. He walked up to the front door and knocked. But as he was soon to discover, Simeon was nowhere to be found. Nor was the beautiful lighthouse matron.

"Simeon!" he called out, hoping that the old man or his companion would be somewhere close by. But still there was no answer, and for a moment, Eddie felt a bit dispirited. Nevertheless, he decided to wait for a while, for he was determined to meet with the old man again, if not to find the answers he was seeking, then at least to bask in his wonderful presence for a few more hours.

Eddie turned away from the door and walked slowly back through the small yard. He went through the little picket fence and off toward a nearby cliff overlooking the San Miguel Passage. He found a second path that wound down the side of the cliff and led to a rocky beach far below. At the entrance of the little trail, someone, probably Simeon, had constructed a comfortable bench. Eddie dusted off a small area and sat down.

The view was absolutely remarkable!

Looking westward across the narrow channel, Eddie could
see three breathtaking sights. The first was the sea, itself, blue
and sparkling in the twilight. The second was the not-so-distant
smaller island, San Miguel. And finally, as it was fast approaching early evening, the setting sun had transformed the distant
horizon with an indescribably beautiful mixture of glowing
reds, yellows, and oranges. It was a sunset like none other.

"Wow," Eddie said quietly, "and I thought I had a terrific
view from my own living room window."

"You do," came a deep, calm voice from behind.

"Wha—" Eddie said, standing up and spinning to face the
unexpected visitor. And as he did so, he saw, to his great relief,
the kind face of the old man he had come to see.

"Simeon! You *are* home. Why, I was quite sure I'd have to
wait the whole night before you returned. I'm so glad to see
you again."

"And you, likewise, my friend," Simeon answered kindly.
"I've been expecting you."

"Expecting me?"

"Well, of course, lad. There are so many discoveries yet to
be made . . . preparations that will require your attention. But
please, Edward, I see that you have already discovered my favorite place of solitude. May I join you?"

"Oh . . . ah . . . sure." Eddie stammered awkwardly, politely
standing to one side so that the elderly gentleman could sit on
the bench beside him. "Please, sir. I'd be honored to sit with
you."

"Thank you, my son," Simeon responded, silently taking
his seat at the crest of the scenic vista. Eddie followed, and for a
moment the two of them sat in complete but comfortable silence, breathing in the warm evening air and collecting their
thoughts. Eddie sensed another warm feeling within and marveled at the serenity that continually prevailed whenever this
magnificent man was near. There was a spirit around Simeon
that could not be seen, but which was most assuredly felt.

"So, most noble Edward, what brings you to our little island
paradise? Are you still troubled, lad?"

But before Eddie could respond, Simeon answered his own
question with an accurate observation. "The trials and burdens
we spoke of during your last visit are upon you now, are they

not? And they are grievous burdens to bear. I sense the magnitude of your pain.

"Do not fear, young Edward," Simeon continued. "They are momentary obstacles, only. And if you are willing to persevere—to remember your greatness, as well as your calling—they will be overcome and will in the end be counted as a marvelous blessing."

Eddie looked with confusion at the white-haired seer. It was difficult, at the moment, for him to think of his recent grief as a blessing. And for just a second it concerned him that Simeon would speak so lightly of such tragic events.

"How can death be a blessing, Simeon?" he responded anxiously. "This storm—you knew it was coming, didn't you?"

"I did."

"Then why didn't you tell me about it?"

"Edward, my friend, search your memory. We did speak of it, and many other things, as well. Have you not understood, even with your eyes open?"

"But it killed people, Simeon! Hundreds, in fact thousands of people perished in that storm, not to mention the unprecedented damage it caused. How can you speak of it so lightly?"

"I do not speak of the matter lightly, my son, not at all. Nor was it a force wrought by mine own hand.

"You must understand, Edward, that the time draws nigh. He is coming. He is coming! It is not a matter for you and I to debate, for it is nothing less than an accurate fulfillment of all that was foretold by the ancients. We cannot alter what is destined to be. Edward, if it were in our hands, we would undoubtedly save everyone. But that is simply not the Master's way."

Eddie stared, almost numb, feeling the power of Simeon's words. Simeon was now looking directly into Eddie's eyes, and without hesitation, he continued. "I do not know, Edward, nor, according to the living prophet, is there any man alive who knows when He will come. But I feel certain that it is soon. And if you will recall, we spoke of that Coming, and of the integral part that you personally would play. Do you remember, Son?"

"Well, I suppose so. But—"

"Remember what I have said," Simeon interrupted gently, "that before He comes, great signs and wonders will appear in places around the earth, as well as in the heavens. The hurricane was only one of many such wonders that will unfold. It served a purpose for the Master, in its own way. Yet it was but a warning. That is why I called upon the heavenly powers to quell the storm before its true fury could be unleashed."

"So it *was* you, then!" Eddie exclaimed suddenly, breaking into the conversation. "I knew that it had something to do with you, Simeon. I just knew it. But why didn't you stop it sooner?"

"I, my friend, stopped nothing. I merely called upon the Creator. It was His mercy that was bestowed upon the inhabitants of the city, not mine."

"Yet so many died," Eddie interjected, not understanding.

"Tragically they did, Edward. But you must know that it was for purposes known to the Master. He takes whom He will, my young friend. And although we cannot always understand, we can know this: his judgments, whatever they may be, are just and undeniably righteous."

Eddie considered that final statement for a moment, then thought about his dearly beloved niece, Megan. How could a just God take from the world an innocent and harmless child like Megan? And as this thought filtered through Eddie's mind, he noticed a sudden warming sensation again. Simeon was smiling.

"Be at peace, my son. Close your eyes, and see . . ."

As Eddie complied, a sensation of well-being and complete serenity filled his soul, and images of graphic clarity began to appear in his mind. The scene was a stretch of desert highway, a place not at all familiar to Eddie. There was a single car on the road, with its blinker on. It was apparently exiting the quiet interstate. Fascinated, Eddie watched on and saw a young Hispanic lad climb out of an old 1957 Chevy and walk toward him in the dark. Strange, Eddie thought, how fascinatingly real it all seemed.

Suddenly, his mind adjusted to the scene and his lower jaw dropped in one quick and fluid motion. For there, beneath the blanket, was his beloved niece, Megan.

"Oh, dear Lord . . ." was all he could say.

PART FOUR

How Great the Price

The power of prayer,
    of hope and of faith,
Shines bright in the hearts of the pure.

For those who believe,
    and then choose to endure,
The ending is sweet, to be sure.

CHAPTER 30

"Excuse me, sir. I do hope I'm not disturbing you, but there is a matter of urgency that I would very much appreciate discussing with you."

Allen Russell turned toward the door of the extraordinarily elegant study in which he had been sitting. He noted that his friend Charlie, the family butler, was standing patiently awaiting a response. In Charlie's hand was a small leather satchel.

"Come in, Charlie," Allen said, using his right hand in a friendly waving gesture. "I was just about to have a glass of orange juice. Care to join me?"

"No, thank you, sir," Charlie replied politely. "But if it's not a bother, sir, I would like to have a word with you."

"No bother at all. Please, come on in and have a seat."

"Thank you, sir."

And as Charlie made his way across the room, Mr. Russell, always alert and forever concerned about his relationship with others, noticed an unusual amount of perspiration on his friend's forehead.

"What is it, Charlie?" he said with growing concern.

"It's your granddaughter, sir . . . Miss Megan. . . ."

"Megan?" the old patriarch asked anxiously. "Have you discovered her body?"

"No, sir," Charlie responded timidly. "Not her body, sir. Something quite different altogether."

"What, Charlie?"

"I do not believe that she is dead at all, sir."

"What are you saying, my friend? I'm afraid that I—"

"May I, sir?" Charlie interrupted, reaching for his leather

satchel. "There are a few things that I'd like to show you. As you know, sir, your granddaughter and I have always shared an affectionate relationship."

"Yes, I've heard her, as well as others, refer to you as 'Uncle Charlie' on more than one occasion."

"Yessir, she does that."

"Well?"

"Well, sir, on the morning of the storm, Miss Megan came to me, saying that she was concerned that the main doors at the west end of the stables might have been left open, and she wanted me to go with her and secure them."

"Did you?" Mr. Russell questioned.

"Yes. But not with Miss Megan, sir."

"Oh?"

"Of course not, sir. Not in those winds! Would have blown her right off her feet!"

"Okay, so you think she went out to check on the horses? What's that have to do with this satchel? What's in there that you wanted to show me, Charlie?"

Charlie handed his employer and friend some photographs.

"What are these, my friend?" Mr. Russell queried.

"They are the tire tracks, sir."

"Tire tracks?"

"Yessir. I took the photos myself, then sent them to your friend Mr. Armbruster."

"Joe?"

"Yessir."

"All right then," Mr. Russell continued, his heart racing, "go on, tell me about these tracks . . . about Megan . . ."

"Well, sir, the night you all came back from Europe, while we were searching for Miss Megan, I remembered her talking about the horses. And later that night, while you were all sleeping, I went out to the stables with a flashlight. There's a small crawl space where the water lines run that might have been a good place for Megan to hole up a while. On a hunch we might have overlooked that area, I went out to search it myself."

"At night?"

"Yessir."

"Well, I don't understand, Charlie. Why didn't you tell me about this 'hunch' earlier?"

"I wanted to be sure of myself before raising everybody's hopes."

"Go on, please."

"Just outside the west entrance, where they bring supplies, I saw something that caught my eye."

"What?"

"Miss Megan calls them her friendship bracelets, sir."

"Friendship bracelets?"

"Yessir," Charlie answered, holding up the small, carefully crafted band. "Like this one here, sir."

Charlie handed him the bracelet and went on with his story. "I knew it was Miss Megan's, just as soon as I saw it, sir, because she showed it to me and told me earlier that her favorite colors were red, yellow, and blue—called them the 'primary' colors, and was real proud to know that."

"Go on."

"Well, sir, when I walked on down to the fence, I saw footprints."

"Footprints?"

"That's correct, sir," Charlie continued, reaching over to assist his employer in sifting through the stack of photographs. "This one here is a photograph of those footprints. There's two sets, small ones and adult-size ones, right here—"

"Are you implying that you think Megan was kidnapped?" Mr. Russell blurted out suddenly, staring deeply into his friend's eyes.

"Well, sir, when I saw what I suspected was Miss Megan's putting up a struggle—by the way the footprints seemed to be dancing down by the west gate—I remembered something important. While I was driving your sons to the airport last week, so they could meet you in Europe, I saw this Mexican boy following us real close. First time I saw him, sir, was just outside the front gate here on Rockingham—"

"A Mexican boy!"

"Yessir. He was driving one of those small economy cars. I have the description written down here in my little notebook, Mr. Russell, sir."

Charlie retrieved the small tablet of paper he carried constantly inside a vest pocket and handed it to Mr. Russell.

"It was a light brown-colored Ford Escort, sir," he went on. "And that's the license plate number."

"California plate?" Mr. Russell queried pensively.

"Yessir. And the number's just below that, sir."

"And you think this Mexican boy, whoever he was, might have come here and kidnapped the child?"

"Quite certain of it, sir. And I'm also certain of the young fellow's nationality. He is Mexican. I saw him real good, sir. Got a close-up. Eighteen, maybe nineteen years old, kinda chubby, dark hair, and Latino skin, sir."

For the next little while, Charlie described in vivid detail all that he had seen that morning at the small grocery market when Larry had insisted on stopping for a package of gum. He didn't, however, trouble his good-natured employer with information about his wayward son's cocaine addiction. He had decided, long ago, that such information was something the Russell family would have to discover, and deal with, on their own.

"So," Mr. Russell interjected finally, "what's the link? What does any of this information have to do with your suspicions that Megan was kidnapped from the estate?"

"That's where Mr. Armbruster comes in, sir. I took the liberty of contacting him and his boy, Hank, with the hopes they might be able to use their ties with the police department.

"It was a difficult process, they told me, because of the confusion that still exists since the hurricane, but they did trace the license plate, sir."

"And?"

"Well, sir, the Ford was a rental car. Seems it was rented to. . . ."

Charlie flipped through his notes.

". . . To a Hispanic named Carlos Antonio, a reporter, or so he claimed, with a Latino newspaper called *La Opinion*. However, Mr. Armbruster was never able to verify anything with the paper, since they haven't yet recovered from the storm."

"So where does that leave us, Charlie?"

"Actually, sir, we don't think this 'Mr. Antonio' was a real person, anyway—"

"And how would you know that?" Mr. Russell asked, growing more interested by the minute.

"Because, sir, the car was only rented for one day, and it was missing for over two weeks."

"I see. Go on, please."

"Just this morning, sir, a friend of Mr. Armbruster's called him and said they found the Ford somewhere downtown. It was abandoned, sir."

"Go on, Charlie!"

"Mr. Armbruster says they got a perfect match, sir."

"What are you talking about, Charlie? What kind of match?"

"The tires, sir. The photos I took out along the west gate match perfectly with the tires on the rental car."

"You mean—" Mr. Russell began.

"I mean just that, sir. Whoever was driving the rental car was the same man who kidnapped Miss Megan!"

"Dear Lord!" Mr. Russell exclaimed, his voice choked with emotion. "Did they check the car for prints, Charlie?"

"Well, that's just it, Mr. Russell, sir . . . there wasn't much left of the car. . . ."

"What do you mean?"

"The car was on fire in downtown L.A., burning like a hot furnace!"

"Oh, no!" Mr. Russell cried out suddenly, thinking that his granddaughter might have been in the car when it was torched. But Charlie was quick to ease his employer's suspicions.

"You needn't worry about Miss Megan being in the car, sir. There wasn't anyone inside. Mr. Armbruster says that the police found the car abandoned, sir."

"But I'm confused, Charlie," Mr. Russell went on, "Why was it burning? Was it purposely set aflame?"

"I'm suspecting that it was, sir. So does Mr. Armbruster."

"But why?"

"Well, sir, whoever kidnapped Miss Megan, we think, had a reason. We're not sure yet what that reason might have been, or just why they haven't made contact with your family. But I suspect they set the car on fire so as not to leave evidence—no prints, sir!"

"And Joe thinks this Hispanic kidnapped Megan for some sort of ransom?"

"Yessir, I suspect he did at that, sir."

"Well, it's already been several days, Charlie, since Megan disappeared. How can you be certain that the kidnappers are after money?"

"I'm not sure, sir. But Mr. Armbruster and I have been trying to piece together the puzzle, and our thinking is that this must be the only logical explanation."

"Then why haven't they made their demands, Charlie?"

"I don't rightly know, sir. Just don't know."

For the next fifteen minutes, a very anxious Allen Russell pored over the information and photographs collected by his faithful butler, Charlie. And he concluded, as Charlie had done, that Megan had indeed been abducted. It was the only logical deduction to make.

Moreover, after placing a telephone call to his lifelong friend, retired detective Joe Armbruster, and then hearing a detailed recapitulation of the story, Mr. Russell sat back on the sofa in his library and spoke.

"I don't care what they want, Charlie! If Megan's alive, we'll give 'em whatever it takes to get her back! But if they harm her . . ." His voice trailed off to a quiet, melancholic whisper. "If they hurt her, they'll pay. Now," he continued, "don't mention any of this to a soul, Charlie. Not a soul!"

"Yessir. No one, sir."

"Good! Now, listen to me—"

But just then their conversation was cut short by a quiet knock at the library door. It was Charlie's wife, Virginia. "Excuse me, Mr. Russell, sir. But there's a little neighbor girl at the front door. Says she's got a message for you—something real important, sir!"

"Thank you, Virginia. I'll be right down."

At the front door, a young freckle-faced girl named Sally Patton stood patiently with her hand clenched tightly around a small soiled envelope. "Mr. Allen Russell" was written on the outside, and nothing more.

"Honey, what can I do for you?"

"I brought you a letter."

"A letter?" Mr. Russell queried, curious at the sight of the small wrinkled envelope the girl was thrusting at him. "Who is it from, darling?"

"The boy on the bicycle," she replied shyly.

"Boy on a bicycle? What bicycle? What boy?"

"Don't know," she replied matter-of-factly. "Just a boy. He gave me a dollar to give it to you."

Mr. Russell opened the envelope carefully, fearing suddenly that there was something terribly wrong with this unusual situation. "Just a moment, my dear," he said, wanting the little Patton girl to stay where she was as he scanned the contents of the envelope. And as he read the words, his heart sank.

He turned to Charlie, who was standing just behind him in the entry hall.

"Look at this!" he exclaimed, his voice beginning to tremble. "But don't touch it anywhere, except on the corner here."

As Charlie examined the handwritten message, Mr. Russell turned his attention back to the little girl in front of him.

"Tell me, sweetheart," he said, "when did the boy on the bicycle give you this note and the dollar?"

"Oh," she answered shyly, scratching her head with the hand that contained the crumpled-up bill, "a few minutes ago."

"Where were you when he gave it to you, honey?" Mr. Russell pressed cautiously.

"Across the street, in front of my house."

"And do you remember what the boy looks like?"

"No."

"And which way did he go after he gave you the note and money? Do you remember, sweetheart?"

"No, sir."

"Well, I'll tell you what, Miss Sally. How would you like five dollars, instead of just one?"

"I would!" she answered excitedly, no longer appearing bashful.

"Okay, here," Mr. Russell withdrew a five-dollar bill from his billfold, then said, "You let me have that one-dollar bill, and I'll give you this five. Okay?"

"Okay," she smiled, handing the crumpled bill to Mr. Russell.

Then, Mr. Russell, turning to Charlie, said, "Charlie here will see you home, Sally. Why don't you go with him now, and tell your parents what happened, okay?"

"All right, come on, Charlie," she said cheerfully, still quite overwhelmed by the five-dollar bill in her possession.

When Mr. Russell was finally alone, he turned, walked back into his study, and absently closed the door behind him. Tears slowly filled his eyes, and for a brief moment he stood with his back to the door and tried to steady his emotions. He felt as if someone had knocked the wind out of him.

Gaining control, he unfolded the note he had received from the Patton girl and placed it next to the dollar bill on the table before him. Then, with shaking hands, he read the note a second time. The words were callous and hateful, and rekindled the fear inside his heart.

> Your granddaughter is alive and well. Whether she stays that way will be your choice. If you contact the police, she will die! If you don't do precisely what we tell you to do, she will die! If we suspect a doublecross, she will die! We will contact you when we are ready. For now, this is all you need to know—
>
> El Tigre Negro

"El Tigre Negro," he whispered. *What kind of a psychopath am I dealing with?*

"What will become of all this?" he sighed miserably. Quietly, he drew in a deep breath of air, turned around, and headed for the door.

"Call, Mr. Tiger," he said defiantly. "Call me!"

CHAPTER 31

Darkness had already fallen by the time Eddie left Santa Rosa Island. And although the skies were clear enough for the stars to shed their light, the darkness out across the water was thick and unnerving. Eddie boarded *Sheriff's Rescue One*, pulled away from the decrepit dock, and set a course for the mainland.

At first, he found the going quite easy. He was able to maintain a visual of Santa Rosa's northern shoreline by navigating the vessel a short distance from the cliffs, then by continuing along an east-by-northeast heading. It remained, nevertheless, a formidable task to see much of anything, and Eddie found himself forever squinting his eyes against the darkness, hoping to avoid a collision with one of the shallow reefs in the area.

The conversation he'd had with Simeon, as the two of them sat together and watched the sun set over the San Miguel Passage, had affected Eddie profoundly. He was grateful, to be sure, to have learned that his niece, Megan, was alive. But at the same time, he was worried about her immediate and future well-being. And there was something else, as well.

Although clearly gifted with extraordinary powers from on high, Simeon had not been able to give Eddie the young child's location. Thus, for a while, Eddie had experienced an emotional frustration that bordered on anger. "Why can't you tell me, Simeon?" he had queried. "You, of all people, must know the location."

"I cannot, Master Edward. It is not mine, but your destiny to learn where the child awaits."

"Awaits!" Eddie had persisted, "What does that mean? Are you saying that you know, but cannot say, or that you don't know and are leaving it up to me to find out?"

Yet with all of his questioning, in the end all Eddie knew was that he should rely on his own instincts and follow the whisperings that would come from within. He did feel, however, that his powers of discernment were becoming sharper. In a unique sense, it seemed that Simeon himself was assisting him. There were great and incomprehensible forces at work, and Eddie seemed to understand that hands unseen were directing his every move.

As he neared the extreme eastern end of Santa Rosa and sailed out into the Santa Cruz Channel, a chilling impression came into Eddie's mind. It was an emotional sensation which took him by complete surprise, and which left him shivering.

Instinctively, he eased back on the throttle and brought the two powerful Chrysler inboards to an idling position. Then, without warning, the engines stopped, and nothing Eddie tried was able to bring them back to life. The vessel simply bobbed up and down in the calm ocean, adding to the silence of the moment.

"No," Eddie cried out in disbelief, "Not now. You can't die on me now!"

But plead as he might, the dual inboards lay dead in the water. Something—an electrical short, a fuel leak, a sudden clogging of the air intakes—something had killed them. And that wasn't the worst of it. For if even one of the independently-operating engines had remained functional, Eddie could eventually have piloted the craft back to the marina at Buenaventura. Yet now there was nothing.

And strangely enough, the navigational lights had failed. Whatever it was, he reasoned, the problem must be electrical. To his horror, he discovered that the boat's police radio was also dead. For a brief moment he just stood there at the helm, doing nothing. He was both worried and frightened, and moreover, he wasn't quite sure how to proceed.

"What am I gonna do?" he cried miserably, trying desperately to formulate some kind of a plan. And as these thoughts rolled through his mind, he felt something cold and eerily moist on his left hand.

"Wha—," he began, jerking his arm away. But at that same instant, more of the coldness moved in. Across his feet and lower legs, then up and over his back and shoulders, and finally onto, and all around, his face.

"What is it?" he cried out a second time, swiping at the chilling dampness with his hands, at the same time stepping awkwardly backwards and away from the craft's edge. But as he did so, he simultaneously knew the answer.

The sudden frigidness was nothing less than the first far-reaching tendrils of a dense fog bank that was moving slowly toward the mainland. A fog bank that had come from somewhere out at sea and that had presumably already engulfed the Channel Islands, leaving a backwards retreat impossible.

Within minutes, the forty-foot *Sheriff's Rescue One*, with its dead engines and sole passenger, was completely enshrouded in the dark grey mist. The fog was unnaturally dense and remarkably cold. In fact, as far as he could remember from his lifetime of living along the California coastline, Eddie had never witnessed so thick or so cold a fog cover.

Then there was silence.

Confusion, dizziness, and utter darkness followed, and before another thought could enter his mind, he slid helplessly and unavoidably into a state of complete unconsciousness. At last, he reasoned oddly, he could rest. . . .

"Arise, my son. Awaken from your weariness, and shake free from your despair."

Slowly, Eddie Allen Russell opened his eyes and stared directly upward. He wasn't sure what he had just heard, but he was certain that it was something, or someone, familiar.

"Do not be afraid, young Edward. That which would do you harm has passed. Arise now, and be about your appointed tasks. There are those who await your arrival and the gifts you shall bestow upon them. However, if you do not act speedily, many will fall and perish! Arise, and witness the strength He has given you. For the hour is come. Your hour. Your appointment."

Once again, Eddie opened his eyes and peered out into the dim light that seemed to be growing steadily brighter through the living room window.

Living room window? What living room window?

He blinked his eyes once, then a second time, and immediately scanned the area around him. Sure enough, there, directly in front of him, was his window. His living room window overlooking the Pacific Ocean and an early morning sunrise!

He tried to speak but could not. His mouth was dry and his lips parched. He felt confused. Hadn't he just heard someone speaking? Yes! As a matter of fact, it had been Simeon's voice. Something about—

"Let's see," he whispered, clearing his throat in the process. "Something about the appointed hour. . . ." He sat upright, yawned and stretched. Then, wiping away the sleep from his eyes, he probed the room a second time.

"Simeon?" he called. But there was no answer. He stood carefully and spoke again, this time with more energy. "Simeon? Are you there?" But the man Simeon was not there. Eddie was very clearly alone.

"Must have been a dream," he reasoned, remembering in vivid detail the horror of the night. But then everything was so clear, so realistic, that he doubted himself for a moment and wondered how any dream could linger with such clarity inside his mind.

Looking up now at a digital clock on the wall, Eddie noted that it was just a little past six o'clock in the morning. He walked into the kitchen, leaned for a moment against the counter, and tried to recall everything he was certain had occurred in the past twenty-four hours.

He did remember his brother Larry's intrusion—probably, he reasoned, because he could still feel the pain in his jaw from where he had been hit. He also remembered thinking that he needed to go and confer with Simeon. That's when he had written a note to Jeff and had left it on the front of the refrigerator.

Had he really gone to visit the old seer? How strange, this feeling of awkward uncertainty. Yet, if he had, then how had he gotten back home? As he searched his mind for answers, Eddie knew with greater certainty that he did not remember piloting Sheriff Haas's rescue cruiser back to the marina, or getting into his Chevy for the drive back home.

"Wait a minute!" he cried out suddenly. "The Chevy!"

Quickly, then, Eddie left the kitchen and hurried out to the garage.

The Chevy was *gone.*

CHAPTER 32

The huge fly that buzzed annoyingly around Megan's head in the early morning sunlight was finally just too much! Repeatedly, the ten-year-old had swatted the pesky nuisance away but to no avail. "Get off me!" she cried out. And of course the fly did get off. Its hundreds of tiny eyes had seen the monstrous hand, and it had taken flight immediately.

Slowly, the young heiress to the Russell fortune turned her head first to the right, then to the left. She was still inside an automobile—the one that belonged to her Mexican friend—what was his name?

For a moment, Megan remained completely still. She turned her gaze back toward the car window and noted that the ugly-looking fly was still there, perched on the glass and trying to free itself from its prison. At least the disgusting fly wasn't attempting again to land on her forehead.

But where exactly was she? In order to learn the answer to that question, she would have to sit up and look outside. Yet Megan hesitated. She wanted desperately to see something familiar outside the car. Perhaps a school yard or a street she would be able to recognize, anything that would assure her that her new friend was taking her back to her grandmother's house.

Of course, in recalling the discussion she'd had with . . . with . . . what was his name? She just couldn't remember. But anyway, in recalling the discussion they'd had yesterday, she did remember something about his poor little sick sister. The girl's name was . . . was. . . .

Sylvia! That was it! Sylvia Maria! There had been talk of

Sylvia's awful condition. Poor little girl. Sylvia was dying, and Megan had agreed to go with her new friend . . . what was his name! . . . to help the little girl in her most desperate hour. . . .

And so, she knew that when she sat up and looked out the window, she would not see any familiar school yard or street sign that would let her know that she was close to home. She wouldn't see anything familiar, because she wasn't close to home at all. She was a long, long way away from home . . . she just knew it!

But that was okay, because she had agreed to go with . . . with Sylvia's brother, and be there for Sylvia. By the way, where was Sylvia's brother? Was he asleep in the front seat of the car? With so many questions needing to be answered, Megan decided, at last, to lift herself up from her prone position of security and look around. And as she did so, she heard a faint noise—a breathing noise—

"What's-His-Name" was indeed in the car with her. He was, in fact, asleep in the front seat, just as she had suspected. "Chava!" came a sudden voice of recollection in her mind. "That's what he'd said his name was, Chava!" And sure enough, her eyes confirmed that he was there and was asleep.

For a moment, Megan could only stare at the man who had saved her life. And with a curious mixture of gratitude, fear, and fascination, she watched as his chubby chest and stomach rose and fell in a quiet and peaceful rhythm of slumber. She wondered what he was dreaming about and hoped that he was not too troubled by fear for his helpless sister back home.

Back home? That was an interesting thought. Where was Chava's home? Were they almost there? Once again, a very curious, yet less-fearful Megan Lynn Russell turned her attention to one of the car windows and looked outside.

What she saw was indeed familiar. Stretched out before her, as far as she could see, was a crystalline blue and green ocean, the same ocean that she'd come to know and enjoy so much at her home in Los Angeles. The Pacific Ocean.

On the other side of the car, peering outside from an opposite window, Megan noted that they were surrounded by a vast desert. And in that direction, there was nothing whatsoever familiar to the little girl. This worried her. Once again, in an effort to recall anything from the previous night's talk that might provide her with a clue as to their ultimate destination, Megan taxed her mind for all she was worth.

"Where are we?" she whispered quietly, looking out into the vast expanse of the open desert before her. This was not a familiar sight at all. It was a beautiful spot, but a very remote one. The road on which they had come to rest was a dirt road. Megan thought that they had come away from the main highway—if highway was the right word—in search of a place to rest.

As these fresh thoughts came into Megan's mind, she suddenly felt an unexpected urge to run away. "But what for?" she countered innocently. Had she something to fear from this "Chava" person in the front seat? And if so, why had he rescued her in the first place?

The kidnapping yesterday afternoon had been a traumatic event for Megan. It was a frightening nightmare. The bad man who had taken her away from the Rockingham Palace stables had been an ugly person. He had had a scar running down his right cheek from the eye to the chin. He was hideous, actually. Just like a monster! And for a while back there, Megan had been quite sure that the bad man was going to do something really awful to her—maybe even kill her.

The lingering thought was upsetting, to say the least. And right now, what she really wanted, more than anything else, was to be home with her sister, Heidi, and her mother and father, and to be tucked safely away inside their home in Santa Monica.

What were her family members thinking, anyway? Did Mr. Chava call her grandmother like he'd promised to do? For some reason, Megan thought not. Once again, the urge to run away from Mr. Chava surged suddenly into Megan's heart and mind. It was now, while he was sleeping, or never!

But, where would she go? She didn't even know where she was, and there was not one building in sight of the car. But wait a minute. What was that?

Something directly to the rear of the automobile caught Megan's eye—something she had not seen before. An old wooden post with a sign nailed to it! Maybe it was a sign that would help her determine where she was. Quietly, she reached for the door handle, held her breath so she could listen carefully for any sign of Chava's waking up from his sleep, then popped the door open.

"Shhsssh," she said to herself as she stepped first one, then a second foot out the door. "Don't wake him up." And within seconds, Megan Lynn Russell was out of the car and shutting the rear door behind her.

Chava did not awaken. He had driven all through the night—until the first rays of morning light had appeared out of the eastern skies—and then had pulled off the main highway to catch a quick catnap.

That had been almost two hours ago. His emotionally and physically exhausted body had succumbed to the need for sleep and had catapulted him headlong into a dreamy void. He would not have awakened even if Megan had slammed the door. His need for sleep had blocked out all external sounds.

Again she felt the compelling urge to run away. But she was now terrified and immobile. Chava was waking up, she just knew it. Megan gathered courage, then took two steps forward and looked inside. Chava was sleeping peacefully. He hadn't awakened, after all.

"Whewww," she sighed, then turned quickly and sprinted down the dirt path. About one hundred yards back along the dirt roadway, Megan came to the wooden sign. It was situated up on top of a grassy knoll that overlooked the ocean from a distance, facing inward towards the mainland.

The sign was well-made, but old and weathered. And although the words were carved into the wooden board and painted white against a dark brown background, Megan could not understand the message—"Decorado Escena."

"Deh-cor-rah-do Es-sec-na?" she questioned aloud, pronouncing each syllable carefully in a futile attempt to understand. "I wonder what that means?" Looking back down the dirt road from atop the grassy knoll, Megan could see that the old Chevy from which she had just emerged was still parked and immobile. Chava was still asleep.

Maybe this was as good a time as any to get away. "Get away?" she again considered, "from what?" Maybe there wasn't a "Sylvia Maria" after all! And that was the disturbing thought that prompted young Megan Lynn Russell to make up her mind at last. She would run. And eventually, if she prayed hard enough, she would find her way back home.

Looking in the opposite direction from the parked Chevy, Megan could see that the dirt road snaked eastward up and over a small hill, just a few hundred yards off in the distance. Where it went beyond that point, she had no idea. But, since that appeared to be the direction from which they had come, she set off on foot with a firm resolve to find someone, anyone who could and would help her get back to her house in Santa Monica or to her grandparents in Brentwood Heights.

CHAPTER 33

The interior of the room was dark. But for Romero Valdez, that didn't matter in the least. He was actually content to be sitting in the obscurity, because it suited his sordid thinking. For the moment, Romero's thoughts were far away—shadows of memories which he would have preferred to bury forever in some ancient tomb where they belonged. The Folsom tomb. He supposed that what mattered most was that he was away from the hideous facility, and that he was now free to roam the streets and to do whatever he chose.

From his position at the window on the second floor of the abandoned warehouse, overlooking a dead-end alley in Venice, California, Romero saw poverty in the faces of four homeless drunks who were sprawled out behind a green dumpster. He, too, understood poverty, and he had vowed that he would never again live such a life. Romero was determined to get money, even if it meant kidnapping and extortion.

Kidnapping. That was an ugly thought, really. And in truth, although Romero was a thief by his own volition and had not hesitated in days past to use a weapon when committing a robbery, he didn't like the idea of kidnapping. He was a thief, nothing more. He was not a molester, or an abuser of children, in any sense of the word. And so he hoped that Megan Lynn was already over the trauma he'd caused.

By now, Romero reasoned, Señor Russell should have received the note. He should already have begun trying to determine just who "El Tigre Negro" was. Romero didn't really expect the wealthy industrialist to keep the abduction or the ransom demands to himself. In the end, he reasoned, only a select handful of skilled criminal investigators would be privy to events as they unfolded.

For this reason, Romero understood that his plans for obtaining the ransom money must be flawless. Above all, he knew that there would be one chance, and one chance only, for success. Besides, if he expected an entrapment of any kind, he would have to abort the mission immediately.

Life inside a United States prison was not worth any amount of money—not ten million, or even twenty million! Especially if he would have to carry the "jacket" of a convicted child abuser. But although he was afraid, Romero was captivated by the lure of "easy money" and the possibility of wealth beyond his and Chava's wildest expectations. He had made up his mind to go through with this deed, and with that decision had assumed the risk of getting caught. If he failed, then he failed. He was prepared to suffer the consequences.

But, if he succeeded—and the chances were very high that he might—he would have the world at his fingertips!

CHAPTER 34

Eddie tried desperately to recall all of the events that had transpired the night before. His goal was to ascertain where he might have abandoned Sheriff Haas's rescue vessel. As his mind groped for answers, he couldn't help but marvel at the circumstances of the night. For, in spite of the mystery surrounding a period of sudden forgetfulness, what stood out in his mind was the sure remembrance that he had seen his niece Megan, alive, in his mind's eye.

Megan was alive! And what's more, she was apparently in the company of some stranger whose malevolent purpose was unknown to Eddie or anyone else. With Simeon's unusual powers to assist him, Eddie grew more confident that a rescue attempt would eventually prove successful. He would intervene.

In fact, in some strange way, Eddie knew in his heart that he must intervene. For truly, all that had been foretold by the old light-keeper and his wife was coming to pass. And Eddie's part in the big picture was becoming clearer with every passing hour. He felt very good inside.

Still, he worried about the unaccounted-for time of the previous night. He would need to call his office and dispatch one or more of his deputies to Ventura, where efforts would be made to locate the expensive *Sheriff's Rescue One* cruiser, which assuredly must still be floating, with its engines dead, somewhere out in the water between the mainland and the Channel Islands. Also, there was the question of his own truck.

Most important, though, was the near-overwhelming desire to get in touch with his brother Larry and inform him of the good news concerning his daughter Megan. He had already forgiven Larry for yesterday's needless aggression. In fact, in a very strange way, he felt a love for his brother that he had never before experienced. In fact, not only had he forgiven his brother's violent assault, but now it went far beyond forgiveness. Eddie discovered that he loved Larry with a love that was deep and rich, and that he cared compassionately for Larry's future well-being and happiness. Actually, not only for Larry, but . . . for everyone.

"How strange," he considered out loud. For it was as though a sudden power had developed within his heart that would not tolerate even so much as a single shadow of darkness. He found himself overwhelmingly in love with his sweetheart, Jennifer. He felt affectionately endeared to his son, Jeff, and was inexplicably drawn to his parents and all other family members.

"What feelings are these?" he asked himself in a quiet whisper, considering the warm sensations. But even as he spoke, he knew in his heart that they were not just feelings, but were actually gifts given to him—a greater capacity, as it were—by a power more encompassing than he could begin to comprehend. They were gifts originating beyond the earth. And he knew also that these gifts had been bestowed upon him through the efforts of his dear friend and patriarchal benefactor, Simeon.

Eddie Russell looked around the comfortable confines of his living room, glanced once more outside at the beautiful morning surf, then decided to head downstairs to Jeff's room. His intent was to awaken the lad so that the two of them could prepare for the busy day ahead. But as he started down the stairs, a noise coming in through the garage caught his attention. It was a vehicle.

Curiously, Eddie glanced up at the small clock above the refrigerator, for he was quite certain that it was still very early in the morning, and he couldn't help but wonder who would be coming to visit at this hour. 6:43 A.M. Still early. Whoever it was, Eddie reasoned, had to be someone close to himself or to Jeff—a friend perhaps. The motor sounded like the engine in a truck—his truck.

That was it. Sheriff Haas had undoubtedly dispatched a search and rescue crew, found the floundering rescue vessel out in the water, and recovered it. And what's more, he or one of his good deputies was returning the Chevy S-10. In any event, Eddie knew well the distinct sound of his own vehicle and was now quite certain that the truck that had just pulled into his garage was indeed the very same truck he'd left up at the Buenaventura beachfront, near the Ventura marina last night.

He rushed toward the kitchen-garage door to greet his guest and began formulating some sort of an explanation about the abandoned rescue boat. For he knew that if indeed this was the sheriff, he would want an explanation almost immediately.

The door suddenly swung open. To Eddie's complete surprise, his son, Jeff, walked into the kitchen holding what appeared to be a paper sack filled with groceries.

"Oh," the lad said cheerily, "hello, Dad! I figured you'd be up and around by now. Honestly, I don't know how you could actually fall asleep in a seated position, anyway. Did you sleep like that all night long?"

Eddie was too stunned to say anything. He just stood there with his mouth hanging wide open and watched in sheer amazement as his son set the paper sack on the kitchen counter. Jeff put the groceries into the refrigerator without noticing anything unusual about his father's silence.

"So," he continued, "what time did you get home, Pop? I got your note. Thanks—" When Eddie still did not respond, but remained momentarily paralyzed with a puzzled look on his face, Jeff interpreted the silence the wrong way.

"Oh," he said, "I'm sorry, Dad! I didn't think you'd mind. We were out of milk and eggs, and when I came upstairs and saw you sleeping like that, with your clothes still on, well, I just figured you were too tired to be bothered. I hope you're not upset that I borrowed your truck—"

"Truck?" Eddie responded at last, although still completely confused. "The truck was here, in the garage?"

"Of course it was in the garage. Where else would it have been?"

Without another word, Eddie went straight for the kitchen door and stepped into the garage. The truck, his truck, was parked in its normal parking spot just as Jeff had left it. And even now, Eddie could hear the internal noises as the Chevy's engine cooled down from its morning jaunt to the Malibu grocery store.

As Eddie walked over to the bed of the vehicle, expecting to find some kind of clue that might help to jog his memory of events immediately following his excursion to the Channel Islands, it dawned on him once more that there were greater powers at work here. It didn't matter how he'd gotten the Chevy back home, or how he'd managed to get back to the marina in Ventura. For in his heart, the serenity and feelings of compassion, charity, and peace indicated the truth behind the experience. He knew that from this moment on, his life would be altered in a significant way.

There was a task to be done. . . . That was what Simeon had told him. . . .

He considered the significance of the idea for a brief moment, pictured last night's experience with Simeon, recalled the image of sweet young Megan as she lay motionless in the back seat of the Chevy he'd "seen," then tilted his head heavenward one last time.

"So be it!" he exclaimed courageously, "If I must be about this appointed task . . . then so be it!"

And with that, Eddie turned briskly on his heels and started back toward the kitchen. Jeff was standing in the doorway. His curious expression now seemed amusing to Eddie, whose own countenance was aglow with his newly acquired conviction and understanding of purpose.

"Are you all right, Pops?" Jeff pressed anxiously.

"I couldn't be better, my dear son! Not in a million years!" Then, grabbing his son by the shoulders, he smiled warmly and said, "Let's have waffles."

At the Rockingham Estate, Eddie's mother, Delores, had taken a serious turn for the worse. The guilt she had imposed upon herself had affected her both mentally and physically. In her mind, Delores just knew that her granddaughter's disappearance was due to her own neglect. Megan, she was certain, had gone unwittingly out into the storm, had been swept up off her feet, and had undoubtedly been hurled mercilessly toward a painful death. And if she had just been a little more responsible as the girl's grandmother, then surely Megan would be alive today. The despair in Delores' mind lingered on.

Meanwhile, in the other room, Mr. Russell was also thinking

about Megan. By now, as the mysterious Tigre Negro had suspected, Mr. Russell had surrounded himself with five high-powered professional friends. From the L.A. Police Department, Earl Streeter and Tommy Kutz. From the FBI, Robert Talley. And Mr. Russell's closest friend, Joe Armbruster, and his son, Hank.

Other than Charlie and himself, Mr. Russell knew that no one in the family had any knowledge about his granddaughter's plight, or the existence of this so-called Tigre Negro. He intended to keep it that way. Family members had too many emotions pulling at them, and he could not inflict further turmoil by bringing them into the "circle."

For a moment, as the six men sat around the library study table, there was complete silence. Each was anxious and focused on his individual concerns. Special FBI agent Robert Talley broke the silence.

"Ten million dollars in unmarked fifties and hundreds?" he asked. "Is he really serious, Allen? I mean, does this Mr. Negro have any idea how much currency that is, or how much it would weigh?"

"I'm beginning to suspect that there is something more to this fellow's plan, Bob," Allen countered. "But in trying to read between the lines and second-guess his overall plan, I'm still as dumbfounded as ever. Negro wants five separate suitcases. Each one is to be arranged in perfect order, with a precise two million in each. He says that he will contact me again and tell me the exact location of each delivery."

Detective Streeter protested suddenly, "You mean this guy wants you to deliver the money to more than one location?"

"That's what I'm saying, Earl!" Mr. Russell reaffirmed. "I couldn't quite figure it, either. Nevertheless, my friend, that's what the note says."

"Here, let me see it," Streeter's partner, Detective Tommy Kutz, interjected, leaning forward in his chair. Kutz, as if attempting to somehow picture the kidnapper, began to read:

> Your granddaughter is well. Whether she stays
> that way is completely up to you. An exchange
> will be arranged for a ransom amount of ten
> million dollars: One-hundred-dollar bills and

fifty-dollar bills—all unmarked currency. Place
the money inside five individual suitcases—
two million in each. Have the suitcases packed
and ready by 5:00 P.M. Friday, and await further
instructions for their delivery at various drop
sites. Don't fool with us, and Megan will live.
Double-cross us in any way, and she will die!

El Tigre Negro

"That seems straightforward enough," Agent Talley said.
"But, why the different drop sites?"

"My point exactly, Bob," Allen affirmed. "It would seem to
me that this 'Tigre Negro' is some sort of leader of a larger orga-
nization. Undoubtedly, there's a band of these renegades working together for some common cause. At least that's the way I
see it."

"So," Agent Talley went on, "you think these guys will really have five different drop sites? I mean, what could possibly
be the purpose of that?" All of the men seated at the table exchanged puzzled glances with one another, shaking their heads
curiously. All, that is, except for Joe Armbruster, who up until
now had been very quiet.

"He doesn't want ten million," Joe said suddenly and quietly.

"What's that you say, Joe?" Allen asked.

"He doesn't want the money, Allen," Joe insisted. "Plain
and simple."

"Doesn't want the money? What are you talking about, old
friend? Who doesn't want the money?"

The retired police detective reached over to where Detective
Kutz was seated and retrieved the ransom letter. Without
speaking, he slid it gently sideways to a position directly in
front of himself and his son. Hank Armbruster was silent. He
had learned well from his father and knew he should listen intently for helpful investigative clues whenever on a case. And
in his own intuitive way, Hank already knew what his skilled
father was getting at.

"The biggest downfall of most criminals," Joe went on, "is
their incessant greed!" All eyes were focused on the silver-
haired private investigator. Mr. Joe Armbruster was revered by

all present, and everyone knew that his hunches were almost always accurate.

"Mr. Black Tiger, as he calls himself, is not some gang leader with a noble cause. And I don't think he's in cahoots with anyone else, other than a single partner, maybe two at the most."

"Go on, Joe," Allen interjected. "What's your theory then?"

"Well," the old man continued, clearing his throat, "if I'm right, Allen, he's not after ten million dollars at all. In fact, I don't even think this guy is after half that much. I think that Mr. Black Tiger is content to escape with a cool two mil, period. And I also think that he has no intention whatsoever of returning your granddaughter to you. If my theory is correct, the five separate drops are intended to confuse us and nothing more.

"Oh, sure," he continued, smiling, "I expect he'd like to have the full ten million. But he understands the folly of greed and has resolved in his mind that two million will set him up like a king, just as ten million would. So he carefully selects five different drop sites, runs us as thin as possible—as he knows with absolute certainty that we will be watching every spot— and preplans a pickup at only one of the five locations. Then, while we are waiting for him to make a move on the other four suitcases, he somehow snatches the one he's after, gets his bundle, and slips away into the night."

"But, what about the one pickup?" Allen queried. "Won't he know that we'll be watching that one, as well?"

"Certainly," Joe agreed. "But this is where things'll get a little more sophisticated."

"What do you mean, Joe?" Allen pressed with mounting curiosity. "Sophisticated in what way?"

"Undoubtedly," Joe continued, "the pickup will not happen immediately. In fact, he will likely insist that you drop the suitcases off at the various locations in some sort of preordered fashion. Let's just suppose that Mr. Tiger instructs you to deliver suitcase number one at say, the telephone booth on Twenty-sixth Street and Wilshire, at five-thirty P.M. this Friday. Then the next one at Sixteenth and Pico, in an old dumpster or something like that, at say, six P.M. the same day. You with me?"

"Yeah," the others chorused.

"Okay, during the night, while you're busy running here and there according to his demands, Mr. Tiger, or perhaps a partner, will be positioned in such a way that he'll be able to see and perhaps even photograph the different suitcases where they stand. He'll get an idea of the size, shape and color of the cases, pick up a duplicate somewhere, and eventually make a switch right under our noses."

"A switch?" Allen questioned. "What do you mean exactly, Joe?"

"Think about it, Allen," Armbruster insisted, glancing at the other men. "One of the drop sites will be a carefully selected site, you can bet on it. In fact, I'm certain that our Mr. Tiger will have carefully prepared one of the five sites in such a way that under the cover of darkness, or through some other means, he'll be able to get his hands on the suitcase full of money without our being able to see him.

"Now I don't know how exactly, but if I guess correctly, he'll pull this off with exceptional skill and speed. Moreover, it will be done in such a way that even if we are looking on, we may not see the switch."

"I think I agree with you, Joe," Agent Talley interposed. "It feels right."

"Hmmmmm," Allen mumbled quietly. Then making a gesture with his hands, he asked, "What about my granddaughter? You say that this fellow's intentions are to keep her? Maybe even harm her?"

"Mr. Tiger is a pro, Allen. More than that, actually. His moves, to this point, have been almost flawlessly orchestrated. Since his principal aim is to extract a king's ransom through this criminal act of kidnapping, and then ultimately flee to some distant paradise for asylum, he will not leave behind one eyewitness—regardless of her youth—who can identify him or his partners.

For the aging billionaire, the very thought of physical harm coming to his beloved Megan was almost more than he could bear. Tears appeared suddenly in his eyes, and he was unable to conceal his emotions. "Excuse me, gentlemen," he said, at last breaking the silence. "I'd better check in on Delores."

As he stood and excused himself from the room, Mr. Allen's equally troubled associates stood as well. They were intelligent men—the best in their fields of expertise. But they were also sensitive men, and together they comprised a group of Allen

Russell's closest friends. They knew of Mrs. Russell's suffering and of the emotional trauma that had the poor woman bedridden. And so they were genuinely supportive of their friend when he excused himself from the meeting.

"Hey, Allen?" Detective Streeter called out quietly, just as the elderly host was about to exit the library. "Perhaps we could all use a bit of a break." He pointed to his watch.

"It's close to noon already, and I for one haven't had any breakfast or lunch. Besides, until we get further word from this Tiger fellow, there doesn't seem to be a whole lot more we can accomplish together . . ." Already the small contingent of skilled criminologists were gathering their belongings, and were heading for the door immediately behind their host.

"I'll take this newest demand letter down to the lab, Allen," Agent Talley suggested, depositing the recently acquired ransom note into a large plastic bag. "Are you sure, though, that you don't want some of my boys to wire your phones? Stay here with you? Maybe see if this guy'll contact you over the wire?"

"He won't," a very-sure-of-himself Joe Armbruster interrupted. "I'm telling you, Bob, the only communications we're going to receive from this Mr. Tiger are going to come like this one and the first one, through some completely uninvolved and youthful courier selected at random."

"Yeah, Joe," the concerned FBI agent agreed, "you're right, of course. Our boy isn't that dumb." And then turning his attention back to Mr. Russell, Agent Talley asked, "What about that youngster, Allen—that neighbor boy who brought this note to you? Any kind of a description from him?"

"Nothing, Bob. Not a thing! The kid's just eight years old, just like the little Patton girl across the street who received the first note."

"Hmmmm," Talley groaned. "Dead ends in every direction."

"And, Bob, it's gonna stay that way until the end." Armbruster predicted. "El Tigre Negro will leave nothing to chance—nothing!"

Then, in the silence that followed Joe's discouraging analysis, a very serious Hank Armbruster spoke up for the first time. Taking in a deep breath, he stated resolutely, "We'll get him. He'll make a mistake somewhere along the line, and we'll get him."

"We will," Talley agreed. "We will, and soon."

Allen Russell stood quietly alone just inside the foyer and watched through a narrow window the departure of his friends as they drove down the lengthy drive of the Rockingham Estate and disappeared out into the street beyond. He was grateful for the collective skills of the five men, and even more so for their genuine concern and willingness to assist him in this ordeal.

Silently, a very pensive Allen Russell turned slowly from his view at the window, made his way over to the stairway, and began his ascent. But just at that moment, a horrifyingly loud scream sounded from somewhere near the master bedroom. The blood inside his aging body turned ice-cold.

The voice was not his wife's, he was certain of it. But, it was a familiar voice . . . a female voice . . . Virginia's voice! "Dear Lord!" he cried out, "what on earth?" Quickly, he raced upstairs toward the master bedroom. There, standing next to his wife's bed, with both hands cupped over her mouth, was Charlie's wife, Virginia.

"What is it, Virginia?" he called out frantically. "What's wrong?" But as the words left his lips, Allen knew the answer in his heart. Delores! His beloved wife, and most precious friend in the world, had taken a serious turn for the worse.

"Call Doctor Rennison, Virginia," Allen instructed, "and then call an ambulance. Quickly, please!" Virginia snapped immediately to her employer's command and headed toward the kitchen, where she kept the emergency telephone directory.

"And get Charlie!" Allen added as the woman raced down the stairs.

Delores' body was still and lifeless. And although he did everything in his power to revive her, the pale blue and purplish color of her face and lips seemed to suggest that the worst had happened.

"No!" he cried, kneeling over the bed and cradling the beautiful form in his arms. "You can't die, Delores! You just *can't!* Help! Somebody help me, please!" No one but Virginia heard his plea.

Over the next several minutes—a time period that seemed more like hours—Allen applied CPR and mouth-to-mouth resuscitation to his beleaguered wife. She did not, however, respond.

"Oh, Delores," he cried again and again, "why? Why do

you choose to leave me now, when I need you the most? Oh, Delores, come back, my darling!"

Just then, a voice from somewhere directly behind the grieving patriarch spoke softly, "She is not gone."

"What?" Allen countered despondently, spinning around to greet the benefactor. It was his youngest son, Eddie, who had just entered the bedroom suite.

"Oh, Eddie, hurry!" he carried on frantically, "It's your mother! She's—"

But Eddie did not hurry. Instead, he walked calmly over to his father's side, placed a hand on his aging, aching shoulder, and continued. "Be at peace, Dad. There are hands unseen at work here. Mother is not dead; she merely sleeps with a broken heart. But now that too will change. For although we have all supposed that Megan was taken from us by the storm, it was not so."

Allen Russell was somewhat stunned by his son's prophetic demeanor and obvious confidence. But what captured his emotions even more was the action that followed. For, without another word, young Edward Russell left his father's side, walked over to his dear mortal mother, placed his hands on her forehead, and reverently bowed his head in prayer. What followed was both astonishing and marvelous. Words were spoken, a plea was made, and a response was granted.

"In the Savior's name," Eddie concluded, "come back to us, Mother. Arise, and breathe the breath of life. Megan is not dead but lives."

And with that prayerful pronouncement, Mrs. Delores Russell, companion to the noble Allen Russell, did in fact take a deep breath and open her eyes! Color returned rapidly to her face and lips, her body and limbs. As the images of two handsome men—her husband and her son—came into focus, a smile came as well.

"Hello, boys," she said weakly. "I just had the most pleasant dream I can ever remember! It was about Megan Lynn."

PART FIVE

The Redemption

Those who listen,
   those who see,
Will surely journey home.

'Tis not the souls
   of evil men
The Savior calls His own.

CHAPTER 35

No more than twenty minutes had passed before Megan Russell recognized the awful magnitude of her plight. The immense vastness of the surrounding desert, with its unfriendly terrain, quickly took away the child's hope. Fear swelled within her, and a longing for home augmented that fear. Where was she? Was she even inside the state of California? And if she was, in which direction should she turn in order to find her way back home?

Cautiously, the little girl turned around and glanced backwards in the direction from which she had come, looking off into the distant horizon where she expected to both see and hear Chava's oncoming Chevy. But still she heard nothing. Only the sound of a chirping cricket at the side of the road.

If, in fact, her Mexican benefactor had awakened and realized that she had vanished, he would undoubtedly come looking for her. She would be able to see the approaching cloud of dust, as Chava would most likely come racing up the dirt road in a panic.

For some reason, it no longer seemed to matter that he'd saved her from the kidnapper the day before. In fact, though she didn't quite understand why, she had begun to fear Chava almost as much as she had the estranged kidnapper. The thoughts were unsettling.

Slowly, Chava rubbed his eyes to clear away the sleep, sat up, and scanned the front windshield of the old Chevy, where he was certain he would find the giant horsefly. It had disturbed his sleep repeatedly over the past little while, and he was tired of fighting it.

"Get out!" he shouted, rolling down the window and shooing the pesky creature away. As he did so, he whispered quietly to what he continued to believe was his young passenger sleeping in the back seat.

"Miss Megan," he said gently, "time to get up, little lady." But the bundled-up sleeping bag and blanket did not move.

"Hmmmm," he said curiously, "must've given her a little too much Benadryl." But as he spoke the words, a sudden siege of anxious apprehension gripped his heart. Chava realized that Megan was gone. Gathering only emptiness as he lifted the blanket, Chava whirled back around in the front seat and slammed a fist against the steering wheel. Instantly, he exited the vehicle.

"Megan!" he called out first toward the vast ocean to the west, then a second and third time in other directions. There was, of course, no response. For, even as he'd suspected, Megan Lynn Russell was gone!

The midmorning sun was rising all too rapidly for Megan's personal liking. As she stopped to catch her breath, she couldn't help but wonder just how hot it would get. After all, her uncle Eddie had cautioned her often about the dangers of too much sun. And now, not only was it getting terribly hot, but there was no shade to provide her sanctuary.

Her grandfather had taught her, a long time ago, that whenever she was faced with a particularly difficult decision in life, a certain "living light" inside her heart would tell her what to do. "You'll know," he had told her, "if you are always doing your best to be honest with others. This light will guide and protect you."

"How will I know, Grandpa?" Megan had queried.

"It comes by way of a special feeling inside your heart, little lady, like when you're helping your mother without her knowing. You just feel this 'living light' inside you, telling your mind and your heart that what you are doing is good."

Now, thinking back on that conversation, Megan wondered if she had indeed made the right choice in leaving Chava, his car, and his water. Suddenly, she was more confused than ever. Should she have trusted her Latino benefactor, or was she right to race out into the desert and hide?

"When you're not sure," Grandfather had instructed, "ask for Heavenly Father's help."

"Hmmmm," she said. "That's what I need to do, pray."

Trembling just slightly, she turned heavenward. "Help me," she pleaded. "Please help me to know what to do, and which way to go." It took only seconds for the response to come, and after wiping away another set of tears, she knew, without understanding why, that she should return to Chava.

Chava felt as if someone had slugged him in the gut. He felt sick. He somehow sensed that Megan had, in fact, grown somewhat fearful of him, and he suddenly hated himself for the lies he'd told and the role he'd played in this whole ordeal. Chava knew well the terrible heat of the southern deserts of Baja and was terrified at the thought of having brought an innocent child into its merciless clutches. Without a moment to spare, he began an immediate search of the area. He was grateful, though not completely relieved, when he located Megan's footprints in the sandy soil where she had exited the rear of the vehicle earlier.

Megan suddenly felt exhilarated, happy beyond words. And in ways she could not understand, she was consumed with passionate feelings of love and charity for all of God's earthly creatures. She was also experiencing renewed feelings of trust for her curious traveling companion, Chava. In fact, something else was happening to her even while she sorted through these feelings.

In her tender and fragile young mind, she understood that Chava wasn't a bad man. In fact, she realized that she'd been wrong all along. She shouldn't have left the sanctuary of Chava's old car. He really did have a young sister who was in trouble—actually dying.

Fearful that Chava might have already driven off in another direction, thereby cancelling her opportunity to assist the invalid child, Megan turned and sprinted as fast as she could toward the beach from whence she'd come.

"Hold on, Sylvia," she whispered courageously. "We're coming."

At that instant, a distinct though distant noise could be heard. It was Chava. As Megan steadied herself, then stood to focus her gaze westward toward the sea, she saw Chava's car coming toward her. Immediately, she realized that her friend was racing forward again. This time, however, it was to liberate her from the suffocating heat of the Baja.

Chava slammed his foot down onto the old brake pedal in the nick of time. He hadn't seen the little Russell girl standing on the dirt road with her back to the sun until it had almost been too late. Yet there she was. Frightened and confused, he threw the gear-shift lever into a neutral position, left the engine idling safely, and leaped out of the vehicle.

"Megan," he coughed upon reaching the small child, "where did you go? I thought you were lost!"

Smiling innocently, Megan did the unexpected. In a gesture that was both genuine and affectionate, she extended her right hand, and delivered a tiny batch of desert flowers to her new friend.

"These are for you," she said confidently.

"What are they?" he asked, confused with her gesture.

"They're flowers for Sylvia Maria," she answered pleasantly. "I wanted to pick her some nice, pretty flowers. You were sleeping, and I . . . well . . . I think we'd better go, 'cause she needs us real bad!"

And with that, Megan placed the bouquet of orange and yellow cactus flowers in Chava's hands, and walked directly around to the passenger side of the Chevy. Chava was nothing less than completely dumbfounded. He watched Megan's light, courageous steps toward the vehicle and then stood silent as she climbed into the front seat of the car.

CHAPTER 36

A thick, dense darkness entered Los Angeles and snaked its way through the crippled metropolis. Initially, as the sun set in the west, no one seemed particularly concerned. In fact, fog was a fairly common sight along most of the southern California coast. But now, like the hurricane's sudden demise, this particular fog bank seemed extraordinary to the beleaguered residents of the valley. It was massive. And coupled with the darkness of the approaching night, the curious mist soon became a suffocating blanket of darkness that was simply impenetrable.

Within hours of sunset, the county of Los Angeles was smothered in a void of nothingness. Street lamps, which had been repaired since Bard's passing, had no measurable effect whatsoever on the paved roadways and sidewalks. This, of course, left hundreds of thousands of residents and travelers in a state of perplexing blindness and mounting fear. For a second time in as many weeks, Los Angeles was under siege.

On the corner of the couch, Romero sat in pensive silence. He at last grabbed a thin leather jacket and threw it over his shoulders. He then fetched a set of car keys from the right side pocket and headed for the front door. But as he placed his hand on the doorknob, a truly unusual sight caught his eye.

Seeping mysteriously and eerily underneath the wooden front door, long tendrils of dense fog snaked into the living room and hung suspended just inches above the rotting carpet.

A surge of apprehension suddenly swept over him and sent a chill up and down his spine. Although he felt a compelling urge to remain indoors rather than travel out into the night, he knew that the wheels of his irreversible plan were already in motion. He also knew that if he wanted the ransom money as much as he claimed he did, then there could be no mishaps. It was now or never!

And so, with renewed determination in his heart and a measure of added courage to see him through, Romero Valdez opened the door and stepped out into the night, out into the fog. The unnatural cover was so complete, so intense, that visibility was less than five feet, at best. It was, to put it mildly, the darkest night he'd ever seen.

"How appropriate," he thought miserably. For he knew that though the obscure cover would conceal him as he performed his mischievous errand, it would also cause him difficulties.

"I'll get there," he vowed, "even if I have to crawl the entire way!"

CHAPTER 37

Jennifer awakened suddenly out of a dream and sat upright in her bed. She didn't know why exactly, but she had succumbed to a curious fear. For a moment, she sat in the darkness and tried to remember the details of her dream. Dreams had always fascinated Jennifer. In fact, it was because of this fascination that she had pursued a career as a clinical psychologist and had chosen to study dreams in depth for her doctoral dissertation.

Because of this, Jennifer was growing more frustrated than frightened by the experience, for in her mind, a dream with such power over the conscious emotions should have been recorded. Even so, probe as she might to bring the nightmare back to the surface, it simply would not come.

"Too bad," she whispered, "I would like to have chronicled that one in my journal." Slowly then, the lovely brunette climbed out of her bed, pulled on a pair of warm slippers, then made her way over to the bedroom window. Everything outside was dark.

"That's strange," she thought. "What happened to the street lamp?" For sure enough, when she pulled back the curtains, the darkness was so complete that she could see nothing. Something was not right. Never in all her life had Jennifer seen such consuming darkness. Suddenly, a noise, faint and almost imperceptible, sounded from somewhere downstairs.

"Huh?" she gasped, partially paralyzed by a surge of panic. "What's that?" Intense fear welled up inside her. She had no idea, even now, what was happening around her. But now there was something more than the darkness, something that seemed to be a part of that darkness. Something, or someone, had entered her condo and was, this very minute, lurking about in the shadows of the first floor.

"Who is it?" she whispered desperately, trying to control the violent shaking of her nerves and muscles. Was it a thief? A prowler? A rapist? She could not move. But, she reasoned, she *had* to move! She would *will* herself to act! Slowly then, she crept cautiously over to the bedroom door and opened it.

Her worst fear was that as she did so the hinges would squeak just a little and possibly alert whoever was downstairs. The hinges, however, did not squeak. "Thank goodness," she whispered, peering out into the upstairs hallway.

A small night-light near the guest bath illuminated enough of the upstairs area for Jennifer to see that no one but herself was up and about. She was momentarily relieved. That mental comfort was short-lived, however, for in that same instant, a second sound broke the silence and reverberated through the darkness. Again Jennifer froze just inside the threshold of her bedroom. She strained her eyes to see what she could down through the stairwell. But nothing moved.

She reasoned that whoever it was had also stopped moving and was even now waiting in the shadows below. How could she face the intruder without a weapon? Jennifer's practical mind reasoned that the prowler was a thief, nothing more. If he'd been a person set on harming her in any way, he'd probably have made his way upstairs already and into her bedroom, where he would have undoubtedly found her still standing at the side of her bed. "Maybe," she thought, "he'll find whatever he's after, take it, and get out. And maybe, just maybe he'll think that I am still sleeping, and—"

Just then Jennifer felt a cold, damp chill slither up and move in around her feet. Through the dimly lit upper hallway, Jennifer witnessed a sight that sent chills throughout her entire body. A thick, greyish mist had crept into her living room and kitchen and was just now slithering upwards and over the stairs.

She could not imagine what the foggy substance was, but she was profoundly startled by the sight and feel. Nevertheless, she knew she had to investigate the sounds coming from down in the kitchen. So, with renewed determination, Jennifer crept out into the hallway, peered over the ornate, wooden banister, and finally tiptoed ever so quietly down the stairs.

Arriving at the base of the stairs, she reached for a decorative fist-size marble egg that was sitting on a small entry table just inside the front door. Jennifer had always been fascinated by collector's eggs. In fact, in the living room, a glass cabinet displayed a formidable and valuable collection. It occurred to Jennifer that the prowler's ultimate target might very well be that collection. Perhaps he'd been a casual acquaintance, had scoped the place out during some previous visit, and had chosen this moment to strike. And if so, he might be in the living room, instead of the kitchen.

In any event, she concluded that she'd certainly rather lose the egg collection than lose her life. So she had grabbed the large marble egg only as a possible defense weapon. Holding the heavy egg high over her head, she moved silently into the living room. When at last she was standing in front of her prized egg collection, a third noise, once again coming from the kitchen, sounded ever so slightly from behind. Jennifer's protective instincts surfaced like a volcanic eruption, and she turned and raced into the kitchen at full speed.

"Who's in here?" she shouted as she ran in through the entryway, wielding her marble weapon high overhead. *"Who's in my kitchen?"*

Jennifer flipped on the overhead lights, and the room was immediately illuminated by the soft florescent glow. Although she half expected someone to leap out of the obscure shadows and attack her right there on the spot, nothing but an empty kitchen and a prevailing silence greeted her.

"Who's in here?" she clamored a second time, now setting her marble egg on one of the countertops and replacing it with a conveniently located butcher knife. Still she heard and saw nothing. There simply was no one there but Jennifer herself. A very intimidated Jennifer. A very frightened Jennifer!

Slowly, then, after shaking off the jitters and replacing the kitchen knife on the counter, she looked up at the wall clock, noted the time, and decided to return to bed. As she was about to extinguish the overhead lighting, she noticed that the window over the sink was open. A thick river of greyish fog was pouring into the room. Quickly and apprehensively, Jennifer stepped up to the narrow window and tried to remember if she had left it open the night before. Carefully, she pulled it shut and secured it so that the slow-moving mist ceased its relentless streaming into her kitchen.

She pulled back away from the window and shook her head slightly from side to side, but then discovered something else that was unusual. Something, she did not know what, was lightly caked across the palms of her hands. Something gritty, something moist. Dirt—muddy dirt. Instinctively, Jennifer whirled around in the darkness and nearly fainted when, to her immediate horror, she found herself face to face with a shadowy male figure.

"Dear Lord!" she managed to say, but she was quickly cut off when an object the man was holding directly in front of her face came suddenly into focus.

It was a revolver—a large revolver!

A rough and filthy hand grabbed her by the throat and shoved her violently backwards, slamming her painfully against the countertop. "Move a muscle, Miss Lapman, and I will kill you without restraint! Make a single sound, and I will blow your head off!"

The man had a nylon stocking over his head. And in the darkness of her kitchen, the overall effect was monstrous. No, she would not move. She would, in fact, do precisely what the man requested of her, although she was so terrified that she simply could not stop shaking.

Within five minutes, a period of time that seemed eternal to Jennifer, the masked abductor had her lying facedown on the kitchen floor, had bound her mouth and hands with an extremely abrasive duct tape, and was even now wrapping the vile fabric around her head and eyes. She was now a prisoner, and the thought that went through her mind as the final strands of tape were being pressed mercilessly against her eyes was that although she had no idea who her abductor was, he had an advantage over her that went beyond his role as abductor and evildoer.

He knew her name.

CHAPTER 38

The hours had drifted away unnoticed by the two men who were sitting in the ornate study of the Rockingham estate. And when Allen Russell looked up at the clock, he was astonished to note that it was already four in the morning. "Can you believe that?" he exclaimed, turning to his son Eddie. "I figured it was about midnight, perhaps one o'clock in the morning."

Eddie turned slowly around in his seat on the plush sofa, noted the time as his father had directed him to do, and then took in a deep breath of air. "It is late," he replied quietly. "And maybe you ought to get some sleep, Dad."

"Maybe we both ought to get some sleep," the old man countered. "In any event, there's nothing more we can do until El Tigre Negro provides us with the locations for the five drop sites. But Eddie . . . you're quite certain that Megan is alive? That she's going to be returned to us?"

"Yes, she is alive and well. But still, I'm not positive of her whereabouts. In fact, as I said earlier, I could not get a clear image of anything in particular near or around the old Chevy. But I did see her abductor's face."

"Yeah," Mr. Russell confirmed, "a perfect description of the Hispanic fellow Charlie told me about. But, tell me, Eddie . . . there's so much more to this than meets the eye. I want to meet this old man, Simeon."

"I don't know much more than what I've already told you, except that when I'm around him or his beautiful companion, I feel immensely peaceful inside. It's like they emit some uncanny power that completely envelopes my soul."

"And you say that it was this Simeon who gave you this . . .

power, this gift, if you will, to bring your mother back from the dead?"

"No, not really. That power, the holy priesthood, was given to me by my bishop, Randy Grimshaw. Simeon has simply enlightened my mind as to the far-reaching impact the use of this priesthood can have."

"Really?"

"I'm serious, Dad. The key to making this power operable seems to be my level of righteousness."

"Righteousness?"

"Yeah," Eddie continued, suddenly feeling very comfortable with his word choice and with his father's acceptance of the strange concepts he was sharing. "Righteousness. You know, a person's choice of right over wrong."

"You sound like a missionary, Son."

"Well," Eddie responded seriously. "I wish I was a missionary, but I'm not. You know something, though? I've found that when my heart is filled with compassion and genuine concern for others, my ability to use the priesthood powers increases significantly.

"Something's happening, Dad—something wonderful is happening. And although we as a family have been faced with the crisis of Megan's kidnapping, there is a reason for it."

"A reason?" the old man questioned.

"Yes, Dad, a reason. Think about it for a moment. The hurricane that suddenly swept up the Baja coastline and almost leveled the city of Los Angeles was quelled instantaneously by a power that was beyond the natural forces of nature. You must know that an omnipotent hand intervened before the full magnitude of Bard's fury was finally unleashed against Los Angeles. And why? Why are there such unusual goings-on in the heavens? Why are so many of us being tested and tried without direction or purpose to sustain us in our most desperate hour?

"I mean," Eddie continued, "who cares anymore about the homeless, about the recently televised atrocities of modern-day concentration camps, or about the frail and dying children of civil-war-torn Somalia, in northeastern Africa? Who cares?"

"Well," Mr. Russell responded gingerly, "I'm not sure, Son. I don't know who really cares anymore. Perhaps it is as you suggest—"

"We have failed, Dad!" Eddie interjected suddenly. "The world we live in is for the most part a cold and callous world, where the common desire is mere self-service and self-aggrandizement! People are out for themselves, period."

"Those are pretty heavy words, Son," Mr. Russell responded, "but I think I see what you mean. We are living in grievous times, aren't we?"

"I believe, especially after conversing with Simeon, that we are living in the ultimate days of time, the eleventh hour. And now, well, you don't need a crystal ball to see the future, for as the prophets of old have declared, the time is at hand."

"What?" the old man pressed, anxious for his son to continue. "The time for what?"

"For His second coming, Dad!" Eddie answered with conviction in his voice.

"You mean . . . " Mr. Russell hesitated for a moment.

"Yes, Dad," Eddie interjected, reading his father's thoughts. "The second coming of Jesus Christ."

"But—"

"Listen to me, Dad," Eddie continued. "Simeon and his wife, Sarah, are messengers of a sort. They are . . . well . . . spending their days under the supervision of the Savior. Simeon and his wife were His friends, Dad."

"Pardon me?"

"They knew Jesus while He was here on earth, almost two thousand years ago."

"They *knew* Him? What on earth are you talking about, Eddie? How could they have known the Christ?"

"They were, and still are, quite literally two personal friends to Jesus," Eddie insisted. "Now, I know this all seems far-fetched, Dad, but please hear me out. I had a difficult time believing the tale myself, but I now know that their testimonials are true. Simeon and Sarah are two thousand years old!"

"What? But, how—"

"They never died, Dad."

"Eddie, I think—"

"No, listen to me, please. I'm sharing this information with you only because Simeon himself told me that I could confide in you. Do you remember," Eddie continued, not allowing his father to interrupt, "the story told in the New Testament about an individual standing in the crowd, who watched Jesus carrying his cross to the hills of Calvary?"

"Who was that?" his father queried.

"The Holy Bible says his name was Simon—Simon of Cyrene. He was an innocent, though truly disheartened, bystander whom the Roman guards picked out of the crowd, and whom they compelled to pick up Jesus' cross and carry it up to Golgotha."

Mr. Russell was now too fascinated by his son's tale to interrupt.

"While Christ was hanging on the wooden cross," Eddie went on, "he inquired of his compassionate friend, Simon, what he, the Savior of the world, could give to the timid Cyrenian. Well, it turned out that Simon had been an ardent follower of the Christ during His earthly ministry, and he wanted nothing more than to continue helping the sons and daughters of God in their mortal quests to follow the Lord. Simon knew of the Christ's promise to come back to earth a second time, and so he asked his dying Master for power over mortal death!"

"What?" Mr. Russell responded skeptically.

"That's right, Dad. Not immortality, for as Simeon explained, that would necessitate resurrection. But a changed state that Simeon referred to as 'being translated.' Sort of an intermediate state of being, like the one the Savior had granted his youngest apostle, John the Beloved. Simeon's companion, Sarah, was given this same gift, and in the centuries that have passed, these two servants have labored unceasingly in the service of Christ."

"Wait . . . uh . . . wait just a moment, Eddie," Mr. Russell insisted. "Are you absolutely certain that these two 'translated beings,' as you call them, are not just a couple of professional cons who have—"

"Dad!" Eddie protested, "look at me. Look closely into my eyes, and into my heart. I promise, in all humility and soberness, that what I am telling you is true. Simon, or Simeon, as he later changed his name in honor of his mortal father, was granted, with his beloved Sarah, a temporary immortality in the flesh. They are messengers of the resurrected Christ and have shown me wondrous things.

"They told me that I had been chosen—before I was born,

no less—to assist them in this final hour of preparation. They told me that great burdens would be placed upon my shoulders, and on the shoulders of my loved ones, while the powers of evil would forever try to prevent us from achieving our pre-assigned tasks.

"Simeon instructed me further to watch and listen, and marvel at the natural wonders that would occur on earth and in the heavens. He told me great calamities would destroy many of the nonbelievers, the evildoers, the workers of darkness, before the Savior would return again to usher in the Millennium.

"In fact, Dad, Simeon told me that earthquakes, volcanoes, horrific hurricanes, and storms would shake the planet violently, signalling the Christ's coming. When Hurricane Bard swept up the coast of Baja and quite suddenly targeted our city, it was the first time that anything like that had ever happened—the very first time in recorded history. And although it was most assuredly on a collision course with L.A. County and would have snuffed out the lives of perhaps even hundreds of thousands, it was quelled by the awesome power of the priesthood that Simeon holds."

"This is incredible, Son, I just don't—"

"That's right, Dad," Eddie again interrupted. "It is incredible. Think about it. If Simeon, or another righteous priesthood holder, had not intervened, the full power of Bard would have been vented against our entire region, and thousands of unsuspecting souls would have perished.

"Of course, Simeon himself would tell you that it was not his power that caused the miraculous silencing of the storm to occur. It was, and continues to be, the craftsmanship of the Master of heaven and earth Himself." Eddie paused, probed the questioning eyes of his father, and continued.

"You know," he began cautiously, "I had to stop and thoroughly examine this whole thing in a very objective way before I began to understand even a small part of it. I asked myself why am I, Edward Allen Russell, a simple dive master with the L.A. Aquatic Rangers, suddenly an integral part of the most significant event in human history? Well, I have concluded that there are two reasons. First, because of my ties with you, Dad . . . "

"With *me*?"

"Yes, Dad . . . with you. You see, I believe that since you are so prominent a figure in global financial and business circles, that perhaps the Savior has foreseen an occurrence in which you and I, and our family, will intervene to assist in His great preparatory work."

"How so?" Mr. Russell pressed.

"I don't really know, Dad," Eddie answered honestly. "But I feel certain that our family was destined to become a part of the work. Because the Lord has given you the gift of acquiring wealth and international prominence for His purposes.

"I mean, think of it, Dad! What an exhilarating feeling of gratitude will be ours, if we, as a family, can in some way assist Him who is called the Christ, as He prepares the world for His second arrival."

Mr. Russell thought carefully about the truly incredible scenario Eddie was proposing, and as he did, he recalled the experience he and his son Warren had had inside their chalet at Zurich. He remembered well the feelings of helplessness when all they could do was watch the television set as it portrayed to a concerned world the awesome fury and devastation being levied against the Los Angeles area by Hurricane Bard. He remembered the breathtaking televised miracle, when Bard suddenly ceased to exist. And, of course, he remembered his own thinking at the time, when he too had discussed, with Warren, the concept of heavenly intervention.

Something wonderful was happening here, yet something terribly frightening at the same time. Nevertheless, Mr. Russell found himself at peace—peace with his son's words, peace with his son's tale of the restoration of the holy priesthood.

"I know why you were chosen, my son!" Mr. Russell smiled affectionately. "I know in my heart that you were selected to assist in this great work because you are who you are, Eddie. And you don't need to explain anything further. I believe you."

"You do?" Eddie countered, feeling in his heart an increased measure of tenderness.

"Yes, Son, I do. You've never lied, to my knowledge, so why should you start now? In my heart, I believe everything you've told me, and I'm gratified that this Simeon has contacted you and is now working with you in this noble endeavor. My only question is where do we go from here? Will Simeon help us locate Megan? Or perhaps more appropriately, do you have a clear direction in mind? Do you know which way to proceed with El Tigre Negro and his lieutenants?"

"Well," Eddie responded pensively, "I don't have all the answers, but—" Just then a feeling of great fear came alive in Eddie's heart! He wasn't sure why, but he realized the voice of warning and was momentarily stunned by the experience.

"Eddie?" Mr. Russell responded with mounting concern. "What's wrong, Son?"

For a moment, Eddie did not respond but sat motionless on the couch while his father continued to stare deeply into his eyes. "Call your friends down at the precinct, Dad! And call Charlie, as well! If my impressions are valid, we have a couple of suspects in the Megan Russell kidnapping case!"

Without waiting for his father to reply, Eddie leaped up from the sofa, ran over to the front door of the Rockingham mansion, then sprang out into the night. In doing so, he ran directly into the fog cover, and before the startled and frightened eyes of his beloved father, he simply vanished like a ghost.

Unfortunately, though the night was ending, the nightmare had intensified.

CHAPTER 39

By now, the enormous fog bank that had rolled inland from the sea had captured the attention of scientists and meteorologists all over the world. Its density and magnitude were unlike anything ever recorded.

In the early morning hours of lingering darkness around the Rockingham estate, Eddie Russell had posted himself as a watch-guard. He was alone in the shadowless fog just outside the cast-iron gates of the opulent mansion and was waiting for two, perhaps three individuals to arrive. For, in truth, he felt that they would arrive, and they would attempt to enter his parents' estate and rob them further of their peace and tranquility.

In a remarkable way, Eddie's power of discernment had increased significantly since his last visit to the keeper of the old lighthouse on Santa Rosa's northwestern point. He had been able to both see and hear a furtive call of warning by, strangely, the one he loved more than life itself—his Jennifer. And although Eddie could not understand, he knew immediately that she, as well as someone with her, was in serious trouble.

"Eddie!" she had called out to his senses, "Help me, please . . . ."

Instantly, Eddie's mind had been taken back to an unusual dreamscape, a place which he suddenly remembered all too well. It was an island setting where, through a thick blanket of impenetrable fog, Eddie had heard the rowing of a small boat. He had also heard the frightened voice of his sweetheart calling out to him for help. And he had leaped blindly into an icy-cold ocean in a futile effort to save her life. This time, however, the terrified plea for his intervention was not a dream, but was, in some unexplainable manner, a voice of reality.

With those words ringing in his mind, Eddie had mentally envisioned two, perhaps three figures. The figures were without faces. They were, in fact, mere shadows of perception, but see them he did, and he understood the vision, instantly knowing that the three were on their way to the home of his beleaguered parents. Their purposes, however, were not made known to Eddie. Yet he was almost certain that they were connected in some way with the kidnapping of his niece, Megan Lynn. That's why he had told his father to call Charlie and the police. He felt sure that these figures had something to do with Megan's abduction.

How had he known that? Things were happening so rapidly that, for a moment, Eddie wondered whether he had experienced a real voice of warning or whether the whole thing had been a dirty trick played against his overly active imagination.

"Dear God," he cried out in humble supplication, "there is such fear in my heart, such anxiety in my soul. I love Jennifer with all my heart. She calls out to me, Lord, and I'm afraid for her life! I need you, dear God. I need the protective powers of the sacred priesthood. For without these, I fear I will be unable to find Jennifer, or my frightened and innocent niece, Megan Lynn.

"Allow my eyes to see through this great blanket of fog, and guide me, Father, to that place where my loved ones can be found. For I fear that harm will befall them and they may very well perish. Help me, Lord! *Please, please help me!*"

Not knowing how or why it had happened, Eddie somehow knew that Jennifer had been abducted by the very group of individuals who had taken young Megan from the estate. He was sick inside at the thought of malicious hands forcing his sweetheart to leave her condo, and perhaps hurting her in the process. But as he tried desperately to capture images of the event, his mind was blank.

Where *was* she? The moment of her voice having cried out to him was past and gone. No further inclinations or whisperings from within could be heard. And so Eddie stood still and waited.

He was curiously aware of the thick fog surrounding him, and he knew instinctively that here too was another sign from heaven that the world was in the eve of a tremendous occurrence. He had no concept at all of the fog bank's magnitude, and he had assumed that it covered just southern California. But even now the fog was quickly rolling eastward, where it would eventually blanket the entire North American continent!

Some distance down the street, Eddie thought he could hear the familiar sound of an approaching automobile. He strained his ears to listen intently. "Courage, Ed," he whispered to himself, thinking again of his beloved Jennifer and his sweet little niece, Megan. "They need you badly, so don't go folding up on 'em now!"

Just then another sound could be heard inside the gates. Someone was behind him and to the left, standing in the middle of the expensive red-brick driveway. "Mister Edward?" a quiet voice called out into the darkness. "You there, sir?" It was Charlie.

"Over here, Charlie," Eddie whispered back. "I'm just outside the gate."

Charlie squeezed through a small opening in the massive iron fence, then crept cautiously over to where he'd heard Eddie's voice. When the two were close enough to see each other's silhouettes in the fog's obscurity, Charlie spoke again. "Your daddy said you might could use some help."

"Shssssh, Charlie," Eddie whispered. "You hear that car coming up the street?"

"Yessir."

"I believe they are coming here to the estate."

"And, who might `they' be, sir?"

"The worst kind of criminals, Charlie."

"What?" Charlie questioned, still in a whisper.

"Yes, my friend. I believe that they are the very ones who kidnapped Megan and Jennifer."

"Miss Jennifer has been kidnapped as well, sir?"

"I believe she was," Eddie whispered back, "although I don't know that for sure." Eddie turned briefly to his black friend.

"Shssssss," he said, putting a finger to his lips. "If they pull into the driveway, one or two will have to get out of the vehicle.

You go over to the other side of the driveway, Charlie. We're gonna have to get the jump on 'em. I'll take the driver. You take the guy in the passenger seat."

"What?" the old butler protested.

"Here they come, Charlie! *Go!*" Quickly then, Charlie scurried to the other side of the estate's driveway and crouched down behind a small bush. Together, he and Eddie waited in the obscurity of the fog bank for the slowly approaching intruders.

The car, an early 1970's Chevrolet Impala, did in fact come to a stop in front of the Rockingham estate. It did not, however, turn into the driveway. Instead, it came to rest a full three feet from the curb, with its engine idling.

Crouching like his counterpart at the other side of the drive, Eddie peered around the small bush in front of him and strained his eyes against the darkness and its blinding fog. Eddie realized that he was going to have to rely completely on his instincts if he hoped to overpower his girlfriend's abductors. But here again, he felt a reassuring surge of confidence. For through his years of intense training at the Elysium, those same instincts had been refined and sharpened hundreds of times over. Jennifer and Megan's lives were at stake. And if this moment was his only chance to find them and ultimately rescue them, then he would prevail. He simply had to!

Suddenly Eddie heard a familiar sound. Someone had opened one of the car doors and had stepped out onto the pavement. But wait a minute. Something else was happening at the same time. Something inside his soul, something inside his heart, something inside his mind.

"Dear Lord," he whispered inaudibly. And in a truly remarkable way, the mist parted. Although it remained as foggy as ever in the immediate vicinity, Eddie was momentarily able to see, with remarkable clarity, the rust-colored Impala and its occupants! The sensation was incredible!

Eddie, however, remained calm. "Use the powers of the priesthood only as you must," he suddenly remembered Simeon telling him. And here he was, faced with another dilemma—a face-to-face confrontation. "What an advantage," he considered gratefully as he watched the three figures exit the vehicle. The thought was comforting.

Eddie leaped silently out onto the driveway, caught the

three unsuspecting Mexicans by complete surprise, and executed two high speed snap-kicks along with a volley of extremely well-targeted, hammer-hard jabs from both fists, which instantly dropped his opponents onto the concrete surface. The three men never knew what hit them.

"Charlie," Eddie called out triumphantly, "they're over here! It's over! We're gonna need to secure 'em before they regain consciousness."

"You got 'em *all*, Mister Edward?" the butler asked shakily. "I mean, already, sir?"

Eddie smiled into the darkness.

"Yes, my friend, I was lucky. They're lying over here at the base of the driveway."

"But—"

"Never mind, Charlie. Listen, one of these guys had a gun. It's laying on the ground, just to your right. You see it?"

"No, sir, I—"

"Here, let me get it for you. I want you to hold it on 'em until I get Dad, and some rope, so we can secure 'em until the police arrive."

Eddie stepped lightly over one of the three prone bodies in front of him and retrieved the handgun that had been kicked out of one of the intruders' hands. It angered him to think of these strangers using such a weapon on his parents, and he was again glad to have been in the right place at the right time. Moreover, he had a sense of deep gratitude in his heart for the intervention of the priesthood power that had allowed him to subdue his family's enemies quickly, with perfect precision, and without having to inflict serious harm or injury.

"Here, Charlie, frisk 'em good. I wouldn't be surprised if they're packing other pieces. And I'll be back as quick as I can, with Dad." Eddie handed the weapon to Charlie, directed him to the three lifeless-looking bodies sprawled out at the base of the driveway, then turned and quickly ran up the driveway to the completely obscured mansion.

Meanwhile, Charlie searched the bodies as he had been instructed to do, and he did in fact find two more weapons. Only this time they turned out to be a pair of knives, rather than firearms. In straddling the bodies during the search, Charlie was amazed to find that the assailants were, in fact, unconscious. He was confused and wondered how it was possible for one lone crusader to so quickly cause such havoc.

Moments later, when Eddie and Mr. Russell returned, a greyish morning light was beginning to filter down through the encompassing fog. And although visibility had not greatly improved from what it had been throughout the night, it was clear that the old butler had everything very much under control.

Two of the young Mexicans were exactly as Eddie had left them—unconscious and immobile—as they remained sprawled out on the turf. The third was just now showing signs of coming around. And as he began to move, Charlie pressed the barrel of the confiscated pistol to his head and whispered a discreet warning: "Move another muscle, and watch ol' Charlie turn out your lights!" The young Hispanic lad did not move.

"That's not necessary, Charlie," Eddie said as he arrived at the scene. "Detective Streeter from the police department and a couple of other friends of Dad's are on their way. Let's let the police handle things from here, ol' friend."

And sure enough, even as Eddie spoke, three different squad cars and one unmarked vehicle arrived at the Russell estate. Within minutes the three very confused and frightened Mexican youths were revived, handcuffed, and placed in custody for questioning, each in a different squad car.

In the emotional aftermath, Mr. Russell and his associates discussed events as they might have transpired if Eddie had not somehow foreseen the trouble before it actually occurred. During the search of the captured trio Eddie had found a note. It had apparently been the final demand letter from El Tigre Negro. Strangely, the note contained not one, but two distinct messages. Using a flashlight provided by one of the officers, Eddie quickly scanned both parts. And when Eddie had read them both, fear and instant anxiety filled his heart. The first had been signed by the Black Tiger, as expected. It read:

> There is no time for delay. You will give the
> money—all of the money—to my home boys!
> They will keep a constant watch as they return
> to me. If they suspect a doublecross, if someone
> follows them, or if they do not return within one
> hour with the money, then your son Larry Russell

will die! Your other son's girlfriend, Jennifer Lee
Lapman, will die, and Megan will be sold on the
black market as a slave to a wealthy landowner in
Mexico! The choice is yours, Mr. Russell. You have
one hour to respond.

El Tigre Negro

This ransom note was followed by a plea for help written by
someone else:

Eddie—I know you'll try to intervene somehow
in your father's business with El Tigre Negro. If you
do, my love, I will die! If anything, just help your
father to make the right decision by putting together
the ransom monies and delivering the package to the
couriers when they arrive! Please, Eddie, do not
intervene. If you do, El Tigre will kill me first, and
then your brother Larry!
I love you, Eddie—

Jennifer

Eddie was shaking all over when he read the second part of
the note. He felt an incredible surge of anger that brought with
it a sudden desire for revenge. But, he knew that he could not
succumb to this latter urge, for if he did, the festering hate
would immediately rob him of his abilities to call upon the desperately needed power that had been granted him. "Jen," he
cried softly, holding back a tear, "hold on, my lady. Hold on."

And with that, he looked down, contemplating his lot.
What was happening here? In fact, what was happening everywhere? Hundreds and thousands of people from all walks of
life were suffering. The hurricane had been disastrous, and now
the coastline was smothered in a foggy and uniquely eerie
abyss. Something amazing was happening. And, like so many
of the world's inhabitants, Eddie turned heavenward for answers.

At that moment, a warm feeling returned to Eddie's heart,
and he was given a glimpse of a future where hope was again

very much alive and well. It encompassed the lives of the Russell family and many others in many parts of the country. Eddie knew that he was a pivotal part of that hope. "Hold on, girls," he sighed, thinking compassionately of his niece and girlfriend. "Just hold on!"

CHAPTER 40

Despite the fact that he was curled up in a fetal position beneath a pile of blankets, Jeffrey Russell was cold. In fact, over the past few hours, he'd had to toss this way and that in an ongoing effort to ward off the frigidity which had greatly disturbed his slumber. Now, however, it was getting ridiculous. Somewhere between his conscious and subconscious minds, Jeff knew that he was going to have to climb out of bed, walk across the cold confines of his basement bedroom, and close the window. The problem was that it was too cold to get out of bed, and too cold not to.

In the end, determined to recapture at least a couple of hours of comfortable sleep, Jeff opened his eyes, peeked out into the seemingly impenetrable darkness, then climbed out from under the covers and walked quickly over to the window. He closed it. But in doing so, he noticed the reason for the icebox temperatures that had enveloped his room. A steady stream of thick, misty fog had been pouring in through the open window. In fact, it was so thick that he found he could actually feel it.

For a moment, Jeff stood by his window and shivered uncomfortably from the lingering cold. He was mystified by the unusual eeriness of the fog and wondered how extensive it might be. But not willing to investigate further, he leaped back into his bed, pulled the sheet and blankets up over his body, and closed his eyes. Gritting his teeth, he tried desperately to fall back into the calm world of a peaceful slumber. But that wasn't going to happen. Instead, Jeff found himself suddenly troubled by something he simply could not understand.

Ten minutes later, he opened his eyes and stared up at the ceiling. Like the rest of his room, it was obscured by the pervading darkness, and although he wanted desperately to fall off into a dreamy chasm, something within him kept his mind awake. Not understanding why, Jeff pulled himself a second time from his bed, threw on some clothes, and exited his room.

Like many times in the past, Jeff had fallen asleep long before his father had returned home for the night. He didn't give it much thought at first—not, that is, until he felt compelled to go check on his dad. Quietly then, Jeff made his way through the darkness of the downstairs family room, climbed the stairs that led up into the kitchen and living area, and headed down the hall toward his dad's bedroom. The door was ajar.

"Dad?" he whispered urgently, "You home?"

But his father was not home. In fact, he hadn't been home all night. He had gone, as Jeff now remembered, to his parents' house in Brentwood Heights. Why he hadn't returned remained a mystery.

Jeff reached over to the light switch, and flipped it to the "on" position. But the lamps at either side of his father's bed did not turn on. As he peered down the hallway toward the kitchen, where a small night-light at floor level normally illuminated a tiny area in the living room, Jeff noted immediately that it too was unlit. No power. Something had in fact caused a temporary power outage.

Suddenly, the thought of being completely alone was terribly unsettling. But why? It wasn't the absence of his father that seemed to stir Jeff's fears. It was something eerily different altogether. With mounting anxiety and an almost overwhelming desire to understand his feelings, Jeff considered making a quick telephone call to his grandparents' home. But there again—what for? To find out if his father was okay? That wasn't necessary. For in truth, Jeff's heart told him that his father was just fine. So what then?

Perhaps he should check all the doors and windows in the house. Not that anyone might try to break in, but just to play it safe. Before he did, though, he'd need a flashlight. "Let's see," he whispered, "where'd I see that?" Quickly he turned away from his father's bedroom and headed for the kitchen. He might have seen the flashlight in the drawer just below the toaster. It was a good place to start.

But as he was about to emerge into the living room, something happened that sent chills racing up and down his back and arms. For somewhere downstairs, he heard two distinct sounds that were immediately recognizable:

Footsteps and whispers.

CHAPTER 41

The mature seagull had already circled a dozen or more times high above the abandoned warehouse in Venice, California. And although the fog was relentless in its march eastward from the vast Pacific Ocean and already had a ceiling height of more than seventeen hundred feet, the gull was undaunted by its immense obscurity.

Something besides the gull's limited vision seemed to be guiding its course, and for reasons that it could not comprehend, the bird felt compelled to drop down through the mist and examine the desolate building below. With incredible accuracy, the seagull floated down through the fog, circled the warehouse twice, then landed quietly on an extended windowsill. The window was slightly ajar, allowing the sleek creature immediate access to the building's interior. The room beyond was completely desolate. There were no signs of activity. Nevertheless, the gull seemed to understand that it was another area of the building, and not this one, that it needed to explore. And so, leaping from the windowsill onto the rotting wooden floor, the gull waddled across the room and eventually exited into a small adjoining hallway.

Cautiously, it tilted its tiny head to the right, then to the left, and finally to the front again as it scanned the dark corridor with its little eyes. The hallway was deserted. At the far end was a series of old offices that once bustled with activity. It could hear voices, and so it waddled on.

Jennifer Lee Lapman was the only human to see the bird when it poked its miniature head around a corner and looked into the room. And although she was still terrified by the bizarre and horrifying events that continued to unfold, she knew in an instant that the gull's presence was a good sign.

Immediately, she thought of the tame gulls that had converged on Eddie's veranda several nights before. "Go, get Eddie!" she pleaded mentally. "Fly! Bring him here, little friend, as quickly as possible. We are in danger—both of us—and if you do not get help, then we will surely die!"

The silent, emotional request was overwhelming, and tears came to her eyes. She did not know what would become of her or of Larry Russell, who like herself was bound tightly with grey duct tape and who waited, as she did, for the next unpredictable assault from their menacing host. The evil Romero had so far shown more mercy for Jennifer than he had for Larry, for she was allowed to see, while his eyes were cruelly taped shut.

Jennifer thought back to the initial assault, just after she'd discovered that someone had climbed through her kitchen window. The prowler/kidnapper had been Eddie's own brother! Eddie's own flesh and blood, Larry, Megan's father! Even now, it was difficult to look at Larry. And although she should have felt pity for him, she was, in some sordid way, delighted that he was getting a taste of his own medicine.

Why? That had been the question that haunted her all through the night. Why had Larry broken into her condo like that? What would he have done with her, had he himself not been abducted?

And there again was that strangest scenario of all. How was it possible that a single person could become the target of not one, but two kidnapping conspiracies in the same night? First, the immense and consuming fog, and then suddenly there was Larry—though she hadn't recognized him at the time—with a woman's stocking over his face.

But then, as if events hadn't been bizarre enough, a trio of gun-wielding Hispanics appeared at her front door, just as she was being hoisted over the shoulder of her first assailant. "Where you think you taking our Señora?" one of them had asked while a very startled Larry Russell had stared into the barrels of three separate guns. And instead of being a kidnapper, Larry, along with Jennifer, had been kidnapped! What Karma!

While Jennifer's mind raced in circles, a very somber Larry

Russell huddled in the far corner of the room. His mind, too, was racing, only with him it was coming to a point of desperation. He needed a fix, and he knew that if he didn't get some of the white powder soon, he'd become miserably sick. As his body broke again into a cold sweat, Larry reeled in self-hatred, for he realized that his anger and his drug habit had caused him to stoop to depths that even a few months ago would have been unimaginable.

Why? he questioned. Why had he ever allowed himself to become addicted? His Elizabeth had grown more distant with each passing day, and now even his children—his remaining children—were afraid of him. If only he could get a hold of his captor's handgun, he reasoned, then maybe he could turn it on himself, end his dismal existence, and ultimately remove the pain in the hearts and lives of so many.

As Larry's mind spun a web of illogical thinking, Jennifer wondered again if she could communicate with the feathered creature. Suddenly, to her complete astonishment, the beautiful bird began moving its tiny body up and down in a strange gesture that seemed to suggest that it might actually have understood her thoughts. After several seconds, it waddled back down the hallway, then leaped up onto the windowsill, peered out into the foggy veil beyond, and took to the skies.

CHAPTER 42

"But Eddie," Mr. Russell reasoned with his son, "how are you going to find this guy? I mean . . . the note said that if we didn't deliver all the cash within the hour, he was going to start killing."

"I can locate Jennifer and Larry. Besides, even if we let these three guys go, and they do in fact take the cash to 'Mr. Black Tiger,' I don't believe we'll ever see Megan, Jennifer, or Larry again."

"Well, tell me this then, Son. How will you find them? I mean Jennifer and the others."

Eddie looked into his father's eyes and noticed that they were filled with fear. He was glad that they had left his parents' bedroom so that his mother would not have to be part of this conversation. Seeing his father's anguish was enough. Eddie wanted to provide his father with all of the assurances he sought. But for the moment, even he was not sure how it would all work out in the end. Still he was confident in his ability to literally *follow* the promptings of the Holy Spirit. Carefully, he put his hands on his father's shoulders and drew him close.

"I don't have all the answers, Dad," he whispered affectionately. "But I have complete faith in my being able to accomplish all that has been placed upon my shoulders. I'll find 'em, Dad, I just know I will! And you know what? I think you know, as well as I do, that God will never require anything of us unless He provides the means for us to accomplish the task. Do you agree?"

"Well," his dad replied, "I suppose I do."

"Then," Eddie continued, "why don't we let Detective

Streeter and your other friends do their job? Let's send them on their way and let them deal with these 'home boys' down at the precinct."

"Don't you think we ought to let Streeter and the others in on the note?"

"Not yet," Eddie answered matter-of-factly.

"But why, Son, why?"

"Well, because it's like I said, Dad. It's a matter between you and me right now. I must have your complete trust, and your blessing, before I can do what I feel that I must do."

"I'm not sure I understand all that, Son," the old man answered, thinking about the professional edge that would be theirs should his friends at the FBI and the police department intervene. "But if you're absolutely sure—"

"Time is of the essence, Dad. In fact, we're running out of it, even as we speak. We simply don't have the time to sit with Streeter, or anyone else, for that matter, and discuss possible alternatives. We must decide on our plan of action right now, and we must see it through to the end."

"Well," Mr. Russell said, "what exactly is your plan, Eddie?"

Again Eddie tried to settle the fears and continued uncertainties of his beloved father. "Help me, Lord," he cried out mentally, then drew his father close a second time, receiving strength from the man who had been such a strength to him throughout his life.

"My plan, Dad," he whispered with conviction, "is to be led by the Spirit."

Mr. Russell could see the warm eyes of his son. They were confident, pure eyes—reassuring eyes—determined eyes! "Very well, Eddie . . ." he sighed, "If it is my blessing you seek, then you shall have it. Follow your feelings, Son; go out and do what you must. I believe in you. Go find them, Eddie. Find them and bring them safely back home to us."

"Count on that!" Eddie exclaimed encouragingly, smiling as he spoke. "You just give your complete attention to Mom. She needs you, Dad. I'll have Charlie keep a sharp eye on things until I get back. And in the meantime, I think we ought to get in touch with Larry's wife."

"Oh?"

"Yes. Get in touch with everyone, as a matter of fact. Have them gather here at the estate this afternoon. I think Elizabeth is going to need support when she discovers that not only Megan, but also Larry, has been abducted."

Less than ten minutes later, the senior Russell had the scene completely cleared out in front of the mansion, although it had been a chore to convince Detective Streeter that he and Eddie would be fine on their own. Eddie had hopped into his Chevy and driven off into the fog to his appointed destiny.

But before he left the estate grounds, Eddie pulled up alongside the front gates, bowed his head in reverence, and asked for direction. He was certain that with much-needed intervention from above, he would ultimately prevail. "Where shall I go?" he pleaded. Even as the words came out of his mouth, something caught his attention and caused him to strain his eyes to see off into the enclosing fog above his head.

He leaned forward and looked up into the morning sky, and strangely he found that his vision through the fog was growing increasingly clear. Warmth and a feeling of well-being flowed through him, and in seconds he saw a small figure approaching from the west. It was a seagull.

When the bird landed on the warm hood of Eddie's S-10, he reached for it through the open window at his left. "Come here, little friend. . . ." But instead of complying, as Eddie fully expected, the gull simply stared motionless into Eddie's eyes.

"What is it?" Eddie asked, searching his heart to understand the meaning of this almost incomprehensible phenomenon. "Did you come for me? Have you come to assist me, my beautiful friend?" And this time, as the words escaped his lips, Eddie heard what he was waiting for. For in that same instant, he received a mental message from the sleek creature before him.

"What?" he whispered questioningly, "follow you?" And sure enough, as if having been cued by the verbal response, the seagull spread its wings once more and lifted off into the foggy morning skies. Eddie did not hesitate for a moment. He threw the Chevy into gear, turned west on Rockingham Avenue, and drove off into the grey mist in hot pursuit.

CHAPTER 43

The drive through the streets of suburban West Los Angeles had been somewhat eerie, since the streets were nearly deserted. But Eddie felt remarkably calm. He could see the fog, there was no dispute about that, and he could also see the crippling effect of its ever-tightening grip on the city. But he could also see beyond the fog. And because of the miraculous manner in which the fog dispersed, he was able to make his way gingerly through the city streets.

Seeing the elegant seagull was an experience all by itself. It too seemed able to travel effortlessly through the morning mist, and it kept low and close enough for Eddie to follow. Within ten or fifteen minutes of leaving the mansion, Eddie had driven through West L.A., Santa Monica, and Mar Vista. This drive would normally have required at least twice that time, but of course the streets were nearly empty.

When at last the gull banked suddenly to the west and flew off toward Venice, just above a remote neighborhood street called Westminster Avenue, Eddie felt in his heart that the two of them, man and bird, had arrived at their destination. Moments later, he saw the seagull swoop up and land on the window ledge of an abandoned warehouse.

Romero Valdez had grown bitterly impatient. It was already well past the one-hour deadline he had given to Señor Russell, and for the first time since he and Chava had begun planning their conspiracy, he wondered what had gone wrong. Something, he concluded, was not right. For even in the fog, his partners should have made it back already. Quite a while ago, in fact. But almost two hours after they should have arrived at the mansion, he alone stood watch over the hostages, and he alone had to decide the next move. That decision, however, was not a difficult one.

The Russell family wasn't concerned for the poor and homeless people—Romero's people. They had more money than they knew what to do with, and yet they became increasingly insensitive to the needs of others. They ate and lived like kings, yet when the truly needy inhabitants of the world put out their skinny, malnourished hands and begged the likes of the Russell family for help, no help came. Where were the Russells when Romero's family were searching through garbage cans in the La Paz ghetto district, looking for food? In fact, what did people like the Russells even know about starvation?

In Romero's mind, there was ample justification for the decision he had made. It was a world where only the toughest of warriors would survive. And if the Russell family wanted to play hardball, then Romero would give them a game they'd never forget!

For a moment, the recently released convict vacillated between the dim light of mercy that remained in his heart and the dark desire that seemed to suggest that now was the time to lash out without restraint. He wanted to make good the promises of El Tigre Negro, to pick up the .44 magnum he and his friends had stolen from the eccentric Larry Russell, and to execute the hostages who were bound and gagged in the adjacent room. Mr. Russell had not responded!

"Two hours," Romero growled, retrieving the weapon and rolling it over in his hands. "Two lousy hours. And I said if the money wasn't in my hands in just one hour, I would kill one of them. Say good-bye, Señor Billionaire. Say good-bye to your worthless son!"

Although the threat was empty, Romero checked the cylinder of his firearm. He walked out the door of his sanctuary and headed for the remote corner of the old warehouse, where Jennifer Lapman and Larry Russell were imprisoned as hostages.

CHAPTER 44

Chava and Megan wound their way through the traffic of La Paz. Within moments, they would arrive at his house, having completed their thousand-mile journey from Los Angeles to this poverty-stricken city on the east coast of the southern Baja Peninsula.

As Chava made his way through the El Fungito ghetto district and entered his own neighborhood, disgust for his family's living conditions consumed his every thought. Thank goodness, he thought, that little Megan was compassionate, for even though she had been born with a silver spoon in her mouth, she would not think herself better than his family.

"Chava?" Megan suddenly spoke, "How many dolls does Sylvia Maria have?"

"My, my, little one. You are so thoughtful to ask. But the answer I do not know. I do remember one doll that sits each day at the foot of her bed. It is blonde, like you, Megan, and Sylvia Maria combs its hair many times each day."

At that moment, Chava pushed on the squeaky brakes of his Chevy, turned sharply down a small dirt street, and came to a stop in front of his family home. He knew this next few minutes would be tricky, for he must introduce Megan Russell to his mother, and to Sylvia Maria and the others, and he would have to place his lies just right, so that his family and Megan would not suspect foul play.

"Dear God, please forgive me," he prayed silently. "I will never harm this lovely child, I promise, no matter how much pressure Romero applies." At that moment, the torn and dilapidated screen door opened, and before the two travelers knew what was happening, their car was surrounded by several delighted, screaming children. Their brother, their special oldest brother, had returned safely to their home.

CHAPTER 45

Jennifer saw the evil Romero enter the room in the deserted warehouse. Larry did not. Jennifer saw the familiar handgun. Larry did not. Jennifer saw the fixed rage in Romero's eyes. Larry did not. And Jennifer saw the confused Latino raise the gun and point it directly at Larry's head.

At the sight of Romero, Jennifer began twisting and turning and moaning frantically from behind the merciless strands of the sticky tape, trying to divert Romero's attention and buy a few more valuable seconds of life for Eddie's brother. "Mmm-mmm!" she pleaded, shaking her head violently from side to side.

"No?" Romero jeered. "And why not, Miss Lapman? You do not care to see this no-good Russell removed from his misery? The very same Russell who was going to take your life himself, only last night?"

"Mmmm—mmmm!" she protested again, beads of perspiration forming on her brow.

"You cannot care for this worthless drug addict, Miss Lapman." Romero went on. "A man who has had the world in his hands, all the money anyone could hope for, and yet wastes his life away by shoveling pound after pound of cocaine into his nostrils! He is no good! And since his own father refuses to negotiate for his worthless life, then as promised, El Tigre Negro must now become his executioner.

"Perhaps, Miss Lapman," Romero continued, obviously enjoying her anguish, "perhaps when they discover that we are serious, they will give us the money we ask."

Jennifer was astounded by the things she had just heard about Eddie's brother. She had no idea how Romero, or El Tigre Negro, as he called himself, had known these things. Nor did she understand why Larry had tried to abduct her, as Romero had said.

Jennifer knew, from talking with Eddie over the telephone that there had been a violent dispute between the two brothers and that Larry had blamed Eddie for his daughter's disappearance. That had to have been the motive for his behavior last night. For although she had not been able to speak with Larry since they had become hostages, she and Larry had learned together what had really become of the tender child.

Someone named Chava, a co-conspirator with the crazy Romero, had taken Megan away. A kidnapping for ransom! And undoubtedly, now that the truth about his daughter was known, Larry probably felt like the greatest fool on the planet earth. Still he certainly did not deserve to die.

"Say good-bye to your boyfriend's brother, Miss Lapman! It is time for justice."

Jennifer could not bear to watch but closed her eyes tightly and gritted her teeth in anguish. She pleaded one last time for God's help. The image of a frightened Larry remained in her mind. Larry could not see, he could not speak, and he could not plead for mercy from the vicious Black Tiger. And now it appeared that he was going to die a truly horrible death.

Romero Valdez did not see the seagull. But before he had actually squeezed the delicate trigger of his Smith and Wesson, he heard the sudden command from Eddie Russell, who stood directly behind him. Like a skilled bird of prey, the gull attacked and hit the would-be murderer squarely in the back of the head. Immediately, Romero discharged his weapon. The bullet sped forward, jarring Larry's head. Jennifer tried to scream as Larry slumped over and fell totally still.

Meanwhile Eddie, upon seeing his two loved ones in danger, bounded into the room and charged Romero with the ferocity of a wild animal. Romero turned around with incredible speed and lifted the .44 out in front of him. He was not, however, fast enough. For even as he squeezed off another round, Eddie was already upon him, initiating two accurate and devastating offensive maneuvers.

The first was a lightning-fast "inside crescent kick" that knocked the .44 from Romero's hand, and the second was a brutally effective "snap kick/roundhouse combination" that lifted the criminal smoothly off his feet, sending him reeling helplessly backwards, where he landed headfirst on the wooden floor.

Instantly the survival instinct that had preserved Romero many times over came alive inside his mind. Although he was in immense pain and quite dazed by the vicious onslaught of his opponent, he leaped up off the floor and attacked.

But once again Eddie proved to be the better fighter. He was skilled in a remarkable way. And as he had learned from the best, a Master of the Korean Ku-Sol school of karate, Eddie was completely relaxed. He waited patiently for Romero's attack, and in reverence to his teacher's memory, he whispered his mentor's name. "Thank you, my friend, Sensei Matthew Yeager! You have taught me well."

And with those words, Eddie leaped high into the air and threw an unparalleled 180-degree windmill sweep that caught the already-dizzy Romero squarely underneath the left temple. The impact knocked the man backwards, rendering him completely unconscious.

Then, being immediately concerned for his brother, Eddie attended to the wound on Larry's face, then moved tenderly over to Jennifer. Stooping down, he removed the tape and cords from his dear sweetheart. Together they collapsed into each other's arms and wept, but then moved quickly to assess Larry's condition.

Meanwhile, the majestic gull, seemingly unconcerned, walked over to the window, glanced up as it unfolded its wings, and lifted silently into the air.

CHAPTER 46

Around the county of Los Angeles, panic was reaching epidemic proportions, and accidents were happening with each passing minute. In an overtaxed hospital, Eddie and Jennifer were affectionately embracing, gathering strength from each other, when Doctor Rennison entered the room. Eddie's father was in tow.

"Our prayers were answered," the smiling patriarch began. "Miraculously, the bullet missed its mark. It hit him in the right ear only. He fainted from shock when it happened, but by the time I arrived at the hospital, he was awake and smiling. He shared something with me," Mr. Russell continued, "that you should both know. He said that he had almost ruined his life, and ours, with a . . . well, a drug habit." Eddie and Jennifer looked at each other and grimaced at the obvious strain that was Mr. Russell's to bear.

"But that's not all," the teary-eyed man coughed, clearing his throat. "Larry . . . uh, he wants to see you both . . . to apologize for his actions . . . and to ask for your help as he enters a rehab facility. Could you find it in your hearts to forgive him?"

"We already have," Eddie smiled. "Drugs do devastating things to a person, Dad, and as Jennifer and I have discussed it, our biggest fear is that Larry won't forgive himself."

"From what I have learned professionally," Jennifer added, putting her arm through Eddie's, "people who succumb to illicit drug use find themselves in a very reactive mode—feeling trapped and sensing, deep within, that they are not in control of their actions. It is a very debilitating feeling, I'm sure. We all must forgive him and now rally around him."

"And," the aging patriarch added, "if I know Elizabeth, she'll do just that."

"Larry," Dr. Rennison interrupted, "would like to speak with you, Eddie and Jennifer. He seems to think it's a matter of life and death."

"What?" Eddie questioned. "What's a matter of life and death?"

"He wouldn't say, Eddie," the doctor continued. "But despite the delirium from the anesthesia I had to use, your brother insists on seeing the both of you in private."

"Is that okay, Dad?" Eddie asked, uneasy with excluding his father from anything that had to do with a member of his family.

"Of course. Just let me know how I can help."

Eddie smiled warmly, then went directly to the recovery room. Arriving at the doorway, he and Jennifer paused for a brief moment, looked into each other's eyes, then went inside. "How're you feeling, Bro?" Eddie inquired affectionately of his brother.

"Alive," Larry answered, "thanks to you." And as he said the words, a long overdue reservoir of emotions broke loose. "I owe you my life," he managed to say between sobs, "both of you. And in truth, I should be shot for my crimes!"

"Nonsense, Larry," Jennifer whispered reassuringly. "Things get confusing at times."

"Listen to me!" Larry suddenly blurted out. "Jeff's in danger."

"What?" Eddie pressed, feeling like he'd just received a powerful blow to the gut. "What are you talking about, Larry? How is Jeff in danger?"

"I . . ." Larry started to weep bitterly. "I sent someone over to your house last night. . . ."

"You did what?"

"I'm so sorry, Eddie."

"To do what?" Eddie pressed, while simultaneously reaching down and grabbing his brother by his hospital gown. "Who did you send to my house?"

"I . . . uh . . . hired a couple of guys. . . ."

And that was all that needed to be said. Instantly, Eddie Russell leaped into action, and reached for the phone at Larry's side. Quickly, he punched in the sequence of numbers and waited. The connection was made within seconds, and the telephone inside Eddie's house began to ring. "Answer it, Jeff!" Eddie cried. But that did not happen.

Finally, Eddie slammed the telephone into its cradle, took Jennifer by the hand, then turned one last time to his weeping, disconsolate brother. "If anything's happened to my boy, Larry—"

But instead of finishing the sentence, he turned and ran with Jennifer out of the recovery room. There was simply no time to lose. They sprinted into the hallway, past a nurses' station where several startled faces popped up from behind the counter, and finally headlong into his father and the doctor.

"What's wrong?" Mr. Russell called out. "Is Larry okay?"

In response, Eddie simply alluded to a possible problem at home and suggested that he needed to take care of something that was "vitally important."

"Larry's fine," he answered, still running, "and we're grateful to you, Doc. But Jennifer and I have something that needs our attention immediately."

"What did you forget?" Mr. Russell asked, confused.

"It's a family matter with Jeff, is all. But hey, Dad, we'll call you later this afternoon. You'll probably be over at Larry's, won't you?"

It was clear to Mr. Russell that Eddie was trying to change the subject, and so he answered, "Well . . . uh . . . I'm sure I will. As long as—"

"Don't worry about us!" Eddie interrupted, stepping into the elevator with Jennifer. "Like I said, we'll call you, as soon as we can. And oh, yeah! If you hear anything from Detective Streeter, I mean if El Tigre Negro talks, if he gives up his partner, that Chava fellow, or lets us in on Megan's possible whereabouts, let me know, okay?"

"Of course," Mr. Russell stammered, "but—"

"We'll call you, Dad!" And with that, the elevator door closed, and Eddie and Jennifer disappeared into the murky obscurity of Los Angeles' immense fog cover.

CHAPTER 47

"Can you see well enough to be driving this fast, Eddie?" Jennifer questioned with mounting fear in her heart. She had grown progressively more concerned as her boyfriend raced through the city streets despite the overwhelming obscurity of the massive cloud cover.

"I can see," Eddie responded. "I'm not sure I can explain it, but I seem to be able to see my way right through it. That's how I found you and Larry at the warehouse this morning." Jennifer looked desperately out into the dense void beyond the Chevy's windshield, strained her eyes to see anything she could, then turned her attention back to Eddie.

Eddie looked over at her lovely face and smiled. "It's a sacred trust, Jennifer, granted to me by Simeon. The priesthood power provides me with strength when I've needed it the most, allowing me, for example, to see through this fog bank."

"Oh, Eddie," Jennifer exclaimed, reaching for his hand. "It's all so . . . incredible."

"It is, my love, it is incredible. But it is an ongoing part of those events we have already discussed. They're happening, honey. They're really happening.

"I mean," he continued, gesturing with his hand, "look at this fog. Have you ever seen anything like it? Or the terribly frightening events that happened to you last night? Think about it, Jen. It's all happening, just like Simeon said it would. Remember?"

"Yes, Eddie, I do remember."

"It's not over yet," Eddie said, "not by a long shot. This isn't just another layer of California fog rolling in off the Pacific. It's much, much more significant than that. I radioed into the Malibu dispatch earlier this morning," he added, "while I was racing out to that Venice warehouse. TC has been swamped with this fog thing, and he told me that there are all kinds of people stranded out at sea. Way out, in fact."

"Oh, really?"

"Anyway, he said that the National Weather Bureau had previously forecasted clear skies—completely clear! And in less than twenty minutes following that report, all of L.A., and most of California, for that matter, was suddenly engulfed inside a fog bank more dense than anything ever recorded. It's what Simeon spoke of when he suggested that signs would appear, great wonders. Unusual occurrences that were to signify the last days and the eminent arrival of Jesus Christ. And I think that He is, in fact, coming!"

"Oh, Eddie," Jennifer again sighed. "You really think so?"

"I honestly do, hon," he answered confidently. "But I'm also convinced that there are other things that need to take place before He comes."

"Like what?" she asked trustingly.

"Like—"

Just then, Eddie's radio crackled, signalling an incoming call from the Malibu Aquatic Ranger Station . . .

"One W-Sixteen," the electronic voice sounded, "come in, Sixteen. Over." Eddie lifted the mike and situated it in his hand.

"This is Sixteen," he responded, "go ahead, dispatch. Over."

"Eddie!" It was TC's voice. "You comin' in? Over."

"That's a negative, TC. I'm on an errand of my own, a matter of extreme urgency. But what's up? Over."

"It's the fog, Eddie. The fog has been rolling in from the west *and* the east!"

"What? What are you talking about, TC? Over."

"They say it's come together somewhere near the Mississippi. The Mississippi, Eddie!"

"What did? What came together, TC? I'm not following you. Come on back." There was another brief pause, and Eddie and Jennifer just waited silently. But then, with panic in his voice, TC began shouting into the mike.

"We're completely covered, Eddie, completely covered! The United States, Canada, Alaska, Mexico, and all the way down to South America! We're completely covered in this fog!"

Eddie held the mike just inches away from his mouth, thought about the image just now implanted into his mind, then glanced anxiously over at Jennifer. She was holding her hand to her mouth in dismay. "Eddie?" the voice on the radio continued, pleadingly, "what's goin' on, Eddie?"

Eddie did not respond. He blocked the mysterious occurences out of his mind and drove speedily past the Malibu Station. Jeff was in danger. There was no time to worry about strange weather incursions or the hysterics of some of his coworkers. Instead, he maintained the radio connection with TC just long enough to rattle off a lengthy list of instructions for the entire department to follow. At the conclusion of the call, Eddie glanced over at his pretty passenger and searched her eyes for a moment. A smile drew across her lips.

"I love you, my lady," he said affectionately, attempting to block the urgency he felt for the safety of his son. "I was so worried back there at the warehouse."

"You were a true darling," she offered in return. "In my heart, I just knew you would come! I like it when you refer to me as 'your lady,'" Jennifer said. "It reminds me of when we first met."

"Oh?"

"Yes," she continued lovingly, "right after your cousin Becky introduced us, you wrote me the sweetest letter. And you began it by writing, 'Greetings, my Lady.' Do you remember?"

"Yes," he answered, wishing there was time to pull the Chevy over to the side of the highway, sweep his sweetheart into his arms, and smother her with kisses. But now as his mind raced back to the extremely urgent matter at hand, he pressed his foot even harder on the gas pedal. Moments later, they reached the turnoff at Pacific View, pulled up in front of the house, and killed the engine.

Together they crept toward the front door, peered in through a small window on the right, and surveyed what they could on the inside. "Shssssh," Eddie whispered into Jennifer's ear, putting a finger up to his lips despite the fact that she couldn't see the gesture. "Let's check to see if the door's open. If it is, we'll go in here. But if it's not, the lock makes too much noise when we use the keys, and we'd be better off going around to the back." Jennifer nodded in silent agreement.

Cautiously, they tested the doorknob. It was locked. "Let's

go," he whispered, leading the way around to the back of the house. "We'll get in through the sliders."

Seconds later, the two were standing just to the side of the sliding glass doors that serviced the downstairs entrance to the beach behind the house. "Get down," Eddie directed, crouching himself as he peered in through the glass panels. "The lamp over by the television is on."

"Can you see anyone inside?" Jennifer whispered back, her own heart beating wildly.

"No," he answered. "It looks pretty quiet." Slowly and cautiously, Eddie slid the door open. "Whewww," he sighed, perspiration trickling down his cheeks. "Come on, Jen, let's go inside."

"After you," Jennifer whispered in compliance. Quickly, then, the two sneaked in through the doors.

"Let's check Jeff's room," Eddie whispered.

"Be careful, Eddie," she insisted.

Quietly, they tiptoed past the small den and approached the boy's room. "Jeff?" Eddie whispered a little louder than normal. "You there, Son?" He was not. "Hmmmm . . ." Eddie questioned. "He was here; the bed's been slept in."

"Upstairs, maybe?" Jennifer interjected. Again they moved quickly and quietly through the shadows and made their way up to the main level.

Arriving on the second floor, they searched the kitchen and the walk-in pantry, peeked out into the garage, and looked around in the living room and hallway. They also checked the bathrooms and the master and guest bedrooms. But in the end, they were forced to conclude the worst. Jeff was not there and had undoubtedly been kidnapped and taken against his will to some unknown destination.

Eddie was sick to his stomach, and Jennifer was on the verge of tears. Suddenly, a noise sounded directly behind them at the far end of the hall. There was a small linen closet that neither had bothered to examine, thinking it too small for a human being. But, as they both had heard the furtive thumping sound at the same time, they turned their attention immediately in that direction and jumped back simultaneously. To their astonishment, the little door swung open and a blurry figure leaped out of the closet, screaming at the top of its lungs!

It was Jeff. And less than a second before he was to slam headfirst into his father's girlfriend, he recognized the woman and his father, standing just inside the master bedroom. He was thus able to veer out of the way. "Dad! Jennifer!" Jeff panted, shaking all over as he put on the brakes. "It's you!"

"Jeff!" Eddie exclaimed, regaining his composure. "What's going on, Son? We've been worried sick about you."

"Oh, Dad," Jeff sighed in obvious relief. "You can't imagine."

"What?"

"How glad I am to see you guys; that's what."

"Glad to see us? Why? What's happened here, Jeff? Why were you hiding in the closet, for heaven's sake? Are you okay?"

"Two men—" Jeff managed to blurt out. "There were two men. They came in through the basement. For some reason, I couldn't sleep last night. The fog . . . It was so cold. I came upstairs looking for you. That's when I heard 'em."

"Hey, bud," Eddie cut in tenderly, "slow down. It's okay. Everything's gonna be all right now. Just take it from the top. Take your time, Jeff."

A few minutes later, the three of them were gathered around the comfortable sofa in the living room. Jeff described, in vivid detail, the two men: a black man with an earring in his left ear and a tall, burly-looking white man with a red bandanna wrapped around his head. They had entered the house by way of the downstairs family room. Jeff related how, by a stroke of good fortune, he had been upstairs at the time.

"Initially, I heard footsteps," he recounted, "but when that was followed by a set of voices whispering in the dark, I knew I was in trouble."

"What'd you do?" Jennifer inquired, feeling the still-very-vivid fear in her own heart as the boy's narrative reminded her of her own ordeal.

"At first," he replied, "I wasn't sure what to do. In fact, I found that I couldn't move."

"Oh?" Eddie interjected.

"That's right, Dad. I was so scared that my legs wouldn't move! I just stood over there in the hallway by your bedroom door and thought that these guys were gonna kill me!"

"So," Jennifer asked, her brow furrowed deeply with concern. "What'd you do then?"

"It was quiet for a minute or so, and I thought that maybe I'd imagined it or something. But then I heard someone's footsteps coming up the stairs."

"And?" Eddie pressed.

"I . . . I saw the tops of their heads. First, the guy with the bandanna—the white guy—then the black guy. . . ." Jeff paused for a moment, stared at the landing on top of the stairwell, and apparently relived the experience all over again. Jennifer could clearly see the fear in the boy's eyes.

"What happened next, Jeff?" Eddie asked.

"That's the weird part, Dad, the part I don't think you or Jennifer will believe. In fact, I'm not so sure I even believe it."

"What are you talking about?" Eddie prodded. "Why wouldn't we believe you?"

"Because—"

Suddenly Eddie knew. He was able to envision what had happened to his son as clearly as if he were watching it on television. Jeff had been frightened so completely by the two intruders that he was unable to move. "Dear God," Eddie whispered reverently, cutting short his son's account. "You saw him, didn't you?"

"Who?" Jeff countered. "Who did I see?"

"Simeon! You saw Simeon, didn't you?"

Jeff's eyes widened with wonder. "Y . . . yes," he said weakly. "That's exactly what happened. The old guy. He just . . . But, how did you know, Dad?"

Jennifer glanced over at Eddie, who seemed to be staring into a void. "Eddie," she whispered. But he did not answer. His eyes and his mind were focused elsewhere.

"Dad?" Jeff queried anxiously. "What's going on, Dad?"

But Eddie was caught up in a vision. He was no longer a part of the conversation. Instead, he had turned his attention to the sliding glass doors, and appeared to be gazing off into the deepening density of the oppressive fog cover.

Slowly, he arose from the sofa and walked over to the doors. For a moment, all was quiet and curiously peaceful between the three. Then suddenly each was given specific answers to pressing questions, and each was edified by a warm and abiding love.

Hope had suddenly come alive in their hearts, and they rejoiced in the knowledge that what was happening was divinely orchestrated. They each knew that soon, very soon in fact, the world would be free of the bitter struggles it had endured for centuries. They knew for a surety that the wars and contentions would cease, that the hunger of so many people living in impoverished nations would end, and that all knees would bow, while all tongues confessed, that the Savior of the world had returned.

But so also did they understand their individual and new-found callings to service. There was work to be done. There were hearts that needed to be changed. People who even now would depend on the charitable contributions of Eddie and his family, and who would, as a result, turn their own hearts heavenward and welcome the Everlasting King to his throne.

"When Simeon appeared," Jeff began again, "everything happened so fast that I'm not sure *what* happened. But I do know that when it was over, I felt good inside."

"Yeah," Eddie agreed, "that's what happens when Simeon is around. But tell me, Jeff, did Simeon say anything? Did he ask for me? Did he leave a message?"

Jeff's memory was suddenly stimulated, and something he'd forgotten earlier popped back into his mind. "The note!" he exclaimed. "Simeon left me a note. Said to give it to you."

Quickly, the beleaguered lad retrieved a crumpled-up piece of notebook paper that had been tucked away inside his pants pocket. "Here," he directed. "See if you can make any sense of it."

Carefully, Eddie scanned the written document, looked over at Jennifer, then refocused his attention on his son. "Numbers?" he questioned. "Simeon left you a set of numbers?"

But just then, Eddie knew. "Get a map!" he shouted. "There in the bookcase. There's a road atlas there on the bottom shelf." Minutes later, all three individuals were huddled around the kitchen table, looking intently at the open text in front of them. And as they did, they ran their fingers along the longitude and latitude markings of one of the maps.

"La Paz!" Eddie shouted suddenly. "La Paz, Mexico. Right here in Baja California. That's where she is! That's where they took Megan!

"Okay," he continued, "we all know what to do. So instead of wasting another minute, what d'ya say we bring her home!"

"I'm with you all the way, Dad!" Jeff exclaimed, delighted by the challenge and marveling at the trust he felt from his father.

"Me, too," Jennifer added, throwing her arms around Eddie's neck. "Let's go to Mexico!"

CHAPTER 48

" . . . And I'll need your assistance, Mr. Presidente!"

The democratically elected leader of the Mexican people held the telephone receiver to his ear. He thought carefully about the unusual request of his lifelong American friend, then smiled.

"You shall have it, Allen. However, when do you expect to arrive?"

"Well, depending on whether or not we can actually fly out of this intense fog, we should be there, say, sometime this evening. Maybe eight or nine o'clock. Is that enough time for your men?"

"Si, amigo, more than enough time," the president responded. "But I am concerned, Allen—"

"About?"

"About you and your people. The fog is everywhere! It is here in Mexico, there in America, and they say that it covers most of the world now. Are you aware of this fact?"

"I am," Mr. Russell replied soberly.

"And how, may I ask, do you intend to land your aircraft through such a fog?"

"Well," Mr. Russell said cautiously, "our jets are equipped with the most efficient state-of-the-art navigational equipment, but once we descend to under five hundred feet, we will be relying completely on your temporary searchlights. They will, as I have suggested, need to be the most powerful available, Mr. Presidente. And as many as you can round up and line up along the sides of the runway."

"They will be there, Allen. You may depend on that."

"Thank you, sir," Mr. Russell answered appreciatively. "I owe you."

"You owe me nothing. It is you who have done so much already. It is my pleasure to assist you in your family's time of need. But tell me, Allen—your granddaughter—how do you know that she is there in La Paz?"

Mr. Russell looked over at his son Eddie, who was standing beside him in the den, and wondered for a moment how he would respond to the Mexican president's inquiry. For indeed, how did he know? Eddie and Jennifer had told him so. And of course, his heart assured him that their words were true. But that would not be an appropriate response. The Latino leader at the other end of the line would think he was totally nuts. So in the end, he decided to avoid the question altogether.

"We've a reliable lead, Mr. Presidente," he answered.

"Do you want the Federalis to follow up on that lead? Perhaps we can get your granddaughter back for you, yes?"

"That is most kind of you, sir," Mr. Russell replied. "But we would like to be there when she is found. And if we're able to work things out as we've discussed, then we will need to fly down anyway."

"I understand, Allen," the president replied. "We will be waiting for you when you arrive. Just call ahead when you are an hour out."

"We will, sir, believe me. Thank you, Mr. Presidente. You are a true friend."

"You are most welcome, Allen. May God bless you."

CHAPTER 49

Four-year-old Sylvia Maria Ayala was wheeled into the operating room at four forty-three that afternoon. She had had a second relapse, since her remission earlier in the year. This relapse was an ominous event, for it had occurred in both her bone marrow and parts of her central nervous system. In order to perform the necessary bone marrow transplant, doctors had needed Sylvia's HLA-matched sibling, Chava! A deposit of no less than ten thousand American dollars had also been required before doctors would even admit the child and her donor brother into La Paz's ill-equipped and sadly outdated hospital.

Chava, of course, had come up with the money for the deposit, even as he had promised his mother he would. And although she had never received an explanation of why he had brought the young white girl to their dilapidated home in the La Paz ghetto, she had become sick with worry for her critically ill daughter. In the end, she did not have the emotional energy to pursue the answers she sought. Instead, she simply accepted the money as a gift from God and rushed the dying girl to their family physician.

In the two days that followed, Megan grew affectionately attached to the tiny, helpless girl. And while Chava awaited word that Romero had acquired the desperately-needed ransom money, Sylvia was admitted to the La Paz facility, and began to undergo presurgical testing.

The medical staff at the La Paz hospital were all worried when Sylvia was brought into their treatment center. The triage physician noted immediately that the child was weak, pale, and lethargic and was in desperate need of a massive transfusion just to restore blood volume.

It was a fight to save her fragile life. Even after the stabilization of her vital signs, Sylvia was so weak that the doctors finally decided that an immediate and complete bone marrow transplant was the child's last and only hope.

For many long hours, both Chava and his mother had consulted with the doctors about Sylvia's ultimate chances for survival. And, although it seemed cruel and unjust, money was a big issue in their discussion.

Inwardly, Chava loathed the doctors for their incessant worrying about money. And although every effort had been made to convince the practicing physician that money was on its way, it was only after the release of the ten thousand U.S. dollars that the old medic had finally allowed Sylvia to be admitted into the hospital at all. Any further financial delays, however, and the child would surely die.

In preparation for the transplant, Chava and his new young friend, Megan, had spent hour after hour at the bedside of the weak child. And although Sylvia didn't speak English, Chava had acted as a translator. As a result, within a very short time, Sylvia Maria and Megan were the best of friends.

"And when your operation is all finished," Megan would tell the child, "you and your whole family can come and live at my grandpa's house."

"Si?" the tiny voice would respond enthusiastically, "and ride the horses?"

"Oh, yes," Megan would respond. "But you have to be brave."

At times the pain would be so intense that the little Hispanic girl would simply lie in her hospital bed and cry. Those were the moments that were most difficult for Megan, because although she could not fully comprehend Sylvia's pain and agony, she sensed it and could only respond by weeping herself.

"It will go away," Megan would say, looking to Chava for a translation. But even with the continual reassurance of her mother, her brothers and sisters, and her wonderful new American friend, Sylvia Maria's ordeal became more intense and more painful with every passing hour.

She *needed* the transplant!

"How will you pay for it?" the hospital administrators had demanded of the child's mother. "We cannot do this operation without receiving, in advance, the cash required for the procedure." The impoverished señora would look to her son for the answers, and Chava, in return, would try to convince the officials that they would be able to pay.

"It'll be here!" he would say to the administrators with mounting concern in his heart. "I will have it from my friend in America in only a few days!"

The money, of course, did not come, despite Chava's relentless insistence that it would. Finally, over the objections of the hospital administrators and some of the doctors, the responsible surgeon simply demanded that the operation proceed. In his heart, he knew that he could not allow the tiny child to die. The transplant was her only hope.

"We will come for you in about one hour, Mr. Ayala," the surgeon had stated, meeting with Chava, his weary-hearted mother, and the young American child he had come to know as Señorita Megan, "so you will please be ready then."

"Si, si," Chava had agreed thankfully, realizing at last that the doctors were going to perform the surgery and trust in him to pay for it when he could. "Where will I go?"

"We will prepare your sister first, a process that will not require your participation," the doctor answered. "Then we will send a nurse to escort you to operating room number four, just down the hallway. She will meet you here in the waiting room in one hour."

"Thank you, Doctor," Chava answered, clearly relieved. "I will be here. And please," he continued humbly, "use as much of my bone marrow as you need to make my sister well again!" The doctor smiled slightly, patted Chava on the back, then exited the waiting room.

"Take care of Megan, Mama!" Chava asked of his trembling and teary-eyed mother. "We must see her safely home to her family after Sylvia's recovery."

"Who is she?" Mrs. Ayala pressed urgently. "You have never even told me who the child belongs to." Chava did not want to get into the conversation right then. He knew that his mother would never have understood, so again he lied.

"I did tell you, Mama. You just don't remember; that's all. She is the daughter of my friend in Los Angeles, who has agreed to loan us the money for Sylvia's operation. He had to go away for a few days, to obtain the money, and so I volunteered to keep Megan until he could come here to La Paz himself."

Inwardly, Chava was relieved that little Megan could not understand or speak Spanish, because he was ashamed of the lies he had been forced to tell. And of course he was certain that the innocent child would not have approved, or cooperated with such a charade.

"Take care of her, Mama," he said again, this time in English so that Megan could understand his words. Then he continued in Spanish, "I need to know that you will do so, before they operate on me and give my bone marrow to Sylvia. Little Megan is so worried about her family, and the immense fog outside, that she needs your comfort desperately."

"But of course," his mother agreed. "I just wish she could speak Spanish."

"Perhaps," he teased, "she wishes you could speak English, yes?"

Mrs. Ayala smiled, then reached out to her courageous son and drew him close. "Don't worry, Chava," she said calmly. "I will watch Megan with my life. How could it be any other way? She is our friend, Sylvia's friend, and she waits, as do I, for the miracle your transplant will bring to our little girl."

Chava then looked over at Megan, who spoke for the first time. "I made this for you," she said in a quiet little voice, handing one of the small friendship bracelets to her friend.

"For me?" he questioned cordially.

"Yes," she said proudly. "It's a friendship bracelet, and sometimes it brings good luck to people. But I have to tie it on for you, or it doesn't work right."

"I see," Chava smiled lovingly, then translated what was being said to his mother. "Thank you, Megan."

"You're welcome," she returned, but then added, "And, oh, would you give this one to Sylvia?"

Chava reached over and retrieved the last tiny bracelet, then held out his arm and allowed Megan to tie his own bracelet around his wrist. He then looked once more into the eyes of his young American friend. "God bless you, little lady," he whispered tenderly, his eyes moistening.

CHAPTER 50

The operation began at 8:38 P.M.

The large contingent, led by Mexico's president, walked into the main reception area at 8:48 P.M. Several feet away, Señora Maria Ayala put her hand to her mouth and could hardly believe her eyes when she recognized the face of her country's elected leader.

Suddenly the young American child leaped up from her chair in the visiting room and raced toward the entourage. "Grandpa! Uncle Eddie!" she shouted jubilantly. "I just knew you would come."

And with that, she leaped from the floor into the outstretched arms of her grandfather, Allen Scott Russell, and started to cry.

"We've been looking a long time for you, Megan," Mr. Russell whispered, holding her ever so tight. "Are you okay?"

"Oh, yes, Grandpa," she whispered between sobs. "But how did you find me?"

"Your uncle Eddie and Jennifer, here, told us where you were hiding."

"I wasn't hiding, Grandpa," Megan said with a smile. "I was helping."

"We know that, Megs," Eddie interjected tenderly, taking his turn to embrace his beloved niece. "And, how is your little friend, Sylvia Maria?"

"You know Sylvia?" Megan asked innocently, looking now at Jennifer.

"Yes, honey," Jennifer answered, "we know all about Sylvia. Is she all right?"

"She's real sick. They're just starting to give her an operation."

The group of adults that surrounded the young child, exchanged concerned glances. They looked over at the president, who in turn focused his attention on the bewildered Mrs. Ayala.

"Señora Ayala," the president asked, taking her hand in his own, "how is she?"

Maria was so startled that for a split second, she could not speak. Finally she whispered almost inaudibly, "Are you referring to my daughter?"

"Yes, ma'am," the president pressed. "We understand that she has leukemia and has gone into surgery for a bone marrow transplant. Salvador, your eldest son, is the donor?"

"Si," she answered timidly. "The doctors have only just begun the operation, Mr. President. I do not know how it goes."

"Perhaps, then," the leader said, "we have come at the right time." Quickly he turned to Mr. Russell and translated into English all that he and Mrs. Ayala had discussed.

"She says they have only just begun to operate," he concluded.

"Then," Mr. Russell instructed boldly, "let's see if we can't intervene immediately."

The aging, compassionate physician in operating room number four was readying his surgical instruments to make the first incision into Sylvia Maria's tiny body when the doors swung open and two renowned American surgeons, who had traveled with the Russell entourage, walked into the room. In front of them, the country's president entered as well.

"Hold up a minute," he instructed. And the old Hispanic surgeon nearly dropped his scalpel right there on the spot!

"El Presidente?" he blurted in complete surprise.

The operation, in the end, had been a grueling experience for all the surgeons. When they had entered the poor child's body, they had discovered that it was riddled with cancerous leukemic clones and that massive numbers of these cells had accumulated in different organs throughout the little girl's body.

Recovery was going to be a long, drawn-out process, even with a transfer to a modern treatment center in Los Angeles. Still, Sylvia *would* recover, and likely live a long and healthy life.

When Chava opened his eyes following surgery, the first thing he saw in the recovery room was his little friend, Megan.

"Hi, Chava," she whispered warmly. "How are you feeling?"

"Oh . . . ah . . . hello, Megan," he groaned. "Is it over?"

"Yes," she affirmed, smiling. "And Sylvia's going to be okay!"

Just then two other faces appeared at the bedside and looked down into Chava's eyes. The one he recognized was his mother, Maria, and the other . . . was . . . a familiar face, to be sure, but he wasn't quite sure how. . . .

"This is my uncle Eddie, Chava," the little girl's voice continued.

"Ed . . . Eddie?" Chava moaned, recognizing the man at last and realizing that he was probably going to go to jail. "Your uncle Eddie?"

"Hello, Salvador," Eddie interjected affectionately, "I've heard a lot about you."

"Oh, Señor Russell," Chava began, "I am so sorry . . . I did not—"

"Shssssh!" Eddie instructed kindly, sensing immediately the fear in Chava's voice. "We know everything that happened, Salvador, everything! And I assure you, you have nothing to worry about. No one is angry with you, my friend. In fact, it is because of you that the life of your sister has been spared."

Chava's eyes widened. "S . . . Sylvia is really all right, then?"

"Yes, my friend, she is recovering nicely. And, although I can't say that I completely approve of your methods, it would appear that your efforts weren't in vain. Thanks to you, Sylvia's going to live! But hey, I want you to meet a few friends of mine." Eddie paused briefly, looked over his left shoulder, then stepped to one side, while his father entered the room with the country's president.

To say that Chava was speechless and shamed would have been an understatement. But steeling himself against the pain of the operation, and the combination of fear and relief he felt knowing that his charade was no longer, Chava held out a weak hand and extended a formal greeting to his visitors.

"I must say, Salvador, that you don't look as mean as I had pictured you." Allen Russell commented, smiling.

"Please forgive me, sir, I—"

"Nonsense, young fellow," Mr. Russell interrupted, letting the man's arm return to his side. "Things have a way of working themselves out. Besides, you opened a few hearts and eyes with your unorthodox antics.

"You see," the aging patriarch continued, "I have learned a great deal these past few days, as have all the Russells. But more about that in a moment. Right now, I've a friend here beside me who'd like to meet you, as well." Mr. Russell stepped politely to one side and allowed the stately president to move closer to Chava's recovery bed.

"Hello, Salvador," the president began, reaching out to greet the young man. "You've given our American friends quite a scare."

"I am truly sorry about that, sir. I—"

"I'm sure that you are, Son. But things seem to have worked out right for you."

"Sir?"

The president looked over at Mr. Russell and Eddie, then turned his attention back to Chava. "You might want to listen for a moment and hear what these gentlemen have to say."

Eddie produced a manila envelope and withdrew some legal documents. "Salvador," he said, we have very much enjoyed meeting your family members and learning how well you have taken care of our little Megan. And if I may ... well ... uh ..." he continued, smiling at the Mexican president, "We have just received clearance from our government officials, and not only have you been pardoned for your actions in Los Angeles, but we have been busy with your president, planning your future."

Chava's face seemed to lose what color was left in it, and he swallowed hard, not understanding where the conversation was leading.

"I have decided," Eddie added, quite pleased with his sense of timing, "that we're going to need you here in La Paz to oversee the construction of the new hospital, as well as a shelter for the poor."

"Shelter? Hospital? You mean ... I ... I'm not going to prison?"

"Well, you can thank my father for that, Salvador. He's decided not to press charges, if you will come to work with us. You've got entire neighborhoods to rebuild. Houses for the poor, jobs for the jobless, food for the needy and hungry. And all of that is to be done under the direction of your president's urban development program."

"That's right, Salvador," Mr. Russell added, while in the background Maria Ayala clasped both hands together over her heart and wept silently. "The Russell-Ayala Construction Company is just waiting for you to get well so it can begin operations immediately. I hope you don't mind, Son, but I have presumed to authorize the immediate construction of a home for your family in the Rio Piedras area. Your president is donating the land."

"Santa Maria!" Mrs. Ayala cried. "How can we ever thank you, Señor Russell?"

"Your son's good heart is more than enough payment, Mrs. Ayala. Besides," he added, allowing the interpreter enough time to translate accurately, "we're counting on your son to repay us himself by accepting a position as director of the shelter renewal program, for, say, twenty thousand dollars a year, starting pay?"

For a moment, Chava was left speechless. It was all so overwhelming, so unexpected. What a great ending to an otherwise-horrible experience. But suddenly he thought about his accomplice and asked, "What about Romero? What's happened to him?"

"As you know, Salvador, Mr. Valdez had just been paroled from Folsom prison. Because of his parole violations, and because of other crimes, his parole was revoked. He's on his way back to Folsom, I'm afraid. A matter that is completely out of our hands. You, on the other hand, have the world at your fingertips, if you're ready to work hard and follow our direction. Are you with us?"

"Oh yes, Señor Russell, I *am* ready!"

"Good! Then, as soon as you're on the mend, you can start immediately."

"Thank you, Mr. Russell! Thank you all! I will do my very best, and that is my sacred promise." Chava and his mother wept while Megan and the others smiled.

And outside, unbeknownst to those in the hospital room, a small break in the massive fog cover appeared directly over the city. It was beginning to dissipate at last.

CHAPTER 51

Simeon sat comfortably alone on the old easy chair in his living room and set the newspaper on his lap. He was feeling warm inside, incredibly warm. For in the relatively short period of time since Eddie's return from La Paz, so many wonderful things had transpired that Simeon was quite certain that a change had begun at last. A real change. Such a change, in fact, that hundreds, perhaps thousands of people were lifting their heads and hearts heavenward and would now be accepted by the Master when He came.

Simeon then picked up the newspaper a second time and looked into the photographed eyes of the young Aquatic Ranger on the front page of the *L. A. Times*. "You did well, Edward Allen Russell," Simeon sighed. "Much of the world's attention will be focused on you now. They will watch with caution at first, my son, but many will listen and will experience a much-needed change of heart because of you."

Underneath the photograph, an advertisement placed by the Russell Foundation pleaded calmly with the citizens of L.A. to free themselves of selfishness and give unrestrained to those in less fortunate nations. There was also an installment of the series the *Times* had been running called "Life and the Russell Foundation." It depicted a truly remarkable and courageous endeavor on the part of Edward Allen Russell, with the Search and Rescue division of the L.A.'s police department.

The story told how, in keeping true to his commitment to help others in need, Eddie Russell had organized a worldwide charity foundation, with the financial muscle of the Russell family fortune to back him, and had already begun massive building projects in Mexico, the United States, Africa, and Europe—to create jobs, stimulate economies, and house the homeless and needy peoples of those regions.

Eddie had made it clear, through his relentless newspaper and television ads, that it was time for change. He had called on people from all corners of the globe to turn their pocketbooks toward the poor and their hearts toward heaven, and to acknowledge the signs and the wonders coming from a caring and compassionate Creator.

Some of his advertisements called for unilateral efforts to feed the poor in all countries, beginning with local regions and reaching out to the starving peoples of Africa. Some called for a cease-fire in nations who were at war with one another. Some called for a peaceful end to racial and hate crimes, while others sought to instill family values and to persuade people to turn away from sexual promiscuity and moral decadence.

All of Eddie's ads, however, centered around a very poignant and straightforward theme. This, of course, was that the Lord of the world was coming back. And that if people would search their hearts, and embrace the simple, though sacred, message of love for one another, then they would rejoice in, instead of fear, the greatest event of all time.

"Oh yes," Simeon reasoned, glancing once more at the photograph of his friend in the *Times*, "He's doing just fine." Slowly then, the ageless patriarch stood up from the comfortable easy chair and walked over to the window.

"Sarah," he called out, smiling gently, "please come in for a moment." From the kitchen, Sarah heard the gentle request of her beloved companion. She set the needlework she had been doing on the kitchen table and walked slowly into the living room.

"And just how might I be of service, darling?" she inquired lovingly upon reaching the top of the landing.

"I just need you near," he answered softly, "to consider, with me, the man, Christ Jesus."

"I wonder," she reasoned, "if He will look different when He comes again."

"The Lord?" Simeon asked innocently.

"Yes, the Savior. Do you think He will look different from when we knew Him?"

"Well," Simeon said, "even if He does, I suspect we'll still recognize Him. But," he continued, "we have guests on their way, so perhaps we ought to prepare for their arrival. Is there anything I might do to assist you, my dear?"

"Everything is ready," she answered with a warm smile. "But maybe you might want to greet them out on the cliffs."

"Hmmmm," the seemingly ageless man reflected, "that sounds great. The fresh ocean air will pour strength into these stiffening legs of mine." Simeon reached out and drew his lovely wife, Sarah, close to him a third time, then hugged her affectionately while kissing her on the forehead. Sarah turned her head and looked up into her husband's eyes.

"I love you, Simon of Cyrene. More, in fact, with every passing century."

"Yes," he affirmed, "I love you too, my dear. And to think that because of the covenants we have made, I will be able to spend the glorious eternities at your side!"

Sarah smiled, and the two of them exited the room.

The waters between the Channel Islands and Santa Barbara were calm and peaceful, and remarkably clear for a warm summer's day. And as Eddie, Jennifer, and Jeff glided effortlessly over its surface in the stately Bayliner, they noted also that the blue-green color of the water was rich and ever so beautiful.

As Eddie stood out on the flybridge, piloting the craft, he felt a tremendous sense of exhilaration and well-being. He was happy. And as he looked momentarily over at his son, a mischevious smile grew across his face.

"What's that all about?" Jennifer asked, having seen the pleasant expression.

"Oh, just something, that's all," Eddie answered, looking a second time toward his son and giving him a quick wink. Jennifer saw the gesture.

"All right, you two!" she stammered, "What's going on?" Jeff looked a little embarrassed.

"Jeff," she scolded humorously, "you're up to something. I can feel it." Jeff just shrugged his shoulders and giggled.

"All right, kiddo," she pressed, "You remember what I've got in my purse?" He shook his head innocently.

"You mean to tell me that you don't remember letting me

drive your new Porsche to the marina this morning? And then depositing the keys right here in my purse?" Jeff was undaunted. He simply continued to giggle like a little kid with a big secret. Jennifer changed her strategy. She walked up behind her boyfriend at the helm, put her arms around his waist, and hugged him closely.

"Hiding something from me?" she whispered softly into his ear. Eddie just smiled. But, still he did not answer.

"Okay," she sighed, repositioning her hands up underneath his arms. "This is your last warning, mister. You either let me in on this secret, or I will tickle you to death, right here and now." And even as she spoke the words, she commenced the attack.

"All right, all right!" Eddie screamed out, twisting from side to side to fend off the assault. "Give it to her, Jeff! Give it to her!" Jennifer wheeled around and stared at the handsome teenager to her left. He was holding a tiny velvet box in his hand.

"What's that?" she squealed, somehow already knowing the contents.

"Oh," Eddie said boyishly, "just a little somethin' I picked up at the store."

Quickly, her heart racing with anticipation, Jennifer reached for the little case and opened it. Inside, as she'd expected, was a beautiful ring, with three individually set diamonds!

"They . . . uh . . ." Eddie began, clearing his throat, "represent the three of us, my lady—you—me, and Jeff. A *family*. That is, of course, if you'll accept my proposal."

Jennifer could hardly contain herself. "Proposal?" she exclaimed. "Are you asking me to—"

"Yes," Jeff interjected suddenly, exasperated by his father's timid approach. "He's *asking*! Will you marry my father, Jennifer?"

Instantly, she threw her arms around Eddie's neck, kissed him without restraint, then pulled back to gaze into his eyes. "Is that what you're saying, my handsome, shy prince?"

"Yes, my love. It *is* what I am saying."

"Say it, then!" Jennifer insisted. "Say it yourself!"

Eddie gave the controls of the rescue vessel to his son. He then stepped over to Jennifer and put both hands up to her warm cheeks.

"My beautiful lady," he whispered warmly, "I love you so very much, and I simply cannot conceive of a life without you. You are my life, my reason for hope and happiness . . . and everything beautiful that exists in this world.

"Will you marry me, Jennifer Lee Lapman?"

"Oh, yes, darling," she answered affectionately. "I will!" She then reached up, drew him close a second time, and smothered him with renewed kisses.

"There is a little beach on the island of Oahu, Jen. A quiet place called Punaluu. I used to sit out on the sand under the stars and dream about wonderful things while I was with my dad on business trips. And I always dreamed of spending my honeymoon on that beach. It was a place I called 'my garden under the sun.'

"Please, Jen, accompany me to the Hawaiian temple, then honeymoon with me in Punaluu, in the garden under the sun."

Again the very emotional Jennifer Lee Lapman reached up and kissed her man, hugged him close, and simply wept with joy. "Yes, my love," she whispered, "I will gladly accompany you to the House of the Lord, and to *our* garden."

Meanwhile, Jeff, who had been watching the approaching land masses, noted a lone figure of a man standing up on the cliffs of Santa Rosa Island. He knew, of course, that it was Simeon, and he felt suddenly very happy for the wonderful experiences of which he had been an intregal part.

As their craft drew closer to shore, Jeff pointed upward, at the same time glancing back to his dad and Jennifer. For there, clearly visible to the three of them, was a lone seagull. It circled effortlessly above them for a while, dancing with the winds aloft. But then, quite suddenly, it dropped out of the sky and landed silently and softly on the bow of the boat. As its head turned toward the passengers, a sweet peace entered their minds, and again they marveled at the almost incomprehensible events of the past few weeks.

For Jeff, life had become exquisite beyond words. As he looked over toward his father and mother-to-be, and saw the obvious love in their hearts for one another, a smile drew across his lips. And although the elderly Simeon was far off, Jeff was quite certain that he could see a smile on his face, as well.

Meanwhile, around the world, meteorologists watched in awestruck reverence as the last of the fog bank disappeared. Satellite photos had chronicled the shrinking of the mist. It had begun in Baja, Mexico, just above a small oceanside community called La Paz. And in the days that followed, the clearing spread outward around the entire planet, until after more than a week of complete obscurity, the peoples of the earth saw the warm glow of the sun shining once again in the heavens.

Tears fell, knees bowed, and hearts were changed forever. Something incomprehensible had begun, and while the world waited, the Savior of the world, Jesus Christ, made final preparations for His global appearance—an event long heralded as the Second Coming.

The Second Coming
of Christ
A Statement of Perspective

Our Savior's second coming is, as was His first advent, one of the most longed-for events in the history of the world. As authors, we felt it would be appropriate and timely to share with readers our understanding of events leading up to and culminating in the Second Coming. At that time, the Savior will usher in the millennial era and administer the affairs of His kingdom from the original Jerusalem, in the Holy Land, as well as from the New Jerusalem, in Jackson County, Missouri.

Upon embarking on such a treatment, we find that to do justice to what the prophets have taught, we could begin here and write another volume much larger than this present novel. The wealth of information, of course, comes not only from biblical passages but also from the Book of Mormon and latter-day revelation.

For the serious reader, we would especially recommend Elder Bruce R. McConkie's treatment of the Second Coming as found in *The Millennial Messiah*. (Deseret Book, 1982). For the purposes of this summary, we will refer to statements made in that book. In addition, the reader may want to examine Gerald N. Lund's book *The Coming of the Lord*. (Bookcraft, 1971), which provides insightful information. Also, the final chapter of Elder James E. Talmage's *Jesus the Christ* (1915; reprint, Deseret Book, 1977) adds perspective to this approaching event in earth's history.

A General Overview

The second coming of our Lord has been preceded by many pivotal moments in the earth's existence. These include various forms of false worship, an abundance of false prophets, and a complete restoration of the gospel of Jesus Christ, which restoration includes true prophets and valid priesthood keys.

Since the Church of Jesus Christ was restored, missionary work has flourished throughout the world, with the unique assistance of the Book of Mormon. The importance of the doctrinal clarity found in this book of scripture cannot be overstated. Because of these truths, the children of Israel (including the Jews and the Lamanites) are being brought to a knowledge of the truth. In addition, with the assistance of the Book of Mormon, the people of the gentile nations are embracing the restored truths in great numbers.

As predicted by the ancients, the Saints have constructed latter-day temples which have been accepted by the Lord Himself. On April 3, 1836, the Savior came to Joseph Smith and Oliver Cowdery in the newly dedicated Kirtland Temple, the first of the latter-day temples (see D&C 110). At this writing, there are forty-five dedicated temples in which saving ordinances are performed. According to Elder McConkie, "we expect to see the day when temples will dot the earth, each one a house of the Lord; each one built in the mountains of the Lord; each one a sacred sanctuary to which Israel and the Gentiles shall gather to receive the blessings of Abraham, Isaac, and Jacob" (*Millennial Messiah*, p. 277).

On a contrasting note, the Savior's second coming has been preceded by an abundance of wickedness and permissiveness, with Satan truly exercising control over the hearts of many. His influence will spread to include world leaders, who shall wage war and bloodshed upon the peoples of the earth. This wickedness is prophesied to include plagues and pestilence, which are even at this hour being poured out upon the face of the land.

Signs and Wonders

In *The Millennial Messiah*, Elder McConkie states that various passages of scripture come together to spell out specific signs and wonders from the heavens that will precede the Lord's second advent. These are the signs and wonders he identifies:

1. Manifestations of blood, and fire, and vapors of smoke.

2. The sun shall be darkened and the moon turn into blood.

3. The stars shall hurl themselves from heaven.

4. The rainbow shall cease to appear in the mists and rains of heaven.

5. The sign of the Son of Man shall make its appearance.

6. A mighty earthquake, beyond anything of the past, shall shake the very foundations of the earth. (Pp. 406–7.)

From what Joseph Smith and other prophets since his time have said, we do not know what the aforementioned sign of the Son of Man will be. We are told, however, that when this sign takes place, the faithful of the earth will recognize it for what it is and the General Authorities will confirm the truthfulness of the same. (See McConkie, *Millennial Messiah*, pp. 418–19.)

Regarding the other signs listed above, Elder McConkie states: "Amid it all, natural disasters shall be everywhere, 'the sea and the waves roaring'—there shall be no safety upon the waters" (*Millennial Messiah*, p. 408).

It is to these natural occurrences that we have addressed the preceding fictional account. Our intent has been twofold. First, we have wanted to demonstrate the potentially catastrophic nature of the calamities mentioned. Second, we have desired to place in perspective the marvelous powers of the Holy Ghost and the sacred priesthood, and to illustrate how totally submissive the earth and its wonders are to priesthood power.

As Latter-day Saint authors, we understand fully the administrative mantle of responsibility of the General Authorities of the Church, who all work under the direction of the First Presidency. Still, our intent in this book has been to focus on the common Church member, to create a fictitious scenario that would awaken the senses of the reader, and to thereby motivate each of us to prayerfully position ourselves to be found worthy of *survival* and of *service* as this great day approaches.